GREAT FRENCH
OCCULT ROMANCES

Great French Occult Romances

**Edited & Translated by
Aaman Lamba**

DEDICATION

The Storytellers and Troubadours of Yore

CONTENTS

IMAGES & FIGURES

Introduction

*F*iction has a way of transporting the reader into the world of the characters, the emotions of the moment and the inevitability of the consequences of their actions, almost as if we were living them for ourselves. We watch the lovers part, knowing they would give anything for a last kiss, for a parting word, if they only knew what lay ahead. We feel a shiver when the Count invites Jonathan Harker into his castle for the night. We grant our belief to tales of monsters and distant planets, in part because we see ourselves in those purple climes, if only we could find a lost book or a little path in the woods.

Fantastic fiction and particularly the *Fantastique* French Literary genre dates back to the middle ages as folklore and myth went underground and religion dismissed earlier beliefs as fictional. This led to a rise in artistic depiction of these themes and the rise of 'supernatural' literature and art. Traveling storytellers and troubadours retold The Song of Roland, circa 1130, the tale of Melusine, the Arthurian myths and the Grail legends of Chrétien de Troyes, often blending them with local events, personages and claimed occult secrets. Marie de France wrote her Breton *lais* in 1170, a series of twelve narrative poems featuring characters such as Tristan and Iseult, a werewolf knight trapped in his lupine form, and the Arthurian knight Lanval, who is wooed by a fairy lady, and then Queen Guinevere, before she accuses him of 'not loving women' before King Arthur, at which point he is forced to reveal his fairy lover, who appears to redeem him.

The Renaissance saw a rise in the popularity of *Contes de Fées* or Fairy tales and an expansion of occult literature, sometimes in fictional form to pass the eagle eye of the Inquisition's censors. King Francis I (1515-47) could perhaps be called the Father of the French Renaissance. He invited many Italian artists to France, including Leonardo da Vinci, who brought with him the Mona Lisa, which the King had acquired for his collection. He standardized the French language, replacing Latin with French as the official language of France, earning the honorific *le Père et Restaurateur des Lettres* (Father and Restorer of Letters). He had renown as a cultural patron and fostered humanism as well as the principle of absolute monarchy. He expanded the royal library, with foreign acquisitions, as well as an ordinance that every book sold in France be housed in the library. His elder sister, Marguerite, produced the classic collection of short stories known as the *Heptameron*. Queen Anne Boleyn and Mary Boleyn were both educated at his court for a time.

The period was particularly productive for fantastic fiction, beginning perhaps with the quatrains of Michel de Nostradame, Rabelais' *Pantagruel* and other satires, publications of folktales such as Puss in Boots and the Beauty and the Beast by Gianfrancesco Straparola in *Nights*, as well as the high creativity across the channel with Edmund Spenser's *The Faerie Queene*, Christopher Marlowe's *The Tragical History of Dr. Faustus*, and William Shakespeare's works such as *The Midsummer Night's Dream*. Pierre de Ronsard had significant royal patronage and produced notable works, such as *L'Hymne des Daimons*.

The Age of Enlightenment, or as the French called it, *La Siecle des Lumieres* or Century of Lights began in the 18th century, under the Sun King, Louis XIV and led to an explosion in supernatural and fantastique writings. Charles Perrault's collections of fairy tales, Madame d'Aulnoy's own *Contes de Fees*, and the various translations of the Arabian Nights, which also included some tales that were original to the French editions. The printing press became the source for many 'blue' and 'red' editions of fantastic works, as well as more serious grimoires, many claiming to be translations from older Hebrew, Greek and Latin works, or referencing Biblical figures such as King Solomon.

The 19th century saw much dynamic ferment in French society and culture, mirroring the chaos and restructuring from the French Revolution, the First Empire, the Restoration, the Second Empire, and the Third Republic. This also led to a division between the *fantastique populaire* and the *fantastique litteraire*, although the distinction was fluid, and often merely due to the fame and notoriety of the authors. Neoclassicism implied a yearning to return to the supposed glories of the past, and grappled with the Revolutionary ethos, which focused on the common folk, depicting the aristocracy in a poor light, and at the same time, an emotional appeal to restore a spiritual aesthetic and a desire to be freed from the weight of history. There was a belief that society and the current time was sick, and there was a sense of loss, or ennui, particularly in the Romantic generation from 1820-48.

The contemporaneous English Gothic novels were mirrored by the French *romans noirs*, which were extremely popular, with authors such as

Charles Nodier, Victor Hugo, and Alexandre Dumas, *père*, who was a fierce competitor of Charles Nodier.

Themes ranged from fairies to vampires to ghosts to angels and demons – they also blended with the esoteric and hermetic tradition. The lingering influence of religious art and literature meant religious matters were well-represented, but not always in a positive light. Mary Shelley references Paracelsus, Agrippa and Albertus Magnus in *Frankenstein*, and the Spiritualist movement had many literary adherents, from Arthur Conan Doyle, Elizabeth Barrett Browning.

The rise of the scientific tradition and the rationality of Charles Darwin, Aldous Huxley, and others notwithstanding, and despite what Max Weber called 'the disenchantment of the world', there was almost a subaltern current of occultism competing and keeping pace with scientism. Roger Luckhurst observes[1] that "every scientific and technological advance encouraged a kind of magical thinking and was accompanied by a 'shadow discourse' of the occult."

Often enough, writers chose to take the scientific high ground and ridicule or show occult themes in a poor light, especially the fraudulent nature of many Spiritualist mediums. Victor Hugo and many other French authors were fascinated with the Spiritualist movement and often dabbled in seances, table-turnings, etc. The French school of Spirituality was a central focus of French Catholicism from the 17th to the 20th century and was a source of inspiration for fin-de-siecle literature. The explosion in occult writings and noted occultists such as Eliphas Levi, or Alphonse Louis Constant, introduced grimoires and the occult tradition to popular attention, and the Blue Library became an impetus for many potboilers and swashbuckling romances with occult themes. The naturalist themes of Emile Zola and J. K. Huysmans went deeper into the origins and motivations of evil in the human condition, especially with the post-Revolutionary rationalist ethos.

Xavier de Maistre (1763-1852) of Savoy was a French writer and soldier, as well as the younger brother of the noted French philosopher and post-Revolution counter-revolutionary Joseph de Maistre.

Charles Nodier was noted for numerous literary achievements, such as

---

[1] *The Victorian Supernatural*, Roger Luckhurst, British Library

popularizing the vampire story, bringing together the luminaries of French Romanticism such as Victor Hugo, Alfred de Musset and becoming librarian of the *Bibliothèque de l'Arsenal*. His romances and short tales were fantasies and satires, steeped in occult symbolism.

Alexandre Dumas, *père*, is known for many significant works and is still one of the most widely read French authors. He saw Charles Nodier as a rival and immortalized his memories of Nodier in a novella *La Dame au Collier de Velours*. He was an ardent social reformer, dealing with capital punishment, prison reform and financial regulation in his books.

This illustrated curation of great French occult romances is intended to illustrate the rich variety of literature from this period. The translations by me are from the original French texts.

The Red Dragon is a translation of a novel by the pseudonymous M. Robville, of whom not much is known, that was written contemporaneously to the earliest known publication of the grimoire of the same name, also known as the Grand Grimoire, to convey a scientific & romantic perspective to the popular fashion around grimoires, or occult magical works. A young man is hoodwinked by a wily old magician but then brought to his senses by a scientific pharmacist. Along the way, he affirms his love, learns science, and folktales about will-o-the-wisps, the legend of Melusine, and much more.

Love and the Grimoire by Charles Nodier features a decadent man about town who almost sells his soul to the devil before a good turn helping a pretty girl saves him from perdition.

The Legend of the Silkworm is an anonymous poem based on the French version by Alexander Ducros about the great King Solomon and a test by the Queen of Sheba, and how he is helped to overcome this challenge by a humble Silkworm.

Alexandre Dumas' *A Thousand and One Ghosts* is a novel with tales that range from talking heads to the horrors of the French Revolution to Polish vampires.

The Leper of the City of Aosta by Xavier de Maistre is about the purest and most tragic love between a leper and his dear sister, and the consequences of war.

THE RED DRAGON

Or THE ART OF CONJURING SPIRITS
DEMONSTRATED by Facts & Examples

by M. Robville

1

Chapter One

*T*his happened in a village in Provence, eight days before the feast of St. John. Father Michu's wheat had been harvested during the day. All the people of the farm assembled in the common room for the evening meal. After a final cup of punch, the women began some sewing work, and the men lit their pipes and engaged in conversation.

Among the assistants was a shy young man, with a timid air, whom the girls sometimes regarded with a smile, and who never spoke without a bit of hesitation. He showed, in brief, all the indications of a weak character, of an intelligence, if not limited, at least somewhat underdeveloped for his age, which was nearly twenty years old.

His name was Claude Michu, the farmer's son.

It must be said, if Claude had none of the manly assurance, this was because he often faced taunts and quibbles from his comrades. He was used to be the target of ridicule from scoffers and had long resigned himself to the role of scapegoat that had been imposed on him since childhood.

Besides, ugly, spindly, and puny as he was, he could hardly triumph over his destiny and sometimes he began to think that a single prodigious event might restore his moral value.

He had wanted to say a few sweet words to the neighborhood girls, but they had laughed at him. He had started some agricultural experiments, following the data from a special book, but none of these experiences had succeeded.

Finally, one might say that Claude was a man pursued by bad luck.

Reflecting on this, we would have seen that this alleged bad luck was quite simply due to the wrong influences on the young person's mind, his intellectual weakness, and his great hesitation in all circumstances, but that was not all.

Whatever might be the reason, Claude had come to convince himself that he would always be unhappy, always weak, always ridiculed by some, beaten by others, and finally that a spell had been cast upon him.

This annoyance was the natural result of the naivety of his spirit.

When his spirit entered his brain, he no longer wished to fight this spell of which he was the victim, but to fight it, he needed, in his opinion, a lot of courage and audacity, and Claude felt that he was severely lacking in these two qualities.

We will see, however, how he decided to revolt against all these setbacks that incessantly swamped him.

The evening was coming to an end when the gate of the farm opened and gave passage to a little old man with a strange aspect and bizarre outfit.

This old man professed to be a shepherd, but he was known in the region as a wise sorcerer, who at a word could change the mountain to the plain and the plain to the mountain, by his whim, according to the good women, who said this while shaking their heads.

1: Paul Cézanne: Maison devant la Sainte-Victoire près de Gardanne (House in Provence), Indianapolis Museum of Art

The truth was that Simounen (as the sorcerer called himself) was a wily old man living on the credulity of the peasants who stocked his purse with fine crowns and made his income from their foolishness.

He was a good companion, cheerful storyteller who knew by heart all the songs and tales of Provence. Simounen was received everywhere with pleasure, perhaps with fear because of his reputation as a sorcerer, which did not fail to cause fear in the weak brains of the local people.

When he appeared at Father Michu's home, the girls, who knew him well, and often bought talismans and charms from him, greeted him with pleasure.

"Well", cried Madeleine, a pretty brunette whom Claude had loved for a long time and wanted to marry, without having the courage to do it, "Well, that is Father Simounen who will tell us a tale!"

"I won't refuse, little one," replied the shepherd, "What would you have me recount?"

"Tell us the legend of the Black Hole. It is interesting and scary."

"Yes!" cried all the voices, "the legend of the Black Hole!"

"Fine, listen to me closely, and do not breathe a word, I do not like to be interrupted."

The circle of listeners huddled around Simounen, and the old man began thus:

"This was a time when Provence was not called so, over a thousand years ago. In this country, two brothers lived together with their father in an old castle on the mountain. The first was called Jehan, the other Andre. Andre, the youngest, was as mean as his brother Jehan was good. Andre left nothing unseen from his evil heart, until the day that his old father was at the point of death.

Then jealousy seized him. He knew that his brother, following the habits of the time, was going to inherit all the fortune and all the paternal titles, and that he, Andre, would be no better than the first servant of Jehan in the castle.

He quickly resolved to kill his elder brother and thus stay the sole possessor of everything.

One night, while everyone was asleep, he crept slowly to his brother's room, and having thrown himself like a wolf on the latter, stabbed him in the chest with a dagger. The poor Jehan cried 'Ah!' and died.

Then the murderer hid himself in his tower and awaited the day.

The next morning, when he learned what had happened, the father of the two young men expired in sorrow, and Andre had what he had wished for so much, the fortune and the honors. Because, no one dared to suspect it, it was believed that Jehan had been assassinated by the thieves who frequented the country. Such was, at least, the rumor that the new lord spread about.

As he was rightly feared in his domain, none dared contradict him.

You believe that he lived a tranquil life, perhaps, as happens to many guilty people? It was not to be so. If the justice of men did not reach him, that of God did not fail.

A year after the death of his father and brother, on a winter evening when the wind blew strong and almost uprooted the rocks, Lord Andre was alone in his room.

In the day, he had received his tenants' rents, and wishing to put them away safely, he had opened the family treasure chest which was piled up with tons of gold, baskets of diamonds and pearls, and large boxes filled to the brim with silver ingots.

He contemplated these riches with pride and congratulated himself on the blow that had made him their master when he heard an extended sigh at the end of the treasure chamber.

His blood froze in his veins and he hardly had the strength to look in front of him.

Suddenly, a voice called out to him twice.

"Andre! Andre!"

He ventured his eyes to the end of the room, and suddenly uttered a cry of terror.

His father stood before him, and by his side was the assassinated Jehan, still bearing two red holes in his chest chiseled by Andre's dagger.

"My father! My father" cried the murderer. "Thanks be to God! Thanks!"

He fell to his knees before the two motionless and menacing specters.

The wind outside began to blow more icy and violent, and the walls of the castle trembled in their foundations.

"Thanks be to God," repeated the miserable wretch.

"God has judged you, your hour has come," the specter of Jehan pronounced slowly. "God gave you one year to repent, and you have not cursed your crime for one moment. You must die, therefore, with all your cursed honors and the ill-acquired riches, and this castle which you have defiled."

The two shades attached themselves to the two pillars which

6

supported the room. As they shook them as if to bring down their fruits, the wind redoubled its rage and the ramparts of the castle trembled under its attacks, like weakly planted stalks.

Soon, Andre heard the cries of superhuman demons around him – the spirits looked at him with flaming eyes, and suddenly the two pillars fell down, a great rolling sound was heard and the soil on which the castle stood collapsed and the towers, walls, gold, silver, diamonds, and all sorts of riches were engulfed in the earth along with their unworthy possessor.

Where there was once a mountain, now opened into a profound abyss. This is what is called the Black Hole today.

2: Ruins of Les Baux-de-Provence, Photographer Berit Wallenberg, Public Domain

The storyteller stopped.

Claude Michu had been listening with interest, mixed with terror.

As for Madeleine, she had not missed a single word of the story, yet she did not declare her curiosity satisfied.

"Father Simounen," she said, "You have not finished. Does one not hear terrible sounds in the region of the Black Hole?"

"Yes, my child. It is said that on some days, the demons make their Sabbath at the place where is buried the body, the castle and the treasures of Andre, the fratricide."

"They also say, don't they," replied Madeleine, "that many people want to conjure the spirits of the Black Hole & search for the hidden treasure?"

"That is true."

"But it is said, none have succeeded."

"One might," ventured Claude timidly, "conjure the demons and appropriate the treasure they guard?"

"No doubt," said Madeleine, "but for that he must be very learned and courageous. As such, it should be anyone but you who should go to the Black Hole, my poor Claude."

Claude did not reply to Madeleine, but questioning once again the sorcerer,

"On which days do we hear these sounds of the Devils' Sabbath?"

"On Christmas, All Saints Day and during St. John Eve," replied Simounen, who had a malicious look on his face at the sight of his credulous listener.

"The Feast of St. John! That is in eight days," murmured Claude. "What else, Master Simounen, must one do to conjure the demons and possess the treasure?"

"You want to know too much too soon, my little child. This knowledge has a high cost, and one may still not fathom what is needed."

Saying so, the shepherd closed his eye in a wink, as if to say, "I know all this myself, and yet I'm not proud."

The wily player had sniffed out in Claude Michele an easy dupe, and at any event he was preparing his ground. Meanwhile, Claude, who was timid by nature, and afraid of being taunted by his comrades, felt braver when he thought and acted alone.

If he possessed the treasure of the Black Hole, Claude believed he would suddenly win the appreciation and respect of all men, the smiles of the girls, and thanks to the strength of wealth, he would be forever rid of that weakness and ridiculousness that prevented him from confessing his love for Madeleine and be able to ask for her hand.

For the first time in his life, he felt the courage and resoluteness to venture on the terrible ordeal of which Simounen had spoken.

For that, he needed to gain the confidence of the old wizard and induce from him even at a high price the secret of conjuration which would render the demons of the Black Hole submissive to his desires.

This demonstrates the extent of credulity and lack of reasoning that a man can be pushed to and the kind of swindling notions that could be pushed by adventurers such as Simounen on the good beasts of the ilk of Claude Michu.

When the shepherd left the farm, it was ten in the evening.

He was at the foot of a sunken road leading to the first slopes of the mountain where he had constructed his hut, when he heard behind him a call to stop.

"Good," he said, while pausing. "The history of the treasure has produced the desired effect – there is my fine man."

Simounen was not mistaken – almost instantly, he heard the breathless voice of Claude behind him.

"Father Simounen! Father Simounen!"

"Is that you, Claude, my boy?" asked the sorcerer with a false note of astonishment.

"I wanted to speak with you, father Simounen. And I did not want to speak in front of everyone, I have followed you here."

"Well, explain yourself."

"It's very difficult…"

"Come, are you afraid? Well! I will spare you the difficulty of speaking. I'll tell you what you want from me."

"You?" whispered Claude, already terrified of the sharp insight of the old shepherd, although it was easy enough to explain after what had happened at the farm in the evening.

"Me!" repeated the old man in a solemn tone.

"Listen: You know that I deal with these terrible sciences, unknown to most men. The history of the treasure of the Black Hole tempts you, and you come to me to know the secrets that will assure you its possession."

"How do you know that?"

"I know everything that I choose to discover. I can do anything I desire, my boy," replied the sorcerer, adopting a graver tone.

"So, you would consent…"

"To teach you the art of conjuration of demons."

"Yes, if you have the courage, but not if you are afraid."

"I will not be afraid."

"But you do not look like a brave man."

"It does not matter. When there is nothing to see to intimidate me, I feel able to do anything."

"So much the better – because what you have to do must be done alone."

"What should be done?

"Gently, my boy. Do you have any money with you?"

"I have a small amount."

"Good, because without that nothing is possible. For the conjurations, you see, you must procure various objects that are not free. Then I have my own secrets and they are worth something to you, I believe."

"I hear you loud and clear."

"All in good time. Well! As it is late tonight, and I have much to tell you, go to sleep quietly. Tomorrow night come find me on the mountain and I will teach you what is to be done.

Simounen started on his path again and Claude returned to the farm, his heart beating fast. He felt agitated by the audacious enterprise that he was undertaking.

Chapter Two

*T*he next day, after dinner, when the boys and girls at the farm were resuming their evening activities, animated by gay comments or rustic songs, Claude slipped away without being noticed and reached Simounen's hut.

The old man was waiting for him, sitting in front of a small table, and reading, by the light of a tallow candle, a torn dusty book.

The interior of the hut corresponded to the public perception of the shepherd.

Birds of prey and bats were nailed to the plastered walls, and in a strange disorder were old weapons, steel-tipped cedar rods, branches of dry mistletoe, and two or three small copper cauldrons. A stuffed iguana hung on the ceiling – a kind of big lizard with a terrible appearance – and a serpent with an open mouth that still displayed a fine forked tongue, hardened by time, and sharpened like a dart.

On rough, square wooden benches were aromatic plants that were drying out. Other plants macerated in a pot beside the table, and there were pots of various forms by the chimney, with strange powders.

The floor of the hut was clay – two black hens pecked away as if they were in a farmyard, and in a dark corner glittered the round eyes of one of those enormous toads, often found in quarries.

The sight of this miserable dwelling did not reassure poor Claude Michu. He paused at the threshold, overcome by apprehension.

He dared not set foot in this cursed place, and he would probably have retraced his steps if Simounen, fearing to see his dupe about to make his escape, had not called out to him in an encouraging tone:

"Good evening, Claude! Come in quickly, my friend. I see that you are a punctual boy."

The aspiring sorcerer saw that it was too late to retreat.

He shivered and ventured into the interior.

The shepherd got up and quickly closed the door.

"We must not be disturbed," he said, speaking to himself. "The police do not believe in anything and if they surprised us, they would be well able to cause trouble in our affairs."

This fear of the police recklessly expressed by the wizard should have inspired some cause for concern in Claude. Instead of saying to himself that he was engaged in a perilous affair, instead of thinking that the wizard who could command demons should not be afraid of men, the credulous peasant considered his dangerous efforts even more tentatively, leading Simounen to take precautions to assure his intended result.

"Come," said the old man after a pause. "We must act fast. Do you want to go to the Black Hole?"

"Yes!"

"And take possession of Andre's treasure?

"If that is possible."

"It will be, if you follow my instructions precisely."

"I will do everything you say."

"And you will do it well, because, think about it, if you miss even one of my conditions, it will mean the loss of the fortune you crave and perhaps even your life."

Claude did not respond. He began to tremble. Yet he recovered, confidently, his initial resoluteness.

"Tell me everything, Father Simounen," he went on, after a brief silence.

The sorcerer left his seat and took a small book printed in red from the mantelpiece.

"What is this book?" asked Claude Michu.

"This book, my son, is the Red Dragon. This is the treasure of science; it is the wizard's code. There, one finds the great conjurations which make the spirits obedient to one's will.

3: Illustration of Der Zauberlehrling. From: "Goethe's Werke", 1882, drawing by
Ferdinand Barth (1842–1892), Public Domain

Claude Michu opened his eyes wide. Simounen continued.

"It is from this book that we must draw the invocation which will open the abyss of the Black Hole."

"One also needs a wand, doesn't one, Master Simounen?"

"Many wizards use a rod or a Blasting Rod, but I do not work like that. The rod is at best good for discovering the sources – for the treasures, one needs something else."

"What is that?"

"One needs the head of an ass, my son."

"The head of an ass!"

"Yes," replied the sorcerer, who had just discovered an excellent opportunity to procure an ass, cheaply, as we will see.

"What do you do with this head of the ass?"

One offers it as a sacrifice to the spirits, burning it on charcoal. The demons choose to respond to your questions if they are satisfied with the sacrifice.

"Bah!" exclaimed Claude, dazed, "the head of an ass!"

"This is what has to be done."

"So…"

"So, you must go to the town before the feast of St. John and buy a two-year-old donkey at the market. Then you must bring him here, leading him by the left hand. Do you hear me well?"

"By the left hand, very well! But what will you do with the animal? Will you chop off its head?"

"Not at all, I will keep it safe for another occasion, and I will give you in exchange the head of another donkey that I have prepared accordingly. The one that you will bring me will be the price of the magical donkey head."

Claude grimaced.

"This does not suit you?" exclaimed the sorcerer, angrily. "So, nothing can be achieved, my boy."

"Yes, Master Simounen, I accept this task. Please continue."

"When you have the magical donkey's head in your possession, you must take it with you without being seen by anyone. Then you will pick a branch of verbena in the moonlight, that you will use to decorate your talisman."

"The head?"

"Yes, of course. Then you will take it to the Black Hole, and after having traced a magical triangle like the one I will show you; you will pronounce the formula mentioned in the Red Dragon, which you will learn by heart."

"Then, Lucifer will appear to you and grant all your desires."

The sorcerer then explained to his adept how he was to construct the magical triangle, as shown below.

4: The magical circle provided by Simounen for the Red Dragon,
from the French novel, circa 1850, public domain

When Claude had been sufficiently informed on this subject, Simounen continued to the final part of the initiation.

He opened the terrible book of the Red Dragon and his finger landed on a page:

Chapter Three

GREAT INVOCATION OF THE SPIRITS WITH WHOM ONE WISHES TO MAKE A PACT, DRAWN FROM THE GREAT KEY

*E*mperor Lucifer, master of all the rebel spirits. I pray I find your favor in this invocation that I make to your Prime Minister LUCIFUGE ROFOCALE, wanting to make a pact with him, I also pray to your Prince Beelzebub to protect me in my enterprise.

O Count Astaroth! Be propitious unto me, and grant unto me that this night, the great Lucifer appears to me in a human form without any bad odor and that he grants me, by means of the pact that I will present to him, all the riches I desire.

O Great Lucifuge! I pray you leave your abode in whichever part of the world that you might be to come and speak with me, or else I will have to compel you by the force of the great living God, by his dear Son and by the Holy Spirit; obey me promptly or you will be eternally damned by the force of the powerful words of the Great Key of Solomon, which he employed to force the rebel spirits to accept his pact. Thus, appear at the earliest before me, or I will continually torment you by these powerful words of the Key:

Aglon, Tetragram, Vaycheon, Stimulamaton y ezpares retragrammaton olyoran irion esytion existion eryona onera erasym moym messias soter Emanuel Sabaoth Adonay, te adore et invoco

Chapter Four

Claude Michu patiently spent a good part of the night memorizing this baroque formula. When he demonstrated this confidently from start to finish, Simounen said to him,

"Now, boy, here you are! The devils of the Black Hole will not be able to stand against you. Go without fear and in eight days you will be rich."

"When should I come back?"

"You must return on the eve of the feast of St. John. You must bring me the donkey that you have bought, and you must bring me four new twenty-franc pieces. In return, I will give you the magical head that will open the treasure gates for you."

Claude Michu found the secret a bit costly – "A two-year-old donkey and 80 francs," he said to himself. "That's a fine price."

He made this observation to the sorcerer.

"Imbecile!" replied the latter, "It is not 80 francs, it is 1000 francs, or perhaps 10,000 francs, that you should offer me. You ask me, why? This is because I give you the means to win millions and you bargain with me!"

Despite his credulity, Claude Michu suddenly discovered an aplomb that shook the composure of the wily conman.

"But Father Simounen," he said, "Since your recipe is so good and worth so much money, why have you not used it to benefit yourself?"

"Why... Because..." stammered the sorcerer, surprised by this objection, "because..."

Then, suddenly recovering his poise, he said, "This mystery need not trouble you, my child, remember in the future not to poke your nose in my affairs, or you might end up in the cooking pot yourself."

This crude defeat and the threat that accompanied it had all the effect that Simounen intended. Claude Michu lowered his head, saying, "Excuse me, Master Simounen, I did not mean to offend you."

Then, he took leave of the wily old man and returned to the farm at the break of dawn.

Chapter Five

$\mathcal{T}$he next Thursday, Claude Michu collected all his savings, squeezed them into a leather purse and left for the town, with the intention of buying the donkey the shepherd magician had asked of him.

After walking for an hour or two in the market, he found what he was looking for – a handsome donkey, two years old, strong on the heels and promising to be a useful auxiliary for the purchaser's campaign.

It was the brave beast that Claude Michu needed, or rather Simounen, because it would be he would enjoy himself the beautiful acquisition of the young man. Claude traded the horse, paying in cash, and having held the halter in his left hand, took him to the village where he hid it in an abandoned stable.

On the eve of St. John, by evening, he came to fetch the beast, and by a roundabout route, led it to Simounen's house.

"Ah! Ah!" he cried, on seeing it, "beautiful beast! You will succeed, my boy, because you have made a fine purchase."

"Do you really think so, Master Simounen?"

"Yes, also, I will take care of my part, but I forget – where are the four twenty-franc pieces?"

"Here they are."

Simounen took the gold, tapping it to hear the tinkling sound and engulfed it in his vest pocket, with an evident satisfaction.

"Come," he said then, "I will give you the magical head."

This famed head was simply that of a poor donkey that had been slaughtered a few days ago, and that Simounen had easily procured. He had cleaned it, stuffed it with straw and modified in a fashion as to suit the needs of the occasion.

He brought it solemnly to the table where he presented it, and then placed it carefully in a basket and handed the same to Claude Michu.

Then he added in an instructive manner: "You will kindle a fire of briar wood and burn the head after having pronounced the invocation that I have taught you. Go, your case is in the bag – but do not forget anything or you will lose your skin and your money.

"Good," said Claude.

He left, filled with hope, and summoning to himself all the courage he would have need of the following night.

During this time, the shepherd began to rub his hands.

"Very well," he thought, "there are still imbeciles in the world, and if this continues, the wizarding profession will not be the worst choice for anyone."

Chapter Six

Claude was returning quietly to the village when he met, not far from the farm, Mr. Bernard Morand, the pharmacist.

"Good evening, Claude," the latter said, who was a friend of his father. "Where are you coming from?"

"Good evening, Mr. Morand, I am coming from the mountain, thank you."

"Ah! Ah! And what were you doing on the mountain if I'm not too curious?"

Claude blushed.

"I went...for a walk...," he murmured.

"Ah! Ah! And your walk has been productive, I see since you return with this heavy basket?"

"Yes...Yes...Mr. Morand," stammered Claude, who had lost his cool.

"What do you have in this basket? Strawberries, without a doubt, it is the season..."

"No! These are not strawberries..."

"What are they, then? Cherries? Did you plunder them, by chance?"

"Oh! Mr. Morand, do you see me as a plunderer? Can you believe that?"

"I believe nothing – but you hide your basket so carefully that there must be some mystery hidden here?"

Claude's natural timidity had returned. Pressed by these questions and unable to dissimulate or lie, he resolved to confess everything to the pharmacist and in return ask him for his confidence and to keep it a secret.

Bernard listened with amazement. He could not resign himself to accepting such credulity on the part of Claude and such duplicity on the part of Simounen.

"So," he asked, when the young man had completed his story, "what are you hiding there – is that the head of a donkey?"

"Yes, Mr. Morand."

"Well, my friend, you are better off than you think – instead of one donkey's head, you have two."

"Two?"

"Yes – the one in your basket, the other…"

"The other?"

"The other on your shoulders, imbecile!"

"Do you not see that Simounen is an old trickster, that he has extorted you of money and that he has fooled you?"

"Do you think so?"

"One must be very simple-minded to ask such a question. How do you, since you have received a certain level of education, still believe in sorcerers, evocations, spells, talismans and all the Cabalistic balderdash? You are sick, my poor boy, you need treatment. Go, quickly throw the head of the donkey into the ditch and remember that true wonders today are those accomplished by science, intelligence, and hard work.

Despite this reprimand, Claude Michel did not move.

"What do you want, Mr. Morand?" he asked. "I promised myself I would try this experiment and I will. I want to have a clear heart."

"As you wish, my boy! But when you are convinced that you have been taken for a fool, come see me and I will remind you, that many things which one believes are spiritual miracles, are only the result of natural operations. Go to the Black Hole, with a clear heart, as you would say.

"With your permission, Mr. Morand."

"Yes, go – and good luck!"

"You will not say anything to my father?"

"Don't worry, farewell!"

"Then, I'll take your leave."

"Good Lord, my boy," mused the pharmacist, who loved a good laugh, "if you go searching for devils in the Black Hole, I hope that you find them."

Chapter Seven

$\mathcal{T}$he dreadful hour arrived too soon for Claude – as it approached, he faltered in his purpose. Yet, he had taken the task too close to his heart to let it go at the last moment.

When the fires of the feast of St. John began to light up the mountain, our future sorcerer left the farm and went towards the Black Hole, which was situated in a gorge, some distance from the village.

It had rained during the day, and the night was starless and dark. Heavy clouds coursed the sky overhead, driven by a strong wind.

The silence of the countryside, barely disturbed by the clicks of the cricket or of the cicada, made a strong impression on Claude Michu.

He quickened his pace, mentally repeating the formula of the Red Dragon, and looking around with a worried eye.

The trees planted by the side of the road were, in his eyes, taking on fantastic appearances, and in the woods, he heard sighs.

Stumbling, out of breath, covered in sweat, he finally arrived at the Black Hole – it was a kind of crater, covered with oaks and ash trees, and although the appearance was not very scary, it inspired a profound horror in Claude Michu.

Simounen's student, over-excited by the situation, chose a place deprived of trees to perform his conjurations, and lighting a fire of heather, he tended it until midnight.

5: The Black Hole was a kind of crater, covered with oaks & ash trees.

During the vigil, which lasted almost an hour, it seemed to Claude Michu that complaints would be raised from the bottom of the Black Hole, but he did not pay much heed, occupied as he was with listening to the sound of the village bell that would toll the twelve strokes of the fatal hour.

At last, midnight struck!

At once, Claude threw the magical head into the fire that he had stoked and uttered with a loud, albeit tremulous voice, the conjuration taught him from the Red Book.

Then he waited, panting, his breath heavy with the exertions of the conjuration.

Nothing happened.

Then, he repeated the invocation in a slow voice.

He had hardly finished, when a terrible noise was heard around him – cries, screams, squeaks of terrible chains.

At the same time, a form, covered with a large red shroud, appeared in front of the blaze, a drawing lit by a sheet of white light, which started from the bottom of the abyss.

"Claude Michu, you who have summoned me, what do you wish of me?" thundered the apparition, in a terrible voice.

Claude fell face down, afraid of the effect that he had achieved.

"The Treasure! The Treasure!" he mumbled, in a muffled voice.

"Before granting you the Treasure that you demand, you must vanquish the spirits of the abyss," replied the Voice. "To me, the demons of the Black Hole!"

Claude, who had got up, full of terror, saw dozens of spirits suddenly surrounding him, resembling the first, who took the leader by the hand and began to perform an infernal dance around Claude.

"Mercy! Mercy!" cried Claude, afraid and at the point of death in the presence of these horrible figures, who were illuminated by the supernatural glow which came from below.

"He is ours! Ours! Ours!" howled the sepulchral voices.

At the same time, Claude was lifted from the earth by strong arms and carried to the bottom of the hole. He closed his eyes and thought himself lost.

The demons let him fall on the grass. He thought he would be thrown into a boiling furnace, when on the contrary, he felt himself wet from head to toe.

The evil spirits had thrown him into a stream which ran along the walls of the Black Hole – this beneficial bath did him good, and he was relaxing in the warm bath when the fantastic light that lit up the scene went out suddenly.

Surprised and bewitched by the darkness and silence that suddenly succeeded the brilliant light and noises, Claude Michu got up and stumbled.

Then an immense burst of laughter resounded around him.

After this, a mocking and cheerful voice spoke, "Well, Claude, are you satisfied, and did my demons do their job well?"

Claude recognized the voice of Bernard Morand.

"Well!" he exclaimed, "Mr. Morand, it is YOU?"

"Me and the devils who have put you in such a fine spot, these are your friends who have kindly joined me to teach you a little lesson."

"My God! My God!" cried Claude, ashamed of the mystification that he had been the victim of. "I will not dare return to the village."

"That will teach you to believe in grandmothers' tales and in the deceits of old Simounen."

"Ah! You gave me a fine fright, Mr. Morand."

"Good! This is a violent remedy – the healing will be guaranteed."

"Oh! I am healed, let's go."

"All in good time, you will see that there are no other demons in the Black Hole than those we have brought to it. In the future, be less timid, less gullible, and more assured in your efforts, and you will succeed in your enterprises, without needing to grease the palm of sorcerers."

"But, Mr. Morand, how did you produce that diabolical light that was as bright as the sun and then went out suddenly in a flash?"

"That was not a diabolical light, but simply an electrical light that I produced by means of this device."

"That is marvelous!"

"A marvel that I will explain to you when you wish."

"Tomorrow, Mr. Morand, and if you wish, I would like to be taught to forget all the nonsense of Simounen and all the jugglery of the Red

Dragon."

"Tomorrow, then. For tonight," said the pharmacist, gathering around him all the actors who had participated in the mystery play presented to Claude Michu, "for tonight, I invite you all to come to my residence to have a glass of mulled wine. It will warm us up. Keep the secrets of our adventure to ourselves and come tomorrow to benefit from the scientific concepts that I will demonstrate to Claude."

"You will thus convince yourself, thanks to some short lessons, that all the power of the sorcerers resides in the knowledge of some practices that will not look too marvelous when the techniques are commonplace."

"What has transpired between Simounen and Claude is nothing more than some complicated adventures of our old shepherd. To common eyes, they appear to be miracles – being able to speak with spirits, moving objects with the power of words – these are in the end how the clever conjurer or cunning rogues misuse their knowledge of science to given themselves supernatural abilities."

"There are few phenomena in the world that cannot be explained by the power of natural laws – this is what I will demonstrate to you, to prevent you from having the urge, like Claude Michu, to throw away your money through the windows of your foolishness."

While having this discussion, Bernard Morand and his companions had returned to the village.

A bowl of mulled wine was awaiting them at the pharmacist's residence. All of them sat down around the table – they toasted the heroes of the evening and the peasants took their leave, promising to return at the appointed time the next day.

Chapter Eight

C laude Michu, still a bit sheepish after his misadventure the evening before, rose the next day with a firm resolve to correct his credulity and seek only within himself the remedy for his weaknesses of spirit.

As a result, and to usher in immediately his new mode of conduct, he put on his finest clothes and walked confidently towards Madeleine's cottage.

His heart was beating fast as he approached the home of the person whom he loved more than anyone, however, he entered with a firm step after knocking twice on the door.

Madeleine and her mother were alone at home. The beautiful girl combed her long brown hair before a small mirror, while the old woman was preparing breakfast.

At the sight of Claude, Madeleine turned around.

"How are you, brave Master Claude," she said to the newcomer. "What brings you here so early?"

"I would like to speak with you."

"With me?"

"With you and your mother."

"What is it about," asked the latter, leaving her work.

"I will tell you when Madeleine has heard what I have to say."

Then addressing the young girl, "Come," he said, "I want to take you to Mass. While passing through the Grand Square, I want to buy you some rings from Beaucaire. The merchant has come today."

So, and without much ado begins a tale of love in the good country of Provence. The rings of Beaucaire, glass rings that are bought by the dozen, which play a big role in the initiation of feeling. To offer them is almost to say – I love you. To accept them, is to implicitly respond – me too.

On hearing the significant proposition of Claude Michu, Madeleine was not too surprised.

"What made you so brave?" she asked him.

"Yesterday, you dared not look at me, and now you speak to me so gallantly."

"I will explain to you, Madeleine, come with me."

With a glance, the pretty girl consulted her mother. This lady, flattered by the attentions of Claude Michu, a boy with good prospects, made an approving gesture, and Madeleine without much fuss, took Claude's arm, which he offered her, who appeared to be a handsome boy since he had given up his shy and embarrassed air.

The two young people went off in this manner on their path and no doubt they got along very well, because when Claude left her, who he already regarded as his fiancée, his face shone, indicating his inner confidence.

The bad luck had, in effect, ended and given way to a newfound resoluteness. He had shown courage and boldness. He had expressed his love to Madeleine in good and honest words, and it appeared that a new life lay ahead for him.

He owed this happy result to Bernard Morand. Thus, he did not fail to go that evening to the pharmacist's residence, looking forward to benefiting from his teachings and advice.

Yet, it was not love that he had questions about that night. The pharmacist had promised to enlighten his young listeners on various points which seemed too obscure for their simple intelligence, more often open to country tales than to healthy science and reason. He wanted to give them to shy away from naïve beliefs and grant the ability to guard them against the maneuvers of fortune tellers, spellcasters, charm merchants and all people of this ilk that took advantage of the superstition and credulity of the people of the countryside.

When Bernard Morand saw he had a full house, he lit his pipe, invited the peasants to make themselves at ease, and started in this manner:

"I have travelled much, my friends, and since I have a curious nature and love learning new things in my travels, I have seen much and learned a lot. Further, I have studied a lot of strange topics that you do not even suspect exist, and that the special nature of my work engaged me deeply.

Therefore, I will be able to speak with you today about many things that will interest you, educate you and perform certain experiments that will prove my theories clearly.

I will not tell you that it is certain that the devil does not exist – religion teaches us that in the world there is a spirit of evil that our virtue must fight but that spirit is not the one described by the storytellers – a horned dark being showing himself to men who know how to evoke him. Nobody can boast of knowing how to bring forth the devil, even those who know by heart the Red Dragon (here, Mr. Morand cast a dark look at Claude who blushed), and yet, since time immemorial, it has been believed that the devil manifests in various forms among us. At all times, the cunning folk have taken advantage of this belief to exploit the common people, and this also proves that there always have been con artists and people who would listen to them.

The apparitions of the devil derive from various beliefs regarding the existence of fantastic beings, endowed with supernatural powers, and according to some, animated by the infernal spirit.

Their names change with the countries where they are found. These include the will-o'-the-wisp, water dragons, treves, leprechauns, werewolves, vampires, goblins, elves, and a host of others, which I will describe to you briefly.

These details somewhat consoled Claude after his witless escape the other night, showing him that he was unfortunately not the only person in the world who believed in the frivolous tales of the storytellers.

The wisps, of which I will speak with you first, because they are the most popular, are, according to folklore, capricious spirits, good or mischievous according to the occasion, and willingly taking the human form when they choose.

It is believed that by showing themselves at night as wandering lights, they like to entertain themselves by misleading travelers and sometimes directing them to precipices, where they fall to their death. It is also believed that they often make friends with some people and put themselves at their disposal. The wisps then do all the housework – they scour the pots, curry the horses, sweep the house, neither more nor less than a good servant at a hundred crowns per year.

*6: Will-o-the-wisp lighting a bog or mire. Artist unknown, Public Domain. Flammarion's
L'atmosphère: météorologie populaire, 1888*

To speak the language of reason, I will tell you that the errant flames which one calls the will-o'-the-wisps, and that one believes are produced by these singular spirits, are simply produced by the inflammation of a gas called hydrogen phosphide, which is formed in the earth's interior by the decomposition of animal matter, and which is spontaneously inflammable as soon as it emerges from the surface. So, if you encounter these will-o'-the-wisps, do not be scared and instead observe them as any one of the thousand diverse phenomena that nature offers each instant to your attention.

The mermaids, or water dragons, that one hears about often in Provence have the reputation of being the invisible proprietors of the rivers and streams. It is believed that they live at the bottom of the waters, and that to attract women and children, their principal victims, they float gold or silver jewels amidst the rushes. They are also called treves. Under this name, they particularly haunt uninhabited houses from where they go out at night to perform their dark deeds.

Werewolves, which I heard you talk about earlier, were popular in the imagination of the Middle Ages. One sees in them magicians able to take any form, choosing in this case that of the wolf and thus metamorphosing to torment their victims.

I could also tell you about djinns who are the Eastern equivalent of our Western elves – elves who live in the fires of the earth or the depths of the sky, or tell you about goblins who flood the fields and smother your workers amidst pestilent vapors, or about Norwegian nickar who raise storms, or vampires who drink human blood, and all the armies of revenants, specters, larvae, and demons that are found in popular legends, but I would rather show you, by a written example, to what extent of madness the belief in spirits can push a man.

In 1821, a man lived in Paris who had so identified with the supernatural world that he had come to believe that nothing was done here on earth without the permission or the help of the spirits, leprechauns to whom he attributed a sovereign influence over even the simplest acts.

This unique character, or rather, as I would term him, this fool who was named Berbiguier, imagined he would write a book in which he would reveal all the tricks, all the evil deeds of the demons that were his obsession.

I have in my hands this book which is a rare curiosity, and I want you to read a certain passage.

Bernard Morand got up, opened his library, and fetched a little book which he handed to Claude Michu.

"Here," he said, reading aloud, "This is the section where the poor fool makes up the nomenclature of spirits constituting the infernal court."

Claude read the following:

Chapter Nine

INFERNAL COURT
PRINCES AND DIGNITARIES

BEELZEBUB, Supreme Chief
SATAN, Dethroned Prince
EURYNOME, Prince of Death *(Mermaid daughter of Oceanus & Tethys)*
MOLOCH, Prince of the country of tears
PLUTO, Prince of Fire
PAN, Prince of the Incubi
LILITH, Prince of the Succubae
LEONARD, Grand Master of Sabbats *(Three-horned goat, Dict. Inf)*
BAALBERITH, Grand Pope (Lord of the Covenant)
PROSPERINE, Arch-devil *(Roman Goddess of Spring, Wife of Pluto)*

Chapter Ten

" "H ere is a well-composed court," interrupted the pharmacist, "and our author does this well, but go on, Claude – read the passage on werewolves to us." Claude Michu turned a few pages and continued:

"Wizards and magicians were once more numerous than today. It is certain that there were kings, queens, princes, and potentates who practiced their arts and who protected them. Also, housewives were often troubled and bothered by the approach of bandits who traveled either alone or in groups. They seized the weak-willed, and as there are such folk in all classes of society, it was among these people that they found their victims quite easily, however they particularly sought them out among the rich and powerful, and to prove this, I will give you an example:

The wretched shysters had seized the spirit of a woman of means and persuaded her that she would have a lot of pleasure and agreed to correct her husband's passion for hunting, which made him spend many days apart from her. They put it in her mind to take the form of a wolf and to surprise her husband by leaping on him when she saw him enter the woods, where she would be hiding in wait.

The gullible wife told her husband that she had to visit a lady in the neighborhood, and with the aid of magical means, she took on the form of a wolf and went to the trail.

By a rather singular chance, her husband did not go out that day – he saw one of his friends passing from his window with whom he would go hunting, and who invited him to join in this pleasure. He excused himself and asked for a tale of the chase – his friend promised to do so.

The hunter, approaching the woods, was attacked by a large wolf. He fired a shot at him which did not hurt the animal, and it continued to approach him. He took the wolf by the ears, knocked it down and cut off a paw which he put in his game bag. When he had finished the hunt, he returned to his friend's home, and took the wolf's paw out of the bag. To their amazement, they found it had transformed into a woman's hand, adorned with a gold ring which the husband recognized as that of his wife. Violent suspicions arose against her, and they searched for her throughout the house, finding her by the kitchen fireplace, warming herself, and taking care to hide her hand, but she was unable to do so for long.

Her husband confronted her, she could not deny what she had done, she confessed that she had attacked the hunter because she believed he was her husband.

7: Image from The Wolf Woman, 1916 silent movie starring Louise Glaum, Public Domain

This case caused a lot of hubbub in the countryside - the woman was arrested and brought before the judge. It was recognized that she had been bewitched by the leprechauns, whose advice she had followed. For having succumbed to such methods which demonstrated her ferocity and premeditation, she was condemned to be burned at the stake for the crime of witchcraft and premeditated murder.

The resources of the leprechauns are rather vast, since they have the power of invisibility, and thus they can torment us without being seen, and further, without being able to be caught. It is hopeless for the poor sufferer, we must therefore consider the bad leprechauns as a moral sickness, which is much more dangerous than physical harm – one might almost consider the cause the remedy. We say in common parlance that the devil is everywhere – this means that all the earth is favorable to exercise his maleficent power that he prepares for us and sends our way. He slips into whatever form he chooses, and counterfeits whichever personality he wishes."

At a word from Bernard Morand, Claude paused his reading.

"That's a curious fantasy," said the pharmacist, "and you see how entertaining are the tales of Mother Goose which have influenced our author. Do not be surprised, after that, if passionately believing in leprechauns and animated by a great fire of charity for his fellowmen, he has looked for ways to save them from this obsession."

"The remedy he found is as pleasant as the rest of his theory. Before letting you know this remedy, I must remind you that Berbiguier was a poor deranged soul, and that we must not see in the exposition of his system anything more than a novel curiosity, worth studying, especially for those, like Claude Michu, tend to exercise their reason a bit feebly and not apply the facts to logical end. Read on, my dear Claude, the history of the Revealing Bucket and the Prison Bottles of Berbiguier.

Chapter Eleven

THE REVEALING BUCKET & THE PRISON BOTTLES

"What do you mean by revealing buckets and prison bottles?" ask most people when I speak of these things. I tell them, you will understand these as I teach you my methods, in a mysterious air – because I can grant myself an air suitable to the occasion.

Would you like to know what I call my revealing bucket and my prison bottles? Let me introduce them to you.

My revealing bucket is a wooden vessel that I fill with water and then place on my window. This serves to unveil the leprechauns who are in the clouds. I think I have already explained to my readers what the power of the scapegoat is – the leprechauns soar and dive on the airstreams when they use their aerial physics. I have therefore invented my revealing bucket to see them travel through the air.

This bucket, filled with water and placed on my window, as I mentioned, serves to reflect for me all the operations of my enemies in the water. I see them argue, jump, dance, and fly much better than all the acrobats like Fortoso and Saqui in the world. I watch them when they conjure time, when they pile up the clouds, when they cause lightning and thunder.

The water which is in the bucket follows all the movements of these wretches. I see them sometimes in the form of a serpent or an eel, sometimes as that of a starling or a hummingbird. I see them and yet I cannot reach them. I must satisfy myself to say to them – Cruel monsters, why can I not drown all of you in this bucket which reflects your ugly iniquities! The unfortunate people whom you persecute would be immediately delivered from your infamy. I see you right now in my bucket on my window. Dear God! What a flock of monsters is assembled here! Begone! They are allied. Incredulous folk look in my bucket, and you will not annoy me anymore with your denials.

"Let me tell you now about my prison bottles. All the operations I have described are nothing compared to what I am doing with these bottles. Formerly, I did not keep my enemies under captivity for more than eight or fifteen days. Now, I can deprive them of their liberty forever if their bottles are not opened or broken. I imprison them in a quite simple way – when I feel them walking and jumping on my bedcovers at night, I disorient them by throwing tobacco in their eyes – they do not know where they are and fall like flies on my blanket, where I cover them with tobacco. The next morning, I carefully pick up the tobacco grains with a card and I empty them into my bottles, in which I also put vinegar and pepper. I then seal them with Spanish wax and thereby deny them any ability to escape the imprisonment to which I condemn them.

Tobacco serves to nourish them, and the vinegar quenches them when they are thirsty. So, they are kept in a state of discomfort, and they are witnesses of my daily triumphs. I place my prison bottles in such a way that they can see everything I do and report to their comrades. As proof that they cannot escape their bottles, I threw the tobacco from one in front of Mrs. Gerand into the fire, at which point we both heard the burning leprechaun sparkle in the brazier as if he were covered in a large quantity of salt grains.

I want to present one of the smaller bottles to the conservator of the Museum of Natural History. He would place it among the menagerie of animals as a new species. It is true that he cannot keep them captive in a cage, as one might place a tiger or a bear, but he would show them in a bottle from which they would be unable to escape.

If among the curious folk who would visit the Botanical Garden and the Natural History Museum, there were perhaps some who did not believe in the existence of leprechauns, the conservator would only have to ask them to stir the bottle to convince them of the existence of evil spirits in their prison, and hear, as I do on a daily basis, the cries of my prisons who seem to ask me for mercy – this would silence the incredulous and the leprechauns would rage on."

"I will not ask you to suspend your disbelief for too long about what you have just heard," said Bernard Morand, when the reader had finished. "We must laugh and do nothing else, at how nonsensical all this, while seeming well-conceived and well-executed. It is too early for us to draw the evening to a close, so let me tell you about the fairies and acquaint you with the legend of Melusine, the serpent woman, one of the fairies who has been well documented by the chroniclers of these tales.

Tomorrow, I will inform you about the enchantments, evocations, divinations, metamorphoses, and other practices of witchcraft. You will see, I hope, that all these are no more acceptable than the existence of leprechauns.

The pharmacist replaced Berbiguier's book in the library and took another in his hand.

"This," he said, handing it over to Claude Michu, who he had, as we can see, elevated to the function of reader, "is a memoir, where is narrated, according to a story by Jean d'Arras, printed in 1699, the legend of Melusine. You will hear about the legend soon enough. Let me tell you first about the fairies, called fados, in the Provencal idiom, who have the specialty of presiding over births and acting as good or bad spirits, over the destiny of the child to whom they are attached. The dark tales say they experience love for men, and never give up, continuing to wreak their vengeance if they are repulsed or abandoned. You have also read the tales of Perrault, and you know, without further explanation, with whom you are dealing. Listen closely – after this, I will bid you goodnight.

Claude, who did not feel tired, as he took much pleasure in this discussion, began immediately to tell the tale of the fairy Melusine.

Chapter Twelve

THE HISTORY OF THE FAIRY MELUSINE

Historical note on the occult sciences, by M. de Fontanelle (Roret Collection), Summary of the novel by Jean d'Arras from a memoir by Mr. Babinet

J ean d'Arras, secretary of the duke of Berri, collected the popular folktales about Melusine in 1387, by the order of Charles V, for the entertainment of the duchess of Bar, sister of the king. Lusignan was the last fortress that the English held in Poitou. After the victory that Dugeusclin won over them at Chize, and the subsequent taking of Niort, the English were forced to return Lusignan. Most of the garrison of Lusignan had perished at the battle of Chize. Poitou and all the provinces ceded to England by the disastrous treaty of Bretigny were delivered to the French. Jean d'Arras composed the novel of Melusine in celebration of the surrender of the last fortress the English held, who was traditionally believed to be the founder of Lusignan.

According to the novel which he published, Melusine was the daughter of Elinas, king of Albania and Perssine. Perssine was a fairy, who met Elinas when he was hunting. As a condition of her marriage, he promised her he would never see her in her bedchamber. She gave birth to three girls – Melusine, Meliar and Palestine.

Nathas, son of the first wife of Elinas, was jealous of his stepmother, and induced his father to break the promise he had made to her. When Elinas entered his wife's bedchamber, the queen and the three girls disappeared instantly.

When Melusine and her sisters grew older, their mother told them of their origins, the betrayal of their father, and the subsequent exile to which they had been condemned to live in, as a result. To avenge the misfortunes of their mother, the three sisters seized their father and imprisoned him in a cavern dug into a mountain, condemning him to a perpetual prison.

Perssine, irritated by the crime of her daughters, and defending a husband who she had never ceased to love, drove her three daughters from her presence, cursing them. Melusine was condemned to transform, every Saturday, to become a snake from her waist down. However, if she found a husband who agreed not to see her on Saturday, her punishment would end in the present life, if he failed to speak with her, she would be condemned until Judgement Day. Meliar was imprisoned in a castle of Armenia, guarded by a sparrow hawk, and Palestine was destined to watch and protect a treasure in the heart of a tall mountain, until a knight from the house of Lusignan came to fetch her to conquer the Holy Land.

Jean d'Arras does not say what happened to Melusine after her mother's curse. He takes his readers to the castle of a Count of Poitiers named Aimery. During a hunting party, the Count and Raimondin, his nephew, were lost in the forest of Colombier at the night.

Skilled in astrology, the Count consulted the stars, and saw that they promised a brilliant future to whoever would kill him that night. Hardly had he informed Raimondin of this sad prophecy when they were attacked by a wild boar, who had chased them all day. Raimondin rushed to his uncle's defense, but the boar turned away and leapt on the Count who had seized a spear. Raimondin pursued the bear and struck him with his sword, but the blade slipped over its bristles and struck the Count, who was stabbed just as he was spearing the wild boar.

Raimondin, terrified by this involuntary crime, mounted his palfrey, and departed from this fatalistic place. Insensate, he wandered until the next morning, so troubled by the misfortune that had struck him, that he did not pay attention to his environs, until he was at last drawn from this state by a sudden movement of his steed.

He recognized then that he was in a very risky place. He was at the foot of a high rock, from which sprung a marvelous fountain called the Fountain of Thirst, the Fairy Fountain, or the Bridge of the Seas, and renowned for the wonders which were witnessed thereabouts.

Melusine was bathing there, with two attendants. She met Raimondin and reassured him that the situation of his uncle and all that had transpired was not his fault. Raimondin, surprised by what he had heard, thought that divine justice had brought him to this redoubtable place, to make him undergo the punishment for the murder of his lord, but reassured by the lady, he gave himself to her counsel and returned to Poitiers to find the people plunged in mourning. The populace, imputing to the boar the death of their sovereign, were burning the body of the wild boar as a felon and false murderer at the door of the church where they were performing the Count's funeral.

Raimondin, following the advice of Melusine, paid tribute to the new count, and asked him to grant him in fief, as much ground as a stag's skin might cover. The count, looking upon this request as having little value, saw no difficulty in granting it, and named the commissioners who would deliver this request to Raimondin.

On leaving the church of St. Hiliers, where the count was receiving the vows of his new subjects, a man presented himself to Raimondin and offered him a stag's skin, which he bought and gave to a saddler to cut into strips, which the workman executed with such skill that the commissioners were surprised when they saw how finely it had been sliced, but they were obliged to literally execute the charter the Count had given them, as demanded by Raimondin.

When they arrived at the Fountain of Thirst, they were surprised to see that an immense trench had been dug in this uninhabited place amidst the surrounding forests. At once, two men appeared, took the skin of the stag and following the path indicated by the trench, they covered a circuit of two leagues (eight kilometers). Returning to the starting point, they discovered they had a surfeit of strips. They unrolled these to enlarge the circle and instead of planting a stake to hold it together, a fountain sprung up in the center and the two men disappeared.

The commissioners, filled with astonishment, returned to the Count's castle, and recounted the marvels that they had witnessed. Some days later, Raimondin returned to Poitiers to invite the Count and all his court to his wedding with Melusine, which further increased the surprise that had been caused by the tale of the commissioners. The count asked Raimondin what was the parentage and country of origin of his new wife. He refused to answer and from that moment on, everyone was convinced he had had an adventure near the Fountain of the Fairies.

The wedding was performed with much pomp and circumstance – the Count and the accompanying lords admired the elegance and number of pavilions prepared in such a short time to receive the nobles of the country. They could not understand where he had found the multitude of servants who hastened to meet the needs of the ladies and knights who had been attracted to this marvelous marriage by the fame of the event.

The gracefulness of Melusine captivated all hearts, and the Count, who had initially felt it a challenge to allow an unknown woman to enter into his family, left the marriage convinced that such an alliance could only increase the honor of his lineage.

We must not forget that Melusine, before agreeing to marry Raimondin, had made him swear that he would never look at her on Saturday, or ask her what she became.

Melusine, in addition to the riches that she granted Raimondin, gave him a nuptial present of two wands which had crystals of great value. The first, that he to whom it would be given in love would not die by the stroke of arms, the second, that he to whom it would be given would be victorious over his enemies, whether individually or in a group.

After leaving the Count of Poitiers, Melusine told Raimondin that his father was originally from Brittany, where he had possessed great property, which he had been deprived of by a conspiracy hatched by a Breton Lord named Josselin, who had the ear of the king of Brittany, and to whom the confiscated property had been granted by his father. Raimondin, on the advice of Melusine, went to Brittany to demand the inheritance of his ancestors.

The king, to know the truth of the claims of the strange knight, ordered a judicial combat between Raimondin and the son of Josselin. Raimondin was victorious and asked for mercy for the vanquished, but the king was too good a judge not to order the hanging of Josselin and his son who were declared traitors in God's judgement.

The Breton king made every effort to keep the brave knight by his side, but his love for Melusine recalled Raimondin to the rock of the Fairy Fountain. He gave the lands he had just conquered to two cousins who lived in Brittany, and left the King as filled with admiration for his courage as for his generosity.

Josselin's parents, wanting to avenge the shame which Raimondin had given them, set a trap for him on his return, which he dispelled by his valor. During his absence, Melusine had not remained idle – by the aid of her magical powers her workmen had constructed a magnificent castle in a few days on the mountain overlooking the Fountain of Thirst.

Raimondin, on his return thought that his eyes betrayed him when he saw a tall fortress and heard a sentry's horn from the high keep of a place he had left in a deserted condition. The new castle was called Lusignan.

Raimondin ruled over this castle for a long time by the power and glory which he had by the wisdom of Melusine. He had nine children – the eldest, Urania, was king of Cyprus; the second, Guyon, was king of Armenia; the third, Regnault, was king of Brittany; the fourth, Geoffrey of the Great Tooth became Lord of Lusignan; the fifth, Fraimon, a monk at Maillezais, the sixth, Antoine, Duke of Luxembourg, the seventh, Raymond, Count of Forests, the eighth, Thierry, Lord of Parthenay, and the ninth, named 'The Horrible', because he had but one eye in the middle of his forehead, was put to death according to the orders of his mother when she was half woman and half serpent. Her magical science had taught her that if he lived, he would destroy everything that she had accomplished for the grandeur of her house. He was therefore stifled under wet hay, which had been set on fire, and was interred in the Abbey of Moutierneuf in Poitiers.

Melusine and Raimondin lived happily until envy disturbed their bliss. The Count of Forests, elder brother of Raimondin, jealous of his prosperity, having known that Melusine disappeared every Saturday and no one knew where she went, induced suspicion in his brother about the fidelity of his wife.

Raimondin, inflamed by jealousy, entered the most secret rooms of the castle, formidable places he had never dared advance to. He was stopped by enormous brass doors. Furious and wishing to see inside these barriers - proof of the accusations directed against his wife – he drew his sword and pressing the point against the door, he turned the hilt and made a hole, which revealed the most deplorable mystery to his indiscreet eye – he saw Melusine performing her punishment as half woman and half serpent. She was struggling with a large basin, from which she poured water into the vaults of the hall.

MÉLUSINE

8: Mélusine découverte par Raymond de Lusignan, artist unknown,
Histoire de la Magie, P. Christian 1870, Public Domain

Raimondin, seized with pity and terror, to see a noble lady in such a miserable state, shut up the fatal hole. His fury turned against his brother, whom he chased from his presence, threatening him with death, if he ever returned to his domain. But, as the fatal secret had not escaped him, the charm was not broken, and after a night filled with anguish, he saw Melusine return to find him as usual. He still hoped for happiness, but an unfortunate servant caused him to lose everything.

Geoffrey, irritated that Fraimon had become a monk, went to the Abbey of Maillezais, and finding the religious folk gathered for divine offices, made an enormous bonfire around the church, and burned the monks and the convent to ashes. Raimondin, angered with this attack, publicly reproached Melusine, that she and her children were only phantoms, and that he was disappointed by her charms and spells and revealed the secret of her Saturday penitence.

Thus, the destiny of Melusine was accomplished – her maternal curse fell on her. She hurled herself out of a window on which remains the mark of her foot and transformed into a half woman, half-serpent form. Raimondin, calming himself from his anger, remained in a long depression, at the sight of disasters that he had called on himself, and to expiate his sins of striking a woman who had showered him with such favor, he renounced all his power and went on a pilgrimage to Rome, before secluding himself in the town of Montserrat.

As for Melusine, she had no dwelling on earth – she was condemned until Judgement Day to the monstrous state which her mother's curse had placed on her. Her tenderness for her children brought her back to their cradle, and their nurses often dragged her enormous tail into their rooms, and she nourished them during the night with her maternal care.

In the following centuries, whenever a calamity endangered her posterity, she was heard on a stormy night, roaming the battlements of the castle of Lusignan. A well-known apparition, if any exist, is described in the following adventure:

After the successes due to the wisdom of Charles V and the bravery of his constable, who had defeated the English power on the continent, Jean, Duke of Berri, and Count of Poitou, brought an army to the walls of Lusignan, the only fortress the English still held in Poitou. Serville, who commanded the castle, was obliged to surrender.

He told the Duke of Berri that the preceding night, a monstrous half-woman, half-serpent being had appeared before him, it had struck his bed with its long tail, about 8-9 feet long. He took his sword to defend himself, but the snake did not harm him, but went to warm herself by a large fire which illuminated the entire room and stayed there all night. She even assumed her human form for some time, but was dressed in only coarse rags, like a penitent, and seemed unable to defend herself.

"Serville" replied the duke of Berri, "how did you, who have been in so many places, have any fear of this serpent? This was the lady of this fortress, that she had erected – you knew that she would never hurt you. She wanted to show you how you had to withdraw from this place."

Serville then added that a local woman, with whom he had charmed the boredom of his garrison, had witnessed the apparition, and had not displayed any fear. In order to not doubt the reality of this fact, it must be remembered that Jean d'Arras, being secretary of the Duke of Berri had written this down by the order of Charles V, victor over the English, and that, this apparition, Melusine, far from being troubled, had been able for a brief time to resume her natural human form, no doubt because the castle she had constructed was about to be delivered from the yoke of the foreigner.

Such is the faithful analysis of the narrative of Jean d'Arras.

One finds such tales everywhere in the Middle Ages, with its naïve credulity and its wondrous imagination.

Chapter Thirteen

The following day, Bernard Morand began thus:

"You, Claude Michu, who would like to be attractive to Madeleine, your pretty little busybody, I will teach you a magic conjuration, which was popular in Germany in the old days to ensure one's true love."

One would take a lock of hair of one's beloved and place it in his clothes, then one would make a general confession – and then perform three masses during which the hair was placed around his neck. At the last gospel, one lit a blessed candle and said, *"O candle, I beseech you by the virtue of the All-Powerful God, by the nine chained angels, by the guardian spirit, to bring me the one I love, so that she belongs to me."*

"What do you think of this process, Claude Michu?"

"I think, Mr. Morand, that you are mocking me."

"I am not making fun of you. I am only describing to you a practice that many lovers had used to their benefit. You will grant me that it is not more ridiculous than that of the Red Dragon, and that it is not as foolish to light a candle as to burn a donkey's head like your experiment at the Black Hole?"

Claude lowered his head in shame.

"Come," said Morand, "compose yourself. I wanted a little laughter before we talk about the many formulas of divination or enchantment used by magical dabblers in all ages."

"Divination has always enjoyed great favor with weak minds."

"To know the future is the most important objective of many people in their lives. They do not think that the future belongs to God and that the duty of man is to live honestly in the present, leaving for Providence the care of future things."

"Heaven would have made us a baneful present if we were given the power to read our own destiny."

"This would have denied us our present happiness – because which man would be bold enough to support himself without succumbing to the power of a science which allowed him to probe the mysteries of time? He would know in advance the future tests he must pass; he would know what term was assigned to his days, and this knowledge would make life unbearable for him. He would calculate the remaining hours and live without the hope in which the mind finds sweetest satisfaction."

"The ancients had many methods of divination."

"Meteors and the shapes of clouds were signs that they interpreted according to the various forms. They also made predictions by means of alectoromancy – that is, by describing on the earth a circle divided into twenty-four parts, in each of which was placed a letter of the alphabet and a grain of wheat.

"A rooster was then introduced into the circle and as the rooster ate one of the grains, one noted the letter that this grain covered. The letters formed the element of prediction."

"They also knew divination by salt. It was considered a bad omen to forget to put the saltshakers on the table, or to fall asleep before they were removed. In our day, superstitious people are still frightened by an overturned saltshaker – there is no other misfortune in this than the loss of the saltshaker when it breaks, or that of the salt when it spills.

9: An augur declares Numa Pompilius king after an oracle of bird flight, etching by Bernhard Rode 1768-69, Public Domain

But the taste for divination was not always limited to these innocent examples. They would commit various crimes, such as to search in human entrails for the secret of future events.

The human sacrifices offered by the Druids, our ancestors have bloodied the soil we cultivate today, and thousands of innocent people have fallen victim to barbaric practices that only Christianity could destroy. *(ed. Ironic)*

The stars, the numbers, the colors, the flight of birds, plants were used for divination.

Regarding plants, one can, without turning to sorcery, agree to one aspect about them that the sorcerers claim. It is certain that by examining some plants, one can almost exactly tell what time it is, but there is nothing marvelous about this fact – it is purely scientific and based on acquired notions with respect to plant habits.

It has been recognized, for example, that the corollas of flowers open and close at a fixed time. With some knowledge of botany, one can compose a floral clock and manage without a solar clock. Linnaeus gave this example and constructed a table which shows the hours of day and night that various plants open and close.

Flowers have been my companions on my long walks, until it was time to return home.

So, seeing the white waterlily fold back it's chalice, I tell myself, "I am late, it is five o'clock, because the waterlily, which blooms at 7 A.M. in the morning, closes at five o'clock in the evening.

All times are indicated in the same manner.

There are plants that especially mark the night hours. These are, for example, the geranium triste, the Night-flowering catchfly, and the large-flowered cactus, which bloom at six, nine and ten o'clock. I imagine that you did not think that you had such charming clocks around you. One day, I will teach you to use them in a more comprehensive manner. Allow me now to speak of dreams in which people still pretend to read hidden warnings.

Do not believe in the interpretation of dreams, my friends – never buy those absurd treatises where one believes one is taught the meaning and significance of dream images. With a bit of reason, you can convince yourself quite easily of the inanity of these observations. What we see in our minds are not representations of future events, but a vague painting, sometimes exaggerated images of past events, and I propose, there are no dreams where one cannot reconstitute the elements.

The role of the soul in dreams cannot be explained. It is certain, however, that in this situation, and despite the physical inertia and moral insensibility that resembles death, the imagination is overexcited and continues to act spontaneously, but it is directionless – it floats in the ocean of sleep, so to sleep, and receives, as if in a cloudy mirror, confused images of the day's events or rough thoughts sketched through the day. Sometimes, it goes back quite far into the past. A forgotten fact is remembered, one forgotten even the day before, and it is reproduced, accompanied with circumstantial details, to create the most material sensation possible.

Thus, after falling asleep under heavy blankets, one sometimes feels a sense of discomfort or even an inexpressible anxiety. So, we think we are gripped by an iron hand – imagination shows us an elf squatting and stomping on our chest. This is a nightmare – one wakes from it with a start, the forehead sweaty, panting breath. One pushes away the heavy blanket. The cause of evil is thus dispelled, and one goes back to sleep calmly.

However, in such a case, if you were to consult a sorcerer like Father Simounen, he will find a host of meanings to your nightmare. He will not say to you – you were too covered. He will take a solemn tone and assert to you without laughing that you have many enemies, that these enemies are pursuing you and preparing to do you harm (which is superabundantly proved by the anxious sensation you had to suffer). He will ask you for thirty sous for the consultation – you will give him the money and you will prove once more that there are still fools in this world.

Here, I must tell you one of my dreams and the studies I have done myself on this subject.

You will see by what induction I arrived at an understanding of what initially seemed inexplicable.

Here is my dream:

I was in a great plain, covered with fragrant flowers and populated by butterflies with glittering wings. A great feeling of well-being filled my soul and I walked slowly, when I realized that I was not alone. A man was coming behind me, following me step by step. Soon, this man put his hand on my shoulder, and it seemed he was pushing me forward. The movement was at first insensible, then he accelerated and acquired a dizzying pace. I was going faster than the wind, and while running it seemed to me that I lost contact with the ground and my feet were moving in the air. I did not run anymore, I flew. I flew whirling, and soon I could not distinguish my surroundings. My heart missed a beat, and I was going to faint, when I found myself suddenly sitting in front of a table laden with fruits and flowers, facing a Turk who was gravely smoking his pipe, and who invited me to refresh myself and have a sorbet. I obeyed, when a black man entered the place where we were sitting, bringing with him a long needle with which he cleaned the pipe of my host. The latter then took the needle and showed it to me:

"You see," he said, "this is to complete my collection."

"And without further ado, he passed the needle through my body. I did not suffer, but I began to shake my arms and legs. Then, I fell in front of the table, and the point of the needle began to spin on the ground, imprinting itself on my body, in which it was wedded, in a rapid rotating movement.

I lost for a moment the sentiment in my situation and I found myself in a church where a large crowd had gathered. I wanted to push through the crowd to reach the door, when it seemed to me that the walls were narrowing around me and were going to choke me.

I cried for help – my voice stopped in my throat. I tried to utter a cry and this effort woke me up.

It was a wonderful day. I got up, and while putting myself to work, I thought of this nonsense verse that I have recounted to you.

"Of course," I thought, "if I consulted a man about this dream, he would not fail to tell me beautiful things. To see flowers is a good omen, entering a church is not always a good one, this Turk who skewered me, after having offered me a sorbet is an enemy who wants my undoing, and who cajoles me to better reach me.

All considered, I applied my usual method to my dream. I reconstructed the previous day, and as you will see, I found all the source elements of my nocturnal visions.

The flower-covered plain was my garden where I had walked for an hour in the morning. While strolling, I had begun to think about aerial locomotion. I had thought of the principle that birds, heavier than air, support themselves in space by the motion of their wings. From these principles I passed to those of gravitation of bodies. I had amused myself by following the thrust of a violently thrown stone, and by calculating how many seconds before it began to descend from the point of departure. This was an easy explanation of my transformation into a flying man. My imagination left to itself during sleep had substituted itself for the bird, and I had seen myself launched into space and supporting myself quite naturally.

But what about the Turk? What was the Turk doing in this affair? I thought about it for a long time, and I managed to understand the origin of the Turk.

While reading my journal, I had found, in foreign news, the story of a feast offered at Constantinople, by the Sultan, to the new ambassador of France. This festival had made me think of The Thousand and One Nights & all the splendors of the Oriental life. This reverie had certainly earned me the unexpected intervention of my Turk.

But why did my Turk pierce me with a needle?

These were just reprisals! Because I had myself stuck, the same day, a magnificent beetle, collected in the fields by father Michu. The poor beast, though pierced from one end to the other, continued to wave its antennae and forewings, just like I myself had shook my arms and legs after my torment.

The rotary movement imprinted on the needle which pierced me was a memory of the first part of my dream. I mechanically returned to my thoughts on gravitation.

However, the situation was critical – by dint of spinning like a top, I had felt the force escape me and it seemed to me that I was going to die. The idea of death had given birth to a religious thought in me, that is how I could explain my presence in a church towards the end of my journey into the land of dreams.

The church explained, all that remained was to justify the anguish produced by the narrowing walls ready to choke me, an anguish that gripped me in my nightmare. Here, my task was easy.

When I struggled in my role as a spinning top, I slipped into an alley and was caught between the wall and the wooden bed. The ever-increasing pressure as I plunged deeper gave me the painful feeling that I spoke of.

So, my friends, I could have linked all the elements.

Nothing of the future was represented in my dream – on the contrary, everything related to the past.

If I have spent so much time on this subject, it is in order to convince you that you must never be afraid of these dreams, and in seeking explanation for them beyond a succession of natural facts that take place, are produced in you or around you, recently.

You will therefore give up all the other divinatory procedures which the malignant tribe of Simounen would prefer to base on the interpretation of dreams.

I condemn in principle all the forms of divination. I have no need, therefore, to dwell on cartomancy, which augurs the future, based on the combination of playing cards, nor on chiromancy, which reads it in the lines of the hand, nor on necromancy, which aims to evoke the souls of the dead in order to interrogate them, nor on the other practices offered to the credulity of the adepts.

I want to present various experiments before you that could not have been tried without danger for the operator, two centuries ago. At that time, it was enough to be a little learned to merit the dangerous qualification of sorcerer. However, the sorcerers were burned alive in the public square, and even if the craft were productive, one would admit that it was not safe from the point of view of the security of the practitioner. There were, I know, among the sorcerers who performed the job of poisoners, and whose loss was by no means deplorable, but how many poor people were condemned to the fire, who had nothing against them but their intelligence and their knowledge?

Albert the Great, who was a saintly man and an illustrious scholar, nearly failed to incur a charge of witchcraft, because, well-versed in the mechanical arts, he had invented automatons and machines that the ignorant public believed were the work of demons.

Del Rio assures us, that in 1515, in Geneva, more than five hundred people perished under the conviction of magic. They burned children who were supposed guilty of infernal practices.

The trials of Edelin, of Urbain Grandier, of the marshal of Ancre and many others are the unfortunate examples of the passion which blinded the spirits.

Very often, it is true, when one comes to the last person that I have just mentioned, the accusation of magic was used to disguise a political or private vengeance, but we must turn our eyes from these horrors to consider the benefits of the civilization that we enjoy today.

In our day, we do not believe in the marvelous, or letting utopias occur in broad daylight. Battling spirits and turning tables have their followers. They can proclaim their doctrines, which must fail before reason. As for the popular diviners, and the printers of the Blue Grimoires, and the sorcerers of Simounen's ilk, one must try to destroy their influence by general education. As long as they confine themselves to telling their absurdities to well-disposed minds, they are allowed to do so by making fun of them, but if they think of making this their profession, the law, which rightly regulates the commerce of fraud, reaches them, and punishes them.

This is what will happen one of these days to Simounen, if he still thinks of playing the kind of dirty tricks of which Claude Michu was the dupe.

With that, my friends, go to sleep and do not have bad dreams. I invite you to come tomorrow to attend my demonstrations. You will convince yourself that science, coupled with a little skill, is nothing but what was formerly called MAGIC.

Chapter Fourteen

hen Claude Michu and his other friends met for the third time at Bernard Morand's home, the pharmacist did not receive them in the room where he had hosted their previous meetings. He took them instead into a large laboratory, setup behind his home, in which he had assembled all the instruments and apparatus necessary for his scientific studies.

The appearance of electrical and pneumatic machines, of batteries, electromagnets, retorts, and balloons astonished his visitors who had never seen anything like it.

Before they could question him, the pharmacist told them, "All that you see here, my friends, is for profoundly serious work, which I will probably initiate you into later. For the moment, I do not want to show you any of that amusing science, instead we will begin by viewing a magical painting.

Bernard Morand then took a frame hanging on the wall and passed it under the eyes of his audience. The frame contained a drawing representing a winter scene. One could see, around a small cottage, some trees and bushes despoiled of their leaves. No birds were visible in the grey and sad sky. In front of the hut, no one was visible. The landscape seemed deserted.

"Very well! Claude Michu," asked Morand, "what do you think of this scene?"

"I say, sir, that I get a chill when I view it. It must freeze in that hut."

"Indeed, it is wintertime."

"And a fine winter, it seems. It appears to be the month of January in this scene."

"Doubtless. Very well! What would you say if I, without touching or removing this painting from its frame, changed it from winter to springtime and gave it the life it presently lacks?"

"By God! I would say that you are a great wizard."

"I am a great wizard, as you call me. How would you say the trees turn green?"

"By the sun."

"By the sun, because of the sun, this is the heat which revives. We do not have the sun, but we can apply some heat and work on the leaves."

"Is that possible!"

"You'll see. Take this lamp reflector in the corner and turn it on. It will provide a warmth strong enough for what we want to do."

Claude obeyed, and Bernard Morand placed the image a short distance from the lamp, which he warmed gently, saying to the peasants:

"Wait and see. Springtime is coming."

All the eyes were fixed on the image. It stayed an instant as they had seen it before, then, little by little, the leaves grow, as if enchanted, on the trees and bushes. Little men, full of cheerfulness seemed to come out of the paper, the sky populated with birds with wide wings, and one saw the rosy glow of dawn appear on the horizon. It was spring in all its splendor. Nothing remained anymore of the simple primitive drawing.

The assistants uttered a single cry of surprise.

"How is this possible!" exclaimed Claude, looking at his friend Morand in terror.

"Stop looking goggle-eyed, my boy," said the pharmacist, "and do not take me for a damned soul. The effect you have just witnessed is quite simple, and I will explain it to you."

"To make this changing picture, we first draw this winter scene in black ink, then with other inks that we call sympathetic inks, which I will explain the composition of, and to which we give all the desired colors, one paints the leaves, the people, the birds and the horizon. These inks have the property to become invisible by drying and reappearing in all their brilliance when exposed to the sun or moderate heat."

"This explains why the landscape, which was earlier in black and white suddenly took on all the nuances that you observe. There is nothing wonderful in this, it is only the adept application of a chemical process. Do you want me to show you how one can inflame a piece of metal by simply throwing it in a bowl of cold water?"

"This seems even more curious to me."

"It is perhaps even more elementary. Here is the object."

Bernard Morand took a capsule of porcelain containing a morsel of the metal called potassium and gave it to Claude Michu.

"What must I do?" asked the latter.

"Do the experiment yourself – plunge the metal in that bowl on the table and observe the results."

Claude timidly extended his hand over the water, expecting some devilry, then, after a short hesitation, he dropped the potassium in the bowl.

The liquid began to bubble, and instantly, innumerable globules of fire which had a bright light and intense heat burst forth.

"It is true," said Claude, amazed. "One could use a glass of water to set a barn on fire."

"This is explained by fact that the water, on contact with the metal, is immediately decomposed. The heat that the latter acquires is enough to immediately ignite hydrogen, one of the elements of water. At the same time, the oxygen contacts the potassium and dissolves it after changing it to potash.

One can also ignite two cold liquids by mixing them together. For this purpose, one mixes in turpentine essence and gasoline, nitric acid and concentrated sulphuric acid and one would see a strong flame suddenly burst forth.

"Certainly," said Claude Michu, "you show us that there are things which would even astonish old Simounen, but pardon me, Mr. Morand, a question for you. You have told us about hydrogen and oxygen in the water, but for my part, I do not know what these are. What do these two words mean?

"Water, my friends, is not a simple element as physicists have long believed. It is composed of two parts of hydrogen gas and one part of oxygen gas."

This truth, long unknown, is demonstrated by an easy experiment, which involves burning hydrogen and oxygen. These two gases, in consuming themselves, form water whose specific gravity is equivalent to their weight.

Oxygen gas, which is also the name of our vital element, exists in nature in an elementary state, and is present in air as well as in water. It is the only one suitable for combustion. A burning object almost extinguished, immersed in a bell filled with oxygen, reignites and burns with a bright flame.

Hydrogen gas burns with a blue flame. Combining with carbon, it produces the lighting gas which you are familiar with.

"But I believe I have occupied myself," reflected the pharmacist, "on a terrain too arid for you."

"To change the subject, I will make you see the devil."

"The devil!" exclaimed Claude Michu.

"Yes, a devil who you will not be able to seize or touch, because, while remaining very visible, it will be as intangible as air."

The pharmacist rolled a small pedestal in the middle of the room, which he arranged at his own pace in some time, then when he had finished his preparations,

"The devil that I will show you," he said to Claude Michu, "will appear to you in the middle of the room, as if it contained all the spirits of its ilk. Turn off the lights first."

The laboratory was once again plunged into darkness. The pharmacist approached the pedestal. Almost immediately the assistants saw a thin blanket of smoke, lit by a white light which they could not explain.

Then amidst the smoke, on the pedestal, they suddenly saw a little demon dressed in red.

"Take a stick!" cried Bernard to Claude, "and come chase the apparition!"

Claude hesitated.

"Do not be afraid," replied the operator. "It is only to prove to you that my little devil is intangible."

The young man then armed himself with a cane and struck the apparition who trembled for an instant but was not otherwise damaged. His cane seemed to only strike the void.

When the experience had finished, the questions began once again.

"What you just saw," said Bernard Morand, "is an application of the magic lantern. Only the image instead of being sent directly by the lantern on a white glass, is projected by the reflection of a mirror, on a cone of smoke coming out of a slot in the pedestal.

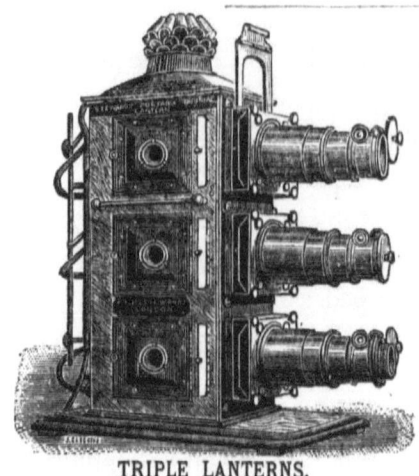

10: Magic Lantern, Colonial & Indian Exhibition, 1886, Public Domain

This is a child's toy which interests everyone, from what I can tell, because you have followed it closely and with much attention. Would you like, Claude Michu, for me to show you how one can leave one's money without fear of it being stolen?

"With pleasure, Mr. Morand."

"Give me a coin. I want you to experience this by your own purse. You will be better persuaded thus."

Claude Michu emptied his wallet into his teacher's hand, who threw all the contents on a metal tile.

Then pushing Claude towards the device, he said, "Try to take back what belongs to you."

Claude guilelessly extended his hand towards the money, but scarcely had he touched it with his fingers that he felt a concussion, which almost knocked him down.

"Put yourself here," said Mr. Morand, "and try again."

This time, the result was satisfactory. Claude Michu touched the copper plate with impunity and retrieved his money without any difficulty.

"If you want to know the reason for the double effect that was demonstrated," concluded the pharmacist, "Look at this iron plate on which you first stood to operate the apparatus. It is connected by an invisible wire with the copper plate on which we placed the money, and which I have heavily charged with electricity."

"Touching the copper plate with your finger, established a circuit between the two metals, copper and iron, a current which in crossing your entire body produced the concussion that you have experienced."

"In the second position, you simply touched the copper plate, and the electricity had no effect."

"Electricity is the instrument of many experiments which are as amusing as they are instructive. It is thanks to electricity that I produced this bright light which frightened you so much the other day, at the Black Hole."

"Where did this light come from?"

"It was produced between two pieces of carbon cut to a point and holding each to one of the conductors of a Bunsen battery."

"In a physics treatise that I want to gift to you, you will find all the explanations about this device in a simple and interesting manner."

The conversation stopped for a moment. Claude Michu took this opportunity to slip in a question that had been pressing him from the beginning of the session.

"Mr. Morand," he said, "while telling us about your changeable painting, you had spoken to us about the sympathetic inks. Could you please explain to us how one makes these inks?"

"Gladly, my boy. Here are some recipes that you can apply quite easily."

INK TO PRODUCE BLUE, RED OR GREEN TEXT

One must write by dipping the feather in a strong infusion of sunflowers, or in the juice of violet flowers. When this writing is exposed to hydrochloric acid vapor, it will turn red; subjected to the action of ammonia gas, it will vary from red to blue, if sunflower ink had been used, and change from red to green, if violet juice had been used.

INK FOR MAKING INVISIBLE WRITING APPEAR PURPLE

For this experiment, a solution of cobalt nitrate is used. The characters traced using this solution remain invisible, but if one passes over them a brush soaked in oxalic acid, a violet hue is produced.

INK TO TURN WHITE TEXT INTO PURPLE

One writes with gold nitro chloride and then wets the writing with tin hydrochloride diluted with water, which is enough to color the text purple.

INVISIBLE INK WHICH IS REVEALED ONLY BY SOAKING THE PAPER IN WATER

This ink consists of a saturated solution of aluminum sulfate and potassium hydroxide. Plunged in water, characters traced using this ink take on a dark hue which makes it possible to decipher them easily by placing them in the light.

"Further," Bernard continued, "one may write with these different colorless liquids and make the text appear by heating it a bit."

"So, with lemon juice, the writing appears in brown, with weak sulfuric acid, in red, with white vinegar, in pink, with onion juice, in blackish brown, with cherry juice, green."

When Mr. Morand had given Claude Michu the explanations that he had asked for, one of the listeners posed a question to him.

"I have seen," he said, "at the city fair, where I had gone lately, an inexplicable thing. Having entered a ring of acrobats, I was sent back for a session of magnetism, during which a man, endowed with what he called second sight, guessed everything that one asked – the age, the country of people, the amount one had in one's pocket, etc., etc."

"That is curious, indeed," replied Mr. Morand. "And did this man operate alone?"

"No, he had a second who was posed questions by the hypnotist."

"That's it! Well then, these two men were two cunning comrades and their second sight a joke. What you saw was simply better than a few others, that's all."

"What! Mr. Morand, do you not believe in magnetism?"

"That depends. I believe in magnetism, as that physical force, which is produced within individuals, by the establishment of an electric current, but I do not believe in the magnetism which claims to probe the future and read through the walls. This seems to me to be a bit of juggling, until serious proof is given for the contrary."

"The second sight has nothing to do with magnetism, and I will explain to you how it is commonly practiced."

"To be successful in this art, one must have a strong memory and also keen attentiveness."

"One of the comrades is blindfolded and placed at some distance from the spectators; the other stands in their middle to collect their questions. All the mystery of the second sight consists of the way in which the questions are asked."

"Are these the numbers?" the operator interrogates his partner so that the latter, following the letter which begins the questions, knows right away which number is used.

So, the word Confitures (Preserves), by example, is composed of ten different letters, which can perfectly correspond to the ten numerals, in the following order:

1. 2. 3. 4. 5. 6. 7. 8. 9. 0.

CONFITURES

If then, the comrade asks the subject: "How many coins do I have in my hand?"

The latter responds boldly: "One!"

Because the letter C which begins the phrase used for the question corresponds with the number 1 in the code word.

And this is done without the public doubting anything.

Thus, for the ten figures, one prepares a series of questions, which can be presented thus:

1. How much? C

2. Oh! say quickly. . . .O

3. Do not you guess? . . . .N

4. Do it promptly. . . .F

5. You must guess. . . .I

6. Try not to go wrong. . . .T

7. Prompt answer, let's go. . . .U

8. Look well. . . .R

9. Well? do you see? . . .E

9 or 10. Please, the answer. . . .S

"This is sufficient for the ten simple digits," observed Bernard's interlocutor, "but if I have, let's suppose, 22 francs."

"Ah well, one repeats the word indicator, that's all."

"For 2, it looks like:"

"Oh! I say quickly."

"For 22, one will say:"

"Oh! I say, Oh!"

"But" replied the controversial inquisitor, "If I have, say, 325. That's difficult"

"No! One pronounces the three phrases representing, 3, 2, and 5, taking care to pause a little between each, so as to make the insider understand this is a compound number."

"For 325, one says therefore:"

"Do not you guess? - Oh ! say quickly. - It is necessary to guess."

"N, O and J which form the initials for the questions easily, following the table that I gave you, for 3,2, and 5, and this method can extend as far as you wish."

"For the objects that the spectators usually carry on them, such as rings, watches, wallets, purses, etc., the operators have similar indicative questions.

But here the initial letters play no role. These are conventional phrases which serve to announce which object is being signaled to the second sight. So:

Looks good may mean --- Ring

Do not hesitate --- Watch

Come on! --- Wallet

Do you see? --- Handkerchief

We are waiting --- Pin

For unforeseen objects, one prepares a secret language, and the word

Attention indicates that we will use it.

So, one interrogates using words of exclamation which begins with the letters used to compose the name of the object.

This is a difficult art, but one gets skilled at it, quite quickly. Other practitioners take less pains, but they can only operate on their terrain, and of course on prepared ground. They use an acoustic duct which goes underground and communicate with the subjects. They affect to interrogate the latter in close detail, with the sole objective of placing the information at the ear of the hidden listener, thus giving their comrade the desired answers.

So, my friends, this is what most of the time is believed to be the second sight. One must admire the method applied, but do not marvel at the supernatural powers of those who exploit it.

"I would like Simounen to have been here," mused Claude Michu, in a reflective manner.

"If Simounen was here, he would have renounced his compromising profession, but Simounen is faithful to the Red Dragon, which pays him his money, waiting for him to take a false step which will put him in prison."

"If Simounen was here, he would have renounced his compromising profession, but Simounen is faithful to the Red Dragon, which pays him his money, waiting for him to take a false step which will put him in prison."

"So, what is this Red Dragon?" asked Claude Michu. "I do not know anything about it but the stupid conjuration that the shepherd had me learn, and I would like to know the substance of the book which Simounen seems to give so much importance."

"I can satisfy you in this regard, because I possess it, myself, as a sample of human foolishness. It is a bunch of absurdities, written a long time ago, by a man named Antonio Venitiana, who did not lack pride and presumption, as you will be able to convince yourself by reading this preface.

Bernard gave the Red Dragon to Claude Michu, who read the following passages amidst much laughter from the audience:

Chapter Fifteen

PRELUDE

(Note: This is virtually identical to the text of the Red Dragon grimoire and an interesting comparison)

J he man who groans under the overwhelming weight of prejudice & presumption will scarcely convince himself that I have been able to contain in this little compendium the essence of more than twenty volumes, which by their expressions and ambiguities, make philosophical operations hardly possible : but the disbeliever and cautious person who takes the pains to follow step by step the route that I guide them on will see for themselves the true banishing from their spirit of the occasional fear one might have from a series of efforts attempted through trial and error, be done out of season, or imperfect circumstances.

One can perform these operations and still be true to one's conscience, the evidence of which is visible by a glimpse at the life of St. Cyprian.

I might dare flatter myself by noting that the scholars of the mysteries of the Divine Science called Occultism will consider this book one of the most precious treasures of the future.

The author of the Red Dragon then adds:

This great book is so rare and sought after that one might, as the Rabbis say, call this the Great Work. It is they who have left us the precious original of which so many charlatans make useless forgeries, wanting to imitate the truth, which they have never discovered, and which they lack the capacity to grasp, while trying to grab the money of the common people, who approach them without searching for the true source.

This book is based on the true writings of the great King Solomon that were discovered by chance efforts. The great king spent his lifetime searching for the hardest, most obscure, and unexpected secrets; but he finally succeeded in all his enterprises, commanding and forcing obedience from even the most secluded spirits by the power of his Talisman or Key. What other man would have the powerful spirit and audacity to express the devastating words which serve God for commanding obedience and dismay from the rebellious spirits, by the force of his will, penetrating unto the vaulted ceilings of heaven by examining the secrets and powerful words that express the force of a terrible and honorable God?

It is this great king, who has captured the most guarded secrets, that serve the grand divinity, since it reveals the influence of the stars, the position of the planets, and the means to manifest all types of spirits, by reciting the great names that you will find later in this book, those which constitute the commanding & powerful Blasting Rod, and the effects that make the spirits tremble, and the effects which make the angels tremble who chased Adam & Eve from the earthly paradise, and from which God struck the rebel angels, thrown by their pride into the dreadful Abyss. The strength of this Rod forms clouds disperses tempests, powerful thunderstorms, hurricanes, and makes them fall on any part of the earth.

These are therefore the true words expressed by him that I have followed step by step, and with which I have complete agreement and satisfaction, having had the good fortune to experience success in my endeavors.

Antonio Venitiana del Rabina

Chapter Sixteen

"One can hardly read," said the pharmacist, taking the book himself, "a fantasy of such bad taste and in such bad French as this one. And do you want to know how the book responds to his pompous preface? We will take some excerpts from the chapter titled:

SECRETS OF THE MAGICAL ARTS OF THE GRAND GRIMOIRE

Bernard Morand flipped some pages, preceded by a rough engraving representing a red demon adorned with three horns and mounted on goat's feet, and continued, with pleasant commentary, the following formulae:

TO SPEAK WITH SPIRITS ON THE EVE OF ST. JOHN THE BAPTIST

From eleven o'clock until midnight, go near a bed of fern and say:

"I pray to God that the spirits which whom I wish to speak appear to me at midnight."

At three-quarters to the hour, say nine times these five words: "*Bac, Kirabace, Alli, Alla, Retragrammaton*

TO BE LOVED

It is necessary to say, while gathering the herb of nine shirts, known as Concordia, "I gather you in the name of Sheba, so that you serve me by bringing me the friendship of N____"

Then, you must put the herbs on the person, without her knowing it or noticing it, and she will immediately love you.

Here Bernard Morand interrupted his lecture and remarked to Claude

Michu that it was improbable for him to only have used this means to have himself loved by his betrothed Madeline. He had arrived at his goal by the honesty of his intentions, a regular conduct and a true love of work was the best herb that one could bring into the household.

TO MAKE ONESELF INVISIBLE

Steal a black cat, and buy a new pot, a mirror, a briquette, an agate stone, coal, and tinder. Take water at the stroke of midnight from a fountain. Then light your fire, place the cat in the pot and hold it covered with your left hand without moving or looking behind you, no matter what sounds you might hear. Then boil it for twenty-four hours and place it on a new plate. Take the meat and throw it over your left shoulder, while saying the following words: Take what you need and do nothing else.

Then place the bones under the teeth one by one, while looking at yourself in the mirror. If this does not look right, throw them over your left shoulder, while saying the same words until you find it, and until your reflection disappears. Retreat backwards, saying:

Father, into your hands, I give my spirit.

TO MAKE THE SEVEN LEAGUE GARTERS

Buy a young wolf, less than a year old, and cut its throat with a new knife, in the hour of Mars, while saying the following words: Adhumatis cados ambulavit in fortitudine cibi ilius

Then skin the wolf and slice the skin into one-inch-thick garters. Write the same words as above on the garters– the first letter in your own blood, the second with the wolf's blood, and so on, until the end of the sentence.

Bernard Morand, closed the book, saying to Claude:

"That's enough, I think, and you have been sufficiently educated about the Red Dragon. When Simounen speaks to you, you can answer him, knowingly, that you know as much about it as he does, and you will have no trouble in showing him that his famous book is good only to throw into the fire."

"We have extended our session this evening to the limits. Continue to come and see me, we will still have cause to speak of things that interest you and I will gladly put the little science I possess at your service."

Claude Michu and his friends took leave of their benevolent professor, and the farmer's son, strengthened by his good resolutions and by the useful lessons he had received, promised himself not to fall back into the faults his weakness had made him commit so often in the past.

Chapter Seventeen

*A*rriving two days later at Bernard Morand's place, Claude and his friends found him in a particularly good mood. The pharmacist held a newspaper and laughed as he went through it.

"Quickly," he said to his usual listeners. "I have something new to teach you."

"What!" said Claude Michu.

"I told you about the country wizards, right now there are sorcerers in Paris."

"In Paris!"

"Yes, indeed. But these were not as pleasant as Father Simounen was with you. The Parisians soon fanned their malice."

"Tell us of this, Mr. Morand."

"With pleasure."

The pharmacist folded his newspaper, settled comfortably in a large armchair and the circle formed around him.

"In speaking with you about necromancy," he began, "that is to say, talking to you about the practices of these jokers who pretend to talk with the dead, I have touched on a particularly important question pertinent to the fashion of our time – the question of Spiritualism."

Spiritualism is nothing but necromancy. Only the thing has changed clothes at the same time as the race.

It is no longer presented in the world, clothed in a scary appearance.

Spiritualists operate in salons. They vow to communicate directly with the invisible world and converse familiarly with the departed souls.

If necessary, they evoke this or that character, deceased for centuries, and write under his dictation.

Other times, they connect their audience with the spirits they frequent, and the layman can feel their icy hands grab their own, a sepulchral breath gliding over their face...

You understand that this is nothing but pure jugglery, and that the so-called spiritualists are all simply skillful tricksters.

However, many people profess belief in this phantasmagoria.

The intervention of the spirits is obvious to them, and badly placed would be any man who put it to himself to convince them of their naivete.

The seances of the spiritualists are well attended. They earn a lot of money from these exhibitions of their abilities.

"This favor granted to a childish show helps increase the number of believers and also those of the operators."

We who do everything with simple eyes and clear senses, we will certainly not give in to the presentation.

And, so long as we were willing to surrender to the training, the story that made me laugh out loud when you arrived, we would be quickly restored to reason.

Do you know that recently two American jokers have recently arrived in Paris, two brothers, demonic cousins of the devil, who claim to have frequent interaction with him?

"A fine tale which comes from far away."

Paris has long been awaiting the two wizards.

The newspapers had announced their coming well in advance, and one has marveled at their powers.

In America, in England, perhaps everywhere, tales have been told by the fervent adepts of Spiritualism that they have performed wonders and confused human voices.

"What have they done?" asked an old man in the group of peasants.

"A singular act. They placed themselves in a cupboard, one facing the other, sitting on a bench with furniture panels.

Once seated, they were tied tightly to their seat by means of strong ropes.

Then the doors of the cupboard were closed, in which were hooked, I must tell you, a large quantity of noisy instruments – bells, tambourines, rattles, etc., etc.

Hardly was the cupboard shut that a dreadful din was heard inside.

The bells rang.

The drum rolled.

The rattles creaked.

White hands showed through a window cut into the door of the cupboard.

The mysterious furniture was opened.

The wizards were still attached to the same place.

Who had done all this?

The spirits invoked by the two brothers, said the believers.

The cupboard was closed once again and reopened a second time.

One found the comrades as attached and motionless as before but stripped of their clothes.

A new marvel!

When the box of wonder was opened for the third time, the Americans were standing and free of their bonds.

Who had set them free?

The spirits, always the spirits, none but the spirits!

The joke lasted until the day when a sly fellow realized that the seat on which the spiritualists were seated was movable and allowed them to leave and resume with the wink of an eye the bonds that had been placed on them.

The false sorcerers had been pulling a fast one on the rest.

This ridicule has driven them from Paris, and spiritualism has received a severe blow, from which it will not recover for a long time.

If the two Americans had presented themselves as clever conjurers, we would have gladly applauded them.

But no! They wanted to introduce the marvelous into their trade, so no one thought of admiring the dexterity with which they had operated. We saw only one thing – that they pretended to take for dupes an audience that rightly passes to be the most intelligent.

The public became angry and exhibited the spirit cabinets, the news of whose misadventure is going around the world.

I knew, in time, a good man who thought himself a medium. In Spiritualism, a medium is an individual armed with the supposed power to communicate with spirits.

My man, whose story is somewhat instructive, was called Philip Larive.

At all events, he boasted of his occult power. According to him, nothing would happen to him without his being immediately warned by his familiar spirits.

You will see how well these spirits treated him.

Inside cabinet, curtains closed, he disengages arm of chair without disturbing bonds.

11: Magician Joseph Dunninger demonstrating an escape from a séance cabinet, 1941, public domain

Philip Larive was married, and his wife had brought him a very restricted dowry, in the sense that it was composed of successive rights sharply constrained by a collateral.

A trial ensued.

Philip Larive was likely to win this trial.

But it was necessary to find certain pieces that had been misplaced for a long time and to search carefully in the archives of his wife's family.

What did Mr. Larive do?

Instead of taking on a writing expert, as advised by his lawyer, and charging him with these inquiries, he simply trusted the spirits and spent his nights and days calling them to his aid, hoping they would not delay in revealing to him the existence of the papers and the place where they were hidden.

The spirits did not respond or rather they responded poorly, it appears, because the day of judgement arrived without Philip being able to show the proofs of his rights. He was sentenced, and his fortune fell so much from this blow that he had to think of setting up his own enterprise.

The Spiritualism he professed threatened to suffer from this sorry state of affairs.

But Philip made a success of leading his business and the marvelous together.

With the debris of his assets, he bought an establishment and began his commercial operations quite favorably.

Then, little by little, he began to neglect these same operations to devote his time exclusively to the practical follies by which he had so obstinately capped himself.

From then on, the business house went downhill.

Philip attended philosophically enough to the run of his hopes.

He always counted on a revelation from above that would open a bright future for him.

His wife reproached him.

He called her crazy.

It was seriously considered whether to shut up this fool who challenged the reason of others. But, as his mania was mild and did not translate into any seemingly extravagant appearances, he was forced to tranquilly consume his losses.

Philip Larive who was a landlord, an established man, having good lands in the sun, was now finishing his life in a hospice of indigent old men. Like the astrologer of La Fontaine, he fell into a well for stubbornly having his nose in the air.

"He believed then," said Claude Michu, "that these spirits would show him the future?"

"Precisely, he pushed to excess his faith in his beliefs – this is what led to his downfall."

"I believe," continued Claude Michu, "that despite what you have told us, I still think the future may be revealed to certain people. One has seen predictions being fulfilled, point by point, and this view is one that I often consider.

"Come on, Claude, you are not as healed as I presumed."

"Oh! I no longer believe in wizards."

"But you still believe a little in the soothsayers?"

"Without believing in them precisely, I suppose that the things predicted can occur occasionally."

"That is true but remember what I told you about prescience. God has concealed the future to safeguard the tranquility of our life. Only he himself can lift the veil of your destiny."

"But like you believe in God, you must believe that sometimes he likes to punish the credulous by which they have sinned."

Those for who misfortune has been predicted will do their best to try and escape it.

Often, led by the hand of God, who wants to test their faith at the last moment and punish them for their lack of self-confidence, they come to the fatal goal they have fled with so much care.

One meets one's destiny
Often by the paths one takes to avoid it

Since this evening, we are talking rather than experimenting, I wish to tell you about a striking and very truthful trait.

Encouraged by the keen attention of his audience, Bernard Morand immediately began the following narrative.

Chapter Eighteen

BEPPO THE BEWITCHED

*B*eppo Fabrini was a young mountaineer near Roquebrune, in the little principality of Monaco. He was used to the mountain and descended only rarely to the town, where he felt as if he was being suffocated.

His character was strongly affected by these habits of isolation.

He was proud, rough, and naïve, all at the same time. His father and mother, with whom he lived, had wanted to send him to school.

But, after a year, he had to be removed.

Beppo was visibly wasting away in the heavy atmosphere of the classroom.

He needed the fresh air of the mountains, the paths in full sun, the wandering life of the goatherds. While keeping his flocks, he hunted and showed great skill. So that, from the products of his hunts, he was able to keep his family fed during part of the year.

Despite his slightly wild instincts, he had a deep amity with his parents.

The thought that he was going to lose them one day was the sole preoccupation of his life.

You see that Beppo was a good sort.

All would have been well if he had not proven so credulous. But, like all people living outside civilization, he loved the marvelous with a passion.

The only reading in his long stations on the mountain was an old volume of magic that he had found by chance in the attic of his father's house.

The symbolic figures of the book made him dream for a long time, and the cabalistic formulae exerted a singular influence on his brain.

One day, when he was on the lookout in the woods, he saw an old woman come to the house in a miserable attire that evoked pity.

This was one of the nomadic gypsies who make a profession out of telling fortunes to all comers for a modest fee.

The old woman was without doubt proud of her chosen profession, because when Beppo tried to slip a coin in her hand, she pushed him away, saying:

"Thank you, I do not ask alms."

"Who are you?" the goatherd inquired curiously, surprised by the charms of the traveler.

"I belong to a gypsy tribe, and I read the future in the lines of a man's hand."

At this moment, a keen interest awoke in the spirit of Beppo.

"Well," he said, "keep the money I gave you. I return, tell me my destiny."

"So be it."

The old woman approached Beppo, took his hand in hers and studied the lines carefully.

"Very well," said the young impatient man, "what do you see?"

"I cannot tell you that."

"Why?"

"Because it would horrify you."

"Tell me everything."

"As you wish. Well, remember this – one day, you will kill your father and mother."

Beppo began to tremble and shake. A dreadful stupor took hold of him.

When he regained his senses, he searched in vain for the prophetess of misfortune around his house. She had left through the woods.

When Beppo returned home at night, he cast a somber and desperate look towards his parents.

The future was clear to his impressionable mind, open to superstitious impressions.

He would be the murderer of those he loved more than himself.

This thought became ever more persistent in his brain, and soon plunged him into a singular depression.

At dawn, he fled his father's home and took refuge on the highest peaks of the mountain. There, he found a bit of calm and relief alone.

His parents were alarmed by the change in Beppo's habits.

They questioned him, with earnest concern.

But the goatherd remained impassive. Without realizing it, he understood the ridiculousness of his preoccupations, and he did not want to admit them.

Six months after the prediction, Beppo disappeared.

His hat and rifle were found on the edge of the precipice.

His parents thought him dead, and wept for their only child, who bore all their solace and a part of their well-being by dying thus.

However, Beppo was still alive.

To escape his destiny, he had not feared to abandon his parents, old and infirm, and preferred to let them believe in his doom.

God would punish him cruelly one day for having yielded to a superstitious terror.

He reached the nearest port and embarked for Corsica, where he entered the service of a rich farmer on his arrival.

He lived there for three years, as quiet as one could be when one has remorse in one's heart.

No news from his parents had reached him, and he had not sought to procure any. After three years in Corsica, Beppo fell in love with a young servant of the farmer and married her.

His master, on this occasion, gave him a small estate to administer where he lived alone with a wife and a plowman.

All was well, Beppo was happy, and he forgot little by little the cause that had made him desert his country.

However, his parents had learned that the young man was not dead. A resident of Roquebrune, who had come to Corsica on business, had encountered Beppo at the market, and, despite the pressing recommendations of the latter, hastened to convey the happy news of his existence to the two old people.

The first thought of the father and mother was to go and embrace their prodigal son.

They left for Corsica, one fine morning and without being preceded by any message, arrived at Beppo's home.

A young woman was sitting on the threshold.

The father came forward trembling towards her and pronounced the name of Beppo.

"My husband!" exclaimed the farm woman. "He is in the city but will return this evening. What do you want of him?"

The old man introduced himself and opened his arms to his daughter-in-law. The latter wished to do honor to her guests. She put the whole house under their orders, and as night fell and Beppo had not returned, she made the old parents go to bed and gave them her own bed. Then, as she was worried about her husband's long absence, went to meet him.

However, Beppo was returning. To reach his home quickly, he had taken a side road. He did not meet his wife. Arriving at home, the young man was astonished not to see his wife sitting at the threshold, as was her custom.

As it was getting late, he thought that she might have gone to bed and slipped quietly into her room. Then, without lighting a lamp, he went to bed to kiss his wife.

Extending his hand in the darkness, he touched the head of a man.

Beppo drew back, stifling a cry of pain.

He could not doubt himself.

His wife had taken advantage of his absence to dishonor him and indulge with another man.

A blind jealousy engulfed him.

He drew his knife and jumping onto the bed, he pierced with a thousand blows those, who in his thought, had done him such a bloody outrage. As came out half mad with rage, a voice gently called out to him.

"Beppo!" And, before him, he saw his wife, smiling and happy at the news she had for him.

"Who did I strike?" he exclaimed; his mind seized with a terrible presentiment.

He returned to the room with a light and recognized the bloody truth.

The prophecy of the gypsy had been accomplished. Beppo had killed his father and mother.

"Well, you see!" said Claude Michu, who realized the story had ended.

"Yes," concluded Bernard Morand, "I note the weak spirit punished by God, and I regard the history of Beppo as a great lesson. If he had resigned himself to living with his parents as a good son, the chance that made him a murderer would not have happened."

Listen and learn well.

Chapter Nineteen

CORRECTIONAL TRIBUNAL OF TOURS (1)

Weak minds and sorcerers – sorceries – illegal exercise of medicine

(1)   The Law, journal of the Courts

$\mathcal{I}$n the countryside, we still believe in sorcerers. Perhaps, people still believe in them a little in the city, but there they are called by another name, and the crooks, to exploit the simple-minded, with so-called somnambulists, who are nothing but crooks. The only difference is that their practices are less coarse.

The Loyau couple live in the village of Beaumont-la-Ronce, where the husband performs his profession of horse-gelding. A gelder, in the countryside, does a little bit of everything – medicine, surgery, etc.

This one, on occasion, undertook necromancy.

They were also warned often of fraud and the illegal practice of medicine.

Their victims, the Lihoreau couple are farmers of Rouziers, a small community not far from Beaumont.

Under the pretext of freeing their cattle and themselves from sorcery, that had enslaved them by contagion, in the picturesque expression of Loyau, the latter swindled them about 1,400 francs.

Mrs. Lihoreau had died recently. She recounted the story of the practices that she and her husband had been the object of to a justice of the peace some days before her death. We will extract some passages which will give a measure of the credulity of these poor people:

Last July, our pregnant cow could not calve, we sent for Mr. Loyau, who managed to get the calf, and then told us that if the mother could not calve, this was because there was a misfortune on her. Then, putting the hands on the reins of the young heifer, he said, "there is also a misfortune on this one, and it will not be like the mother if you do not do what I tell you."

He took my husband to Beaumont and gave him a vial with the recommendation of pouring the liquid it contained on the four spurs of the heifer, as well as in the toes.

...This time, he asked us for money, and I saw my husband give him 300 fr. in front of me! As well as a dozen fowls, on which Loyau told us he would pass the evil which was upon us.

A second time before the harvest, Loyau arrived at our house at night, between eleven o'clock and midnight.

He knocked on the door. We opened and he entered, he told us that that a great evil had fallen on us, on our animals, on our children; that the sole means of conjuring this away is known only to him, but he can do nothing if we do not give him 375 fr. Then, he asked us for a plate, which he placed in the middle and poured some liquid on it and set it on fire with paper from his pocket. A blue flame rose as he uttered words we could not understand.

When all was burned, he said, "See, the bottom of your plate is dry, whoever harms you must be dry as well, but you cannot use this plate anymore. It must be thrown in the underbrush.

We were scared to death, my husband and me. We gave him 375 fr. He asked us for a dozen more fowls. He also demanded twelve pounds of butter.

...The next morning, Mrs. Loyau returned my basket.

She told us that the perpetrator intended to set us on fire, and to preserve us, she took three spoonsful of cold ashes from the hearth with three extinguished pieces of charcoal, placing everything it in a corner of her choice, then asked to visit all the rooms of the house...

Finally, she asked for 200 fr. 75 c., to save us from burning... we gave her this sum. ...A third time, Loyau brought two rosaries to the house for which he asked 200 fr. But my husband, having no more money, promised to give it to him some time later.

My husband also made a journey to Chartres, following the orders of Mr. Loyau, and there he found himself with another gentleman who we did not know. This unknown person has taxed my husband to give Mr. Loyau four bushels of wheat, to be able to harvest more, he recalled.

Mr. Loyau's threats and practices deeply frightened my husband and me, and that's why we gave him our last penny, and had to borrow for our needs.

After having the witnesses removed, the President of the court questioned the defendants.

The President to the defendant: Loyau, you lived at Beaumont-la-Ronce, what role did you exercise there?

A. That of the postman.

Q. Maybe, but you were practicing another industry, and if you gave cures to the animals, you also gave them to people gullible enough to believe your so-called science.

A. Only once, I gave sedative water to a young girl who complained of a severe headache.

Q. What you have prescribed is not as simple as you would have us believe. Do you know the Lihoreau couple?

A. Yes, sir.

Q. You've looked after their cattle... What do you say about everything they have claimed? The examining magistrate has informed you...

A. That it is not true.

Q. So they lie. They say that in many circumstances they have given you money and they must have been singularly moved by your practices to get rid of all they had, being so stingy!...

A. How then could they have given me all this? Lenoir still has a ticket of mine that I gave him following a loan he made me of 130 fr.

Q. Why? Because you had persuaded them that they were lost, that they were frenzied, enslaved, these were the words you used.

A. It is not possible for a man to be so limited as to believe these stupid things!

Q. If there were no people simple enough to believe such absurdities, there would be no rogues, and you would not be here.

A. If they accuse me, it is because they desire me. I challenge them to bring forth witnesses.

Q. Indeed, there are none, because you have always arranged to work in the shadows. But these poor people have spoken, and their story has such an accent of truth that it is difficult not to believe them.

You will hear, moreover, witnesses who will recount very compromising things about you.

Mrs. Loyau, you have attended many interviews, and you have taken an active part in all these practices?

A. I never helped my husband in these things-

Sit down, both of you. Usher, show Mr. Lihoreau in.

One heard several voices in the witness room. These were those of the usher and some witnesses who attempted to make it clear to Lihoreau, who was deaf, that the court was awaiting his attendance.

The usher finally entered, supporting Mr. Lihoreau by his arms, who presented himself with a dazed air.

The President: Come forward.

Lihoreau looked to the right and the left, then went towards the usher to whom he held out his hat.

The Witness: I hear hard, my good sir, I hear hard.

The usher brought him to the bottom of the court steps.

Q. Your name?

A. I hear with difficulty. (He put a hand to his ear in the shape of a horn)

Q. (To the usher) Repeat to him my questions.

Q. You are called Lihoreau? Your age?

A. I will soon be twelve years…Ah! Damn! Yes, Seventy-two.

Q. Do you know Loyau?

A. I know him without knowing him – for having cared for my horse and my ox, when he brought a bottle for my cattle who was sick, after which he told me that the poor beasts were enslaved. There he put the names of God. He said we were lost… I gave him whatever he wanted.

Q. After?

A. After that he told me: "You are not likely to double the sum you have given me three or four times…" I still had two hundred gold francs. I gave them to him. After that, as he said, we were bewitched. I borrowed from my wife. My poor deceased wife who has died… also gave me a lot of money.

Q. Did he not come at night?

A. Yes, he came in the middle of the night. Yes, yes…

He retreated back and appeared frightened by Loyau, whose eyes had just met his.

Q. What was it?

A. A lot of stories – I was caught like a feeble headed sort. He has enlisted us in this business. (Laughter in the room)

Q. What else has he done?

A. He gave each of us a rosary and told us that we had to take money to the crossroads.

Q. How much?

A. 200 francs.

Q. When he told you that you were bewitched, what did you say?

A. I was sick.

Q. If you were sick, how did you feel?

A. My faith, only that it choked me. (General hilarity)

Q. Did he not burn something on a plate?

A. Yes, and he even told me not to use the plate.

Q. What did you do with it?

A. (muffled) we threw it into the bushes, my good sir.

Q. So you were afraid of the devil?

A. Ah! Damn!

Q. And that is why you gave him money?

A. Yes, since he said I was lost.

Q. So he spoke so loudly that you heard everything he said? Have you since gone deaf?

A. Ah! I heard him well, to my misfortune!

Q. Loyau and his wife claim that you organized a plot against them, that you have invented what you have recounted?

A. No, no, I have always been faithful, and I will be faithful unto death. (Hilarity)

Q. Did you borrow money?

A. Yes, since I gave him everything.

Loyau: All this is false. He takes revenge because he pretends that I took too dear a price from him.

Q. He does not look like a man who makes things up, and I believe that he has never invented anything, the poor devil.

The witness. I would have had more than 1,600 francs in my pocket if it were not for him.

Q. And Mrs. Loyau, did you see her?

A. Yes, she came, and my wife gave her money…

Ah! The poor deceased soul!

We then heard several witnesses to whom Mr. Lihoreau had told what had happened. These were others from whom they had borrowed money.

Mrs. Roussetet: By St. John, my two girls, who were sick, told me that they wanted to purge themselves.

I said to them: So, go to the doctor. But they were found by Loyau, who gave them two bottles. When I found out what was happening, I did everything to prevent it.

Q. Why did they go to Loyau?

A. Sir, this is because it was much cheaper.

After the testimony of the witnesses, the transcript was given to Mr. Perrot, who required a severe application of the law against the defendants and declared that he did not insist on the count of illegal practice of medicine, that he retained the trial only as an inquiry of morality.

Mr. Brisard then introduced the defense of the two accused.

The court dismissed the count of illegal practice of medicine and sentenced Loyau to thirteen months in prison, his wife to one month, and both were fined 100 francs.

"Well done!" exclaimed the chorus, who had found this lecture instructive.

"Here," said Bernard Morand to Claude, handing him the paper, "you will give this account to Simounen. This will give him pause."

"Thank you, Mr. Morand. I believe we would preach to an empty choir."

"That is quite possible. Good night, my dear children, and see you soon."

Chapter Twenty

$\mathcal{T}$he following evenings were occupied by similar conversations. Always more attentive to the extent that their understanding was bent on the lessons of the pharmacist, the peasants took a real pleasure at these familiar instructions and saw the hours flow with a fabulous pace.

In these reunions, Bernard Morand explained to them many things that had hitherto been unknown to them.

He spoke with them on the century's progress, gave them short but precise explanations of electricity, steam, and all modern inventions. He turned their minds towards the study of agricultural questions and showed them that the true wonders were those which could be accomplished by the will placed in service of a civilizing idea.

In a word, those whom he had assembled around him were children by the simplicity of their minds – he sought to make men of them.

As for Claude Michu, he owed Bernard especially for the conquest of his own self. He was no longer that shy and indecisive boy we knew. He drove out the old man forever and showed himself well-disposed to undertake many things which had hitherto frightened him or excited his mistrust.

Under his able direction, Father Michu's farm became a model establishment.

In place of the Red Dragon or other books of its sort, Claude sought the agricultural treatises, the serious works – he was encouraged in this by the pharmacist, who obligingly placed at his disposal the journals that he received from Paris.

Our young man drew excellent theories from them and applied them with an intelligence and care which were completely successful.

Sometimes he would think of his past efforts, often unhappy trials, and he rightly said to himself that one succeeds in the world only on the condition of deploying, on every occasion, a great deal of firmness and perseverance, precious qualities which he had been deprived of for a long time.

From time to time, Claude would visit Madeline.

Seeing this good looking, tanned, resolute young man entering her house, the pretty girl did not laugh as much as before.

She held out her hand and it was clear that she would be happy on the day when she would be called Mrs. Michu.

Amid his preoccupations and new ideas, Claude had kept a spiteful thought against old Simounen, and he promised himself to tell the shepherd what he had done.

Unfortunately, he had left the country momentarily. He had gone to drive herds in the Crau, at the confluence of the Durance and the Rhine, and would return in the spring.

Claude Michu gradually forgot his rancor when the unexpected return of Simounen came to remind him.

The valiant farmer was overseeing the work of the estate one day, when he heard not far from him on the road, the mocking voice of the old man, who cried to him: "Hello Claude, how are you?"

Simounen would doubtless have been safe from the reproaches of his former dupe if he had presented himself poorly. Unfortunately, he had risen in the fine year that he owed to Claude's naivete.

This circumstance rekindled all the sleepless anger in his mind and reminded him of his old foolishness.

"Good morning," he answered curtly.

"How are you, my boy, what fly has stung you?"

"I know I'm talking with a cunning rogue. The affronts! I will confront you before the judge."

"Bah! Why don't you release two or three of the demons you command!"

"And if I did so?"

"You are free to do so; it would be amusing!"

"Oh well! Little one," said the shepherd, who was embarrassed by Claude's ironic tone and wanted to take the conversation to another level, "Oh well Have you not been successful at the Black Hole?"

"Yes, I have succeeded in being extorted of 80 fr. and the fine beast I see before me! That is all I have won, not counting the jokes from my friends."

"That is not my fault. You have perhaps overlooked some detail."

"What do you say, father Simounen, what a joke! I will give you some advice. Keep my money and my donkey since you have them, but do not boast of what you have done. I do not want to denounce you to the law; however, you must keep quiet in the future, do you understand?

On this account, we will still be good friends, and I will not close the door on you, when you come to ask me for a glass of wine and a slice of cheese."

"Well said, my boy," said the shepherd, reassured, "but do you not believe in anything?"

"Yes, I believe in many things."

"That is good to hear."

"I believe, for example, that I have been an imbecile and that you took advantage of me. I also believe that if you could sell the means to procure treasures, you would be extraordinarily rich indeed. I also believe, finally, as Mr. Morand says, that there are no other means of success in the world than probity, intelligence and hard work."

"There is truth in what you say, but, bah! A little bit of mystery hurts no one and is good for many people."

"Which means, Father Simounen, that you have not improved and that you would be willing to sell yourself to exploit more good souls."

"Why not, if it be so!"

"Good? And if it so happens that they arrest you and put you in prison?"

"One is smart, my boy."

"Very well, all the better. God grant that your predictions are not realized.

Goodbye, father Simounen!"

"Goodbye, my boy."

Despite his boasting, Simounen did profit a little from the selfless advice of Claude Michu. He stopped pretending to be familiar with the supernatural world, but at the same time that he was getting rid of his necromantic robes, he devoted himself to another branch of operations no less dangerous than magic, from the point of view of his personal tranquility.

In brief, he began to sell remedies in which the marvelous element also played a part. They were drugs of unusual energy that had to be administered or absorbed by pronouncing certain formulae and that the old shepherd delivered to the consumers with all sorts of recommendations concerning their use and all kinds of praise about their indisputable efficacy.

Claude Michu was quick to learn what was going on and he spoke with his friend Bernard Morand.

"Yes," said the latter, "I know that old Simounen is competing with me, but besides being indifferent to his competition, I am in no mood to put him to the test with the law. A day will come, where he will deliver himself, by committing some of those blunders which are the end of the story of all the merchants of old wives' remedies."

In the countryside, where doctors are scarce, it would be desirable for peasants to have certain rules of hygiene, the application of which would prevent many diseases and avoid the risk of placing them in the hands of snake oil salesmen and their various evil deeds.

One of our great practitioners said, "The wealth of the poor is cleanliness."

I would like our countrymen to consider this maxim. Cleanliness is the sister of good health. It must reign everywhere, in man and around him.

The body must be kept clean, but also the clothes, the linen and the hands should be clean.

I see, with regret, many of our neighbors have piles of garbage near their homes.

This is a bad habit - filthy deleterious gases emerge from these piles which can cause and spread contagious diseases.

Any farm scraps that cannot be used as fertilizer must be carefully burned, dead animals must be buried deeply and not abandoned on the roadside, as is commonly done in the countryside.

The question of food must also be the subject of great attention. It is necessary to eat little and at fixed times. To eat when you have time and to consume too much, under the pretext that it takes longer, is a habit that can become harmful.

The stomach is a well-organized machine, without doubt, but it breaks easily; it needs a strict diet. To have too much or too little food induces irregularity in digestion, which compromises the order of its functions.

We can gain from this approach a terrible affliction called gastritis.

One must eat a little meat, but it must be digested. Meat gives blood and muscles the strength needed for field work. Plant foods must be intelligently combined with meat in the ordinary course of daily meals. They can be taken in fairly large quantities, avoiding as much as possible the acidic foods which can be dangerous.

Fruits are good, provided they are eaten when ripe. They refresh moderately, when eaten too often, they overload the stomach and weaken the bodily economy.

All these principles, I would grant, cannot be consistently applied by the poor people who take what God gives them; but it is good to know them and conform to them as far as possible.

Country clothes should be loose to facilitate body movements. It is necessary to avoid choking the neck, because this causes frequent congestion, especially during the heat.

Canvas is good for summer war, and light wool even better. In the sun, wool lets in less heat than canvas, and although it is heaver, it is less warm.

Cotton should be preferred closer to the skin because it absorbs sweat better and keeps the skin warmer than usual.

In winter, it is necessary to avoid staying in an apartment that is too hot. Do not go outside without increased layers of clothing.

It is better to prefer exercise over fire as a remedy against the cold. Natural warmth is the best; that of fire, especially that from cast iron stoves, dries the skin, irritates the nervous system, and sometimes causes violent headaches.

During the hot days, when one is covered in sweat from field work, one must carefully refrain from the shade of walnut trees and certain other trees whose foliage keeps an unhealthy and sometimes mortal freshness.

It is better to let sweat slowly vaporize.

Drinking fresh water when one is hot is also harmful; when one is very thirsty, it is better to dip one's hands in water, and if one can, take a bath.

The water then enters the body through the pores, which are like many small moths, and the thirst disappears without having to load the stomach with a quantity of liquid which cannot be digested without fatigue.

Such are the principles which I would like to see engraved on the minds of our peasants.

But these are just preventive approaches.

When an illness occurs, do not wait for possible aggravation before claiming the care of a doctor. Those who, by economy, procrastinate, or ignorantly apply old wives' remedies, which we spoke of a moment ago, lose more money than they save, because the worse the disease becomes, the more expensive it is to treat.

To this purely material care, I would like to add others, if I were free to arrange the affairs of this world at my pleasure. I would like to take care of the mind as well as the body, of the intelligence as well as that of the health.

Nowadays, there are few communities who do have a schoolmaster. Thanks to the current laws, the instruction tends to be generalized. Well, in my opinion, we still find too many peasants who refuse the benefits of this instruction which is so freely offered to them.

The child is sent quite willingly to the school as long as his little arms are too feeble to handle the wheelbarrow or the rake, but as soon as he reaches the age of ten or twelves, his education is cut short and he is sent to the fields with the men, whether he can read or not. What we see in him, above all else, is another menial helper.

I do not like these tendencies – besides the fact that they lead to a selfishness that cannot be excused, they are contrary to the interests of the farmer. If he considers primary instruction as useless, or at least as indifferent to his interests, he is wrong, and greatly misled.

A man, even if he must push the plow all his life, should be able to at least read, write and count.

These three notions will inspire in him the desire to acquire new ones.

During the leisure, his labors grant him, his spirit will find a serious repast – he will go less to the cabaret and his purse will be heavier. He will read from time to time some simple books appropriate to his nature. Which will give him useful lessons on the things he ought to know. He will be able to calculate more exactly the yield of his lands, and on these calculations, he will base more productive enterprises.

Finally, it builds morale, because I do not believe in this honesty that some people claim resides in the absolute ignorance of everything.

"There may be a good reason which prevents the farmers from giving his children a higher education," objected Claude Michu, "because he fears he will be disdained by them when they are more learned than him."

"True, there are evil spirits and bad hearts who blush at the ignorance of their parents, but the remedy is easy against them."

To take one example – I have a friend named William Hervieux. His father was a rich proprietor near Marseilles. Having received only a limited education, this good man said to himself that his son, who went to school regularly would be an able assistant to him in the future.

For this purpose, he imposed sacrifices on himself and placed him in one of the good hostels of the city. In three years, the child was a very distinguished student.

His masters urged Hervieux to push his education further. The farmer did not hesitate, despite the ridicule of his friends.

When William returned for the second time, he set himself heartily to the work of the house, but one day, Hervieux wanted to send him to the market to sell two oxen, he revolted against this demand.

"You refuse?" asked the farmer sternly.

"Yes, my father, you have not educated me so well, to make me a leader of oxen."

The father did not respond, but when William wanted to get up the next day, he found, in place of his clothes from the night before, a nasty shirt, canvas trousers and clogs.

"From today," announced Hervieux, "I do not want to feed a useless mouth. If you want to eat, earn your bread. My workman left me yesterday, I give you his place."

William threw himself repentantly in the arms of his father. He had understood this hard lesson.

From that moment on, he took care of all the hard work of the farm, and thanks to his knowledge, he made the estate the richest and best kept domain in the department.

"I will take advantage of everything you have taught me, Mr. Morand," said Claude Michu, "and I will make my children profit by it, I promise you."

"Your children? You should get married first."

"This is what I'm going to do. In a month, I will lead Madeleine to the church, and if you will be my witness, it will be a great honor to me."

Bernard Morand promised this to him.

One month later, Claude and Madeleine were the happiest couple in all Provence.

What became of old Simounen? Alas! The prediction of Claude and Bernard was realized.

Simounen sold one of his unbelievable remedies to a grubby farmer one day, which he was paid dearly for, doubtless in consideration of the magical virtue it granted him.

The drugs were so harsh and worked so well that in two days, the patient died.

Simounen consoled himself, but justice was less philosophical. It wanted to know the reason for the event, and our old shepherd received a visit from the police whom he dreaded so much.

We then discovered all the maneuvers which he had been engaged in for a long time. It was known that he abused the credulity of the people to exploit them, and that his so-called beneficent practices left much to be desired in terms of probity.

In short! Father Simounen was sentenced to several months in prison.

The prison activities must have inspired him with salutary reflections and healed him forever from the unfortunate idea of applying to the poor world the supernatural recipes of the Red Dragon.

LOVE & THE GRIMOIRE

by CHARLES NODIER

12: Original image of Charles Nodier by Michael Gallant

*D*o not be frightened, gentle and easily scared folk, by the incendiary title of this story. I attest to you that I do not believe I am damned, and that it is at most a case of conscience that the least firm priest of your village would settle amicably, but finally, I am aging quickly, since the world no longer amuses me, and I am angry to have my heart cleared of the last of my scruples.

I therefore confess that I had two great and childish passions in my life, and that they absorbed me entirely.

The first of my two grand childish passions that I had in my life was to see myself as a hero of a fantastic tale, to don Fortune's hat, to wear the Ogre's boots, or perching foolishly on the golden branch, beside the blue bird. You will excuse such a taste in a well-read and intelligent person, but for me, it was a mania.

The second of my dear interests was to write such a fantastic story before my death, in an extravagant and innocent manner, in the style of Miss de Lubert or Mrs. d'Aulnoy, because that of Mr. Perrault seemed too strong for me, and to amuse them, at least for a few generations, the posterity of playful and chubby children with pink cheeks and alert eyes, who would happily remember my inventions during their hours of leisure, and even in those delicious hours when one does nothing.

As for the other form of posterity that you know, a pale, slender, insignificant, stupid figure will be shown to you in the next room, and which hangs suspended, at the end of two ugly arms, two ugly plaster laurel wreaths, I swear on my honor that I never had such a thought.

Anyway, I cannot hide from myself that these two frenzies have singularly influenced my real-life profession and my sad job of storyteller of nonsense. It has to be so. Forbid me to recite a common fact, an event that happened *in public & to the Senate,* one of those stories about sincerity without invoking the devil or flights of fantasy.

I am talking about three lovely women who I have loved entirely, in all honor, and whom I saw die within fifteen years. Three women dead in fifteen years! But this is a tall tale! Fantastic! Wait, sir, please, the truth is that I liked seven hundred women in that period and that makes the mortality figure a little less hyperbolic! Besides, I have spoken to you on purpose and exclusively of my posthumous loves because another kind of confidence would have been in bad taste in my youth, and I do not suppose anything has changed in my decorum. The modesty of these mysteries was only freed from its veils by taking those of mourning and widowhood, and it was only then that the pain of the survivor was allowed the respectful outpouring of a long-hidden feeling!

Well! All the more reason! Fantastic, if ever there was one!

Fantastic! If it pleases you, as fantastic as it could be! Alas! I could not ask for better – I would like to find something fantastic in my memories, fantastic! Eh! What would I not have exchanged for a bit of fantasy, especially when I have known the truth of this world, when experience has made me perceive and absorb it through every pore? Fantastic, my God! But, I would have given ten years of my life, and I would have made a big deal to meet a sylph, a fairy, a sorcerer, a sleeping prophet, an ideologue who made sense, a gnome with flamboyant hair, a ghost in a robe of fog, of a will-o'-the wisp as great as nothing, the devil the most succinct in body and the most feeble in spirit who has ever nibbled on the parsley of the devil of Papefigure. Not possible, sir! If there was anything fantastic three thousand miles away, I would have found my way there, but there was no such thing!

I do not know what would have happened in my poetic faith in the marvelous world if I had not yielded one day to the strange idea that I told you of – that of giving myself to the devil. This is, frankly speaking, a somewhat harsh resolution, but it simplifies the question admirably.

At the time of which I speak, I would have been deeply sorry to pass up an evil topic just because it was fashionable, and then because it was pleasant to occupy the women who never entertain themselves with such bad themes. I therefore made myself a bad subject, and I had taken the freedom to do this to the great regret of my excellent father, who paid dearly for my teachers to make me take more honorable degrees, but I must say this immediately, in order to protect the reader against the infallible disgust which is attached to the reputation of Lovelace and Mr. Faublas, the Chevalier.

Oh! I was not like that – I was incredibly careful, really. You would not find, in all my history, three pages which would make you envy the good fortunes of your valet, if you have one, which I do not wish you, for it is a great embarrassment. I was a bad subject, without prejudice to morality and sentiment, timid for all that could command respect, for everything that might frighten decency, one of those amicable conquerors, who only attempts their invasions in countries of good will.

However, it was known that I was a bad person because I was an infamous individual, a notorious libertine, seducer in title of all who wished to be seduced, and this did me honor. Except for this enormous defect, I dare say that no one had more fixed principles on morals, and I presented a degree of Judaic observance, the combination of which, incredible as it might seem with my expansive disorders, had no compare in my time. We could call this now eclectic debauchery, a doctrinaire libertinism, but it would not be worth it, because it would never be seen again – the times have become too bad.

To understand my philosophy, because it was a philosophy if you will, you have to free yourself from your definition, and I am still afraid that people will not understand me. The idea of carrying a secret of trouble in an innocent heart that society denied me, induced me to release the least of the world, by a criminal effort, from a bond that society had formed. This would have been enough to make me sabotage the real evils from hell. I would have run away from Clarence at the first smile from Julie, for fear of her unending kisses. I would have left my coat in the hands of the pretty wife of Potiphar, had it been that of Elijah and made one a prophet, but nothing stopped me from tasting a fruit which had lost its flower, and which had fallen from its nourishing branch without being collected by the gardener's disdainful hand.

Well, I say, it is pleasant and sweet, and I savor it without doing any harm to anyone. So that if the master were there by chance, I would have answered his reproaches thus: *"Pardon, master! I am not a marauder; I merely sample the bounty."*

This conviction had given me the invaluable security of the heart, which is the first reward of virtue. This is precisely why I was then a bad person, and what made me call myself the worst person, par excellence, like a true prototype of the species.

I have just said such flattering things about myself, that I must claim some modesty to add to them. However, I owe you and myself, as they say, to stick to the accuracy of this account, which is almost the only thing of the kind that I have written. That it is the most marvelous thing is another matter, as it depends on one's taste. The most extraordinary result of my system is that I have made many good and worthy young people my students, with a singular aptitude and perfectibility, and whom I had luckily managed to divert from crime by the facility of vice, while waiting for my lessons to bear better fruit and convert them altogether.

Twenty years later, they were model men. Time has not harmed them, but it appears to me that they must have no remorse, sweet and precious for their old age. I do not know how it was done, but women of good company hated us.

The best of my acolytes was called Amandus. He was my lieutenant, my Menaechmi[2] in all the matters of the heart where the heart is not interested, which multiply by the sole act of will, which are complicated by the slightest condescension of politeness, and who would reduce a pasha without a helper to go to war in eight days.

Amandus was in truth a pretty boy, with a flair for painting, a stunning vocabulary, an overwhelming sufficiency. He played all games to perfection, and never played without losing, rode a horse like a centaur, and broke some limb every month, drew weapons like St. George, and regularly came out of these duels with an arm in a sling. Heir to a pretty fortune, he had dissipated it in six months, which proves a lot of wit, and he still found debts to be settled, which proves much more. Finally, there was only one cry on his account when he crossed any room – that Amandus was charming, and that he had no commonsense.

The excellent education of Amandus had been neglected on a point that some common minds take to their advantage. There are spots on the sun, after all. Either by capacity or preoccupation, Amandus had never been able to learn to write. I am inclined to believe that it is because he did not feel the need for it, and this disdain hides a very philosophical idea. It is not that Amandus could not have written if he had wanted to, but it would have been better if he had not tried.

It is not that Amandus did not know spelling, far from it! His spelling was perfect! If I told you that the spelling of Ms. Marie would be the standard next year of the Academy, you would no doubt say to me that there is no harm in writing like the Academy, especially if you are from the Academy, but this was not the spelling of the Academy – it was the

---

[2] Twin brothers in the eponymous play by Plautus

spelling of Amandus, a miraculous spelling. Amandus was aware, unlike Ms. Marie, that the genius of writing consisted in disguising the spoken word in all its forms and syllables.

For him, all the articles, all the pronouns, all the particles, all stray letters from the least letter of the plurals of the verbs were fodder for his verbose writing style. He threw in accents on the letters, mute or atonic, umlauts on the diphthongs, apostrophes amidst words, beautiful ornate capital letters, and commas, damn, commas all over! Never has one seen so many commas!

In the habits of vulgar love of which I have spoken, this did not draw much attention, since most of our heroines could not read, but if they had known how to read, they would have been cruelly embarrassed. There were, however, difficult occasions, situation of gallantry in which I was of immense help with my simpler spelling, where I did not intend to enrich it with all this magnificence.

The only friend of Amandus, who remained loyal to him since he was ruined, I devoted myself bravely to the interpretation of these hieroglyphs whose impenetrable obscurity would have thrilled the learned Champollion. I had to leave my study of Hebrew, I put myself at the study of Amandus. I managed to read quite fluently after three or four months, and I finally ventured to put my own ideas instead, when a scabrous and rebellious text confused my erudition or tired my patience. Translators often take the same approach when they no longer understand their author. Amandus, stripped of his grammatical luxury, then copied word for word and letter for letter, as Homer had prepared the Anthology under the dictation of Apollo. The comparison is a little prideful, but it is not too disproportionate. This time, I will admit, was not wasted, for my studies, because I thus learned how to turn out a proper love letter. I had been obstinate until then and not written a single one. The letters remain unwritten.

We did not frequent what is called bad society, but the nature of our occupations rarely drove us through what one calls good society. Nomadic travelers in the middle of life, we planted our adventurous tent every evening between two worlds in which we also participated, selected at first by the forces of education and habit, and attracted at any time towards the second by convenient pleasures and conquests without alarms.

If the topography of this double hemisphere is not exactly known to you, I will have the advantage of teaching you that the contingent point is occupied by the theater, and to better characterize the locality, by the gallery of premieres in good provincial towns. As soon as the canvas was lifted, a dozen black or blue eyes (I'm talking about the overall scenes), lifted us up on our couch and welcomed us with delicious reproaches or seductive promises.

The furtive gaze of a beauty that sighed from the box seats before making its entrance, spied us stealthily behind the coat of the Harlequin, or sprung as if by lightning through the enormous yawning of an adjustable chassis, between tufts of painted roses. She finally entered by exercising the riches of a nightingale's throat. She entered amidst the flattering whispers of an assembly which seemed to applaud only for us, because we gave half of all ovations. It seems to me that we also had our share in the whistles, but you have to know how to accommodate in such circumstances.

I even think I'm sure that between us, I was the most interested in disgrace, because my impatient & fluid character was lucky, but we shared our bounty as brothers, Amandus and I, and we were not counting our victories. I remember, without going into much detail, that my bad destiny had imposed on me that month a mezzo-soprano who was five feet seven inches tall and overweight, more suited for the overcoat of a Swiss drum major than the corset of the shepherdess.

When she played Babette, (My Lord, what a Babette!) and sometimes struck me down with a kind eye, rummaging through a basket of nasty flowers with large hands and singing in a delicious voice that her formidable person,

It is for you that I arrange this bouquet,

Oh! You can believe me when I say that I would have blessed the beneficent dagger that would have pierced my breast at that moment! But what was there to do? It was one of the essential conditions of my happiness because it was one of the impregnable backups of my innocence. I forgot to say that she was very ugly and squinted horribly.

The other part of the world was in the boxes, and this is clear if one were kind enough to follow my metaphor. Our morals forbade us to go to the boxes – to look, but not to see, and yet by dint of having seen what is good to see, we look at it. This is because in one of the boxes of a little theater in a small city, and I won't tell you exactly which city it is, otherwise you would be perfectly free to seek it out, there was, I say, in the third box from the right, one of those figures of angels who damn men and the saints dream of.

133: auditorium of the Théâtre Historique, 1850

I don't know how to paint, but one paints wonderfully when one has a palette at hand. Sixteen years old, thin as a reed, with white yet lively skin, under which blood flowed animatedly, coloring everything without blushing, blond hair that flowed like vapor on the shoulders, raised from what purity I know not, and more celestial than one can describe – traits that would have caused the sculptor of Venus to cut his throat with his chisel, and a wide regard with blue eyes that enchanted like the sky and shone like the sun – you have no idea of the thousandth part of the perfections of Marguerite.

Marguerite had lost her father and mother young. The poor little girl had an annuity of eighty thousand francs and was in the care of a widowed maternal aunt, very annoying and just under forty, whom no one accused of being insensitive to the sighs of a loving heart. I found myself very keenly and even very significantly in love with her one or two years ago (I'm speaking of the aunt), and it cost me I don't know how many deadly hours of projects, anguish, and expectations, but with no other result, because my grand passion had just occurred to the day before, and this was the memorable era of my philosophical love affairs.

I hadn't thought about her once, even in those ecstatic moments when the soul rocks between the two nightly sleeps, and my imperturbable memory, if it were true to the names of flies and butterflies, may well have forgotten the aunt's name, if the aunt had no niece. I need not say that the age and innocence of this charming child (this is the niece that is the present question) threw between her and me an unbridgeable space. With an annuity of eighty thousand francs, it was much worse! I barely had this much passive capital.

"You breach our conditions!" Amandus said to me one day, "you watch the boxes!"

"As unbaptized dead children watch from limbo," I replied, "and without calling from so high 'a look for a look!' Besides, I have my reasons, and I make no secret of it. Time is marching forward mercilessly, while we believe we are atomizing the present in a few hours of madness, and all pretty boys that we are, we will age too as much as the seven sages of Greece. You still have a pretty sweet life to flow between the pleasant leisure of laziness and the gallant fox hunts in the halls of the Vulpiniere, if your uncle, disarmed by more exact conduct, leaves you his dilapidated castle, it's lofts and brushwood at his death, which will not be long coming.

"I have no uncle, no castle, no loft, no brushwood, neither hopeful happy foxes. When my creditors will share my said spoils, I hope they find an audience of sufficient size to read my novels, and especially to buy them! So I need to be inspired by someone who lives and never hope of dreaming, petting, feeding in my thoughts some adorable figure, and when I meet her, I will take her."

"Little Marguerite," said Amandus, focusing his binoculars and turning them brazenly on this divine figure before which my eyelids droop in indignation and respect.

"She is really that good. Thank you for pointing this out to me. There's something in her, like you say, that excites the imagination, and which however calms the heart – a Raphael-esque morbidity, don't you think?!"

"One feels purer to see her, one feels better to think of her. The delightful privilege of the strange sympathy of beautiful souls! Alas! My virtuous friend, what a pearl, what a diamond in a milliner's counter or in a group of mute figures! Blind fortune has it all, but she never grants it to others. It must be admitted that destiny is bitterly stupid enough to perch this delicious face in a carriage, instead of showing it to us this evening between two weeks in the wings."

I shivered with indignation. He was looking at the fourth box to the left of the wings.

"Well, take your inspiration," continued Amandus, leaning his head on my shoulder, and sprawling on the seat, to my great scandal, because Marguerite could see us. "Take inspiration from Marguerite, if that suits you, because I'm more concerned than ever with your inspirations. Write novels, Maxime, write novels!

"As for me, if I am not mistaken, I will have a happy denouement. My uncle is not lacking in goodwill for me, and I know he is determined to secure his thin fortune for the day when I perform my first wise act by marrying honorably."

"Marrying honorably!" I cried. "Are you thinking about getting married, Amandus?"

"Why not?" he continued, with a burst of laughter, "Do you think I am incapable of a serious idea and a firm resolution?"

"My God! That Aglaé[3] is badly presented today! And her grooming is badly matched with the elephant menagerie!"

"We must end things, Maxime, a reasonable end, a serious and formal end, when one has no more money. This is the opinion of my uncle and it is wise. You do not appreciate it yet, this wisdom, but you will, when that time comes."

"Look! She is singing out of tune now!"

---

[3] A nymph in the lyrical drama, Echo et Narcisse by Christoph Gluck, 1779

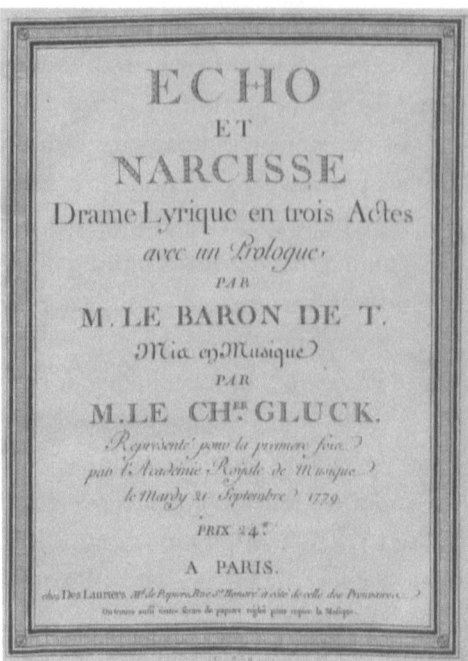

144: Echo et Narcisse, 1779 edition of the score, Public Domain

"So get inspired to give me a little statement – very expressive, passionate, very sincere, a direct appreciation of my weaknesses, my errors, of all you wish to say. I don't care. A small slice – increase it if you can, subtract if you so choose! You are my conscience, you have my heart, you know all that rests with tenderness and good feelings in this fraternal breast which beats against yours."

"Do you notice this possessed creature who has not lost sight of me all evening? But she pinches her lips, she is missing two teeth!"

"Still, it would be fitting," I went on without being distracted, "that I have some idea of happiness. She who is fixed as one's choice, as the proposition has it: *Moderation in all things, these are the fixed ends.*"

"There is neither finesse nor an enigma, Maxime, and if you guess, you will really know more than me about the future where I lower my head down to save myself from the present. If you guessed, I would ask you to tell me who I am thinking of, and who is the object of the first of my reasonable loves. I do not ask you to guess, by the devil! I ask you for a graceful and formal description in beautiful terms, like *Telemachus*, or *The Princess of Cleves*, which is familiar to all, everywhere – an inventive description you might give me that I might venture to play at the marriage lottery.

"Speak of candor, virtue, beauty – don't get involved in hair color, because that could cause a few misunderstandings. I will copy everything you say accurately, take it to the post office, and my lucky star will take care of my hopes, and my worthy uncle, who wants me to take a wife, will have nothing to blame me for when I show him that I was refused by fifty women. Or else, there will come two, three, a dozen, I don't know how many – and then you will choose immediately after me, better than me, maybe you are more fortunate!"

"The traitor!" I thought, as Aglaé sang.

"Me? Then leave!" I replied bitterly, "I haven't the wealth and domains of Vulpiniere."

"What! Would this faint hope be held to heart? I am going to play against your horse or against Aglaé, from the first rows."

"I sold my horse yesterday. I give you Aglaé this evening if you wish. As for the letter, I will write it, if I can."

The correspondence was sent on its way, because to my surprise, and no doubt of Amandus, his initiative did not cost too much. I did not judge his progress, because he had become discreet, and I have never been curious. When the results were evident, I almost fell down. I was wounded by the idea that he had found himself a woman sufficiently intrepid to believe in his incredible oaths.

We still went to the show, but very rarely, especially Amandus, who began to keep, according to his promise, a certain air of respectability. I was unfortunately attracted to the theatre by another inducement – my colossal shepherdess had not yet left the stage, and she had not yet met a man bold enough to flush me out, although it was a good time for the cavalry to make their appearance.

I did not feel at ease with the arrival of a regiment of dragoons, all shining with their epaulettes, covered in dust and glory, whose horses cantered beneath the windows of the cheering crowds. Vain hope! The hussars followed, and these pavilions of pleasure and war which foraged everywhere did not deign to touch Aglaé with a stroke of their angel wings. I dreaded needlessly the effects of the courage of the cuirassiers. Aglaé retained all the honors of a cloudless fidelity in this long trial and asserted all her rights. She was impregnable, with an unshakeable constancy. Her virtue quelled all the annoyances that I suffered in love which gave me an endless headache.

I was only looking for a pretext to exile myself from the world, and it was the purest of my moral feelings that provided it to me at the moment when I least expected it.

I had already noticed that Marguerite paid more attention to us than I would have liked. This preoccupation had even taken on for some time a character which worried me – the expression of an affectionate interest, with a dreamy sensitivity with that vague *je ne sais quoi*, tender and idealistic which expresses on the forehead of a young girl the development of a secret inclination.

Misfortune and desolation! I said to myself, would you be condemned by your unlucky stars, poor and gracious child, to love one of us damned souls?

Ah! At least I won't be complicit in my complaints! The examinations were approaching, and I had not even opened a book to prepare. Well! I gave up all these transient disappointing people with their voluptuousness. I set myself to read, as one must, the ten volumes of Jacobus Cujacius in the Annibal Fabrioti edition, *in chambers*. I will read them, as a reference before paying attention to the women, and I take as my witness the shade of Justinian!

Vowing the above, I left the room, and I went home to send a definitive note to Aglaé. I need not tell you that this resolution relieved me of a great burden.

There was probably a persuasive assurance in the communication which I sent the next day to my father of this new plan of life, because he presented me that very instant, to recognize my sacrifices, with his entire library and the pretty pavilion which housed it. Those were the two things he liked best after me. I spent the day disposing of everything that could serve my studies well or embellish my voluntary exile, and I felt a sense of satisfaction fill me with this pleasant care, that happiness had more than one aspect.

What did I mean? That the pure happiness of a contented soul prevails over one's imaginary happiness for a temporary infatuation while it lasts. I was happy until evening – this had never happened to me before.

In the evening, I yawned. I looked at my watch twenty times in ten minutes. The first notes of the orchestra pursued me. The almost discordant noise of the open and closed boxes resounded in my ear, my nostrils smelt the familiar odors in the air in vain, alas! It was too pure, the gloomy aroma of the vapor of the smoking lamps and the exhalation of perfumes was absent in the dry atmosphere. I searched for the delicious image of Marguerite in all the attics, all the paneling. I looked in vain at all the shelves of the library, and my eyes only met the Jacobus Cujacius of Annibal Fabroti.

"I would be curious," I cried at last, "to know if her appreciative looks were for him, or if they were reserved for me, and as he borrowed a post chair this morning, he must be traveling. I will never get a better opportunity to clear my doubts, and this will clear my mind, whatever the result of this test, for the reasonable designs I have conceived. I will work harder tomorrow!"

This time, I did not have to make a mistake. I declare it to you with all the confidence that love can inspire in a fool that these looks were for me, for me alone! You will tell me that I was alone, and like a marvelous luminescent fossil whose light-loving pores still glow after sunset, perhaps I was merely a simulacrum of Amandus for Marguerite. This idea did not occur to me, and I know myself well, this idea appealed to me all too well. I tried, I shuddered to understand, I armed myself with heroic courage, and I fled, dead in the heart, by dint of believing myself happy!

No, no, Marguerite! I will not violate the sanctuary of your innocent soul to ignite it or to maintain a passion that loses us both! No, I will not transplant into the sterile desert of my life a stem so fresh and so delicate with its fragrant flowers!

And yet, who other than me will love you as you should be loved? I would have worshipped the altar of your feet, the harp of your sighs, the vase of your perfumes! I would have burned in front of you like incense! I would have wiped myself out in a ray of your eyes like a drop of dew in the fires of midday! Oh! I don't think I would have untied the cords of your virgin dress with manly hands! I would have purified myself on the crater of a volcano before approaching you and my lips would not even touch your veil, for fear of profaning it. But you are rich, Marguerite, and there is no event possible that can strip you of so many useless goods to reduce you to the equal of my fortune! You would still be too much above me and too worthy of kings!... No, Marguerite, I will never see you again... - unless the devil gets involved.

Finishing this poetic apostrophe, the trivial end of which I have shared with you, I fell overwhelmingly into my armchair, which was fortunately flexible, supple, and deep. Three candles were lit on my desk by Dine, an unusual luxury of my nights, which gave me further proof of my family's satisfaction, and I was left to my studious solicitude.

I leaned for a moment on my balcony. The sky was crystal-clear like a lake, enameled like a meadow. One could hardly hear the breath of air in the branches of my young trees, and the breeze seemed to pass through them, as if in play, bringing back sweet emanations. The nightingale sang in the distance, moths rustled gently, fluttering under the leaves. It was a beautiful evening for a love other than the kind known to me – a magnificent empyrean domain which I would have liked to traverse through its innumerable spheres with the rapidity of the fires which flashed on all sides, but which my soul could do no more than probe the depths with my eyes. I closed everything to free myself from these immense distractions, and I sat down, with the intention of putting myself to serious work, after having a last smile of satisfaction at the admirable order of my cabinet, its description is no less necessary to provide here than the map of Latium in Virgil's Aeneid.

My father had had this pavilion built, in happier times, between his courtyard and his garden, above a long, quaint alley, which could have easily stored in its wings the cabriolet I never had. The whole building contained only one long parallelogram-like room, lit to the east and to the west by pointed windows, and which opened to the south on a garden of little extent, but fairly well-designed in its composition. This point was the only side by which one could reach my room – either one came from the courtyard or from the garden, which was not difficult, it's narrow enclosure connecting on all aides by doors always open to the wide enclosures of our neighbors.

They were excellent old men, accustomed to seeing each other since childhood, like Plato and his philosopher friends meeting in the Academy. The twisting staircase which led to my balcony was no more than six degrees, because it rose from a terrace. The second of the narrow sides of the long square which faced the entrance was occupied by my bed, a student's modest berth, around which a white curtain with long folds was tied with a bell, passed over a golden arrow. The rest of the interior walls offered nothing to the eye that was not like the back of an old catalogue. My black table cut in a smaller proportion to this little monastic edifice stood in the middle of the room, and its memory still charms me. There was enough space to circulate conveniently around the table, and to measure the sides in twenty-four or twenty-five steps, in a span of time which rushed and slowed, depending on the emotions of the walker. I made a lot of progress around the table that evening.

However, I sat down, and casually throwing my hand behind me on the shelf on which my armchair was leaning, I tried to extract the first volume of the beautiful Treatise on Civil Procedure by Robert Joseph Pothier, and I brought before me the *History of Apparitions* by D. Calmet[4], which is, as everyone knows, one of the best collections of hellish tales that one can read.

The tale was curious. I read through six pages. What misery, I thought at last, that such a learned man could have written such nonsense, like an old village woman who dreams of spirits and demons by picking up dead leaves and a few green twigs at the edge of the wood!

I would really like it if the devil appeared before me, and I must mention this, since I have here the authentic manuscripts of the Key of King Solomon and the Enchiridion of Pope Leo, the precious heritage of a Dominican of our family, who had used these grimoires a thousand times for the deliverance of the possessed.

The devil's conversation in person would be as amusing and as instructive, if I am not mistaken, as that of Pothier and Cujas, and if it is difficult to obtain this favor from him, which Agrippa[5] and Cardan[6] paid for dearly, one at least deserves to be tempted by a resolute spirit.

It depended, in effect, on a simple act of kindness, for I had this wicked grimoire right in front of me, between my writing desk and my hourglass.

---

4 *Traité sur les apparitions des esprits et sur les vampires ou les revenants de Hongrie, de Moravie*, &c. by Augustin Calmet, 1751
5 Heinrich Cornelius Agrippa von Nettesheim, 1486-1535, German polymath, physician, soldier, theologian, author of *Three Books of Occult Philosophy*
6 Giralomo Cardano, 1501-76, Italian polymath, influential in probability, binomial theorems, natural philosophy

I don't know who the hell had put it there.

I stretched out trembling fingers towards it, as if merely the slightest contact with the scratchy parchment would carry some cursed influence on my senses. It was only cold, dirty, and sealed up. I opened its eight folds without it exhaling the slightest atom of sulfur or burning bitumen. The earth did not shake, the flame of my candles continued to rest calm and white on their blue stands, my unshakeable volumes remained asleep under the learned webs of their bibliophile spiders.

I emboldened myself. I tried to read, I spoke aloud the solemn formulas of the spirit of Python, with which I began to be animated, until my innocent windows, which had never vibrated, resounded under such words.

But it was quite another grimoire than the one I had thought. I hadn't read through twelve lines of the fatal book than I found myself stopped by unintelligible and truly diabolical signs, by impenetrable symbols and letters unnamed in the alphabets of the earth, which cut me off.

Anyone else would have lost courage at the appearance of these heterogeneous monograms, of these hieroglyphs of the other world, which could well be, in the end, only the whim of a charlatan of a copyist. Unwise, but determined, I encamped myself proudly among my candles, exclaiming in an energetic voice:

> *Come to me, saint and credulous Sperberus[7], scholar Khunrath[8], immortal Knorr von Rosenroth[9]! And you, good Gabriel de Collange[10], who once used such a worthy life to make you the incomparable translator of the indecipherable Tritheme[11]! Come, and develop for me these mysteries of which only ignorance can be frightened!...*

---

[7] Julius Sperber 1540-1616, physician & advisor of Prince Christian von Anhalt zu Dessau, mystical writer, cabalist, and alchemist. He is considered the co-founder of the Rosicrucian Order

[8] Henrich Khunrath, 1560-1605, German physician, hermetic philosopher, and alchemist author of *Amphitheatrum Sapientiae Aeternae,*

[9] Christian Knorr von Rosenroth 1636-1689, privy counsellor of Christian Augustus, Count Palatine of Sulzbach, author of *Kabbala Denudata* & multiple hymns

[10] Gabriel de Collange 1524-1572, valet-de-chambre to Charles IX. A Catholic, he was taken for a Protestant & assassinated in the massacre of St. Bartholomew in 1572. He translated Trithemius.

[11] Johannes Trithemius 1462-1516, lexicographer, chronicler, cryptographer, and occultist. Author of *Steganographia*. His students included Heinrich Cornelius Agrippa and Paracelsus.

The devil did not move any more than before, for I must warn my readers – these are not the names of demons that I have just uttered, they are simply the names of cabbalists.

Perhaps for the first time, these brave authors saw their yellowed bookmarks floating on pages exposed to the light of torches, and whose tattered edges had aged under the dust. I did not feel surprised by understanding, and through this long labyrinth of a mad science, all that was necessary for leisure, patience, and especially good will, to find so many lost languages, excepting that of the angels, which is the surest, but work does not terrify me when I am amused. I finished my study of this topic in twenty minutes, which would be enough to know all that was useful to know if used well.

I declaimed the words of the grimoire clearly, and I dare say, without mistakes. Midnight rang as I was finishing, and the devil, who is essentially rebellious, did not appear. The devil comes very rarely – he may not even appear in the familiar form, and should not be trusted, because he has all the necessary ability to take on more attractive forms, when needed to win his objective.

I must admit, I said to myself, plunging back into my cushions, that I played a grand game and now feel very dizzy. How embarrassing it would have been for me if the devil had appeared to me and asked, according to the custom, in a hollow and terrible voice what I demanded of him? He is not called with impunity. His questions demand to be answered, and he is not an opposing party one can get rid of easily like some clumsy litigant, with some devious appeals of inadmissibility.

What grace would I try to impregnate with his dark power, in exchange for my poor Soul that I had thrown on the carpet of damnation, as a stake of little value?

Money? What is the point? The cards were so favorable to me this week that the price of my horse almost increased tenfold in my purse; one more gold coin would not matter much, and I could pay three creditors instantly, if I so chose.

Knowledge? I have more than I need, without vanity, for my particular use, and the honest people who are kind enough to take a little interest in my successes still to come do not hesitate to predict that I will spread over my works, if I ever do, a pedantic varnish that would taste bad enough.

Power? God forbid! One can only get it at the cost of rest and happiness.

The gift of foresight perhaps? That would be a fatal advantage, which must be paid for with all the sweetness of hope and all the delights of uncertainty! The vicissitudes of life – this is what makes it charming!

Women and adventures! It would be abusing the poor devil's complacency – one has done all too well on this chapter. Yet, I went on, half-asleep, as if the devil had presented me the young Marguerite, so fresh, so delicate, so blonde, so rosy…. By the Devil! These are another pair of sleeves, as Mr. Buffon might say… as if Marguerite moved, pulsating, a little disheveled, a lock of hair hanging on her breast, and her bosom almost free from a badly attached kerchief…

If Marguerite had suddenly climbed my staircase with a furtive step; if, arriving at my door, she had knocked on it with a timid hand, which desires and yet fears to be heard, three small discreet blows. Tap, tap, tap.

I was half asleep, as I mentioned, and I repeated vaguely… tap, tap, tap… almost falling asleep completely.

Tap, tap, tap… This, o incomprehensible wonder! It no longer appeared to be a faint image in the dark regions of my sleepy ruminations. I almost believed it for a moment, however, I pinched my fingers hard to make sure I was awake.

Tap, tap, tap… There were indeed knocks. I cried, my limbs trembling. The clock struck one.

Tap, tap, tap… I got up, stumbling. I walked precipitously forward, then collected myself and my frightened spirits.

Tap, tap, tap… I armed myself with one of my candles. I stepped resolutely towards the balcony. I opened the shutters. O terror! Never has nature shown anything more delightful in the eyes of love – I thought I would die that very moment.

It was Marguerite, leaning against the glass of the door frame, a thousand times more beautiful than I had seen her last, more beautiful than I could dream of. Marguerite, moved, pulsating, a little disheveled, a lock of hair hanging on her breast, and her bosom almost free from a badly attached kerchief… I sighed, commended myself to God, and opened the door.

It was her – my trembling hand touched her soft, velvet delicate fingers without burning myself. I led her in, completely forbidden, to my chair and I waited for a sign from her eyes to sit a few steps away on a folding chair. She rested her arm on one of the arms of the chair, her head on her hand, and veiled her forehead with her pretty fingers. I waited for her to speak, but she did not say anything, she merely sighed.

"I would ask you, miss," (I broke the silence), "what inconceivable fortune am I indebted to that such a step has been made to surprise me?"

"What! Sir!" she replied quickly, "my approach would astonish you? Was it not an agreed thing?"

"Agreed, miss, agreed, yes, this is true, although the convention has not been stipulated in all the required forms to make it so, and this is far from being as positive and as valid as good justice as you seem to believe. Strange ideas do arise in a sick mind that imprudent love leads astray. Finally, to tell you the truth, I did not count on this happiness at all – it overwhelms me…"

I no longer knew what I was saying.

"I understand you, sir, the denouement puts you off the business. Accustomed to brilliant, yet easy pleasures, you have never measured the scope of the sacrifices of true love…"

"Stop, Marguerite, don't outrage my heart! The scope of the sacrifices of true love – I know them well… I flatter myself if I do not."

(I found this expression a bit strong, however)

"But still, why did he not come? Why did he not accompany you? At least, there should be between us this exchange of words which is the first condition of the synallagmatic[12] contract. I don't know if you understand…"

"After fetching me, he left me at the bottom of the stairs, and he will only come to take me at daybreak."

"Take you, my dear child? I beg you to believe me that I have not agreed this only to entertain myself. If I could, I would tell him this if he was there."

"He did not dare to come up to you because he foresaw your scruples."

"He did not dare to come up, you say! Not possible! I didn't think he was so shy."

---

12 Mutual agreement, a contract in which each party to the contract is bound to provide something to the other party.

"I suppose he must have been afraid of the irritability of your feelings, of the delicacy of your principles."

"I am deeply obliged to him, that is always a pleasure, but I must finally see to it that I discuss this with him…"

"At sunrise, in three or four hours from now."

"Three or four hours!" I exclaimed, coming closer to her, "Three or four hours, Marguerite!"

"And during this time, Maxime," she continued gently, approaching me, "I have only you to shelter and protect me, since the city doors must open to let him pass through in his carriage…"

"Ah! The doors have to open to let him pass through…" I sighed, rubbing my eyes like a man who was just waking up to the situation.

"He would have spared you the worry and responsibility for the service that you provide to both of us, if his respected mother had not died of an enlarged heart."

"Wait, miss," I cried, pushing my folding chair the other end of the cabinet, "his mother died of a swelling of the heart? Who are you talking to me about?"

"I am speaking to you about Amandus, good Maxime, about Amandus, who is so attached to you and whom you love so much. Since you ignore these details, I will tell you that he came to pick me up this evening at the agreed time between us to remove me from my aunt's house, because she insisted on refusing him my hand. It was the only way, you will agree, to obtain a more favorable resolution to the situation, but as it was evening, the court was full of people coming and going, other visitors and servants who would have watched our flight. We were saved only when we reached the gardens."

"No sooner had he seen your illuminated window than he said to me with joy, "See, Marguerite, the wise and studious Maxime is still hard at work. Maxime, who is my brother, my confidant, my providence. Maxime, who is aware of all my secrets, and who will be only too happy, I know in my heart, to give you asylum until daybreak. Go upstairs and knock with confidence, Marguerite, while I go and arrange everything for our departure."

"Thereupon, he left me, and I came upstairs. I knocked several times without response, and now you know everything."

"I know everything all too well, but on the whole, I like it even better than anything else. The main thing is that you will be happy. So you have a decided passion for Amandus. This is true, is it not?"

"Who is it for? I only spoke to him three times, but he writes with such penetrating warmth, with such persuasive tenderness! He expressed with such passionate energy the feelings he felt for me. Amandus, my dear Amandus!"

"Wait, wait! Are you talking about his letters?"

At the same instant, I stopped short, because I had expressed an enormous stupidity. I meditated on my words. I took refuge like a melodramatic character in a mysterious aside to myself.

No, no, my friend, I said to the demon, you have not entered on the weaker side of love – you will not enter, I mean it, by that of vanity.

"So you feel that Amandus writes well?" I whispered with affected carelessness, biting my tongue between my teeth.

The truth is, I thought to myself, she is as spiritual as she is pretty.

"You were distracted by another idea, Maxime, and that is not what you wanted to say to me."

"Your observation is correct, my lady. I was doing what you should have done, suffer me to tell you, before taking such as haphazard resolution as you have."

"What then?"

"Let me put it this way. Amandus was out of his mind, and there is much to be said about that, when he thought of making you spend a night, beautiful and wise Marguerite, in the room of a reckless young man of my kind, a man without principles, who has neither faith nor law, and who almost gave himself to the devil, half an hour ago – a bad character, in short."

"You speak too rigorously, perhaps with irony, of two or three foolish actions of a young man, which do not compromise the character, and which did not make you lose anything in the esteem of honest people. Amandus, who has a few faults of the same kind to blame himself for, justifies himself in his letters with an eloquence which touched my aunt herself, although she is extraordinarily rigid by nature."

"A bad character, Maxime? Oh, you don't look like one!"

"Thank you miss, for the good opinion you have of me. But this long, mysterious meeting, embarrassing to excess, let's cut to the point, for all the virtue you are willing to grant me, is at least likely to make your innocence suspect before such a vulgar common miserable person who you claim would make a less favorable judgement of my juvenile purity, and I shudder for you to think of the consequences. Allow me, in the name of your reputation, and out of compassion for mine, to find you another resting place until morning. I will come back to you in a moment, and I leave you sovereign mistress of all your actions, except to go out alone from her, and to open the door to anyone."

I awaited her consent; I got it and did one better. I made sure, not to be fooled, by closing the door with a double twist of the lock.

I had made my resolution, because I had the lively and sudden ideas that come easily in one's youth. Marguerite's aunt was having one of her evening soirees, I had just learned, and the provincial soirees are disproportionately long in all respects.

When I approached, the last carriages had just moved away from the entrance. I slipped in, swift and subtle like a bird, between two lackeys who were about to close the doors.

"Where is my lord going?"

"To Madame's place."

"Everyone has left."

"But, I have just arrived."

"Madame has retired for the evening."

"That is as it may be, but I am here nevertheless."

There was no objection to this decisive answer, and ten seconds later, I was in Madame's bedroom, where I had never set foot, neither so late nor any earlier, although I had thought of it a few times.

The noise I made while entering the room made her turn away from her dresser, just as she was about to untie, God forgive me, the penultimate of her dress fastenings.

"How awful!" she cried. "You, sir! To meet me at this hour in my bedroom! Without being announced! Without regard for the most common proprieties!..."

"As one might say, my lady, I don't know when I might obey the impulse of my heart."

"Well, sir, are you returning to your old frenzies? Please keep to yourself, I implore you, all this display of feelings which are expressed with so much vehemence, and which will be forgotten so quickly, for a more appropriate moment."

"It would be difficult, madam, to choose one better, if I had to speak with you about the subject to which you attribute my visit this evening, but I am called to your place by more serious reasons, which do not suffer any delay."

"In heaven's name!" I continued, grabbing her hand quickly, "Clarice, listen to me!"

"Some more serious motives, perhaps, some desperate resolution of which you are only too capable?... You terrify me, sir, you frighten me terribly! I know your outbursts – I have violence to fear, sir! I am going to sound the alarm."

"Take care, madam," I went on, taking hold of her free hand, and forcing her abruptly to sit on the sofa.

"This must remain between us, madam, in the deepest confidence, secret from all eyes and ears. It is at your knees that I beg you to listen to me for a single moment! We have no time to lose!"

"Woe is me," she sobbed in a stifled voice, "If only I had not sent my maids away!"

"They would be too much of an audience, and if they were here, I would demand they leave – the slightest public attention would destroy you."

"But this is an ambush! An assassination! It is an unimaginable crime! Monster! What do you demand of me?"

"Almost nothing, and if you had listened to me, you would know what it is. Give me the grace to say where Marguerite is."

"Marguerite? My niece? What a strange question! What has Marguerite to do with the outrageous scene that you present me? Marguerite retires early, especially when I have people over for the evening. This is one of the scrupulous practices of tender and regular education that I have given her. Marguerite is in her room. She is in her bed. Marguerite is asleep – I am as sure of it as of my own existence!"

"God, who is the master of all, could have allowed it, like so many inexplicable things that it is impossible to deny, but that is very curious! Besides, here is her door if I remember correctly. It is quite easy for you to convince yourself that she has not gone out of the house, and thereby rid us both of an afflicting doubt which concerns the responsibility of an aunt more closely than that of a neighbor."

"Awaken the child, Maxime, and awaken her when there is a man in my apartment?"

"Oh, but you will not awaken her," I replied, reassuring myself that the key to my room was safely in my pocket.

"She is, by the way, wide awake, I say, wide awake if ever one was, and if you find her asleep in her bed, the devil knows more today than in Dom Calmet's time."

She took a candle, entered the adjoining room, took a few steps, and returned just in time to pass out on the sofa.

As I went towards her, I noticed a bottle of salt on her dresser. I untied the clasp and tapped the bottle lightly on ten chubby fingers that tightened under my hand, and I kissed the ends more lightly still with all the modesty of which I am capable.

I had to compose myself to avoid a nervous attack myself, for it would have weakened me and I needed all my strength at this moment.

"We don't have time to indulge in unnecessary emotions, beautiful and adorable Clarice (*how the hell was she going to take these words?*)! The circumstances call for prompt resolution."

"Alas! I know this well! But who do I turn to, if not you, Maxime, the accomplice of this attack? The culprit, perhaps?"

"Well, no," I said, sighing.

"You know where she is, Maxime! You know it, my friend! You can't deny it!... Give her back to me!"

"This, madam, is forbidden to my loyalty. I have the secret, but it will not leave my heart, and you will despise me if I abuse it. What I attest is that she is in the care of a man of honor, who will only place her back in your hands when you have consented to let them pass into those of her spouse, as you must. Clarice! Yesterday it was a possibility, today it is a necessity! This is what I have to say to you."

"A husband? Amandus, no doubt! A madman, a debauch, a dissipated sot! A beautiful wedding, indeed!"

"We don't get married the way we want. Madam, when one has been kidnapped, the man who touches lightly on such scruples, in consideration of an opulent dowry, is a thousand times worse than a madman – he is a wretch!"

I continued, "Amandus is not a very exemplary character, I agree, but a noble love must correct him. My heart has never understood better than today the ease of this metamorphosis."

"I know this for a fact because it was he who told me that his uncle's fortune will be assured to him in the marriage contract. The area is not very productive, but it is beautiful hunting country."

"As for the dowry of the minor, it is easy to insure it against the depredations of an extravagant husband, by fifty precautions which I will make my duty to indicate to you, as soon as I have completed my intense study of Cujas, and it won't take long. I have spent days and nights at it and will be done in a few moments more."

"The alliance is, in all other respects, as suitable as one might desire, and even Amandus' faults do not obscure his brilliant and honorable qualities: he is frank, obliging, brave!"

"And he writes wonderfully – he turns a letter into perfection, this credit must be given to him." She exclaimed.

"Do you think so, madam? It is an effect of your indulgence."

"Do you not share this opinion? I am afraid, Maxime, that you will not say this out of envy."

"On the contrary, my lady, I blindly defer to your taste," I replied, taking up the case again. "I only wish you did not find him a little lacking in style. But his style does nothing for the case if I hear something about matrimonial proprieties. There are other precautions and conveniences than oratory ones. You will judge in ten minutes of reflection, and the urgency of the current position leaves you no more time, of the nature of means to take to divert from your house the scandal that threatens it."

I enumerated the conditions for the jury to arrive at the logical conclusion.

"First, this does not change your state of fortune. Marguerite is mature, as you can see, she is very advanced for her age! Sooner or later, you would have decided to have her married, when you saw her choosing her husband on her own. Oh! She is a kind child! It is a great happiness that she has fallen in love with a reckless person who her upbringing makes her submit in advance to all the concessions, instead of throwing herself at a man of money or a man of law. The process would have entered your house through the same door as the sacrament, if she had had the courage to be passionate about a lawyer."

"With Amandus, there is no embarrassment to experience. He is so fluent in business, this worthy Amandus, that there are days when he would allow you to acquire the whole estate for a thin sheaf of notes, and still he would make sure to pay the notary and keep a big gratuity for the master clerk – a sublime character indeed!"

"On another note, the girl was growing up. Her childlike beauty, which is very remarkable, would have ended up displaying the impertinent pretension of competing with yours, and I have already heard drunken sots cry from one box to another, "This pretty person must get married very young!" – they pronounce you for the mother!"

"As if that were possible, Maxime! I was not yet in boarding school when she was born!"

"Who are you saying this to? Finally, the event has occurred, and I am grateful to him for putting an end to your irresolution."

"You talk about this with such ease! The event, the event! It is unknown if she will return, and I am counting on your discretion."

"My discretion, madam, is foolproof, but Marguerite will not return tonight, and the happy event is rumored to be tomorrow, but if Marguerite discovered that the event would not happen by chance tomorrow, it could probably occur on…" Permit me, I continued, pretending to guess the date on my fingers, because it was only necessary to appeal to her imagination with the captivating argument of peroration, well recommended by rhetoricians.

Then I leaned over her ear and whispered a couple of words into it.

"What a horrible idea!" she cried, almost fainting on her cushions.

"It appears I took the liberty of telling you the world is walking on a dangerous path."

"My good sir," she went on, rising with dignity, "You know where Marguerite has been hidden. Go and fetch her and promise her on my faith that in a fortnight she will be Amandus' wife, since she wished it so."

"Well, you haven't left?"

"On your faith, madam? What can one not count on for his happiness as for that of others?"

"Come on, come on, Maxime, kiss my hand, and bring my niece back."

"Wait, don't go out without helping me arrange my clothes! I think he is in a fine state!"

I retrieved Marguerite after having convinced her, by fresh entreaties, of the sincerity of the promises I had just received for her. The aunt was austere but reasonable, the young one respectful but resolute. Things transpired to perfection on both sides. Marguerite kissed me, which I would have gladly dispensed with.

"You have accommodated so many difficulties in a short time," said the aunt to me, leading me back. "You are an admirable man to end family debates. I hope we will see you at the wedding?"

"Yes, my lady, and we will resume the conversation of this night when it all began."

"If you wish, but you will not lose anything by taking it back to where it ended."

This was very pretty talk, but there are delicious words which lose much of their pleasure when spoken aloud.

It must be agreed, I said to myself as I returned to my pavilion, that I have indeed accomplished in a few hours such undertakings of intelligence and works of heroism which have little to yield to the works of Hercules. First, I learned the Grimoire without missing a word, a letter, a spirit or a sephiroth. Secondly, I caused the marriage to her lover, against all odds, a young girl with whom I was passionately in love, and who did not seem too ill-disposed on her side to wish me well, since she was doing me the favor of coming to spend the night without much ado in my bedroom, and thirdly, I courted a forty-five-year-old woman, if not older. Fourthly, I gave myself to the devil, which is pretty much the only way to explain how I came across so many wonders.

This last idea crushed my mind so much when I had finished turning my key in the lock that I did not have the strength to take two steps across the carpet laid just inside the door. I stumbled over the folding chair that I had brutally launched there while receiving the unexpected confidence of Marguerite, and I sat there, legs crossed, hands crossed, my head hanging under the weight of a sorrowful meditation, sighing from time to time like a soul in perdition awaiting judgement.

My eyelids tired of old women and worries lifted slowly. Two or my three candles were out, the last one died with pallid and vacillating gleams which lent to all the objects in the room strange movements and unusual colors or shadows. Suddenly, I felt my hair stand on end and my blood froze in horror. My chair was occupied like that of Banquo in the tragedy of Macbeth. There was no doubt someone was sitting there.

My first thought was to run directly towards the apparition, but my limbs chained by fear refused to lend their offices to my helpless will. I was reduced to observing with a startled look the small, emaciated specter, livid, who had come to take Marguerite's place, as if to punish me for sin by a hideous parody of the illusions which had produced it.

It must have been a woman's ghost, judging by the long strands of her black hair, beneath which I vaguely and frighteningly sketched out, I cannot say what, but which looked like the glimmer of a face, or where one might be. From the level where one would have expected shoulders in a normal person, descended on the arms of the chair, two thin and inarticulate limbs which clung on either side, end to end, to a pair of pale claws, whose whiteness, as of morocco leather contrasted with the accoutrements of the funeral larva housed within.

"By the Lord's Protection!" I cried, while raising my hands to the heavens.

"Will you abandon me in this terrible moment? Will you not deign to show pity to the unfortunate Maxime, who, without knowing it, and unwittingly, My God, have I called the devil in person in his father's house?"

"This is precisely what I imagined," replied the ghost in a sour voice, rising to his full height and falling as if struck by lightning. " May the heavens have mercy on us!"

"What? Dine? Did you speak? By what miracle are you here now?"

Dine, who I had mentioned earlier without introducing her, had been, half a century before, my mother's nurse, and during my mother's lifetime, she had never left her. Since her death, she had remained in the family, as a housekeeper and absolute governess to all the children. I loved Dine dearly.

"I did not appear here as if by a miracle," replied Dine, grumbling. "I entered with the double key which I use to watch and care for all the house, and to prepare the apartment for the gentleman, in his absence."

"This is good, my dearest friend, but one hardly makes the apartment at two in the morning, and you will allow me to say," I added, smiling, because this episode had given me a little confidence, "that with your fresh physiognomy and cheeky air, it is a rather singular moment to visit a young man who has proven himself to be quite reckless."

"It had to be, well, a bad joke, since you didn't let me sleep all night, and what a night, blessed Virgin! Noises of imprecations to thrill! More evil words and names than there are saints in the litanies! Wandering lights floating about, black and white spirits falling from the clouds in the garden, black spirits going away on all sides, white spirits who open your windows, as if get fresh air, while humming romantic tunes, and most terrible of all, to see you before my eyes as if drawn from some purgatory by my prayers, you! Maxime! What have you done?"

"All this can be explained wonderfully, my poor Dine, and Mr. Calmet himself would not, however, have represented these infernal hallucinations with more energy and naivete. But, since you are awake, you must hear my story, because you are a woman full of spirit, of judgement and of experience, and there is only you who can free me from my scruples. So listen to me carefully if you are not sleeping."

I told her all about what had transpired that evening, and what I have shared already, (and I suppose you would not be curious enough to hear it told twice). I told her, with such penetrating compunction and such sincere concern about the results of my faults that the devil himself would have been touched if he had heard me.

When I had finished, I waited, trembling, for Dine's response, as my supreme judgement. It was so late that I feared she might have fallen asleep while I was telling the story. It could have happened.

Finally, she solemnly took off her glasses, which she had put on to follow my facial expressions closely, by the light of the candles, renewed by her care since my return. She rubbed one edge on her sleeve, put them in their case and then put it back in her pocket. (the worthy housekeepers who pride themselves on their precaution and accuracy never let them out of their pockets). Then she got up and walked in a straight line to the folding chair where I was still sitting.

"Go to bed, kid," she said, knocking my cheeks softly with a flick of the back of her hand. "Go to bed, Maxime, and sleep quietly, my child. No, really, you're not damned yet, not this time anyway, but it's not the devil's fault!"

THE LEGEND OF THE SILKWORM

Author unknown, original French translation by
Alexander Ducros

155: Original Image of Alexandre Ducros by Michael Gallant

Original Translator's Note

My

Dear Aline,

This is the Legend that I translated for you, twenty years ago.

It was in Alais, in the Cévennes.

You were given a few silkworm eggs; you set out to hatch them. I remember your joy when you saw these precious insects go up to the fragrant briar heath, with which you had covered our little nest of artists and spin their red cocoons like Indian gold or white like virgin snow.

In the evening we went, marauding, to pick leaves of mulberry, and while singing, we spelt these words that my friend Frédéric Mistral, from Maillane, had already put on the lips of Mireille and Vincent, also double picking !

Twenty years ago ! ! !

Alexander Ducros

The Legend of the Silkworm

I see you every day, Aline, worried,
  Watching carefully for these cherished insects,
    That you care for, that you feed
  With silky antlers
From the tree with golden veins, in the country of the Chinese,
  I believe,
Traucat knew how to steal, oh charming breeder.
Well, I want to brighten your dreary work with a story.
An Oriental tale, if you like it,
  I'm not asking for a salary,
  Just a kiss for the storyteller,
This tale, I'm sure, will fill you with joy,
  Because it is about a silkworm!

From the Sabean country, the Queen came one day
    To find Solomon at his court.
    His glory was talked of everywhere,
The Sabean wanted
To see it for herself, and this is a notorious tale,
    Since I read it myself,
One evening, near El-Arouch, in an old grimoire
    That my friend had given me,
        Old Ben-toumi.
The Queen therefore came. I passed the procession,
    Or the Caravane, what do I know?
I cannot speak of it, I did not witness it,
    But the Queen came from far away!
If the weather was superb or if there was a storm,
I don't know yet, but the grimoire says,
    That she had a very good trip,
And, like me, I think that's enough for you.
    She was beautiful, this Queen!

S olomon noticed this all too well!
She had a noble demeanor, a sovereign air;
Her teeth were of mother-of-pearl and hair ebony,
And his gaze was… was like yours!
I leave you to consider how it was
That Solomon received the Queen of Sheba?
Dances, games & feasts, of course, nothing was missed
    In this Court of hospitality;
Jerusalem was covered with dust,
    So one wiggled through it!

One day, when they were alone, Solomon & the Queen,
Alone in a grand garden lit by the moon,
    The king, taciturn, distracted,
    By the Royal Sabean
    Wished to share a secret
Close to a tall mastic tree, beside a fountain,
Spoke with her with emotion in a low voice.
The Queen, however, did not answer him.
But then, changing her mind – "You love me?" she asked
"Do you admit it? Certainly from such a great King,
    "Love must flatter any beautiful woman,
    Were she Queen like me…
Your love inspires me with some terror.

*I*f I know how to count, you have eight hundred wives
     Who languish in the harem?
          In a word, you burn, Sire, with so many flames,
That you could very well from your firs....Polygamists!
     Burn Jerusalem!
Eight hundred women, Lord! And your extreme love,
     Offered to me... gallantly,
     To be the eight hundred and first?...
     Well... I accept!... Honestly!"

Solomon, transported, delighted, beyond himself,
Falls at the feet of the Queen, and his emotion,
Prevents him from speaking. "But," continues our Queen,
I place on this hymen a condition,
If you fulfill it, under your laws I am enchained"
     "What is this condition? Speak!
To win your heart, nothing is impossible!
     Tell me what you wish!"
He replied, "Is there a terrible neighbor,
Who we should invade? Order, and I will charge there,
To fight for you, one must be invincible!
     Or is it help you need for the arts,
In the middle of the desert, should we build temples?
Spacious palaces, magnificent examples

*T*he power of love? Just say a word, and suddenly
  Marble, cedar, brass,
  Will stand in basilicas,
In famous monuments with thousands of porticos,
Wonderful masterpieces from the splendid Orient!
O Queen! Express your wish! Say! What should be done?"
  "Neither buildings nor invasions,"
  Responds the Queen, smiling,
Look at this pearl, it comes from Golconda,
From Golconda or Ormuz, under the waves profound,
The diver who took it had never sinned
Pearl most precious and most beautiful and most pure!
  Capricious Nature,
  (Is it for a hidden purpose?)
Made it a strange, wonderful pearl;
See, it's pieced! And not in a straight hole,
Sire, but wavy! – Be clever enough,
  (Success is glorious!)
Be clever enough to pass this thread.
  If you do, I swear
To belong to you." With these words, the figure
Of the great King darkens. "Alas! Alas!" he says,
"You make fun of me, I can't do it,
This is a fatal arrest for my disappointed hopes,
  Revoke this severe judgement!"
  "No! You have heard my request,
You must pass the thread," replies the Sabean,
  Or give up my hand.
Sire, here is the thread and the pearl – Until tomorrow!"

S olomon was deeply worried!
The rest of the night he only thought
By means of being able to pass
The thread through this pearl, and all week
He only looked for a means to do so,
He delved his head and couldn't find anything!
Sleep fled from his eyes, on his table
The food remained intact. To all strangers,
He continued to pursue this untraceable means!
Unable to bear it any longer, the King ordered to travel
And come to his court, people of all sects:
One saw mages and soothsayers,
Augurs, priests, doctors
Famous geometers and learned architects,
They all came from distant lands.
Solomon assembles them and in a mournful voice
He shares with them his torment:
"Find for me," he said, "all you praised people,
What I'm looking for in vain,
And I will shower you in glory and riches.
But hurry, because time is short;
The Queen of Sheba wishes to leave, and I want
To keep in my Court the one that torments me,
And for whom, alas! My mad love increases.
Imagine a thousand means,
And find a good one, so that I might soon
Satisfy the caprice of my proud beauty,
And pass the thread through the pearl!" With these words,
Solomon adjourned the court.
Then he secluded him to taste some rest,
Which flees from him, despite his power.

So, one could see
From morn to eve,
    The magi, soothsayers, sages,
All the famous personages,
    Coming, going, worried.
They looked like escaped madmen,
Just by looking at their faces.
    One put his finger on his forehead
And murmured a corollary
On the secant and the plumb.
    The other, on the wall or on the floor,
With an air of mystery
Without saying anything, traced a circle.
    And soon the people themselves...
    To find the solution to the problem,
    Began to search in turn!
Jerusalem was moved by this,
One met another on the street,
But without exchanging greetings!
    And each one with a serious or swift step,
    Walking along made the gesture
Of threading a needle, in spite of the scoffers.
It looked like the world-renowned city,
    Was no longer inhabited
    Save by an army of tailors!
How creased were the heads!
How many projects were combined,
    To find the famed means!
Despite the most beautiful promises
From Solomon and his riches,
    We found nothing! Nothing! Nothing!
And the great King Solomon wept! – says the grimoire.

*T*he Queen was leaving the Court that day.
      It was all over with her lover!
      "What good is greatness, fortune, glory?
What good is all this, Lord?" he murmured.
      "Vain qualities, I despise you,
      Since your power is naught
      In front of nothing, before a thread!
A pitiful spectacle of nothingness!
      O vanity of vanities!
All is vanity under the exalted skies!
      Who can I turn to? Which Oracle
Holds the secret of the pearl?" – Suddenly,
A small voice spoke in the garden,
Where the King, sorrowful, had come,
      To invent a new proverb
      Against mad human pride.
That voice said, "Come here! O Great King!
Your tears disturb me in my abode of grass,
      And I pity your state of sorrow…"
David's heir, listening to these words,
      Was filled with great joy.
"Where are you hiding?" he asked, "Appear! Let me see you!
You, who come to bring a remedy to my ailments,
      I bless the one who sends you!"

"$\mathcal{I}$ stand at your feet and if you wish to see me,
Bow down, Solomon!" replied the soft voice.
"Hey! Careful! Your foot almost stepped on me,
Crush me and it would have been a great pity … for you."
  "I'm looking and I don't see anyone!" said the King.
"Eh! Bend over, I say! Again…let's go…again!
Do you see me?" – "No, really!" –"You are touching me!"
"I only touch a worm!" –"Well, this worm is me!
  Me, crawling from dawn to dusk!"
  "It is indeed an insect, indeed,
Who is speaking to me?" replies the stupefied Solomon.
"Eh? Yes! I was born, alas, in the kingdom of insects!
I am a humble worm! However I claim,
  I am better than your wise men, your scholars,
  Your soothsayers and your architects,
  Whose mind is not too subtle,
To give you the means to pass the subtle thread
  In the pearl that pains you.
What do I mean? I mean myself, in the blink of an eye,
I will introduce the thread and cast down the pride
  Of the Royal Sabaean."
"Ah! If you that!" –"I will, really!...
Place the thread in my mouth and hold the pearl, now leave,
Leave me to maneuver at my ease now."
Solomon was watching, filled with astonishment!

*T*he humble worm, with agility,
   Enters the pearl, it glides,
   With the thread, he promenades,
The pearl of the Queen
The capricious dance,
It stretches, it folds back,
The thread is drawn effortlessly,
And then, his work complete,
In triumph he leaves.
"Here, take it!" he says to the king, "the pearl is traversed,
Now the Queen can wear it around her neck
Suspended from this thread, gently balanced.
Your scholars have searched, well, I know not where…"
But, not listening, Solomon heads
Towards the palace. The insect in a low voice, says,
"Without so much as a thank you, he strides away,
I must admit, this process distresses me!
Not for me, but for him… See, am I crazy?
Men, people, kings – are all cut from the same cloth:
All ungrateful, forgetful, but I am a philosopher, am I not?
Let's get back to my hole, safe and true."

ho was surprised? It was the Queen,
As she saw Solomon
Coming fast, breathless,
And palpitating with emotion,
Presenting her the pearl with the thread passed through!
The whole court was in awe and admiration,
And the Queen kept her promise,
The hymen was solemnized…but without witnesses!
The grimoire is silent on this,
Because there is no single person
Whose scrupulous examination
Could certify what day was the marriage.

What of the worm? What of the poor worm? – The story,
Non, I mean the grimoire,
Adds that one morning the king
Looked for him everywhere. – "What do you want from me?"
He said, to those who found him.
"The King wishes to speak." –"Let him come! I'm here!"
The Messengers withdrew.

"Do you come now, perhaps a little late, to *thank* me?"
Said the philosopher worm to the sumptuous monarch.
"A king who remembers! This is worthy of note,
So I don't want to be outdone by you!"
"What do you mean, insect?" exclaimed our King.
"I wish to make you a gift for the price of your memory,"
The worm expresses to him, "and I like to believe
That you will appreciate it. Carry me in your hand,
        Over there, up to that tree
Which lends its shade to this marble basin,
Put me on it and… you will see tomorrow!
        My gift will be wonderful!
In memory of the thread in the pearl
You will have the richest tunic woven with it,
The richest coat ever woven!…
Well! Here I am on the tree, goodbye!… I'm in a hurry!"

The next day, oh wonder!
        As soon as the rust of dawn
Illuminated the horizon,
        Solomon,
Followed by his entire Court,
Went into the garden,
To see the tree by the basin,

*T*he worm was absent, but in its place one saw
An object that one would have taken for a very small egg,
And the worm spoke from it!
"O Solomon!" he said, "with the humble abode
Where I'm enclosed, I leave you a treasure,
It was I who built it with long golden threads.

I will come out in good time,
But I will appear as a butterfly,
And I will produce the germs, in one sense
Which will give in abundance

Silk for my labors! Listen Solomon!
Give this tree care; it's foliage
Will serve as sustenance for the worker insect
Which cannot finish his striving without it;
God for the silkworm planted the mulberry tree;
He placed gold threads in each green leaf,
The threads with which I built the house

That one calls the *cocoon*.

Farewell! I will leave now; my house is open!...

Listen again, Solomon:
That on the frame, the shuttle
Quickly pass these numerous strands
And man will conquer
This useful, wonderful art!
O King! My promises are true,
I tell you the truth!
I feel wings forming…

I crawled; I fly away… freedom to me!

*D*ear Aline, here, syllable by syllable,
    What I read one evening in the Arabic grimoire,
    I have translated for you, translated in its entirety.
Happy, if indulgent smiles welcome it,
And if you allow me, when I dare ask you,
To come with you in the evening to pick the leaf,
    The green leaf of the mulberry tree.

Alais, 1857

THE THOUSAND AND ONE GHOSTS

By Alexandre Dumas

166: Original Image of Alexandre Dumas, Père by Michael Gallant

To Mr. ***,

My dear friend, you have often told me - in the middle of these evenings, which have become too rare, where everyone chatters at leisure, or saying the dream of his heart, or following the whim of his mind, or wasting the treasure of his memories, - you often told me that since Scheherazade and after Nodier[13], I was one of the funniest storytellers you have ever heard.

Here you are today writing to me that while waiting for a long novel from me, - you know, one of those endless novels as I write, and in which I cover a whole century, - you would like some tales – two, four or six volumes at most, poor flowers of my garden, which you intend to throw in the middle of the political preoccupations of the moment, between the trial of Bourges, for example, and the elections of May.

Alas! my friend, the era is sad, and my stories, I warn you, will not be gay. Only you will allow that, tired of what I see happening every day in the real world, I go to seek my stories in the imaginary world. Alas! I am afraid that all minds a little high, a little political, a little dreamy, will not be in search of the ideal, the only refuge that God leaves us against reality.

Here, I am in the middle of fifty open volumes about a story of the Regency that I have just finished, and that I beg you, if you realize it, to invite the mothers not to let read to their daughters. Well! I am there, I told you, and, while writing to you, my eyes stop on a page of the Memoirs of the Marquis d'Argenson[14], wherein I read the following:

> *"I am convinced that, when the Rambouillet Hotel set the tone for good company, we listened well and reasoned better. We cultivated taste and spirit; I still saw models of this kind of conversation among the old men of the court that I attended. They had the proper word, energy and finesse, some antitheses, but epithets which increased the meaning; depth*

---

[13] Charles Nodier, author of Love & the Grimoire, various dream writings and many *contes fantastiques*, Librarian of the Bibliothèque de l'Arsenal

[14] René-Louis de Voyer de Paulmy, Marquis d'Argenson, 1697-1757, friend of Voltaire, who was the Minister of Foreign Affairs and whose *Mémoires* are a valuable chronicle of the time.

without pedantry, playfulness without malignity."

It is just a hundred years since the Marquis of Argenson wrote these lines, which I copy in his book. - He was, at the time when he wrote them, about the age we are, - and like him, my dear friend, we can say: We have known old men who were, alas! what we are no longer, that is, men of good company

We have seen them, but our sons will not see them. This is what makes us, although we are not worth much, better than our sons will be worth.

It is true that every day we take a step towards freedom, equality, fraternity, three big words that the Revolution of '93, you know, the other one, the dowager, launched in the middle of modern society, as she would have done with a tiger, a lion and a bear dressed in lambs' fleeces; empty words, unfortunately, and that we read through the June smoke on our bullet-riddled public monuments.

I go like the others; I am the movement. God save me from preaching stillness! Stillness is death. But I'm like one of those men Dante talks about - whose feet are walking forward - that's right - but whose head is turned towards his heels.

What I am looking for above all - what I regret above all - what my retrospective gaze is looking for in the past is society which leaves, which evaporates, which disappears like one of those ghosts whose story I'll tell you.

This society, which made elegant life, courteous life, this life, which was worth living, finally (forgive me barbarism, not being of the Academy, I can risk it), is this society dead or did we kill it?

Here, I remember that, as a child, I was taken by my father to meet Madame de Montesson. She was a great lady, a woman from the other century altogether. She had married, nearly sixty years ago, the Duke of Orleans, grandfather of King Louis-Philippe; she was eighty years old.

She lived in a large and wealthy hotel in Chaussée-d'Antin. Napoleon had made her an annuity of a hundred thousand crowns.

- Do you know on what title this rent was registered in the red book of the successor of Louis XVI?

- No.

Well ! Mrs. Montesson received from the emperor a rent of one hundred thousand ecus *for having preserved in her living room the traditions of good society of the times of Louis XIV & Louis XV.*

This is just half of what the House gives her nephew today to make France forget what her uncle wanted that she had remembered.

You would not believe a thing, my dear friend, it is that these two words which I have just had the imprudence to pronounce: The Room, which bring me straight back to the to the Memoirs of the Marquis of Argenson.

- What do you mean?

- You'll see.

"We complain," he said, "that there is no more conversation these days in France. I know the reason. The fact is that the patience to listen decreases daily among our contemporaries. We do not listen well, or rather we do not listen at all. I made this remark in the best company I frequent."

Now, my dear friend, what is the best company you can hang out with today? It is certainly one that eight million voters have deemed worthy of representing the interests, opinions, and genius of France. This is the House, finally.

Well! enter the Chamber, at random, on the day and at the time you want. You can bet a hundred to one that you will find in the gallery a man speaking, and on the benches five to six hundred people, not listening to him, but interrupting him.

It is so true what I'm telling you, that there is an article in the 1848 Constitution that prohibits such interruptions.

So count the amount of bellows and punches given to the House in the past year or so since it gathered: - it is countless!

Always in the name, of course, of freedom, equality, and fraternity.

So, my dear friend, as I told you, I regret a lot of things, right? although I've been around half of my life; well! the one I most regret among all those who have gone or who are leaving, is the one that the Marquis of Argenson regretted a hundred years ago: courtesy.

And yet, in the time of the Marquis of Argenson, we had not yet had the idea of calling ourselves citizens. So judge.

If we had said to the Marquis of Argenson, at the time when he wrote these words, for example:

> *"Here is where we came from in France: the canvas*
> *falls; all spectacle disappears; there are only whistles*
> *whistling. Soon, we will no longer have elegant*
> *storytellers in society, no arts, no paintings, no built*
> *palaces, but envy of everything and everywhere."*

If we had told him, at the time when he was writing these words, that we would come to - for me at least - envy that time, he would have been astonished, wouldn't you say, this poor Marquis of Argenson?

Also, what am I doing? I live with the dead a lot, with the exiles a little. I try to revive extinct societies, missing men, those who smelled amber instead of smelling the cigar, who were hitting each other rather than punching themselves.

That is why, my friend, when you chat, you are surprised to hear a language you no longer speak. That is why you tell me that I am a fun storyteller. This is why my voice, an echo of the past, is still heard in the present, which listens so little and so badly.

In the end, like those eighteenth-century Venetians who were forbidden by sumptuary laws to wear anything other than cloth and wool, we always like to see silk and velvet unfold, and the beautiful gold brocades in which royalty carved the clothes of our fathers.

Yours,
Alexandre Dumas

Chapter One: The Rue de Diane in Fontenay–aux–Roses

O n September 1st of the year 1831, I was invited by one of my old friends, the office manager of the king's private estate, to inaugurate, with his son, the opening of the hunt at Fontenay-aux-Roses.

I really liked hunting at that time, and, as a great hunter, the choice of country where the opening had to be done each year was a serious matter to me.

We usually went to a farmer's house or rather to a friend of my brother-in-law. It was at his home that I had made, by killing a hare, my beginnings in the science of Nimrod[15] and Elzéar Blaze[16]. His farm was located between the forests of Compiègne and Villers-Cotterêts, halfway through the charming village of Morienval, one league from the magnificent ruins of Pierrefonds.

The two or three thousand arpents[17] of land which form its demesne present a vast plain almost entirely surrounded by woods, cut in the middle by a pretty valley at the bottom of which we see, among the green meadows and the trees with changing tones, swarming with houses half lost in the foliage, and which are hinted at by the columns of bluish smoke which, first protected by the shelter of the mountains which surround them, rise vertically towards the sky, and then, arriving at the upper layers of air, bend, widened like the tops of palm trees, in the direction of the wind.

It is on this plain and on the double slope of this valley that the game of the two forests comes to frolic as on neutral ground.

One finds everything on the plain of Brassoire: deer and pheasant along the woods, hare on the plateaus, rabbit on the slopes, partridges

---

[15] Biblical figure, "a mighty hunter before the Lord"

[16] Captain Elezar Blaze, one of Napoleon's distinguished officers, author of *Life in Napoleon's Army : The Memoirs of Captain Elzear Blaze*

[17] A pre-metric French unit of area, having various official measures. Derived from Late Latin arepennis ("surface of a field"), & Gaulish are-penno- ("end, extremity of a field")

around the farm. Mr. Mocquet, our friend, was therefore certainly glad to see us arriving; we hunted all day long, and the next day, at two o'clock, we returned to Paris, having killed, between four or five hunters, one hundred and fifty pieces of game, of which we have never been able to make our host accept a single one.

But, that year, unfaithful to Mr. Mocquet, I had yielded to the obsession of my old office companion, seduced as I had been by a painting sent to me by his son, a distinguished student at the School of Rome, and which represented a view of the plain of Fontenay-aux-Roses, with steeds full of hares and alfalfa full of partridges.

I had never been to Fontenay-aux-Roses: no one knows the surroundings of Paris less than I do. When I cross the barrier, it is almost always five or six hundred leagues. Everything is therefore a subject of curiosity in the slightest change of place.

At six o'clock in the evening, I left for Fontenay, my head out of the door, as always: I crossed the barrier of Hell, I left the Rue de la Tombe-Issoire on my left and I took the road to Orléans.

We know that Issoire is the name of a famous brigand who, in Julien's time, used to kidnap for ransom travelers who went to Lutèce. He was hanged, I believe, and buried in the place that bears his name today, some distance from the entrance to the Catacombs.

The plain that develops at the entrance to Petit-Montrouge is strange in appearance. In the middle of artificial meadows, fields of carrots and flowerbeds of beets, are laid out in squares, marked out by white stones, dominated by a cogwheel like a skeleton of extinguished fireworks. This wheel carries on its circumference wooden sleepers on which a man alternately presses one and the other foot. This squirrel cage[18], which gives the worker a large apparent movement without actually changing places, aims to wrap around a hub a rope which, by coiling, brings to the surface of the ground a cut stone at the bottom of the quarry, which slowly comes to the surface.

A hook brings this stone to the edge of the hole, where rollers await it to transport it to the place which is intended for it. Then the rope

---

[18] A treadwheel crane or *magna rota*, is a wooden circular hoist dating to Roman times and popular in the Middle Ages for construction of castles, quarryworks, etc.

descends into the depths, where it will seek another burden, giving a moment of rest to the modern Ixion, to which a cry soon announces that another stone awaits the work which must make him leave his native career, and the same labor begins again.

By evening, the man has traveled ten leagues without changing places; if he actually climbed up one degree each time his foot landed on a step, after twenty-three years he would have arrived in the moon.

177: 13th c art of a treadmill crane, Artist Unknown, Public Domain.

It is especially in the evening, that is to say at the time when I was crossing the plain that separates the Petit from the Grand-Montrouge, that the landscape, thanks to this infinite number of moving wheels that stand out in force on the fiery sunset takes on a fantastic aspect. It looks like one of these engravings by Goya, where, in the halftone, the hangmen hunt for the hanged.

Around seven o'clock the wheels stop; the day is over. These rubble stones, which are large squares fifty to sixty feet long, six or eight high constitute the future Paris being torn from the earth. The quarries from which this stone comes out are growing every day. It is the sequel to the

Catacombs from which old Paris came out. These are the suburbs of the underground city, which will incessantly gain the country and extending to the circumference. When we walk in this meadow of Montrouge, we walk on abysses. From time to time we find a depression of the ground, a valley in miniature, a ripple in the ground: it is a badly supported cave below, whose ceiling of gypsum has cracked. A crack was established through which water entered the cavern; water swept away the earth; from there we see the movement of the ground: this is called a melt.

If you don't know that, if you don't know that this beautiful layer of green earth that seems so inviting does not rest on anything, you can, by putting your foot above one of these cracks, disappear, as you might disappear at Montanvert between two walls of ice.

The population living in these underground galleries has, like its existence, its character, and its physiognomy apart. Living in the dark, it has a bit of the instincts of the night animals, that is to say that it is silent and fierce. We often hear about an accident: a forestay failed, a rope broke, a man was crushed. On the surface of the earth, it is believed to be a misfortune: thirty feet below, it is known that it is a crime.

The aspect of the carriers is generally sinister. During the day, their eyes blink, in the air their voices are deaf. They have flat hair, folded up to the eyebrows; a beard that only gets to know the razor every Sunday morning; a waistcoat that reveals sleeves of large gray canvas, an apron of leather bleached by the contact of stone, blue canvas pants. On one of their shoulders is a jacket folded in half, and on this jacket poses the handle of the pickaxe or the besaiguë[19] which, six days a week, digs the stone.

When there is some riot, it is rare that the men we have just tried to paint a picture of do not get involved. When we say at the barrier of Hell: *"Here are the quarries of Montrouge coming down!"* The residents of the surrounding streets shake their heads and close their doors.

This is what I looked at, what I saw during this hour of twilight which, in September, separates day from night; then, at night, I threw myself back into the car, from which certainly none of my companions had seen what I had just seen. It is the same with all things: many people look, very few

---

[19] A carpenter's tool combining a chisel and a mortise on a long handle.

see.

We arrived at half past eight at Fontenay; an excellent supper awaited us, then after supper a walk in the garden. Sorrento is a forest of orange trees; Fontenay is a bouquet of roses. Each house has its rose bush which rises along the wall, protected at the foot by a case of planks. Arriving at a certain height, the rose blossoms as if it were a gigantic fan; the passing air is embalmed, and when instead of air it blows, it rains leaves of roses, as it rained at Corpus Christi when God had a party.

From the end of the garden, we would have had a beautiful view if it had been day. The lights scattered in the darkness indicated the villages of Sceaux, Bagneux, Châtillon and Montrouge; at the bottom stretched a large reddish line from which came a deafening noise similar to the breath of Leviathan: it was the breath of Paris.

We had to force ourselves to go to bed, as one does with children. Under this beautiful sky all embroidered with stars, in contact with this fragrant breeze, we would have gladly waited for the day.

At five o'clock in the morning, we set off on our chase, guided by the son of our host, who had promised us mountains and wonders, and who, it must be said, continued to boast of the game-rich fertility of his territory with a dignified persistence of a better fate.

At noon we saw a rabbit and four partridges. The rabbit had been missed by my companion on the right, a partridge had been missed by my companion on the left, and, of the other three partridges, two had been killed by me.

At noon, in Brassoire, I would have already sent three or four hares and fifteen or twenty partridges to the farm.

I like hunting, but I hate walking, especially walking across fields. So, on the pretext of going to explore an alfalfa field located on my far left and in which I was sure I could not find anything, I broke the line and stepped aside.

But what there was in this field, what I had hoped for there in the desire for retirement which had already taken hold of me for more than two hours, was a sunken path which, hiding me from the eyes of other hunters, was to bring me back, by the rue de Sceaux, straight to Fontenay-aux-Roses.

I was not mistaken. As one o'clock was striking at the parish bell tower,

I reached the first houses in the village. I was following a wall which seemed to me to close off a fairly fine property, when, arriving at the place where the rue de Diane branched off with the Grande-Rue, I saw a man coming towards me, near the church, who was so strange in appearance, that I stopped, and instinctively cocked the two barrels of my rifle, moved as I was by the simple feeling of personal preservation.

Pale, with spiky hair, eyes out of his orbit, dressed in messy clothes and bearing bloody hands, this man passed by me without seeing me. His gaze was fixed and dull at the same time. His gait had the invincible outburst of a body that would descend a mountain too fast, and yet his gasping breath indicated even more dread than fatigue.

At the junction of the two lanes, he left the Grande-Rue to throw himself into the rue de Diane, on which opened the property which, for seven or eight minutes, I had followed the wall. This door, on which my eyes stopped immediately, was painted green and was topped with the number two. The man's hand stretched out toward the doorbell long before he could touch it; then he reached it, rang it violently, and, almost immediately, he leaned on one of the two arches which served as support for this door. Once there, he remained motionless, arms hanging, head tilted on his chest.

I retraced my steps, as I understood that this man must have been the actor of some unknown and terrible drama.

Behind him, and on both sides of the street, a few people, on whom he had no doubt had the same effect as I did, had come out of their houses, and looked at him with an astonishment similar to that which I experienced myself.

When the doorbell rang violently, a small door set into the large one opened, and a woman aged forty to forty-five appeared.

"Ah! It's you, Jacquemin," she said. "What are you doing there?"

"Is the mayor at home?" the man asked in a low voice.

"Yes."

"Well ! Mother Antoine, tell him that I have killed my wife, and that I have come to surrender."

Mother Antoine uttered a cry to which were heard in reply two or three exclamations torn by terror from people who were close enough to hear this terrible confession. I took a step back myself and encountered the trunk of a lime tree on which I leaned.

Besides, all those who were within earshot had remained motionless. As for the murderer, he had slipped from the doorstop to the ground, as if, after having spoken the fatal words, he had lost all his strength.

However, Mother Antoine had disappeared, leaving the small door open. It was obvious that she had gone to accomplish with the mayor the commission which Jacquemin had charged her with. After five minutes, the gentleman she had gone to fetch appeared on the doorstep. Two other men followed him. I can still see the scene.

Jacquemin had slipped to the ground, as I said. The mayor of Fontenay-aux-Roses was standing near him, towering over him, tall as he was. In the opening of the door crowded the two other people whom we will speak about at greater length later. I was leaning against the trunk of a lime tree planted in the Grande-Rue, but from where my gaze plunged into the rue de Diane. To my left was a group of a man, a woman and a child, the child crying for his mother to take him in his arms. Behind this group a baker poked his head through a window on the first floor, chatting with his boy who was downstairs, and asking him if it was not Jacquemin, the carrier, who had just run past; then finally there appeared, on the threshold of his door, a blacksmith, black in front but his back lit by the light of his forge from which an apprentice continued to pull the bellows.

So much for the Grande-Rue.

As for the rue de Diane, apart from the main group that we have described, it was deserted. Only, at its end, we saw two gendarmes appear who had just made their round in the plain to check for arms permits, and who, without suspecting the work which awaited them, approached us while walking quietly in step.

The clock tolled a quarter past the hour.

Chapter Two: L'Impasse des Sergents

*T*he last vibration of the bell mingled with the sound of the mayor's first word.

"Jacquemin," he said, "I hope that Mother Antoine is crazy: she comes to tell me that your wife is dead, and that it was you who killed her!"

"It is the pure truth, mayor," replied Jacquemin. "I would like to be taken to prison and judged very quickly."

Saying these words, he tried to get up, clinging to the top of the post with his elbow; but, after an effort, he fell back, as if the bones of his legs had been broken.

"Come on! you are crazy!" said the mayor.

"Look at my hands," he replied.

He raised two bloody hands, to which their clenched fingers gave the form of two talons.

Indeed, the left was red up to the wrist, the right to the elbow. In addition, in the right hand, a trickle of fresh blood flowed down the thumb, from a bite that the victim, in wrestling, had, in all probability, done to her killer.

Meanwhile, the two gendarmes approached, halted ten paces from the main actor in this scene, and were looking down from their horses.

The mayor made a sign to them; they got down from their horses, throwing the bridle of their mounts to a boy wearing a police cap and who appeared to be a troop follower.

After which, they approached Jacquemin and lifted him under the arms. He gave in without resistance, and with the dullness of a man whose mind is absorbed by a single thought.

At the same instant, the police commissioner and the doctor arrived; they had just been warned of what was going on.

"Ah! come on, Mr. Robert! Ah! come, Mr Cousin!" said the mayor. Mr. Robert was the doctor and Mr. Cousin was the police commissioner.

"Come - I was going to send for you just now."

"Well ! Let us see, what is it?" asked the doctor with the most jovial air in the world; "a little assassination, they say?"

Jacquemin said nothing.

"Say, Father Jacquemin," continued the doctor, "is it true that it was you who killed your wife?"

Jacquemin did not breathe a word.

"He has at least just accused himself," said the mayor; "however, I still hope that it is a moment of hallucination and not a real crime that makes him talk."

"Jacquemin," said the police chief, "answer. Is it true that you killed your wife?"

The same silence.

"In any case, we'll see," said Dr. Robert; "does he not stay at *L'impasse des Sergents*[20]?"

"Yes," replied the two gendarmes.

"Well! Mr. Ledru," said the doctor, addressing the mayor, "let's go to the *L'impasse des Sergents.*"

"I am not going! I am not going!" cried Jacquemin, snatching himself from the hands of the gendarmes with such a violent movement that, had he wanted to flee, he would certainly have been a hundred paces before anyone thought of pursuing him.

"But why don't you want to go?" asked the mayor.

"Why do I need to go there, since I admit everything, since I tell you that I killed her, killed her with this big two-handed sword that I took from the Artillery museum last year? Take me to jail; I have nothing to do there, take me to jail!"

The doctor and Mr. Ledru looked at each other.

"My friend," said the police commissioner who, like Mr. Ledru, still hoped that Jacquemin was under the weight of some momentary disturbance of mind, "my friend, the matter is urgent; besides, you must be there to guide justice."

"How does justice need to be guided?" said Jacquemin; "you will find the body in the cellar, and, close to the body, in a plaster bag, the head; as for me, take me to prison."

"You must come," said the police commissioner.

"Oh! My God! My God!" cried Jacquemin, overcome by the most dreadful terror; "Oh! My God! My God! If I had known..."

"Well! what would you have done?" asked the police commissioner.

"Well! I would have killed myself."

Mr. Ledru shook his head, and, looking at the police chief, he seemed to say to him: there is something hidden in that statement.

"My friend," he went on, addressing the murderer, "come on, explain

---

[20] Jacquemin's residence. L'impasse typically refers to a cul-de-sac or a dead end. This is a clever choice of name, referring to the Impasse the Sergeants find themselves in.

it to me."

"Yes, to you, whatever you want, Mr. Ledru, ask, question."

"How is it, since you had the courage to commit the murder, that you do not have any to find yourself in front of your victim? Has something happened that you are not telling us?"

"Oh! yes, something terrible."

"Well! come on, tell me."

"Oh no! You would say it's not true, you would say I'm crazy."

"Anything! What happened? Tell me."

"I'll tell you, but only you."

He approached Mr. Ledru.

The two gendarmes wanted to detain him; but the mayor made a sign to them, they left the prisoner free.

Besides, if he had wanted to save himself, the thing had become impossible; half of the population of Fontenay-aux-Roses encumbered the rue de Diane and the Grande-Rue.

Jacquemin, as I said, came close to Mr. Ledru's ear.

"Do you believe, Mr. Ledru," asked Jacquemin in a low voice, "do you believe that a head can speak, once separated from the body? Mr. Ledru uttered an exclamation that looked like a cry, and visibly paled."

"Do you believe it? Tell me," repeated Jacquemin.

Mr. Ledru made a start.

"Yes," he said, "I believe it."

"Well! ... well! ... she spoke."

"Who?"

"The head ... Jeanne's head."

"You don't say!"

"I saw that she had her eyes open, I say she moved her lips. I say she looked at me. I say that when she looked at me she called me: *Miserable!*"

By saying these words, which he intended to say to Mister Ledru all by himself and which however could be heard by everyone, Jacquemin was frightening.

"Oh! How clever!" cried the doctor, laughing; "she spoke ... a severed head spoke. Well! Well! Well!"

Jacquemin turned around.

"I tell you it did!" he cried.

"Well!" said the police commissioner, "all the more reason for us to go to the place where the crime was committed. Gendarmes, take the prisoner."

Jacquemin cried out, writhing.

"No, no," he said, "cut me to pieces if you want, but I'm not going!"

"Come, my friend," said Mr. Ledru. "If it is true that you committed the terrible crime of which you are accused, it will be an act of public expiation of sorts."

"Besides," he added, speaking to him in a low voice, "resistance is useless; if you don't want to come willingly, they will take you there by force."

"Well then!" said Jacquemin, "I am willing; but promise me one thing, Mr. Ledru."

"What?"

"During all the time that we will be in the cellar, you will not leave me."

"No."

"You will let me hold your hand."

"Yes."

- Well, he said, let us go!

And, taking a checkered handkerchief from his pocket, he wiped his brow soaked in sweat.

We made our way to the *L'impasse des Sergents*. The police commissioner and the doctor walked first, then Jacquemin and the two gendarmes. Behind them came Mr. Ledru and the two men who had appeared at his door at the same time as him.

Then rolled, like a torrent full of swell and rumors, the whole population, with which I was mixed. After about a minute's walk, we reached the *L'impasse des Sergents*. It was a small alley located to the left of the Grande-Rue, and which led to a large dilapidated wooden door, with two large doors and a small door cut out from one of the two large doors.

This little door was hanging from a hinge. Everything, at first glance, seemed calm in this house; a rose was blooming at the door, and near the rose, on a stone bench, a large red cat warmly blissfully warmed itself in the sun.

When he saw all these people, hearing all this noise, he got scared, ran away and disappeared through the basement window of a cellar. When we got to the door we described, Jacquemin stopped. The gendarmes wanted to force him in.

"Mr. Ledru," he said, turning around, "Mr. Ledru, you promised not to leave me."

"Well! here I am," replied the mayor.

"Your arm! your arm!"

He was tottering like he was ready to fall.

Mr. Ledru approached, motioned for the two gendarmes to let go of the prisoner, and gave him his arm.

"I answer for him," he said.

It was obvious that, at the time, Mr. Ledru was no longer the mayor of the town pursuing the punishment of a crime, but a philosopher exploring the realm of the unknown. Only, his guide in this strange exploration was an assassin.

The doctor and the police chief entered first, then Mr. Ledru and Jacquemin; then the two gendarmes, then a few privileged ones, among whom I was included, thanks to the contact I had with the gendarmes, for whom I was no longer a stranger, having had the honor of meeting them in the plain and show them my permit to bear arms.

The door was closed on the rest of the population, who milled outside. We walked towards the door of the little house. There was nothing to indicate the terrible event that had taken place there; everything was in its place: the green serge bed in its alcove; at the head of the bed the crucifix of black wood, surmounted by a branch of boxwood dried since the last Easter. On the mantelpiece, a baby Jesus in wax, lying among the flowers, between two Louis XVI-shaped candlesticks, formerly silver; on the wall, four colored engravings, framed in black wooden frames, and representing the four parts of the world. On a table, a cutlery set, on the hearth a boiling hot pot, and nearby, a cuckoo in an open hutch.

"Well!" said the doctor cheerfully, "I don't see anything so far."

"Take the door on the right," whispered Jacquemin in a low voice.

We followed the prisoner's instructions, and we found ourselves in a sort of cellar at the corner of which opened a hatch at the opening of which trembled a gleam which came from below.

"There, there," whispered Jacquemin, clinging to Mr. Ledru's arm with one hand and showing the opening of the cellar with the other.

"Ah! ah!" said the doctor to the police chief in a low voice, with that terrible smile of people whom nothing impresses because they believe in nothing, "it seems that Madame Jacquemin has followed the precept of Master Adam;" and he hummed: *If I die, let me bury myself in the cellar where is ...*

"Silence!" interrupted Jacquemin, livid face, spiky hair, sweat on his forehead, "don't sing here!"

Struck by the expression of that voice, the doctor fell silent.

But almost immediately, going down the first steps of the stairs:

"What is that?" he asked.

And, stooping down, he picked up a broad-bladed sword. It was the two-handed sword that Jacquemin, as he said, had taken on July 29, 1830, from the Artillery Museum; the blade was stained with blood.

The police commissioner took it from the doctor.

"Do you recognize this sword?" he said to the prisoner.

"Yes," replied Jacquemin. "Come on! come on! Let us finish this."

It was the first milestone in the murder investigation. We entered the cellar, each holding the rank we had already established. The doctor and the police chief first, then Mr. Ledru and Jacquemin, then the two people who were at his house, then the gendarmes, then the privileged ones, among whom I was one.

After descending the seventh step, my eye plunged into the depths of the cellar and embraced the terrible scene that I will try to paint.

The first object on which the eyes stopped was a headless corpse, lying near a barrel, whose tap, half open, continued to let out a trickle of wine, which, as it flowed, formed a channel which got lost under the corpse.

The body was half twisted, as if the torso, turned over on its back, had started a dying movement that the legs could not follow. The dress was rolled up to the garter on one side.

We could see that the victim had been struck when, kneeling before the barrel, she began to fill a bottle, which had escaped from her hands and which was lying by her side.

The whole upper body was swimming in a pool of blood. Leaning in a plaster bag against the wall, like a bust on the column, one could see, or rather guess at, a head buried in its hair; a line of blood reddened the bag, from the top to half.

The doctor and the police commissioner had already circled the body and found themselves in front of the stairs. Towards the middle of the cellar were Mr. Ledru's two friends and a few curious people, who were in a hurry to get in there.

At the bottom of the stairs was Jacquemin, who could not have been pushed further than the last step. Behind Jacquemin, the two gendarmes. Behind the two gendarmes, five or six people, among whom I was, were standing with me on the stairs.

This gloomy interior was lit by the flickering light of a candle placed on the very barrel from which the wine flowed, and in front of which lay the corpse of the Jacquemin woman.

"A table, a chair," said the police commissioner, "and let's verbalize."

Chapter Three: The Interrogation

*T*he furniture requested was passed to the police commissioner. He took over his table, sat down in front, asked for the candle, which the doctor brought to him, stepping over the corpse, drew from his pocket an inkwell, feathers, paper, and began his report.

While writing the preamble, the doctor made a movement of curiosity towards the head placed on the plaster bag; but the commissioner stopped him.

"Do not touch anything," he said, "regularity above all."

"That is right," said the doctor.

He resumed his place.

There were a few minutes of silence, during which we only heard the pen of the police commissioner scratching on the government's rugged paper, and we saw the lines succeeding each other with the speed of a usual formula to the writer. After a few lines, he looked up and looked around.

"Who wants to serve as our witnesses?" asked the police commissioner, addressing the mayor.

"Well," said Mr. Ledru, pointing to his two standing friends, who formed a group with the police chief seated, "let us propose these two gentlemen to begin with."

"Good."

He turned to me.

"Then, sir, if it is not unpleasant for the gentleman here to have his name entered in the minutes."

"Not at all, sir," I replied.

"Then let the gentleman come down," said the police commissioner.

I felt some reluctance to approach the corpse. From where I was, certain details, without completely escaping me, seemed less hideous, lost in a semi-darkness which threw the veil of poetry over their horror.

"Is it really necessary?" I asked.

"What?"

"For me to come down."

"No. Stay there, if you wish."

I nodded, saying, "I want to stay where I am."

The police commissioner turned to the closer one of Mr. Ledru's two friends.

"Your last name, first name, age, position, profession and domicile?" he asked with the volubility of a man accustomed to asking these kinds of questions.

"Jean-Louis Alliette," replied the one to whom he was speaking, "you might say Etteilla by anagram, a man of letters, living in rue de l'Ancienne-Comédie, number 20."

"You forgot to state your age," said the police commissioner.

"Should I say the age I am or the age I am given?"

"Tell me your age, good Lord! we are not two ages."

"That is to say, Commissioner, there are certain people, Cagliostro, the Count of Saint-Germain, the Wandering Jew, for example ..."

"Do you mean that you are Cagliostro, the Count of Saint-Germain, or the Wandering Jew?" said the commissioner, frowning at the mockery.

"No; But..."

"Seventy-five years," said Mr. Ledru; "put down seventy-five years, Mr. Cousin."

"So be it," said the police commissioner, and he noted seventy-five years.

"And you, sir?" he continued, addressing the second friend of Mr. Ledru.

He repeated exactly the same questions he had asked the first.

"Pierre-Joseph Moulle, sixty-one years old, ecclesiastic attached to the church of Saint-Sulpice, residing in rue Servandoni, number 11," replied in a soft voice the gentleman he had questioned.

"And you, sir?" he asked, addressing me.

"Alexandre Dumas, playwright, aged twenty-seven, living in Paris, rue de l'Université, number 21," I replied.

Mr. Ledru turned to my side and made me a gracious sign, to which I replied in the same tone, as best I could.

"Good!" said the police commissioner. "See if that's right, gentlemen, and if you have any comments."

And, in that nasal and monotonous tone that belongs only to public officials, he read:

"Today, September 1, 1831, at two o'clock in the morning, having been warned by public rumor that a crime of murder had just been committed, in the commune of Fontenay-aux-Roses, on the person of Marie-Jeanne Ducoudray, by the name of Pierre Jacquemin, her husband, and that the murderer had gone to the home of Mr. Jean-Pierre Ledru, mayor of the said commune of Fontenay-aux-Roses, to declare, on his own initiative, to be the perpetrator of this crime, we hastened to go, in person, to the home of the said Jean-Pierre Ledru, rue de Diane, number 2; where we arrived in the company of Mr. Sébastien Robert, doctor, living in the said commune of Fontenay-aux-Roses, and there we already found in the hands of the gendarmerie the named Pierre Jacquemin, who repeated before us that he was the author of the murder of his wife; whereupon he was ordered to follow us to the house where the murder had been committed.

Which he refused to do at first; but soon, having yielded, at the request of the mayor, we headed for the L'Impasse des Sergents, where the house inhabited by Mr. Pierre Jacquemin is located. We arrived at this house, and the door closed to prevent the population from invading it, we first entered a room where there was no indication that a crime had been committed; then, at the invitation of the said Jacquemin himself, from the first bedroom passed into the second, at the corner of which a hatch giving access to a staircase was open. This staircase having been indicated to us as leading to a cellar where we were to find the body of the victim, we began to descend the said staircase, on the first steps from which the doctor found a sword with cross handle, wide blade and sharp, that said Jacquemin confessed to us to have taken, during the July Revolution, from the Artillery Museum, and to have served him for the commission of the crime.

On the cellar floor we found the body of the Jacquemin woman, overturned on her back and swimming in a pool of blood, having her head separated from the trunk, which head had been placed upright on a plaster bag leaning against the wall, and said Jacquemin having recognized that this corpse and this head were indeed those of his wife, in the presence of Mr. Jean-Pierre Ledru, mayor of the commune of Fontenay-aux-Roses; Mr. Sébastien Robert, medical doctor, living in the Fontenay-aux-Roses commune; of Jean-Louis Alliette, known as Etteilla, man of letters, seventy-five years old, living in Paris, rue de l'Ancienne-Comédie, number 20; Pierre-Joseph Moulle, sixty-one years old, clergyman attached to Saint-Sulpice, living in Paris, rue Servandoni number 11; Mr. Alexandre Dumas, playwright, aged twenty-seven, living in Paris, rue de l'Université, number 21, proceeded as follows to the interrogation of the accused."

"Is that correctly stated, gentlemen?" asked the police commissioner, turning to us with an air of evident satisfaction.

"Perfectly, Sir!," we all answered in one voice.

"Well! Let us question the accused."

Then, turning to the prisoner, who, during all the reading that had just been done, had breathed loudly and like an oppressed man:

"Accused," he said, "your last name, first name, age, domicile and profession?"

"Will this take long?" asked the prisoner like a man at the end of his strength.

"Answer: your first and last names?"

"Pierre Jacquemin."

"Your age?"

"Forty-one years old."

"Your residence?"

"You know it well, since you are there."

"No matter, the law requires you to answer this question."

"L'Impasse des Sergents."

"Your job?"

"Carrier."

"Do you admit the perpetration of the crime?"

"Yes."

"Tell us the cause that made you commit this crime, and the circumstances under which it was committed."

"The cause that made me commit this... it's useless," said Jacquemin; "it's a secret that will stay between me and the one who lies there."

"However, there is no effect without cause."

"The cause, I tell you that you will not know it. As for the circumstances, as you say, do you want to know them?"

"Yes."

"Well! I will tell you. When we work underground as we do, in the dark, and then we think we have a reason for sorrow, we eat our souls, you see, then we have bad ideas."

"Oh! Oh!" interrupted the police commissioner, "do you admit the premeditation?"

"Hey! Since I tell you that I admit everything, isn't that enough?"

"Even so, speak."

"Well! that bad idea that came to me was to kill Jeanne. It troubled my mind for more than a month, the heart prevented my head, finally a word that a comrade said to me decided me."

"What word?"

"Oh! That is one of the things that does not concern you. This morning I said to Jeanne, "I will not go to work today; I want to have fun as if it were a party; I'll go bowling with my classmates. Take care that dinner is ready at one o'clock."

"But..."

"No observations; dinner at one o'clock, you hear?"

"That is fine!" said Jeanne, and she went out to get the stew.

"Meanwhile, instead of going to play boules, I took the sword that you have there. I had sharpened it myself on a sandstone. I went down to the cellar, and hid behind the barrels, saying to myself: she will have to go down to the cellar to prepare wine; then we will see."

"All the while, I was squatting there, behind the barrel which is standing in the corner ... I do not know; I had a fever; my heart was beating, and I saw everything glowing red in the night. Then there was a voice repeating to me and around me this word that the comrade had told me yesterday."

"But what is this word?" insisted the commissioner.

"It's useless. I already told you that you would never know. Finally, I heard a rustle of a dress, a step approaching. I saw a light tremble; the bottom of her body going down, then the top, then her head. I could see her, her head... She was holding her candle in her hand."

"Ah! I say, very well! And I repeated the word that my comrade had told me. Meanwhile, she was approaching. Word of honor! It looked like she suspected things were going wrong for her. She was afraid; she looked on all sides; but I was well hidden: I did not move. So she knelt before the barrel, approached the bottle and turned on the tap. I got up. You see, she was on her knees. The sound of wine falling into the bottle prevented her from hearing any noise I might make. Besides, I stayed silent. She was on her knees like a culprit, like a condemned man. I raised the sword, and ... Wham! ... I don't even know if she cried out; her head rolled."

"At that time, I didn't want to die; I wanted to save myself. I was planning to make a hole in the cellar and bury it. I jumped on the head, which rolled while the body jumped on its side. I had a plaster bag ready to hide the blood. So I took the head, or rather the head took me."

"See."

And he showed us his right hand, a large bite had mutilated the thumb.

"How? Or rather, what took you?" said the doctor. "What the hell are you saying there?"

"I say she bit me with her teeth, as you can see. I say she did not want to let go of me. I put the head on the plaster bag, leaned it against the wall with my left hand, and tried to pull away my right hand; but after a while the teeth loosened on their own. I withdrew my hand; so, you see, it may have been madness, but it seemed to me that the head was alive; eyes were wide open. I could see them clearly, since the candle was on the barrel, and then the lips, the lips moved, and, while stirring, the lips said:

Miserable, I was innocent!

I do not know the effect this deposition had on others; but as for me, I know that the water was running on my forehead.

"Ah! That is too strong!" cried the doctor, "the eyes looked at you, the lips spoke?"

"Listen, doctor; as you're a doctor, you don't believe anything, it's natural; but I tell you that the head you see there, there, do you hear? I tell you that the head bit me, I tell you that that head said to me: *Miserable, I was innocent!* And the proof that she told me, well! is that I wanted to run away after I killed her. - Jeanne, right? - and that instead of running away, I ran to the mayor's house to denounce myself. Is that true, mayor, is that true? Answer!"

"Yes, Jacquemin," replied Mr. Ledru, in a tone of perfect kindness; "Yes, it is true."

"Examine the head, doctor," said the police commissioner.

"When I'm gone, Mr. Robert, when I'm gone!" cried Jacquemin.

"Are you afraid that she's still talking to you, fool!" said the doctor, taking the candle and approaching the plaster bag.

"Mr. Ledru, in the name of God! said Jacquemin, "tell them to let me go, I beg you, I beg you!"

"Gentlemen," said the mayor, "making a gesture that stopped the doctor, you have nothing more to take from this unfortunate man; let me take him to jail. When the law ordered the confrontation, it assumed that the accused would have the strength to support it."

"But the minutes of the verbal interrogation?" said the commissioner.

"It is almost finished."

"The accused must sign it."

"He will sign it in his prison cell."

"Yes! Yes!" exclaimed Jacquemin, "in the prison I will sign anything you want."

"That is good!" said the police commissioner.

"Gendarmes! Take this man away!" said Mister Ledru.

"Ah! thank you, Mr. Ledru, thank you," said Jacquemin with an expression of deep gratitude.

And, taking the two gendarmes himself by the arm, he led them up the stairs with superhuman force.

This man gone; the drama was gone with him. Only two hideous things remained to be seen in the cellar: a headless corpse and a bodyless head.

I too leaned over to Mr. Ledru.

"Sir," I said to him, "is it permissible for me to withdraw while remaining at your disposal for the signing of the minutes?"

"Yes, sir, but on one condition."

"And that is?"

"You will come and sign the report at my house."

"With the greatest pleasure, sir; but when?"

"In about an hour. I will show you my house; it belonged to Scarron - you will find it interesting."

"In an hour, sir, I will be at your house."

I saluted, and I went up the stairs in my turn. Arriving at the highest level, I took a last look in the cellar.

Dr. Robert, candle in hand, brushed the hair out of his head: it was that of a still beautiful woman, as far as one could judge, because the eyes were closed, the lips contracted and livid.

"That Jacquemin fool!" he said, "to maintain that a severed head can speak! Unless he was trying to pretend he was crazy; it would not be so badly played: there would be extenuating circumstances."

Chapter Four: The Scarron Mansion

*Q*n hour later, I was at Mr. Ledru's house. Chance made me meet him in the courtyard.

"Ah! he said when he saw me, "there you are; so much the better, I'm not sorry to chat with you before I introduce you to our guests, because you're having dinner with us, right?"

"But, sir, you will excuse me."

"I don't admit excuses; you come on a Thursday, too bad for you: Thursday is my day; everyone that comes into my house on Thursday belongs to me in full ownership. After dinner, you will be free to stay or leave. Without the event earlier today, you would have found me at the table since I invariably dined at two o'clock. Today, by extraordinary chance, we will have dinner at half past three or four."

"Pyrrhus that you see," and Mr. Ledru showed me a magnificent mastiff, "Pyrrhus took advantage of the emotion of Mother Antoine to seize the cooked leg: it was his right, so we were forced to get another from the butcher. I said that it would give me time not only to introduce myself to my guests, but also to give you some information about them."

"Some information?"

"Yes, it is here that the future wife of King Louis XIV, while waiting to amuse the immovable man, looked after the poor legless cripple, her first husband. You will see his room.

"Madame de Maintenon?"

"No, Madame Scarron[21]; Let us not confuse ourselves: Madame de Maintenon's room is at Versailles or Saint-Cyr. Come."

---

[21] Françoise d'Aubigné, Marquise de Maintenon 1635-1719 was the second wife of King Louis XIV of France. She was known during her first marriage as Madame Scarron, and subsequently as Madame de Maintenon.

18: Françoise d'Aubigné, Marquise de Maintenon, Public Domain

We went up a large staircase and found ourselves in a corridor overlooking the courtyard.

"Here," said Mr. Ledru to me, "is what moves you, my dear poet; it's the purest Phoébus that was spoken in 1650.

"Ah! ah! the map of Tendre."

"A round-trip ticket - traced by Scarron and annotated by the hand of his wife; just that."

Indeed, two cards held the gap between the windows. They were drawn in pen, on a large sheet of paper glued to cardboard.

"You see, continued Mr. Ledru, this big blue snake is the Tendre river; these little dovecotes are the hamlets Petits-Soins, Billets-Doux, Mystère. Here is the Inn of Desire, the Valley of Sweetness, the Bridge of Sighs, the Jealousy Forest, all populated by monsters like that of Armide. Finally, in the middle of the lake where the river takes its source, here is the Palace of Perfect Contentment: it is the end of the journey, the goal of the race."

"By the Devil! What do I see there, a volcano?"

"Yes ; it sometimes upsets the country. It is the volcano of passions."

"Isn't it on Mademoiselle de Scudéry's card?"

"No. It is an invention of Mrs. Paul Scarron."

"The other one?"

"The other is the Return. You see, the river overflows; it is magnified by the tears of those who follow its banks. Here are the hamlets of Boredom, the Inn of Regrets, the Isle of Repentance. It could not be more ingenious."

"Will you be good enough to let me copy this?"

"Ah! as long as you want. Now do you want to see Madame Scarron's room?"

"I think so!"

"There it is."

Mr. Ledru opened a door; he made me pass in front of him.

"It's mine today; but, apart from the books with which it is cluttered, I give it to you for what it was in the time of its illustrious owner: it is the same alcove, the same bed, the same furniture; these toilets were hers."

"What about Scarron's room?"

"Oh! Scarron's room was at the other end of the corridor; but, as for that one, you will have to deprive yourself of the pleasure of seeing it; we do not enter. It is the secret room, the cabinet of Bluebeard.

"By the Devil!"

"It is like that. I too have my mysteries, mayor that I am, but come, I will show you something else.

Mr. Ledru walked before me; we went down the stairs and entered the living room. Like all the rest of the house, this living room had a special character. His wall hanging was a paper whose primary color would have been difficult to determine; all along the wall reigned a double row of armchairs, bordered by a row of chairs, all in old tapestry; from place to place, game tables and pedestal tables; then, in the middle of it all, like the Leviathan in the middle of the fishes of the Ocean, a gigantic desk, extending from the wall, which supported one of its ends, to the third of the living room, a desk all covered with books, brochures, newspapers, in the midst of which dominated like a king *The Constitutional*, favorite reading of Mr. Ledru.

The living room was empty, the guests were walking in the garden, which you could discover in its full extent through the windows. Mr. Ledru went straight to his desk, and opened a huge drawer, in which was a crowd of small packets similar to packets of seeds. The objects in this drawer were themselves enclosed in labeled paper.

"Here, there is still something more curious for you, the historical man, than the Tendre card. It is a collection of relics, not of saints, but of kings."

Indeed, each paper wrapped a bone, hair, or beard. There was a patella of Charles IX, the thumb of François I, a fragment of the skull of Louis XIV, a rib of Henri II, a vertebra of Louis XV, the beard of Henri IV and hair of Louis XIII. Each king had supplied his sample, and of all these bones we could have reconstructed, more or less, a skeleton which would have perfectly represented that of the French monarchy, which has long lacked the main bones.

There was also an Abelard's tooth and a Heloise's tooth, two white incisors, which, from the time when they were covered by their quivering lips, had perhaps met in a kiss.

Where did this ossuary come from?

Mr. Ledru had presided over the exhumation of the kings at Saint-Denis, and he had taken from each tomb what he liked. He gave me a few moments to satisfy my curiosity; then, seeing that I had pretty much reviewed all of its labels:

"Come on," he said, "that is enough time to care for the dead, let us move on to the living."

He took me to one of the windows through which, as I said, the view plunged into the garden.

"You have a lovely garden there," I said.

It was a parish priest's garden, with its quincunx of linden trees, its collection of dahlias and roses, its cradles of vines and its espaliers of peach and apricot trees: one might see all this, but, for the moment, let's take care, not of the garden, but of those who walk there.

"Ah! first tell me who is this Mr. Alliette, calling himself Etteilla by anagram, who asked if we wanted to know his real age, or only the age he seemed to be; it seems to me that he looks much younger than the seventy-five years that you gave him."

"Exactly," replied Mr. Ledru. "I intended to start with him. Have you read Hoffmann?"

"Yes, why?"

"Well ! He is a Hoffmann man."

"All his life, he has sought to apply maps and numbers to the divination of the future; everything he owns goes to the lottery, which he started off by winning, and which he has never won since. He knew Cagliostro and the Count of Saint-Germain: he claims to be from their family, to have like them the secret of the elixir of long life. His real age, if you ask him, is two hundred and seventy-five: he first lived a hundred years, without infirmities, from the reign of Henry II to the reign of Louis XIV; then, thanks to his secret, while dying in the eyes of the vulgar, he accomplished three other revolutions of fifty years each. At this moment, he starts the fourth again, and is therefore only twenty-five years old. The first two hundred and fifty years only count as memory. He will live like this, and he says it out loud, until the last judgment."

"In the fifteenth century, we would have burned Alliette, and one would have been wrong; today we just complain, and we're still wrong. Alliette is the happiest man on earth: he only talks about tarot cards, cards, spells, Egyptian sciences of Thoth, mysteries of Isis. He publishes on all these subjects, small books which nobody reads, and which however a bookseller, as crazy as him, publishes under the pseudonym, or rather under the anagram of Etteilla; he always has his hat full of brochures. Here, see it; he holds him under his arm, he is so afraid that he will be taken from his precious books."

"Look at the man, look at the face, look at the coat, and see how nature is always harmonious, and how exactly the hat goes to the head, the man in the coat, the doublet in the mold, as you say – you romantics."

Nothing could be truer.

I examined Alliette: he was dressed in a greasy, powdery, threadbare, stained coat; his hat, with shiny patent leather braces, widened disproportionately from above; he wore black terry breeches, black or rather red stockings, and rounded shoes like those of the kings under whom he claimed to have received his parentage.

As for the physique, he was a big little man, stocky, figure of a sphinx, hoarse, a large mouth deprived of teeth indicated by a deep grin, with sparse hair, long and yellow, fluttering like a halo around his head.

"He is chatting with Father Moulle," I said to Mr. Ledru, "the one who accompanied you on our expedition this morning, an expedition to which we will return, isn't it?"

"And why will we come back to it?" asked Mr. Ledru, looking at me curiously.

"Because excuse me, but you seemed to believe in the possibility that this severed head might have spoken."

"You are a physiognomist. Well! It is true, I believe; yes, we will talk about that again, and if you are curious about stories like that, this is the place to talk about it. But let us talk about Father Moulle."

"He must be," I interrupted, "a man of charming commerce; the softness of his voice, when he answered the police chief's interrogation, struck me."

"Well ! this time again, you guessed right. Moulle has been a friend of mine for forty years, and he's sixty: you see, he's as clean and as neat as Alliette is threadbare, greasy, and dirty; he is a man of the world in the first degree, thrown long before into the society of the Faubourg Saint-Germain. It is he who marries the sons and daughters of French peers. These marriages are an opportunity for him to deliver short speeches that the contracting parties print and keep preciously in the family."

"He almost became bishop of Clermont. Do you know why it did not come to pass? Because he was once a friend of Cazotte, and because finally, like Cazotte, he believes in the existence of superior and inferior spirits, good and bad genii. Like Alliette, he makes a collection of books. You will find in his library everything that has been written on visions and on apparitions, on specters, apparitions, ghosts."

"Although he hardly speaks, except among friends, of all these things which are not entirely orthodox, in short, he is a confident man, but discreet, who attributes all that happens in this world to the extraordinary power of hell or the intervention of celestial intelligences."

"You see, he listens in silence to what Alliette says to him, seems to be looking at some object that his interlocutor does not see, and to which he responds from time to time with a movement of the lips or a nod. Sometimes, in our midst, he suddenly falls into a dark reverie, shivers, trembles, turns his head, comes and goes in the living room. In this case, you have to let it happen; it might be dangerous to wake him up, I say wake him up, because then I think he is in a state of somnambulism. Besides, he wakes up on his own, and, you will see, in this case he has a charming alarm clock."

"Oh! but, I dare say," I said to Mr. Ledru, "it seems to me that he has just mentioned one of those spirits you were talking about earlier?"

And I pointed to my host a real walking specter who came to join the two talkers, and who carefully placed his foot between the flowers, on which he seemed to be able to walk without bending them.

"This creature," he said to me, "is still a friend of mine, the knight Lenoir ..."

"The creator of the Petits-Augustins museum? ..."

"Indeed, he himself. He almost died of grief from the dispersal of his museum, for which he had, in '92 and '94, ten times been almost killed. The Restoration, with its ordinary intelligence, had him shut down, with orders to return the monuments to the buildings to which they belonged, and to the families who had rights to claim them."

"Unfortunately, most of the monuments were destroyed, most of the families were extinct, so that the most curious fragments of our ancient sculpture, and therefore of our history, were scattered, lost. This is how everything goes from our old France; only these fragments remained, and from these fragments there will soon be nothing left; and who are those who destroy? The very people who would have the greatest interest in conservation."

And Mr. Ledru, as liberal as he was at the time, sighed.

"Are they all your guests?" I asked Mr. Ledru.

"We may have Dr. Robert as well. I am not telling you anything about that one, I presume you have judged him. He is a man who has all his life experimented on the human machine as he would have done on a mannequin, without suspecting that this machine had a soul to understand pain, and nerves to feel it. He is a bon vivant who killed a lot."

"Fortunately for him, he does not believe in ghosts. He is a mediocre spirit, who thinks he is spiritual because he is noisy, a philosopher because he is an atheist. He is one of those men we receive, not to receive them, but because they come to you. As for going to get them where they are, one would never have the idea."

"Oh! Sir, how I know this species!"

"We were to have yet another friend of mine, younger than all of the gentlemen, who stands up to Alliette on fortune-telling, to Moulle on demonology, to Chevalier Lenoir on antiques; a living library, a bound catalog in Christian skin, whom you must know yourself."

"The bibliophile Jacob?"

"Exactly."

"And he will not be able to come?"

"He has not come yet, and, since he knows that we usually have dinner at two o'clock, and that it's going to be four, there is slim chance that he will visit us this evening. He is looking for some book printed in Amsterdam in 1570, a princeps edition with three typographical errors, one on the first sheet, one on the seventh, one on the last.

At that moment, the door to the drawing-room opened, and Mother Antoine appeared.

"Dinner is served," she announced.

"Come on, gentlemen," said Mr. Ledru, opening the garden door. "To table, to table!"

Then, turning to me:, he said, "Now, there must still be somewhere in the garden, in addition to the guests you see and whose history I have told you of, a guest whom you have not seen and whom I have not spoken about. This one is too detached from the things of this world to have heard the crude call that I have just made, and to which, you see, all our friends have responded.

"Look for her, it concerns you; when you have found her immateriality, her transparency, *eine Erscheinung*[22] as the Germans say, you will try to call her yourself, you will try to persuade her that it is good to eat sometimes, if only to live; you will offer her your arm and you will bring her to us."

I obeyed Mr. Ledru, guessing that the charming spirit I had just appreciated in a few minutes had some pleasant surprises in store for me, and I walked into the garden, looking around.

The investigation was not long, and I soon saw what I was looking for. It was a woman sitting in the shade of a quincunx of lime trees, and whose

---

[22] An apparition

face and shape I could not see: the face, because it was turned towards the countryside; waist, because a big shawl wrapped it. She was dressed all in black.

I approached her without her making a movement. The sound of my steps did not seem to reach her ear: she looked like a statue. Besides, everything I saw about her was gracious and distinguished.

From afar I had already seen that she was blonde. A ray of sunshine, which passed through the leaves of the lime trees, played on her hair and made it a golden halo. From close up, I could notice the delicacy of her hair, which would have rivaled those threads of silk that the first breezes of autumn detached from the Virgin's cloak; her neck, a little too long perhaps, a charming exaggeration which is almost always a grace if not a beauty, her neck was rounded to help her head rest on her right hand, whose elbow supported her on the back of the chair, while her left arm hung beside her, holding a white rose with the tips of her slender fingers.

Her neck was rounded like that of a swan, hand folded, arms hanging, all of her was of the same dull whiteness; she looked like a Paros marble, without veins on its surface, without a pulse inside; the rose that was beginning to wilt was more colorful and more alive than the hand that held it.

I looked at her for a moment, and the more I did, the more it seemed to me that she was not a living being that I had before my eyes. I had come to doubt that when I spoke to her she would turn around. Two or three times my mouth opened and closed without saying a word.

Finally I made up my mind.

"Madam," I said to her.

She started, turned around, looked at me in astonishment, like someone who comes out of a dream and recalls her ideas. Her big black eyes were fixed on me, with the blond hair I described (contrasting with her eyebrows and black eyes), she had a strange expression.

For a few seconds we remained without speaking, she was looking at me, examining me.

She was a woman between the ages of thirty-two and thirty-three, who must have been of marvelous beauty before her cheeks had sunk, before her complexion had turned pale; besides, I found her perfectly beautiful as well, with her pearly face and the same tone as her hand, without any shade of crimson, which made her eyes seem jet-black, her lips coral.

"Madam," I repeated, "Mr. Ledru claims that by telling you that I am the author of Henri III, Christine and Antony, you will be kind enough to present me, and accept my arm up to the room at eat."

"Sorry, sir," she said, "you've been here for a while, haven't you? I felt you coming, but I could not turn around; it happens to me sometimes when I look from certain sides. Your voice has broken the spell, so give me your arm, and let's go.

She got up and put her arm under my own, but hardly, although she did not seem to be in any way constrained, I felt the pressure of this arm. It looked like a shadow walking beside me.

We arrived in the dining room without having said either word. Two places were reserved at the table. One to the right of Mr. Ledru for her. One in front of her for me.

Chapter Five: The Assault of Charlotte Corday

*L*ike everything else at Mr. Ledru's, this table had its own character. It was a large horseshoe leaning against the garden windows, leaving three-quarters of the huge room free for service. This table could accommodate twenty people without any being inconvenienced. The company always ate there, whether Mr. Ledru had one, two, four, ten, twenty guests; or just him alone: that day there were only six of us, and we barely occupied a third of it.

The menu was the same every Thursday. Mr. Ledru thought that, during the past eight days, the guests had been able to eat something else either at home or at the other hosts who had invited them. So we were sure to find Mr. Ledru, every Thursday, serving soup, beef, chicken with tarragon, a roast leg, beans, and a salad. The chickens doubled or tripled according to the needs of the guests.

Whether there were few or many people, Mr. Ledru would preside at one end of the table, his back to the garden, his face towards the courtyard. He had been sitting in a big inlaid armchair for ten years in the same place; there he received, from the hands of his gardener Antoine, converted, like master Jacques, into a footman, in addition to ordinary wine, a few bottles of old burgundy which were brought to him with religious respect, and which he uncorked and served to him - even to his guests with the same respect and the same religion.

Eighteen years ago, we still believed in something; in ten years, we will no longer believe in anything, not even old wine.

After dinner, we went to the lounge for coffee.

Dinner flowed like dinner does, testing the kitchen, praising the wine. The young woman ate only a few crumbs of bread, drank only a glass of water, and did not speak a single word. She reminded me of the Arabian Nights ghoul, who sat at the table like the others but only to eat a few grains of rice with a toothpick.

After dinner, as usual, we went to the living room. It was naturally up to me to give the arm to our silent guest. She walked towards me half the way to take it. It was ever the same softness in her movements, the same grace in the turn, I would say almost the same impalpability of the limbs.

I led her to a lounge chair where she lay down.

Two people had been brought into the living room while we were dining.

They were the doctor and the police commissioner.

The police commissioner came to have us sign the minutes that Jacquemin had already signed in his prison. A slight bloodstain stood out on the paper.

I in turn signed, and, signing, asked, "What is this stain? Does this blood come from the wife or the husband?"

"It comes," replied the commissioner, "from the wound which the murderer had in his hand, and which continues to bleed without being able to stop the bleeding."

"Do you understand, Mr. Ledru," said the doctor, "that this brute persists in asserting that his wife's head has spoken to him?"

"And you believe it to be impossible, don't you, doctor?"

"My Lord!"

"Do you even think it impossible that the eyes reopened?"

"Impossible."

"You do not believe that the blood, interrupted in its flight by this layer of plaster which immediately blocked all the arteries and all the vessels, could have restored to this head a moment of life and feeling?"

"I do not believe that."`

"Well!" said Mr. Ledru, "I believe it."

"Me too," said Alliette.

"Me too, " said Father Moulle.

"Me too, " said the knight Lenoir.

"Me too, " I said.

The commissioner and the pale lady alone said nothing: one, probably because he was not interested enough, the other, perhaps, because it was too much.

"Ah! If you are all against me, you'll be right. Only if one of you was a doctor..."

"But, doctor," said Mr. Ledru, "you know that I am almost one."

"In that case," said the doctor, "you should know that there is no pain where there is no longer any feeling, and that the feeling is destroyed by the section of the spine."

"And who told you that?" asked Mr. Ledru.

"Reason, by the way!"

"Oh! The right answer! Isn't that also the reason that told the judges who condemned Galileo that it was the sun that was turning and the earth that remained motionless? Reason is a fool, my dear doctor. Have you experimented with severed heads yourself?"

"No never."

"Have you read Sommering's essays? Have you read Dr. Sue's minutes? Have you read the protests of Œlcher?"

"No."

"So, you believe, don't you, Mr. Guillotin's report, that his machine is the safest, quickest and the least painful way to end life?"

"I believe him."

"Well! You are mistaken, my dear friend, that is all."

"Ah! For example?"

"Listen, doctor, since you made a call to science, I'm going to talk to you about science: and none of us, believe it, is foreign enough to this kind of conversation not to take part in it."

"The doctor made a gesture of doubt."

"No matter, you will understand on your own, then."

We got closer to Mr. Ledru, and for my part, I listened eagerly; this question of the death penalty applied either by rope, by iron or by poison, having always singularly preoccupied me as a question of humanity.

For my part, I even did some research on the different pains that precede, accompany and follow the different kinds of death.

"Come on, talk," said the doctor incredulously.

"It is easy to demonstrate to anyone who has the slightest notion of the construction and the vital forces of our body," continued Mr. Ledru, "that sensation is not entirely destroyed by the torture, and, what I advance, doctor, is based, not on assumptions, but on facts."

"Let us see these facts."

"Here they are. One: the seat of feeling is in the brain, right?"

"It is possible."

"Can the operations of this consciousness of feeling be continued, although the circulation of blood by the brain is suspended, weakened or partially destroyed?"

"It's possible."

"If therefore the seat of the faculty of feeling is in the brain, as long as the brain retains its vital force, the victim has the feeling of his existence."

"Proofs?"

Here they are: Haller, in his *Elements of the Physique, Vol IV*, p. 35 said,

> *A severed head opened its eyes and looked at me*
> *from the side because, with the tip of my finger, I*
> *had touched its spinal cord.*

"Haller, perhaps, but Haller may have been wrong."

"He made a mistake, I mean it. Let us move on to another. Weycard, in *The Philosophical Arts,* p. 221 says:

> *I saw the lips moving of a man whose head had been*
> *severed.*

"Well; but to move is not to speak ..."

"Wait, we are getting there. Here is Sommering[23]; his works are there, and you can search them for yourselves. Sommering said,

> *Several doctors, my colleagues, have assured me*
> *that they have seen a head separated from the body*
> *cringe in pain, and I am convinced that if the air were*
> *still circulating through the vocal organs, the head*
> *would speak.*

"Well! Doctor," continued Mr. Ledru, turning pale.

"I am more advanced than Sommering: a head has spoken to me."

We all started. The pale lady rose from her chaise longue.

"To you?"

---

[23] Samuel Thomas von Sömmerring, 1755-1830, German physician and anatomist, who conducted deep investigations on the brain and central nervous system.

"Yes, to me; will you also say that I am crazy?"

"My lady!" said the doctor, "if you tell me that yourself."

"Yes, I tell you that this thing happened to me. You are too polite, aren't you, doctor? To tell me out loud that I'm crazy; but you will say it in a whisper, and it will be absolutely the same."

"Well! Come on, tell us about it," said the doctor.

"It is easy for you to say. Do you know that what you ask me to tell you, I have never told anyone in thirty-seven years that it happened to me; Do you know that I do not answer for fear of fainting by telling you, as I passed out when that head spoke, when those dying eyes fixed on mine?

The dialogue became more and more interesting, the situation more and more dramatic.

"Come on, Ledru, courage!" said Alliette, "and tell us about it."

"Tell us about it, my friend," said Father Moulle.

"Tell us," said the knight Lenoir.

"Sir..." murmured the pale woman.

I said nothing, but my desire to know more was in my eyes.

"It is strange," said Mr. Ledru without answering us and as if talking to himself, "it is strange how events influence each other! You know who I am," he said, turning to my side.

"I know, sir," I replied, "that you are a very educated man, very spiritual, who give excellent dinners, and who is the mayor of Fontenay-aux-Roses."

Mr. Ledru smiled, thanking me for a nod.

"I'm telling you about my origin, my family," he said.

"I don't know your origin, sir, and don't know your family."

"Well ! Listen, I'll tell you all about it, and then maybe the story that you want to know, and that I dare not tell you, will come after. If I am able to tell you, well! you will listen; if it doesn't come forth, don't ask me again: it's because I lacked strength to tell you."

Everyone sat down and made themselves comfortable to listen at ease.

Besides, the drawing-room was a real drawing-room of tales or legends, large, dark, thanks to the thick curtains and the dying day, whose angles were already in full darkness, while the lines which corresponded to the doors and windows retained only a remnant of light. In one of these angles was the pale lady. Her black dress was completely lost in the night.

His head alone, white, motionless, and resting on the sofa cushion, was visible. Mr. Ledru began:

"I am," said he, "the son of the famous Comus, a physicist of the king and the queen; my father, whose burlesque nickname classified him among the retractors and the charlatans, was a distinguished scholar of the schools of Volta, Galvani and Mesmer. He was the first in France to take care of phantasmagoria and electricity, giving mathematics and physics sessions to the court."

Poor Marie-Antoinette, whom I saw twenty times, and who more than once took my hands and kissed them when she arrived in France, that is to say when I was a child, Marie- Antoinette loved him. When he passed in 1777, Joseph II declared that he had seen nothing more curious than Comus.

In the midst of all this, my father took care of the education of my brother and mine, initiating us to what he knew of the occult sciences, and to a host of galvanic, physical, magnetic knowledge, which today are in the public domain, but which at that time were secrets, privileges of only a few. The title of physicist of the king granted to my father, served, in '93, to imprison my father; but, thanks to some friendships I had with La Montagne[24], I managed to get him released.

My father then retired to the same house where I am, and died there in 1807, aged seventy-six.

Let us come back to me.

I talked about my friendships with the Montagnards. I was indeed linked with Danton and Camille Desmoulins. I had known Marat more as a doctor than as a friend. Finally, I had known him well. As a result of this relationship that I had with him, however brief it was, that the day that Mademoiselle de Corday was taken to the scaffold, I resolved to witness her torment.

"I was just going to help you in your discussion with Dr. Robert on the persistence of life by telling you about the fact that history has recorded in relation to Charlotte de Corday."

---

[24] Radical group in the French Revolution, led by Robespierre, which unleashed the Reign of Terror.

"We are getting there," interrupted Mr. Ledru, "let me speak. I was a witness; therefore from what I will say you may believe. At two o'clock in the afternoon I had taken my post near the Statue of Liberty. It was a hot July morning; the weather was heavy, the sky was overcast and promised a thunderstorm.

At four o'clock the storm broke out; it was then, it is said, that Charlotte got on the cart.

She had been taken to his prison when a young painter was busy painting her portrait. Jealous death seemed to want nothing to survive the girl, not even her image.

The head was sketched on the canvas, and strange thing! at the moment when the executioner entered, the painter was working on the point of the neck that the iron of the guillotine was going to cut.

Lightning flashed, the rain was falling, the thunder was rumbling, but nothing had been able to disperse the curious populace; quays, bridges, squares were congested; the rumors of the earth almost covered the rumors of the sky. These women, who were energetically called guillotine harpies, were cursing her.

I could hear these roars coming to me like you hear those from a cataract. Long before anything could be seen, the crowd rippled; finally, like a fatal ship, the cart appeared, plowing the stream, and I could make out the condemned, whom I did not know, whom I had never seen.

She was a beautiful young girl of twenty-seven, with magnificent eyes, a perfectly shaped nose, lips of supreme regularity. She was standing, head raised, less to appear to dominate this crowd than because her hands tied behind her back forced her to hold her head like this.

19: Execution of Charlotte Corday, assassin of Marat, 1793, artist unknown, Public Domain

The rain had stopped; but, as she had endured the rain for three-quarters of the way, the water that had flowed on her drew the contours of her charming body on the damp wool: it looked like she was coming out of the bath. The red shirt which the executioner had put on her gave a strange appearance, a sinister splendor to this head so proud and so energetic. As she arrived on the square, the rain stopped, and a ray of sunshine, sliding between two clouds, came to play in her hair, which radiated like a halo.

In truth, I swear to you, although there was a murder behind this young girl, a terrible action, even when it avenges humanity, although I detest the cause, I could not have said if what I saw was apotheosis or torment. When she saw the scaffold, she turned pale; and this pallor was noticeable, especially because of the red shirt, which went up to her neck; but almost immediately she made an effort, and finished turning to the scaffold, which she looked at with a smile.

The cart stopped; Charlotte jumped to the ground without wanting to be helped to descend, then she climbed the steps of the scaffold, made slippery by the rain that had just fallen, as fast as the length of her towed shirt allowed her. embarrassment of his tied hands. When she felt the hand of the executioner land on her shoulder to tear off the handkerchief that covered her neck, she paled a second time, but, just then, a last smile came to deny this pallor, and herself, without being attached to the infamous seesaw, in a sublime and almost joyful impulse, she put her head through the hideous opening. The cleaver slipped, the head detached from the trunk fell on the platform and bounced.

It was then, listen to this, doctor, listen to this, poet, it was then that one of the executioner's valets, named Legros, seized this head by the hair, and, by a vile adulation to the multitude, gave her a slap. Well! I tell you that at this blow, the head blushed; I saw it, the head, not the cheek, can you hear me? Not just the affected cheek, but both cheeks, with an equal redness, because the feeling lived in this head, and she was indignant for having suffered a shame that had never ended.

The people also saw this blush, and they took the side of the dead against the living, of the tortured against the executioner. They demanded, immediately, revenge for this indignity, and, immediately, the wretch was handed over to the gendarmes and taken to prison.

"Wait," said Mister Ledru, who saw that the doctor wanted to speak, "wait, that's not all."

"I wanted to know what feeling this man could have brought to the infamous act he had committed. I asked where he was; I asked permission to visit him at the Abbey where he had been locked up, I got it and I went to see him.

A revolutionary court order had just sentenced him to three months in prison. He did not understand that he had been condemned for such a natural thing as the one he had done. I asked him what had brought him to this action.

"Well," he said, "that's a fine question! I am a Maratist; The law had just punished her, I wanted to punish her for my own account."

"But" I said to him, "didn't you understand that there is almost a crime in this violation of respect due to death?"

"Oh that!" Legros said to me, staring at me, "so you think they are dead, because they were guillotined, do you?"

"Without a doubt."

"Well! We can see that you do not look in the basket when they are all there together; that you don't see them twisting their eyes and gnashing their teeth for another five minutes after the run. We are forced to change the basket every three months, as they ransack the bottom with their teeth.

It's a bunch of aristocrat heads, you see, who don't want to die, and I wouldn't be surprised that one day some of them would scream:"

Long live the king!

"I knew everything I wanted to know. I went out, pursued by an idea: if indeed these heads were still alive, and I resolved to confirm this."

Chapter Six: Solange

During Mr. Ledru's story, night had fallen quietly. The inhabitants of the drawing room appeared as shadows, shadows not only mute, but also motionless, so much was it feared that Mr. Ledru would stop; because we understood that, behind the terrible story he had just made, there was an even more terrible story.

So you could not hear a breath. The doctor alone opened his mouth. I grabbed his hand to keep him from speaking, and, indeed, he fell silent.

After a few seconds, Mr. Ledru continued.

"I had just left the Abbey, and I was crossing the Place Taranne to go to the rue de Tournon, where I lived, when I heard a woman's voice calling for help.

They couldn't be criminals: it was barely ten o'clock in the evening. I ran to the corner of the square where I heard the cry, and I saw, in the moonlight coming out of a cloud, a woman struggling in the middle of a patrol of sans-culottes.

This woman, for her part, saw me, and, noticing in my suit that I was not quite a man of the people, she rushed towards me, exclaiming:

- Hey! Here is Mr. Albert whom I know; he will tell you that I am indeed the daughter of Mother Ledieu, the laundress. At the same time the poor woman, all pale and trembling, grabbed my arm, clinging to me like the shipwrecked man on the board of his salvation.

- You can be Mother Ledieu's daughter as long as you like, but you don't have a citizenship card, beautiful girl, and you're going to follow us to the guardhouse!

The young woman squeezed my arm; I felt all the terror and prayer in this pressure. I understood. As she called me from the first name that was offered to her mind, I called her, myself, from the first name that appeared to mine.

- What ! It's you, my poor Solange! I said, what is happening to you?

- There! You see, gentlemen, she went on.

- Why don't you say: citizens?

- Listen, sergeant, it's not my fault if I speak like that, said the girl; my mother was experienced in the big world, she used to be polite to me, so it was a bad habit that I took, I know it well, an aristocratic habit; but what do you want, sergeant, I can't get rid of it.

There was in this response, made in a trembling voice, an imperceptible mockery that only I recognized. I was wondering who this woman could be. The problem was impossible to solve. All I was sure of was that she was not the daughter of a laundress.

"What I am doing here?" she went on, "citizen Albert, let me explain. Imagine that I went to deliver laundry; that the mistress of the house had gone out; that I waited for my money to come back. Lady! these days, everyone needs their money."

I waited until nightfall. I thought I would come home. I had not taken my citizenship card, I fell in the middle of these gentlemen, sorry, I mean these citizens; they asked me for my card, I told them I didn't have one; they wanted to take me to the guardhouse. I shouted, you came running, just an acquaintance; so I was reassured. I said to myself: Since Mr. Albert knows that my name is Solange; since he knows that I am the daughter of mother Ledieu, he will answer for me; right, Mr. Albert?"

- Certainly, I will answer for you, as I have done.

- Well ! said the chief of the patrol, and who will answer for you, Monsieur le Muscadin[25]?

- Danton. Are you okay with that? Is he a good patriot, that one?

- Ah! if Danton answers for you, there is nothing to say.

- Well ! it's society day at the Cordeliers; let's go there.

"Let's go that way," said the sergeant. "Citizens sans culottes, forward, walk!"

The Cordeliers club was held in the former Cordeliers convent, rue de l'Observance: we were there in an instant. When I got to the door, I tore a page out of my wallet, wrote a few words in pencil, and gave them to the sergeant, inviting him to take them to Danton, while we were in the hands of the corporal and the patrol.

The sergeant entered the club and returned with Danton.

"What!" he said to me, "you are the one they have held! You, my friend, Camille's friend! You, one of the best Republicans out there! Come

---

[25] Dandy, or coxcomb

on! Citizen sergeant," he added, turning to the chief of the sans-culottes, "I answer for him. Is that enough for you?"

- You answer for him: but do you answer for her? replied the obstinate sergeant.

- Her? Who are you talking about?

- This woman, Good Lord!

- Him, her, everything around her; are you happy?

- Yes, I'm glad, said the sergeant, especially seeing you.

- Ah! Good Lord! You can give yourself this pleasure for free: look at me as you please while you hold me here.

- Thank you. Continue to support the interests of the people as you do, and rest assured, the people will be grateful to you.

- Oh yes! I count on it! said Danton.

- Will you give me a handshake? continued the sergeant.

- Why not ?

And Danton gave him his hand.

- Long live Danton! cried the sergeant.

- Long live Danton! repeated the whole patrol.

And she went away led by her chief, who ten paces away, turned around and waving his red cap, shouted once more: Long live Danton! A cry which was repeated by his men.

I was going to thank Danton when his name, repeated several times inside the club, reached us.

- Danton! Danton! cried several voices; at the podium!

- Excuse me, my dear, he said to me, you hear; a handshake, and let me in. I gave the sergeant the right, I give you the left. Who knows? the worthy patriot may have had scabies. And turning around: - Here I am! he said in that powerful voice which raised and calmed the storms of the street; here I am, wait for me.

And he threw himself into the interior of the club.

I was left alone at the door with my stranger.

"Now, madam," said I, "where must I take you? I am at your command."

- To Mother Ledieu's house, she replied, laughing, you know very well that she is my mother.

- But where does Mother Ledieu live?

- Rue Férou, No. 24.

- Let's go to Mother Ledieu's, rue Férou, No. 24

We went down rue des Fossés-Monsieur-le-Prince to rue des Fossés-Saint-Germain, then rue du Petit-Lion, then we went up place Saint-Sulpice, then rue Férou.

All this was done without us having exchanged a word.

By the rays of the moon, which shone in all its splendor, I was able to examine her at my ease.

She was a charming twenty- to twenty-two-year-old brunette with big blue eyes, more spiritual than melancholy; a fine and straight nose, lips with a mocking air, teeth like pearls, queen's hands, children's feet, all of which, under the vulgar costume of the daughter of mother Ledieu, retained an aristocratic appearance which had, rightly awakened the susceptibility of the brave sergeant and his belligerent patrol.

When we got to the door, we stopped, and we looked at each other for a moment in silence.

- Well! what do you want with me, my dear Mr. Albert? said my stranger, smiling.

- I wanted to tell you, my dear young lady Solange, that there was no point in our meeting to leave so quickly.

- But I'm asking you for a million pardons. On the contrary, I think it is completely worth it, since, if I had not met you, I would have been taken to the guardhouse; I would have been recognized for not being the daughter of Mother Ledieu; it would have been discovered that I was an aristocrat, and most likely my neck would have been cut.

- So do you admit that you are an aristocrat?

- I don't admit anything.

- Come on, tell me at least your name?

- Solange.

- You know very well that this name, which I gave you by chance, is not yours.

- Anything! I love it and will keep it, at least for you.

- What need do you have to keep it for me, if I don't have to see you again?

- I do not say that. I'm just saying that if we meet again, there's no need for you to know what my name is as my name is. I named you Albert, keep that name Albert, as I keep the name Solange.

- Well! So be it, but listen, Solange, I said to her.

"I'm listening to you, Albert," she replied.

- You are an aristocrat, you admit it?

- When I wouldn't admit it, you'd guess it, wouldn't you? So my confession loses much of its merit.

- And as an aristocrat, are you being prosecuted?

- There is something like that.

- And are you hiding to avoid prosecution?

- Rue Férou, 24, at the home of mother Ledieu, whose husband was my father's coachman. You see that I have no secrets from you.

- And your father?

- I have no secrets from you, my dear Mr. Albert, as these secrets are mine; but my father's secrets are not mine. My father is in hiding too while waiting for an opportunity to emigrate. That's all I can tell you.

- And you, what do you intend to do?

- Leave with my father, if possible; if that's not possible, let him go alone and join him later.

- And this evening when you were arrested, did you return from seeing your father?

- I was coming back.

- Listen to me, dear Solange!

- I'm listening to you.

- Did you see what happened tonight?

- Yes, and that gave me the measure of your credit.

- Oh! my credit is not great, unfortunately. However, I have a few friends.

- I met one of them tonight.

- And you know, this one is not one of the least powerful men of the time.

- You intend to use his influence to help my father's escape?

- No, I reserve it for you.

- What about my father?

- For your father, I have another way.

- You have another way! cried Solange, grabbing my hands and looking at me anxiously.

- If I save your father, will you keep a good memory of me?

- Oh ! I will be grateful to you all my life.

And she said those words with a lovely expression of anticipation. Then, looking at me with a pleading tone:

- But will that be enough for you? she asked.

- Yes, I replied.

- Let's go! I was not mistaken; you have a noble heart. Thank you on behalf of my father and mine, and if you do not succeed in the future, I am no less in your debt for the past.

- When will we meet again, Solange?

- When do you need to see me again?

- Tomorrow, I hope I have something good to share with you.

- Well! see you tomorrow.

- Where then?

- Here, if you want.

- Here on the street?

- My God ! Don't you see that it is still the safest; in the half hour we have been chatting at this door, not a single person has passed.

- Why don't I come up to your house, or why don't you come to my house?

- Because, coming to my house, you are compromising the good people who gave me asylum; because when I go to your house, I compromise myself.

- Oh good! Here – I will take the card from one of my relatives and give it to you.

- Yes, so that we can guillotine your relative, if by chance I am arrested.

- You are right, I will bring you a card in the name of Solange.

- Perfectly! you will see that Solange will end up being my one and only real name.

- What time?

- The same as when we met today. Ten o'clock, if you like.

- Ten o'clock then!

- And how will we meet?

- Oh! It is not too difficult. At ten minutes to ten you will be at the door; at ten o'clock I will come down.

- So tomorrow at ten o'clock, dear Solange.

- Tomorrow at ten o'clock, dear Albert.

I wanted to kiss her hand; she presented her forehead.

The next evening, at half past nine, I was on the street. At quarter past ten, Solange opened the door. Each of us was early. I stepped up to her myself.

- I see you have good news, she said smiling.

- Excellent; first here is your card.

- First my father?

And she pushed my hand away.

- Your father is saved – if he wants to be.

- If he wants to, you say, what should he do?

- He has to trust me.

- It's already done.

- You saw him?

- Yes.

- You exposed yourself.

- What else could I do? It must be done; but God is with us!

- And you told everything to your father?

- I told him that you saved my life yesterday, and that you might save his life tomorrow.

- Tomorrow, yes, precisely; tomorrow, if he wants, I will save his life.

- What do you mean? Say; come on, talk.

What an admirable friendship I would have made if all this succeeded!

- Only ... I said hesitantly.

- Well?

- You can't go with him.

- As for that, did I not tell you that I had made my resolution?"

- Besides, later, I'm sure I will have a passport for you.

- Let's talk about my father first, we'll talk about me afterwards.

- Well ! I told you I have friends, right?

- Yes.

- I went to see one today.

- You did?

- A man you know by name and whose name guarantees courage, loyalty, and honor.

- And that name is ...

- Marceau.

- General Marceau?

- Exactly.

- You are right; if he has promised his word, it will hold.

- Well! he promised.

- My God! how happy you make me! Let's see, what did he promise? Tell me.

- He promised to serve us.

- What do you mean?

- Ah! in a quite simple way. Kléber has just had him appointed general-in-chief of the Western army. He leaves tomorrow evening.

- Tomorrow evening? But we won't have time to prepare anything.

- We have nothing to prepare.

- I do not understand.

- He's taking your father.

- My father !

- Yes, as secretary. Once he arrives in Vendée, your father must commit his word to Marceau not to serve against France, and, that one night, he wins a Vendean camp: from Vendée, he goes to Brittany, to England. When he's settled in London, he gives you the news, I get you a passport, and you will join him in London.

- Tomorrow! cried Solange. My father will leave tomorrow!

- There is no time to waste.

- My father has not been warned.

- Warn him.

- Tonight?

- Tonight.

- But how, at this hour?

- You have a card and my arm.

- You are right. My card ?

I gave it to her; she put it beside her breast.

- Now your arm.

I gave her my arm and we left. We went down to Place Taranne, that is to say to the place where I had met her the day before.

- Wait for me here, she said.

I bowed and waited. She disappeared around the corner from the old

Matignon hotel; then, after a quarter of an hour, she reappeared.

- Come, she said, my father wants to see you and thank you.

She took my arm and led me to rue Saint-Guillaume in front of the Mortemart hotel. When she got there, she took a key from her pocket, opened a small hidden door, took my hand, guided me to the second floor, and knocked in a particular way.

A man between the ages of forty-eight and fifty opened the door. He was dressed as a worker and appeared to exercise the status of bookbinder. At the first words that he said to me, at the first thanks that he addressed to me, the great lord had betrayed himself.

"Sir," he said to me, "Providence has sent you to us, and I receive you as an envoy from Providence. Is it true that you can save me, and above all that you want to save me?"

I told him everything. I told him how Marceau took it upon himself to take him as secretary and asked him for nothing other than the promise not to bear arms against France.

- I promise you this oath, and I will renew it to him.
- Thank you in his name and mine.
- But when does Marceau leave?
- Tomorrow.
- Should I go to his house tonight?
- Whenever you wish; he will be waiting for you.

Father and daughter looked at each other.

- I think it would be wiser to go there tonight, father, said Solange.
- It is. But if I am stopped, I do not have a citizenship card.
- Here's mine.
- But what about you?
- Oh! I am known to the police.
- Where does Marceau live?
- Rue de l'Université, No. 40, at his sister's, Miss Dégraviers-Marceau.
- Will you accompany me?
- I will follow you from behind, so I can bring back your daughter when you enter.
- And how will Marceau know that I am the man you told him about?
- You will give him this tricolor cockade; it is the sign of recognition.
- What will I do for my deliverer?

- You will charge me with the salvation of your daughter, as she charged me with yours.

- Let's go.

He put on his hat and turned off the lights. We went down by the light of a moonlight that filtered through the staircase windows. At the door, he took his daughter's arm, leaned to the right, and by the rue des Saints-Pères, reached the rue de l'Université. I followed them ten paces away. We got to No. 40 without meeting anyone. I approached them.

- It bodes well, I said; now do you want me to wait or come up with you?

- No, do not compromise yourself further; wait for my daughter here.

I bowed.

- Again, thank you and goodbye, he said, holding out his hand. Language has no words to translate the feelings I have for you.

- I hope to God that I will one day be able to express my gratitude to you.

I replied with a simple handshake.

He went in. Solange followed him. But she too, before entering, shook my hand.

After ten minutes, the door reopened.

- Well? I said.

- Well! she went on, your friend is well worthy of being your friend, that is to say that he has all the delicacies. He understands that I will be happy to stay with my father until I leave. His sister is helping me make a bed in his room. Tomorrow at three in the afternoon my father will be out of harm's way. Tomorrow, at ten o'clock in the evening, like today, if you think that the thanks of a girl who owes her father's life to you is worth the trouble of bothering you, come and get her on rue Férou.

- Oh! I will definitely come. Didn't your father tell you anything about me?

- Thank you for your card, here, and please send it back to me as soon as possible.

- It will be when you want, Solange, I replied with a tight heart.

- At least I need to know where to join my father, she said. Oh! you haven't gotten rid of me yet.

I took her hand and pressed it to my heart, but she, presented her

forehead to me as the day before

- See you tomorrow! she said.

Pressing my lips against her forehead, it was no longer only her hand that I pressed against my heart, but her quivering chest, her leaping heart.

I went home, happy at heart like never before. Was it the awareness of the good deed that I had done, did I already love this adorable creature? I do not know if I slept or if I stayed up; I know that all the harmonies of nature sang within me; I know that the night seemed endless, the day immense; I know that, while pushing the time ahead of me, I would have liked to hold it back so as not to waste a minute of the days I still had to live.

The next day, I was at rue Férou by nine. At half past nine Solange appeared. She came to me and threw my arms around my neck.

- Safe! she said, my father is saved, and it is to you that I owe his salvation! Oh! how I love you!

A fortnight later, Solange received a letter announcing that her father was in England. The next day, I brought her a passport. Upon receiving it, Solange burst into tears.

- So you don't like me? she says.

"I love you more than my life," I replied, but I committed my word to your father, and, above all, I must keep my word.

- So, she said, I'm the one who will break mine. If you have the courage to let me go, Albert, I don't have the courage to leave you!

Alas! she stayed.

Chapter Seven: Albert

As with the first interruption of Mr. Ledru's account, there was a moment of silence.

A silence more respectful than the first, because we felt that we were approaching the end of the story, and Mr. Ledru had said that he might not have the strength to finish it. But almost immediately he went on:

- Three months had passed since that evening when there had been talk of Solange's departure, and, since that evening, not a word of separation had been spoken.

Solange wanted accommodation on Taranne Street. I took it for her under the name of Solange. I didn't know her under any other name, like she didn't know me other than Albert. I had brought her into a young girls' institution as a sub-mistress, and that more surely shielded her from the investigations of the revolutionary police, who became more active than ever.

We spent Sundays and Thursdays together in this little apartment on rue Taranne: from the bedroom window, we saw the place where we had met for the first time.

Every day we wrote letters to each other; she in the name of Solange, me in the name of Albert. These three months had been the happiest of my life.

However, I had not given up on the plan which had come to me following my conversation with the executioner's valet. I had asked for and obtained permission to do experiments on the persistence of life after the ordeal and these experiments had shown me that the pain survived the ordeal and must be terrible.

- Ah! this is what I deny! cried the doctor.

- Come on, said Mr. Ledru, would you deny that the knife strikes at the place of our most sensitive body because of the nerves that are there? Would you deny that the neck contains all the nerves of the upper limbs: the sympathetic, the vague, the phrenicus, finally the spinal cord, which is the very source of the nerves which belong to the lower limbs? Would you deny that the breaking, that the crushing of the bone spine produces one of the most excruciating pains that a human creature is given to experience?

"So be it," said the doctor; but this pain only lasts a few seconds.

- Oh! that's my point! cried Mr. Ledru with deep conviction; and then, if it lasted only a few seconds, during these few seconds, the feeling, the personality, the ego, remain alive; the head hears, sees, feels, and judges the separation of its being, and who will say if the short duration of the suffering can compensate for the horrible intensity of this suffering?

- So in your opinion, the decree of the Constituent Assembly which substituted the guillotine for the gallows was a philanthropic error, and was it better to be hanged than beheaded?

- Without a doubt, many hanged themselves or were hanged who came back to life. Well! they were able to describe the sensation they experienced. It is that of a lightning apoplexy, that is to say of a deep sleep without any particular pain, without any feeling of any anguish, a kind of flame which springs before the eyes, and which, little by little, changes to blue color, then to darkness, when one falls in syncope.

- Indeed, doctor, you know this better than anyone. The man whose brain is compressed with the finger, in a place where a piece of skull is missing, this man experiences no pain, only he falls asleep. Well! the same phenomenon occurs when the brain is compressed by a heap of blood. Now, in the hanged man, the blood collects, firstly because it enters the brain through the vertebral arteries, which, crossing the bony channels of the neck, cannot be compromised; secondly because, tending to flow back through the veins of the neck, it is stopped by the link which ties the neck and the veins.

- So be it, said the doctor, but let's go back to experiments. I can't wait to get to that famous head who spoke.

I thought I heard a sigh escape from Mr. Ledru's chest. As for seeing her face, it was impossible. It was completely dark.

- Yes, he said, in fact, I'm getting off topic, doctor, let's go back to my experiences. Unfortunately, the subjects were missing. We were at the height of the executions, we guillotined thirty or forty people a day, and so much blood flowed on the Place de la Révolution, that we had been forced to construct around the scaffold a ditch of three feet deep. This ditch was covered with planks. One of these planks turned under the foot of an eight- or ten-year-old child, who fell into this hideous ditch and drowned.

It goes without saying that I was careful not to tell Solange what occupied my time on the days when I did not see her, moreover, I must admit that I had first felt such strong repugnance for these poor scraps of human debris, that I was frightened of the after-effects that my experiences might add to the ordeal. But still, I told myself that these studies that I was doing were done for the benefit of society as a whole, since if I ever managed to share my convictions at a meeting of legislators, I would perhaps be able to abolish the death penalty.

As my experiments produced results, I wrote them down in a memoir.

At the end of two months, I had learned enough on the persistence of life after the ordeal to validate all the experiences that one could have. I resolved to push these experiments even further if possible, using galvanism and electricity.

I obtained access to the cemetery of Clamart, and all the heads and all the bodies of the tortured were placed at my disposal.

A laboratory was set up for me in a small chapel which was built at the corner of the cemetery. As you know, after driving out kings from their palaces, they kicked God out of his churches. I had an electric machine there, and three or four of these instruments called exciters.

Around five o'clock the terrible convoy arrived.

The bodies were jumbled up in the cart, the heads jumbled up in a bag. I took at random one or two heads and one or two bodies; we threw the rest into the mass grave.

The next day, the heads and bodies on which I had experimented the day before were added to the convoy of the day. Almost always my brother helped me in these experiences.

In the midst of all these contacts with death, my love for Solange increased every day. For her part, the poor child loved me with all the strength of her heart.

Very often I had thought of making her my wife, very often we had measured the happiness of such a union, but, to become my wife, Solange had to announce her name, and her name, which was that of an emigrant, an aristocrat, an outlaw brought death with it. Her father had written to her several times to hasten her departure, but she had told him of our love. She had asked him for his consent to our marriage, which he had granted; so everything was fine on that side.

However, in the midst of all these terrible trials, one trial more terrible than the others had deeply saddened both of us.

It was the trial of Marie-Antoinette.

Started on October 4, this trial was pursued with alacrity: on October 14, she had appeared before the revolutionary tribunal; on the 16th, at four in the morning, she had been sentenced; the same day, at eleven o'clock, she climbed on the scaffold.

In the morning, I had received a letter from Solange, who wrote to me that she would not let such a day pass without seeing me. I arrived around two o'clock at our little apartment on rue Taranne, and I found Solange weeping. I myself was deeply affected by this execution. The Queen had been so good to me in my youth that I had fond memories of this kindness.

Oh! I will always remember this day; it was a Wednesday: in Paris – there was more than sadness, there was terror. As for me, I felt a strange discouragement, something like the presentiment of a great misfortune. I wanted to try to give strength to Solange, who was crying, enfolded in my arms, and I had missed the consoling words, because the consolation was not in my heart.

We spent the night together as usual: our night was even sadder than our day. I remember a dog trapped in an apartment below ours howling until two in the morning.

The next day we inquired: his master had gone out carrying the key; in the street, he had been arrested, taken to the revolutionary tribunal; sentenced in three hours, he had been executed in four.

We had to leave; Solange's classes started at nine in the morning. Her boarding school was located near the Jardin des Plantes.

I drove a carriage forward and drove it to the corner of rue des Fossés-Saint-Bernard; there I stopped to let her continue on her way. Throughout the road, we had been kissing without saying a word, mixing our tears, which flowed down to our lips, mixing their bitterness with the sweetness of our kisses.

I got out of the cab; but, instead of going to my side, I stayed in the same place, to see her carriage move further. After twenty paces, the car stopped, Solange poked her head through the door, as if she guessed that I was still there. I ran to her. I climbed back into the cab; I closed the windows. I hugged her again. But nine o'clock struck at Saint-Etienne-du-Mont. I wiped her tears, closed her lips with a triple kiss, and, jumping out of the car, ran away. It seemed to me that Solange called me back; but all these tears, all these hesitations could not be noticed. I had the fatal courage not to turn around.

I returned home desperate. I spent the day writing to Solange; in the evening I sent her a volume. I had just mailed my letter when I received one from her. She had been very admonitory; she had been asked lots of questions and the headmistress threatened to take her out of the school for the first time.

Her first outing was the following Sunday; but Solange swore to me that in any case, should she give up her position with the boarding school mistress, she would see me that day.

I too swore it; it seemed to me that if I went seven days without seeing her, what would happen if she didn't use her first outing, I would go crazy.

Especially since Solange expressed some concern: a letter which she had found at her boarding school on returning there, and which came from her father, seemed to her to have been opened.

I had a bad night, and a worse day the next day. I wrote as usual to Solange, and, as it was my day of experiments, around three o'clock I passed by my brother's house to take him with me to Clamart. My brother was not at home; I left alone.

The weather was awful; nature, sorry, melted in rain, the cold and torrential rain which announces winter. All along the way I heard the town criers screaming in a hoarse voice the list of convicts of the day; it was numerous: there were men, women, and children. The bloody harvest was abundant, and I would not miss subjects for the session I was going to conduct in the evening.

The days ended early. At four o'clock I arrived at Clamart; it was almost dark. The appearance of this cemetery, with its vast, freshly moved tombs, with its rare trees rattling in the wind like skeletons, was dark and almost hideous.

All that was not turned over was grass, thistles, or nettles. Every day the turned earth invaded the green soil. In the midst of all this blistering of the ground, the pit of the day was gaping and awaiting its prey; more prisoners were expected, and the grave was larger than usual.

20: Cemetery of Clamart, 1827, Artist Unknown, Public Domain

I approached it mechanically. The whole bottom was full of water; poor naked and cold corpses that we were going to throw into this cold water like them!

When I got near the pit, my foot slipped, and I almost fell into it; my hair stood on end. I was wet, I was shivering, I was on my way to my laboratory.

It was, as I said, an old chapel; I was looking with my eyes, why was I looking? I don't know that; I looked for any signs of worship on the wall, or on what had been the altar; the wall was bare, the altar was low. In the place where the tabernacle, that is to say God, that is to say life, was once, there was a skull stripped of its flesh and hair, that is to say the dead, that is, nothingness.

I lit my candle; I put it on my experimental table, loaded with these strange-shaped tools that I had invented myself, and I sat down, dreaming of this poor queen whom I had seen so beautiful, so happy, so loved; who, the day before, followed by the imprecations of a whole people, had been driven in a cart to the scaffold, and who, at this hour, with her head separated from the body, slept in the bier of the poor, she who had slept under the gilt paneling from the Tuileries, Versailles and Saint-Cloud.

As I sank into these dark reflections, the rain redoubled, the wind passed in great gusts, throwing its lugubrious complaint among the branches of the trees, among the stalks of the grass which it made shiver.

This noise soon mingled like a lugubrious thunder roll; only this thunder, instead of rumbling in the clouds, bounded on the ground, which it made trembling. It was the rolling of the red truck, which came back from the place de la Révolution and which entered Clamart.

The door to the small chapel opened, and two men dripping with water entered carrying a bag.

One was the same Legros I had visited in prison, the other was a gravedigger.

'Here, Monsieur Ledru,' said the executioner's servant, 'that's your business; you don't have to hurry tonight; we leave you the whole caboodle; tomorrow we will bury them; it will be in broad daylight. They will not catch a cold for spending a night in the air.

And, with a hideous laugh, these two deathly stooges put their bags in the corner, near the old altar on my left, in front of me.

Then they went out without closing the door, which began to rattle against its doorframe, letting in gusts of wind which made the flame of my candle flicker, which rose pale and almost dying along its blackened wick.

I heard them unhitch the horse, close the cemetery, and leave, leaving the cart full of corpses.

I had really wanted to go with them, but I don't know why something kept me in my place, all shivering. Certainly, I was not afraid; but the sound of the wind, the whipping of this rain, the cry of these twisting trees, the hissing of that air which made my light tremble, all that shook a vague dread on my head which, from the damp root of my hair, was spreading all over my body.

Suddenly, it seemed to me a soft and lamentable voice came from the dim enclosure of the small chapel and I heard it pronounce the name of Albert.

Oh! For once, I started. Albert! ... Only one person in the world called me that. My wandering eyes slowly went around the little chapel, which, as narrow as it was, my light was not enough to light the walls, and stopped on the sack dumped at the corner of the altar, and whose bloody, bumpy canvas indicated its funeral contents.

As my eyes stopped on the bag, the same voice, but weaker, more dismal, repeated the same name:

- Albert!

I straightened in horror: the voice seemed to come from inside the bag.

I fumbled to know if I was sleeping or if I was awake; then, stiffly, walking like a stone man, with outstretched arms, I walked towards the bag, into which I plunged one of my hands. It seemed to me that still warm lips were leaning on my hand. I was at that level of terror where the excess of terror itself gives us courage. I took this head, and, returning to my chair, where I fell, I placed it on the table.

Oh! I uttered a terrible cry. This head, whose lips still seemed lukewarm, whose eyes were half closed, was Solange's head!

I thought I was crazy.

I screamed three times.

- Solange! Solange! Solange!

The third time the eyes opened again, looked at me, dropped two tears, and, throwing a damp flame as if the soul were escaping, closed again so as not to reopen.

I got up mad, insane, furious; I wanted to flee; but, getting up, I hung the table with the hem of my coat; the table fell, causing the candle to go out, the head rolled, confusing me even further. Then I seemed, lying on the ground, to see this head slide towards mine on the slope of the flagstones: her lips touched my lips, a shiver of ice passed through my whole body; I groaned, and passed out.

The next day, at six in the morning, the gravediggers found me as cold as the slab on which I was lying. Solange, recognized by her father's letter, had been arrested the same day, condemned, and executed the same day. This head which had spoken to me, those eyes which had looked at me, those lips which had kissed my lips, were the lips, the eyes, the head of Solange.

- You know, Lenoir, continued Mr. Ledru, turning to the knight, that was when I almost died.

Chapter Eight: The Cat, The Usher, & The Skeleton

$\mathcal{T}$he effect produced by Mr. Ledru's story was terrible; none of us thought of reacting against this impression, not even the doctor.

The Chevalier Lenoir, called out by Mr. Ledru, replied with a simple sign of support; the pale lady, who had lifted herself for a moment on her sofa, had fallen back in the middle of her cushions, and had only given signs of existence with a sigh; the police chief, who did not see in all this any matter to verbalize, did not breathe a word. For my own part, I noted down all the details of the disaster in my mind, in order to find them, if I liked to tell them one day, and, as for Alliette and Father Moulle, the adventure aligned too completely with their ideas for them to try and fight it.

On the contrary, Father Moulle was the first to break the silence, and, in a way, summing up the general opinion:

"I fully believe what you have just told us, my dear Ledru," he said, "but how will you explain these facts, as we say in material language."

- I can't explain myself, said Mr. Ledru; I tell it; that is all.

- Yes, how do you explain it? asked the doctor because finally, whatever the persistence of life, you do not admit that after two hours a severed head speaks, looks, acts?

"If I had been able to explain it, my dear doctor," said Mr. Ledru, "I would not have suffered such a terrible sickness after this event.

- But, doctor, said the knight Lenoir, how do you explain it yourself? Because you do not admit that Ledru has just told us an invented story to plead; his illness is a material fact too.

- By the Lord! This is no big deal! By hallucination. Monsieur Ledru thought he saw, Monsieur Ledru thought he heard; it's exactly like he's seen, heard. The organs that transmit perception to the sensorium, that is to say to the brain, can be disturbed by the circumstances that influence them; in this case, they get confused, and, when they get confused, transmit false perceptions: you think you hear, you hear; we believe we see, and we see.

The cold, the rain, the darkness had disturbed Mr. Ledru's organs, that's all. The madman also sees and hears what he thinks he sees and hears; hallucination is a momentary madness; we keep its memory when it has disappeared.

- But when it doesn't go away? asked Father Moulle.

- Well! Then the disease falls into the category of incurable diseases, and one dies.

- And have you sometimes treated these kinds of illnesses, doctor?

- No, but I knew some doctors who treated them, including an English doctor who accompanied Walter Scott on his trip to France.

- What did he tell you about this?

- Something similar to what our host has just told us, perhaps something even more extraordinary.

- And that you would explain by physical means? asked Father Moulle.

- Of course.

- And this fact, which was told to you by the English doctor, can you tell us?

- Without a doubt.

- Ah! tell, doctor, tell!

- Is it necessary?

- No doubt! cried everyone.

- Very well, then. The doctor who accompanied Walter Scott in France was named Dr. Simpson: he was one of the most distinguished men of the faculty of Edinburgh, and consequently was linked with the most important people of the city.

Among these was a criminal court judge, whose name he did not tell me. The name was the only secret he found fit to keep in this whole affair. This judge, to whom he gave the usual care as a doctor, without any apparent cause of disturbance in health, was dying visibly: a dark melancholy had taken hold of him. His family had, on different occasions, questioned the doctor, and the doctor, for his part, had questioned his friend without drawing anything from him other than vague answers which had only irritated his concern by proving to him that a secret existed, but that, this secret, the patient did not want to tell.

Finally, one day Doctor Simpson insisted so much that his friend confessed to him that he was sick, and held his hands with a sad smile:

- Well ! yes, he said, I am sick, and my illness, dear doctor, is all the more incurable since it is entirely in my imagination.

- What! In your imagination?

- Yes, I'm going crazy.

- You are going crazy! In what way? You have a lucid look, a calm voice (he took his hand), an excellent pulse.

- This is precisely what makes my condition serious, dear doctor, it is that I see it and that I judge it.

- But finally, what is your madness?

- Close the door, don't be disturbed, doctor, and I'll tell you.

The doctor closed the door and returned to sit near his friend.

- Do you remember, said the judge, the last criminal trial in which I was called to pass judgment?

- Yes, on a Scottish bandit who was sentenced to be hanged by you, and who was.

- Exactly. Well, as I delivered the judgment, a flame spurted from his eyes and he showed me his fist threatening me. I didn't pay attention. Similar threats are common among convicts. But, the day after the execution, the executioner came to my house, humbly asking forgiveness for his visit, but declaring to me that he had thought he should warn me of one thing: the bandit had died while pronouncing a sort of curse against me, saying that the next day at six o'clock, the hour at which he had been executed, I would hear from him.

I believed his companions might have some surprise planned for me, some sort of armed revenge, and, when six o'clock came, I locked myself in my study, with a pair of pistols on my desk.

Six o'clock struck on the mantelpiece clock. I had been preoccupied all day with this revelation from the executioner, but the last hammer blow vibrated on the bronze without my hearing anything other than a certain purring of which I did not know the cause. I turned around and saw a big black cat, with a fiery streak. How did he get in? It was impossible to say; my doors and windows were closed. He must have been locked in the room during the day.

I did not like the taste of this experience; I rang, my servant came, but he could not enter, since I had locked myself in: I went to the door and opened it. I told him about the black and fiery cat: but we looked for him unnecessarily, he had disappeared.

I didn't care anymore. The evening passed, night came, then the next day. It passed as usual, then six o'clock struck. At the same instant I heard the same noise behind me, and I saw the same cat.

This time he jumped on my lap. I have no antipathy for cats, and yet this familiarity gave me an unpleasant feeling. I chased him off my knees. But hardly was he down than he jumped on me again. I pushed him away, but as unnecessarily as the first time. So I got up, walked through the room, the cat followed me step by step. Impatient at this insistence, I rang as I had the night before, my servant entered. But the cat had fled under the bed, where we looked for it, but he was gone.

I went out during the evening. I visited two or three friends, then I returned to the house, where I returned thanks to a master key. As I had no light, I climbed the stairs slowly for fear of hitting something. When I got to the last step, I heard my servant talking with my wife's maid.

Hearing my name made me pay attention to what he said and then I heard him tell the whole story of the previous day and the day; only he added:

- My lord has gone crazy. There was no more black and fiery cat in the room than there was in my hand.

These few words frightened me: either the vision was real, or it was false; if the vision were real, I was under the weight of a supernatural fact; if the vision were wrong, if I thought I saw something that did not exist, as my servant said, I would go mad. You can guess my dear friend, with what impatience mixed with fear I waited for the next evening.

The next day, under the pretext of tidying up, I kept my servant close to me; six o'clock struck while he was there; at the last blow of the clock I heard the same noise and I saw my cat again.

He was sitting next to me.

I remained for a moment without saying anything, hoping that my servant would see the animal and speak to me first; but he came and went in my room without seeming to see anything.

There was one moment when he had to pass almost over the cat to accomplish the order I was going to give him,

"Put my doorbell on my table, John," I told him.

He was at the head of my bed, the doorbell was on the fireplace; to get from the head of my bed to the fireplace, he had to walk on the animal.

He started to move; but, as his foot was about to land on him, the cat jumped on my lap.

John didn't see him, or at least didn't seem to see him.

I admit that a cold sweat passed over my forehead, and his words: "The man must be going mad!" represented themselves in a terrible way at my thought.

- John, I said to him, don't you see anything on my lap?

John looked at me. Then as a man who takes a resolution:

- Yes, sir, he said, I see a cat.

I breathed.

I took the cat, and said to him:

- In this case. John, put it outside, please.

His hands came to meet mine. I put the animal in his arms, then, at a sign from me, he went out.

I was a little reassured; for ten minutes I looked around with some anxiety; but, having seen no living thing belonging to any animal species, I resolved to see what John had done with the cat.

So I left my room intending to ask him, when I stepped on the threshold of the living room door, I heard a big laugh that came from my wife's bathroom. I tiptoed over and heard John's voice.

- My dear friend, he said to the maid, sir is not going mad: no, he is already so. His madness, you know, is to see a black and fiery cat. Tonight he asked me if I couldn't see this cat on his knees.

- And what did you say? asked the maid.

- Good Lord! I said I saw him, said John. Poor dear man, I didn't want to upset him; so guess what he did.

- How do you want me to guess?

- Well! he took the alleged cat on his lap, put it in my arms, and he said to me:

"Take it away! Take it away!" So I bravely took the cat away, and he was satisfied.

- But, if you took the cat, did the cat exist then?

- No! the cat only existed in his imagination. But what good would it have been if I told him the truth? To be kicked out. My faith! No, I'm fine here, and I'm staying here. He gives me twenty-five francs a year to see a cat: I see it. Let him give to me thirty, and I'll see two.

I didn't have the guts to hear more. I sighed and returned to my room. My room was empty.

The next day, at six o'clock, as usual, my companion found himself near me, and did not disappear until the next day.

- What can I tell you, my friend?, continued the patient, for a month, the same apparition was renewed every evening, and I began to get used to its presence when, the thirtieth day after the execution, the clock rang six times without the cat appearing.

I thought I was rid of it; I could not sleep with joy. All morning the next day I pushed time ahead of me, so to speak; I was looking forward to arriving at the fatal hour. From five to six o'clock, my eyes never left my clock. I followed the progress of the needle advancing minute by minute. Finally, it reached the number XII; the quiver of the clock was heard.

Then, the hammer struck the first blow, the second, the third, the fourth, the fifth, finally the sixth! ...

On the sixth knock, my door opened, says the unhappy judge, and I saw a sort of usher in the room, dressed as if he had been in the service of the Lord Lieutenant of Scotland.

My first idea was that the Lord Lieutenant was sending me some message, and I reached out to my stranger. But he did not seem to have paid any attention to my gesture; he came to stand behind my chair.

I didn't have to turn around to see him – I was in front of a mirror, and in that mirror I saw him.

I got up and walked around the room; he followed me a few steps. I returned to my table and rang the bell. My servant appeared, but he saw the usher no more than he had seen the cat.

I sent him away, and I stayed with this strange character, whom I had time to examine at my ease.

He wore court attire, his purse, his sword at his side, a jacket embroidered with a drum, and his hat under his arm.

At ten o'clock I went to bed; so, as if to spend the night as comfortably as possible, he sat down in an armchair, in front of my bed.

I turned my head to the side of the wall; but, as it was impossible for me to fall asleep, two or three times, I turned around, and two or three times, in the light of my night light, I saw him in the same chair.

He didn't sleep either.

Finally, I saw the first rays of day creep into my room through the interstices of the blinds. I turned to my man one last time: he had disappeared, the chair was empty.

Until evening, I was stripped of my vision.

In the evening, there was a reception with the Grand Commissioner of the Church. Under the pretext of preparing my ceremonial costume, I called my servant at five minutes to six, ordering him to lock the door.

He obeyed.

At the last stroke of six o'clock, I fixed my eyes on the door – it opened, and my usher entered.

I went immediately to the door: the door was closed; the locks did not seem to have come undone. I turned around: the bailiff was behind my chair, and John came and went around the room without seeming the least bit concerned about him.

It was obvious that he did not see the man any more than he had seen the animal.

I got dressed.

Then something strange happened: very attentive to me, my new companion helped John in everything he did, without John noticing that he was being helped. So John was holding my coat by the collar, the ghost supporting him by the sides; thus, John presented my pants to me by the belt, the ghost held them by the legs.

I have never had a more informal servant.

The time for my departure came. Then, instead of following me, the usher preceded me, slipped by the door of my room, descended the staircase, held the hat under the arm behind John, who opened the door of the carriage, and, when John had closed it and had taken its place on the back shelf, he climbed into the driver's seat, which pulled to the right to make room for it.

At the door of the high commissioner of the Church, the carriage stopped; John opened the door; but the ghost was already at his post behind him. No sooner had I dismounted than the ghost rushed before me, passing through the servants who were blocking the front door, and looking to see if I was following him.

So I wanted to perform the test I had done on John on the coachman himself.

- Patrick, I asked him, who was the man who was near you?
- What man, Your Honor? asked the coachman.
- The man who was in your seat.

Patrick rolled his large, astonished eyes as he looked around.

- It's good, I said, I was wrong.

And I entered in my turn.

The usher stopped on the stairs and was waiting for me. As soon as he saw me resume my way, he resumed his, entered before me as if to announce me in the reception hall; then, when I entered, he went to take the place that suited him in the anteroom.

As with John and Patrick, the ghost had been invisible to everyone.

It was then that my fear changed to terror, and I realized that, really, I was going crazy.

It was from that evening that everyone realized the change that was taking place in me. They asked me what preoccupation held me, like you have done yourself.

I found my ghost in the anteroom. As when I arrived, he ran before me when I left, climbed back into the seat, came home with me, followed me to my room, and sat in the chair where he had sat the day before.

I wanted to make sure that there was something real and above all tangible in this appearance. I made a violent effort to move backwards to sit in the chair. I didn't feel anything, but in the mirror I saw him standing behind me.

Like the day before, I went to bed, but only at one in the morning. As soon as I was in my bed, I saw him in my chair. The next day he disappeared.

The vision lasted a month. After a month, he broke his habits and one day failed to appear. This time, like the first apparition, I no longer believed in a total disappearance, but in some terrible modification, and instead of enjoying my isolation, I waited the next day with dread.

The next day, at the last stroke of six o'clock, I heard a slight rustling in the curtains of my bed, and, at the point of intersection that they formed in the alley against the wall, I saw a skeleton.

This time, my friend, you understand, it was, if I can put it that way, the living picture of death.

The skeleton was there, motionless, looking at me with empty eyes. I got up, made several turns in my room; the head followed me in all my evolutions. The ghastly eyes did not leave me for a moment; the body remained motionless. That night I did not have the courage to go to bed. I slept, or rather stayed with my eyes closed in the chair where the ghostly usher usually sat, whose presence I had come to regret.

In the day, the skeleton disappeared.

I ordered John to move my bed and close the curtains.

At the last stroke of six o'clock, I heard the same touch; I saw the curtains flutter; then I saw the ends of two bony hands spreading the curtains of my bed, and the skeleton took the place it had occupied the day before in the opening.

This time I had the courage to go to bed. The head, which, like the day before, had followed me in all my movements, then tilted towards me; my eyes, which, like the day before, had not lost sight of me for a moment, then fixed on me.

You understand the night I spent! Well ! my dear doctor, twenty such nights have passed. Now you know what I have; will you still try to heal me?

- At least I will try, replied the doctor.
- What do you mean ? let's see.
- I'm convinced that the ghost you see only exists in your imagination.
- What does it matter if it exists or if it doesn't exist, if I see it?
- Do you want me to try to see him?
- I ask nothing better.
- When?
- As soon as possible. Tomorrow.
- Tomorrow then... Until then, good luck!

The patient smiled sadly.

The next day, at seven in the morning, the doctor entered his friend's room.

- Well ! he asked him, the skeleton?

"He just disappeared," he replied in a weak voice.

- Well ! we're going to make it so, yes, that he doesn't come back tonight.

- Do it.

- First, you said that it comes in at the last stroke of the clock striking six o'clock.

- Without fail.

- Let's start by stopping the clock.

He stared at the pendulum.

- What do you want to do ?

- I want to take away your ability to measure time.

- Good.

- Now let's keep the shutters closed, fasten the window curtains.

- Why do you want to do that?

- Always for the same purpose, so that you cannot realize any progress of the day.

- Do it.

The shutters were secured, the curtains drawn; we lit candles.

- Have lunch and dinner ready, John, said the doctor, we don't want to be served at set times, but only when I call.

- Do you hear, John? said the patient.

- Yes sir.

- Then give us cards, dice, dominoes, and leave us.

The requested items were brought by John, who withdrew.

The doctor began to distract the patient as best he could, sometimes chatting, sometimes playing with him; then, when he was hungry, he rang the bell.

John, who knew what the bell was for, brought lunch.

After lunch, the game started, and was interrupted by a new bell from the doctor.

John brought dinner.

They ate, drank, had coffee, and started playing again. The day seemed longer than ever, passing time idly. The doctor thought he had measured time in his mind, and that the fatal hour must have passed.

- Well! he said, getting up, victory!

- How? Or rather what victory? asked the patient.

- Without a doubt ; it must be at least eight or nine o'clock, and the skeleton has not come.

- Look at your watch, doctor, since it is the only one working in the house, and, if the hour has passed, well! like you I will declare victory.

The doctor looked at his watch but said nothing.

- You were wrong, doctor? said the patient; it's just six o'clock.

- Yes, it is.

- Well! Here is the skeleton coming in.

And the patient threw himself back with a deep sigh. The doctor looked around.

- Where do you see it then? he asked.

- In its usual place, in the lane of my bed, between the curtains.

The doctor got up, pulled the bed, went into the alley, and went to take the place between the curtains that the skeleton was supposed to occupy.

- And now, he said, do you still see him?

- I no longer see the bottom of his body, since yours hides it from me, but I see his skull.

- Or this ?

- Above your right shoulder. It's like you have two heads, one alive, the other dead.

The doctor, incredulous as he was, shivered in spite of himself. He turned around, but he saw nothing.

"My friend," he said sadly, returning to the patient, "if you have some testamentary arrangements to make, make them."

And he went out.

Nine days later, John, entering his master's room, found him dead on his bed.

It had been three months to the day that the bandit had been executed.

Chapter Nine: The Tombs of Saint-Denis

"Well! what does that prove, doctor?" asked Mr. Ledru.
- This proves that the organs which transmit to the brain the perceptions they receive can be disturbed as a result of certain causes, to the point of offering the mind an unfaithful mirror, and that in such cases we see objects and we hear sounds that don't exist. That is all.

- However, said the chevalier, M. Lenoir with the timidity of a bona fide scientist, however, certain things happen that leave their mark, certain prophecies that have an accomplishment.

How will you explain, doctor, that blows by specters could have created black spots on the body of the one who received them? how will you explain that a vision could have revealed the future ten, twenty, thirty years ago? Can what does not exist bruise what is or announce what will be?

- Ah! said the doctor, you mean the vision of the king of Sweden?
- No, I mean what I saw myself.
- You!
- Me.
- Where was this?
- In Saint-Denis.
- When?
- In 1794, during the desecration of the tombs.
- Ah! yes, listen to that, doctor, said Mister Ledru.
- What? What did you see? Tell us.
- In 1793, I was appointed director of the Museum of French Monuments, and, as such, I was present at the exhumation of the corpses of the Abbey of Saint-Denis, when enlightened patriots had changed the name to Franciale. I can, after forty years, tell you the strange things which signaled this desecration.

The hatred that we had managed to inspire in the people for King

Louis XVI, and that the scaffold of January 21 had not been able to satisfy, had risen to the kings of his race: we wanted to exterminate the monarchy to its source , the monarchs to their graves, throw the ashes of sixty kings to the wind.

Then also, perhaps we were curious to see if the great treasures that were said to be locked in some of these tombs had been kept as intact as they said.

The people rushed therefore onto Saint-Denis. From August 6 to 8, they destroyed fifty-one tombs, the history of twelve centuries. Then the government resolved to regularize this disorder, to search the tombs for its own account, and to inherit the monarchy, which it had just struck in Louis XVI, its last representative.

Then it was a question of annihilating the name, the memory, the bones of kings; it was a question of wiping out fourteen centuries of monarchy from history.

181: Looting of Royal Tombs in Saint-Denis Basilica, October 1793, Hubert Robert, Public Domain

Poor fools who don't understand that men can sometimes change the future – never the past!

A large mass grave had been prepared in the cemetery on the model of the pits of the poor. It is in this pit and on a bed of lime that the bones of those who had made France the first of the nations were cast, from Dagobert to Louis XV.

Thus, satisfaction was given to the people, but above all, enjoyment was given to those legislators, to those lawyers, to those envious journalists, birds of prey of revolutions, whose eyes are injured by all splendor, like the eyes of their brother, the night owl, is injured by any light.

The pride of those who cannot build is to destroy.

I was appointed inspector of excavations; it was a way for me to save a lot of precious things. I accepted.

On Saturday October 12, while the Queen's trial was being conducted, I had the Bourbon vault opened on the side of the underground chapels, and I began by removing from it the coffin of Henri IV, who was assassinated on May 14, 1610, fifty-seven years old.

As for the Pont-Neuf statue, a masterpiece by Jean de Bologne and his pupil, it had been melted down to make big money.

The body of Henri IV was wonderfully preserved; the facial features, perfectly recognizable, were indeed those which the love of the people and the brush of Rubens had consecrated.

When we saw him first come out of the grave and appear in his shroud, well preserved like him, the emotion was great, and the cry of *"Long live Henri IV!"* hitherto so popular in France, sounded instinctively under the vaults of the church.

When I saw these marks of respect, I would even say of love, I stood the body upright against one of the columns of the choir, and there everyone could come to contemplate it.

He was dressed, as in his lifetime, in his black velvet doublet, on which stood out his ruffs and his white cuffs; his doublet-like velvet case, silk stockings of the same color, velvet shoes.

His beautiful graying hair still made a halo around his head, his beautiful white beard always fell on his chest.

Then began an immense procession as at the shrine of a saint: women came to touch the hands of the good king, others kissed the hem of his coat, others made their children kneel, murmuring softly: "Ah! if he lived, the poor people would not be so unhappy! And they could have added: neither so fierce; because what makes people ferocious is misfortune.

This procession lasted all day through Saturday October 12, Sunday October 13, and Monday October 14.

On Monday, the excavations started again after the workers' dinner, that is to say around three o'clock in the afternoon.

The first corpse which surfaced the day after that of Henri IV, was that of his son Louis XIII. He was well preserved, and although his facial features were weakened, he could still be recognized by his mustache.

Then came that of Louis XIV, recognizable by his broad features which made his face the typical mask of the Bourbons; only it was black like ink.

Then came successively those of Marie de Medici, second wife of Henri IV; Anne of Austria, wife of Louis XIII; of Marie-Thérèse, wife of Louis XIV, and of the grand dauphin.

All these bodies were putrefied; only that of the grand dauphin was rotting liquid.

On Tuesday, October 15, the exhumations continued.

The corpse of Henry IV was still there standing against his column, an impassive assistant to this vast sacrilege which was accomplished both on his predecessors and on his descendants.

Wednesday 16, just when Queen Marie-Antoinette had her head severed on the Place de la Révolution, that is to say at eleven in the morning, Louis XV 's coffin was taken from the Bourbon vault.

He was, according to the ancient custom of the ceremonial of France, lying at the entrance of the vault, where he awaited his successor, who was not to join him there. They took it and opened it in the cemetery on the edge of the grave.

First, the body was removed from the lead coffin, and well wrapped in linen and strips, appeared whole and well preserved; but, freed from what enveloped it, it no longer offered anything but the image of the most hideous putrefaction, and there escaped from it a smell so foul that everyone fled, and that we were obliged to burn several pounds of incense to purify the air.

We immediately threw into the pit what was left of the hero of Parcaux-Cerfs, the lover of Madame de Châteauroux, Madame de Pompadour and Madame du Barry, and, falling on a bed of quicklime, we covered these filthy relics with even more quicklime.

I was the last one to burn the fireworks and throw the lime in when I heard a loud noise in the church; I went in quickly, and I saw a worker struggling among his comrades while the women were punching him and threatening him.

The wretch had left his sad work to go and see an even sadder spectacle: the execution of Marie-Antoinette; then intoxicated with the cries he had uttered and heard uttering, from the sight of the blood he had seen spilling, he returned to Saint-Denis, and, approached Henry IV erected against his pillar and always surrounded by curious people, and I would almost say devotees:

"By what right," he had said to him, "do you stay standing here, when you cut off the heads of kings on the Place de la Révolution?"

And, at the same time, grabbing the beard with his left hand, he had pulled it out, while, with the right, he was giving a strong blow to the royal corpse. The body had fallen to the ground, making a sharp noise, like that of a bag of bones that had been dropped.

Immediately a great cry arose from all sides. To such a king as he was, one might have risked such contempt; but to Henry IV, the king of the people, it was almost an outrage to the people. The sacrilegious worker therefore ran the greatest risk when I ran to his aid. As soon as he saw that he could find support in me, he put himself under my protection. But, while protecting him, I wanted to leave him under the burden of the infamous action he had committed.

- My children, I said to the workers, leave this wretch; the one he insulted is in a fairly good position up there to get God's punishment for him.

Then, having taken from him the beard which he had torn from the corpse, and which he still held with his left hand, I chased him from the church, announcing to him that he was no longer one of the workers I employed . Hoots and threats from his comrades chased him into the street.

Fearing further outrages against Henri IV, I ordered that he be carried into the mass grave; but, until then, the corpse was accompanied by marks of respect. Instead of being thrown like the others, at the royal mass grave, he was taken down there, laid down gently, and laid down carefully at one of the angles; then a layer of earth; instead of a layer of lime, was piously spread over him.

When the day was over, the workers withdrew, the caretaker alone remained: he was a good man whom I had placed there, lest at night we would enter the church, either to carry out new mutilations, or to operate new flights; this guardian slept during the day and kept watch from seven in the evening until seven in the morning.

He spent the night standing and strolling to warm up or sitting by a bonfire against one of the pillars closest to the door. Everything in the basilica presented the image of death, and the devastation made that image of death even more terrible. The vaults were open, and the flagstones stacked against the walls; broken statues littered the cobblestones of the church. here and there, broken coffins had restored the dead, which they believed they would not have to account for until the day of the last judgment. Finally, everything brought the spirit of man, if that spirit was elevated, to meditation; if he was weak, to terror.

Fortunately, the guardian was not a spirit, but an organized master. He looked at all this debris with the same eye as he would have looked at a sectioned forest or a mown field and was only concerned with counting the hours of the night, monotonous voice of the clock, the only thing that had remained alive in the desolate basilica.

As midnight struck and the last hammer struck the dark depths of the church, he heard loud cries coming from the side of the cemetery. These cries were loud, long complaints, painful lamentations.

After the first moment of surprise, he armed himself with a pickaxe and advanced towards the door which communicated between the church and the cemetery; but, at this open door, perfectly recognizing that these cries came from the pit of kings, he dared not go further, closed the door, and ran to wake me up at the hotel where I was staying.

I refused at first to believe in the existence of these clamors emerging from the royal pit; but, as I was living just opposite the church, the guard opened my window, and, in the midst of the silence disturbed by the mere rustling of the winter breeze, I actually thought I heard long complaints which seemed to me not only to be the lamentation of the wind.

I got up and accompanied the guard to the church. When we got there, and the porch door closed behind us, we heard the complaints he had spoken of more clearly. It was all the easier to tell where these complaints were coming from, that the door to the cemetery, badly closed by the guard, had reopened behind him. So these noises were actually coming from the cemetery.

We lit two torches and headed for the door; but three times, as we approached it, there was a gust of air almost blocking us from passing through. I understood that these would be challenging straits to cross, and once we were in the cemetery, we would no longer have the same struggle to support ourselves. Besides our torches, I lit a lantern. Our torches went out, but the lantern persisted.

We crossed the gate, and, once in the cemetery, we relighted our torches which the wind respected. However, as we approached, the clamor was dying, and by the time we got to the edge of the pit they were pretty much extinguished.

We shook our torches above the large opening, and in the midst of the bones, on this layer of lime and earth all pierced by them, we saw something formless struggling.

This thing looked like a man.

- Who are you and what do you want? I asked this shadow.

- Alas! he murmured, "I am the wretched worker who gave Henri IV a blow.

- But how are you there? I asked.

- Get me out of there first, Mr. Lenoir, because I'm dying, and then you'll know everything.

As soon as the guardian of the dead was convinced that he was dealing with a living being, the terror that had first taken hold of him was gone; he had already erected a ladder lying in the grass of the cemetery, holding this ladder upright and awaiting my orders.

I ordered him to lower the ladder into the pit and invited the worker to climb out. He dragged himself to the bottom of the ladder; but when he got there, when he had to stand up and climb the rungs, he noticed that he had a broken leg and arm.

We threw him a rope with a noose; he passed this rope under his shoulders. I kept the other end of the rope in my hands; the guard went down a few steps, and, thanks to this double support, we managed to get this living man out of the company of the dead.

As soon as he was out of the pit, he passed out. We carried him by the fire; we laid him on a bed of straw, then I sent the guard to get a surgeon.

The guard returned with a doctor before the wounded man regained consciousness, and it was only during the operation that he opened his eyes. Once he was bandaged, I thanked the surgeon, and, as I wanted to know by what strange circumstance the defiler was in the royal tomb, I in turn dismissed the guard. This good soul asked for nothing better than to go to bed, after the emotions of such a night, and I remained alone near the worker. I sat on a stone near the straw where he was lying, and in front of the hearth whose trembling flame lit the part of the church where we were, leaving all the depths in a darkness all the thicker, the part where we were was in a greater light.

I then questioned the wounded man. This is what he told me.

His dismissal had little concern for him. He had money in his pocket, and until then he had seen that with money there was nothing lacking. As a result, he went to spend time at the cabaret.

At the cabaret, he had opened a bottle of wine, but at the third glass he had seen the host come in.

- Are you finished? had asked for this one.

- And why is that? replied the worker.

- But because I heard that it was you who had given Henri IV a blow.

- Well! Yes it's me! said the worker insolently. And so what?

- So what? I don't want to give a rascally villain like you a drink, who will call the curse on my house.

- Your house, your house is everyone's house, and as long as we pay, we're at home.

- Yes, but you will not pay.

- And why is that?

- Because I don't want your money. Now, as you will not pay, you will not be at home, but in my house; and, as you will be in my house, I will have the right to throw you out.

- Yes, if you are the strongest.

- If I'm not the strongest, I'll call my boys.

- Well! Call a few, let us see.

234

The cabaret owner called in three boys, warned in advance, who entered on his voice, each with a stick in his hand, and this was forceful enough for the worker that although he wanted to resist, he withdrew without saying a word.

So he went out, wandered around the city for a while, and at dinner time he went into the shop where the workers used to have their meals.

He had just finished his soup when the workers who had completed their work for the day entered. When they saw him, they stopped at the door, and, calling the host, told him that if this man continued to eat there, they would desert his establishment, one and all.

The baker asked what had this man done, to cause him to be prey to general disapproval.

They said that he was reputed to be the man who had given Henri IV a blow.

- Then get out of here! said the guy, walking towards him, and may what you eat turn to poison!

There was even less possibility of resisting at the innkeeper's than at the cabaret. The cursed worker stood up threatening his comrades, who were angry, not because of the threats he had made, but because of the desecration he had committed. He went out, rage in his heart, wandered part of the evening in the streets of Saint-Denis, swearing and blaspheming. Then, around ten o'clock, he made his way to his garni[26].

Against the custom of the house, the doors were closed. He knocked at the door. The landlord appeared at a window. As it was dark, he could not recognize the knocker.

"Who are you," he asked. The worker named himself.

- Ah! said the landlord, it was you who gave Henri IV a blow: wait there.

- What! What should I wait for? said the worker impatiently.

At the same time, a package fell at his feet.

- What is that? asked the worker.

- All there is for you here.

- What! All there is for me here?

---

[26] Small hotels in France, typically without a reception or night porter, and which provide limited refreshments.

- Yes, you can go to sleep wherever you want; I don't want my house to fall on my head.

The workman, furious, took a paving stone and threw it into the door.

- Wait, said the landlord, I'll wake up your companions, and we'll see.

The worker realized that he had nothing good to wait for. He withdrew, and, having found an open door a hundred paces from there, he entered into a shed.

In this shed there was straw; he lay down on that straw and fell asleep. At a quarter to twelve, it seemed to him that someone was touching his shoulder. He awoke and saw before him a white form that looked like a woman, and which signaled him to follow her. He believed that she was one of those unhappy people who always have lodging and pleasure to offer to those who can pay for it; and as he had money, as he preferred to spend the night covered and lying in a bed, to spend it in a shed and lying on the straw, he got up and followed the woman.

The woman skirted the houses for a moment on the left side of the Grande-Rue, then she crossed the street, taking an alley to the right, still signaling the worker to follow her.

The latter, accustomed to this nocturnal carousel, knowing from experience the alleys where women of the type he followed usually lived, did not make any fuss, and entered the alley.

The alley ended in the fields; he believed that this woman lived in an isolated house, and still followed her.

After a hundred paces they crossed a breach; but suddenly, having looked up, he saw before him the old abbey of Saint-Denis, with its gigantic belltower and its windows slightly tinted by the interior fire, near which the guard watched.

He looked for the woman; she was gone.

He was in the cemetery.

He wanted to go back through the breach. But in this dark, threatening breach, his arm stretched out towards him, he seemed to see the specter of Henry IV.

The specter took a step forward, and the worker a step back. At the fourth or fifth step, the earth failed under his feet, and he fell backwards into the pit.

He seemed to see all these kings, predecessors and descendants of

Henry IV, standing around him, so it seemed to him that they were raising their scepters, others their hands of justice, shouting: *"Woe! Sacrilege!"*

It seemed to him that in contact with these hands of justice and these scepters weighing like lead, burning like fire, he felt his limbs break one after the other. It was at this time that midnight struck, and the guard heard his screams.

I did what I could to reassure this unfortunate man; but his reason was lost, and, after a delirium of three days, he died crying: *"Mercy!"*

"Sorry," said the doctor, "but I don't quite understand the consequence of your story. Your worker's accident proves that, with his head preoccupied with what had happened to him during the day, either in a waking state or in a state of somnambulism, he began to wander at night; that while wandering, he entered the cemetery, and that, while he looked up, instead of looking at his feet, he fell into the pit, where naturally he fell, in his fall , broke an arm and a leg. Now, you talked about a prediction that has come true, and I don't see the smallest prediction in all of this."

"Wait, doctor," said the knight; the story I just told, and which, you are right, is just a fact-based story, leads straight to this prediction which I will tell you, and which is a mystery.

Here is the prediction:

Around January 20, 1794, after the demolition of the tomb of François I, the tomb of the Countess of Flanders, daughter of Philippe le Long was opened. These two tombs were the last to be excavated; all the vaults were collapsed, the tombs were empty, all the bones were in the mass grave. A final unknown burial remained: it was that of Cardinal de Retz, who, it was said, had been buried in Saint-Denis.

All the vaults had been closed or nearly closed, the vault of the Valois, and vault of the Charles. Only the Bourbon vault remained, which was to be closed the next day.

The caretaker spent his last night in this church where there was nothing left to guard; permission had therefore been given to him to sleep, and he was enjoying the rest. At midnight he was awakened by the noise of the organ and religious chants. He woke up, rubbed his eyes, and turned his head towards the choir, that is to say, where the songs came from.

So he saw with astonishment the choir stalls furnished by the monks of Saint-Denis; he saw an archbishop officiating at the altar; he saw the chapel lit; and, under the burning candelabra, the large sheet of mortuary gold, which usually covers only the body of kings.

By the time he woke up, mass was over, and the funeral ceremony had begun. The scepter, the crown, and the hand of justice, placed on a red velvet cushion, were given to the heralds who presented them to three princes, who took them.

They advanced immediately, sliding rather than walking, and without the sound of their steps making the slightest echo in the room. The gentlemen of the chamber, who took the body and carried it into the vault of the Bourbons, left alone open, while all the others were closed.

The sergeant at arms went down there, and when he got down he called out to the other heralds to come and do their office.

The sergeant and the heralds were five in number.

From the bottom of the vault, the sergeant at arms called the first herald, who came down, carrying the spurs; then the second, who came down, wearing the gauntlets; then the third, who went down, carrying the shield; then the fourth, who went down, carrying the stamped helmet; then the fifth, who went down, carrying the coat of arms.

Then, he called the first valet, who brought the banner; the captains of the Swiss guard, the archers of the guard and the two hundred gentlemen of the house; the great squire, who brought the royal sword; the first chamberlain, who brought the banner of France; the grandmaster, in front of whom all the butlers passed, throwing their white sticks into the vault and saluting the three princes bearing the crown, the scepter and the hand of justice, as they paraded; the three princes, who in turn brought the scepter, hand of justice and crown.

Then the sergeant at arms cried aloud and three times:

The king is dead; long live the king! The king is dead; long live the king! The king is dead; long live the king!

A herald, who had remained in the choir, repeated the triple cry.

Finally, the grand master broke his baton as a sign that the royal house was broken, and that the king's officers could provide. Immediately the trumpets sounded, and the organ woke up.

Then, while the trumpets faded away, the organ moaned lower and lower, the lights of the candles dimmed, the bodies of the assistants faded, and, at the last moan of the organ, at the last sound of the trumpet, everything disappeared.

The next day, the guard, all in tears, related the royal burial he had seen, and which he, a poor man, attended alone, predicting that these mutilated tombs would be put back in place, and that, despite the decrees of the Convention and the work of the guillotine, France would see a new monarchy and Saint-Denis new kings.

This prediction was worth the prison and almost the scaffold to the poor devil, who, thirty years later, that is to say on September 20, 1824, behind the same column where he had had his vision, said to me, pulling me by the basque[27] of my coat:

- Well! Mr. Lenoir, when I told you that our poor kings would one day return to Saint-Denis, was I wrong?

Indeed, that day Louis XVIII was buried with the same ceremonial honor that the tomb guard had seen practicing thirty years before.

- Explain that one, doctor.

---

[27] The part of the waistcoat extending below the waist.

Chapter Ten: L'Artifaille

Either he was convinced, or more likely, that denial seemed difficult vis-à-vis a man like the Chevalier Lenoir, the doctor fell silent.

The doctor's silence left the field open to commentators; Father Moulle rushed into the arena.

"All of this confirms my system," he said.

- And what is your system? asked the doctor, delighted to resume the controversy with less harsh jousters than Monsieur Ledru and the Chevalier Lenoir.

- That we live between two invisible, populated worlds, one of hellish spirits, the other of celestial spirits; that at the time of our birth two geniuses, one good, the other bad, come to take our places by our side, accompany us all our lives, one blowing us good, the other bad, and that at the hour of our death the triumphant takes hold of us. Thus, our body becomes either the prey of a demon or the abode of an angel; with poor Solange, good genius had triumphed, and it was her who said goodbye to you, Ledru, by the silent lips of the young martyr; as for the brigand condemned by the Scottish judge, it was the demon who had remained master of the place, and it was he who came successively to the judge in the form of a cat, in the habit of a bailiff, with the appearance of a skeleton; finally, in the last case, it is the angel of the monarchy who avenged the terrible sacrilegious desecration of the tombs, and who, like Christ manifesting himself to the humble, showed the future restoration of royalty to a poor guardian of tombs, and that with as much pomp as if the fantastic ceremony had witnessed all the future dignitaries of the court of Louis XVIII.

"But still, Father," said the doctor, "any system is based on conviction."

- Without a doubt.

- But conviction, for it to be real, must be based on a fact.

- It's also a fact that mine is based on fact.

- Was it a fact that was told to you by someone you trust?

- On a fact that happened to me.

- Ah! the abbot; let's hear the fact.

- Gladly. I was born in this part of the heritage of the ancient kings that we now call the department of Aisne, and that we used to call Ile-de-France; my father and my mother lived in a small village in the middle of the forest of Villers-Cotterêts which is called Fleury. Before my birth, my parents had already had five children, three boys and two girls, all of whom were dead. As a result, when my mother became pregnant with me, she clad me in white until the age of seven, and my father promised a pilgrimage to Notre-Dame de Liesse.

These two vows are not rare in the provinces, and they had a direct relationship between them, since white is the color of the Virgin, and Our Lady of Liesse is none other than the Virgin Mary.

Unfortunately, my father died during my mother's pregnancy: but my mother, who was a pious woman, no less resolved to fulfill the double vow in all its rigor; as soon as I was born, I was dressed in white from head to toe, and as soon as she was able to walk, my mother undertook the sacred pilgrimage on foot, as it had been vowed.

Fortunately, Notre-Dame de Liesse was located only fifteen or sixteen leagues from the village of Fleury; in three stages, my mother arrived at her destination.

There, she made her devotions, and received from the priest's hands a silver medal, which she tied to my neck.

Thanks to this double blessing, I was free from all the accidents of youth, and, when I had reached the age of reason, either due to the result of the religious education I had received, or the influence of the medal, I felt drawn to the ecclesiastical state. Having studied at the seminary of Soissons, I left as a priest in 1780, and was sent vicar to Étampes.

Chance attached me to that of the four churches of Étampes which is under the invocation of Notre-Dame. This church is one of the marvelous monuments that the Roman era bequeathed in the Middle Ages. Founded by Robert le Fort, it was completed only in the twelfth century; today it still has admirable stained-glass windows which, during its recent construction, had to admirably harmonize with the paint and gilding which covered its columns and enriched the capitals. As a child, I loved these marvelous blooms of granite that faith had brought out of the earth from the tenth to the sixteenth century, to cover the soil of France, this eldest daughter of Rome, with a forest of churches, and which stopped when faith died in the hearts, killed by the poison of Luther and Calvin.

As a child, I played in the ruins of Saint-Jean de Soissons; I had delighted my eyes with the fancies of all these moldings, which seem petrified flowers, so, when I saw Notre-Dame d'Étampes, I was happy that chance, or rather Providence, had given me, whether I be swallow, a small nest; or Alcyon[28], such a grand vessel.

So my happy moments were those I spent in the church. I don't want to say that it was a purely religious feeling that kept me there; no, it was a feeling of well-being that can be compared to that of the bird that we pull from the pneumatic machine, to return it to space and to freedom. My space was that which extended from the portal to the apse; my freedom was to dream, for two hours kneeling on a grave or leaning on a column.

What did I dream of? it was certainly not some theological quibble; no, it was this eternal struggle of good and evil that tugged at man since the day of sin; it was these beautiful angels with white wings, these hideous demons with red faces, who, with each ray of sunshine, sparkled on the stained glass windows, some resplendent with celestial fire, others flamboyant with the flames of hell; Finally, Notre-Dame was my home: there I lived, I thought, I prayed. The little Presbyterian house that I had been given was just my base, I ate and slept there, that's all.

Often, I did not leave my beautiful Notre Dame until midnight or one in the morning. We knew that. When I was not at the presbytery, I was at Notre-Dame. They came to get me there, and they found me there. Very few sounds of the world reached me, confined as I was in this sanctuary of religion, and especially of poetry.

However, among these noises, there was one that interested everyone, young and old, clerics and laymen. The surroundings of Étampes were desolate by the exploits of a successor, or rather a rival of Cartouche and Poulailler, who, for all his audacity, seemed to follow in the footsteps of his predecessors.

This bandit, who attacked everything, but particularly churches, was

---

[28] Poetic description of the kingfisher from its legendary ability to nest on the sea, calming the waves.

called L'Artifaille[29].

One reason that made me pay more attention to the exploits of this brigand was that his wife, who lived in the lower town of Étampes, was one of my most assiduous penitents. She was a brave and worthy woman, who had the deepest remorse for the crime-filled life into which her husband had fallen, and who, believing herself responsible before God, as a wife, spent her life in prayer and in confession, hoping, by her holy works, to attenuate her husband's impiety.

As for him, as I have just told you, he was a bandit who feared neither God nor the devil, claiming that society was badly made, and that he was sent to earth to correct it; that, thanks to him, balance would be restored in fortunes, and that he was only the precursor of a sect that we would see one day, and who would preach what he put into practice, it is the community of goods[30].

Twenty times he had been taken to prison, but almost always, on the second or third night the prison had been found empty; since no one knew how he realized these escapes, it was said that he had found the grass that cuts iron.

So there was some wonderful air that attached to this man.

As for me, I thought about him, I admit, only when his poor wife came to confess to me, confessing her terrors and asking me for my advice.

So, you understand, I advised her to use all her influence on her husband to bring him back on the right track. But the poor woman's influence was very weak. He therefore had only the eternal recourse to grace that prayer opens before the Lord.

The Easter Holidays of 1783 were approaching. It was in the night from Thursday to Good Friday. I had heard a large number of confessions during the day on Thursday, and by eight o'clock in the evening I had become so tired that I fell asleep in the confessional.

The sacristan saw me asleep; but knowing my habits and knowing that I had a key to the door of the church on me, he had not even thought of waking me up; what happened to me that night had happened to me a hundred times.

---

[29] Rubbish, old pieces of iron or tin, ordure.
[30] Collectivism, as practiced in the Paris Commune.

So I was sleeping, when in the middle of my sleep I felt a double noise. One was the vibration of the bronze hammer striking midnight, the other was the rustling of a step on the flagstone.

I opened my eyes, and was about to leave the confessional when, in the ray of light cast by the moon through the stained glass of one of the windows, I seemed to see a man passing by.

As this man walked cautiously, looking around him with each step he took, I understood that he was neither one of the assistants, nor the beadle, nor the cantor, nor any of the regulars of the church, but some intruder coming there with bad intention.

The nocturnal visitor made his way to the choir. When he got there, he stopped, and after a moment I heard the sharp blow of iron on a flint; I saw a spark, a piece of tinder ignite, and a match fixing its wandering light at the end of a candle placed on the altar.

By the light of this candle, I could then see a man of mediocre stature, carrying on his belt two pistols and a dagger, with a mocking rather than a terrible face, and who, casting an investigative look throughout the extent of the circumference lit by the candle, seemed completely reassured by this examination.

Consequently, he drew from his pocket, not a bunch of keys, but a bunch of these instruments intended to replace them, and which are called nightingales [31]probably from the name of the famous Nightingale who boasted of having the key to all the numbers. Using one of these instruments, he opened the tabernacle, first drawing the holy ciborium[32], a magnificent cup of old silver carved under Henry II, then a massive monstrance, which had been given to the city by Queen Marie-Antoinette, then finally two burettes of vermillion.

Since that was all that the tabernacle contained, he closed it carefully, and knelt down to open the underside of the altar, which was being built.

The underside of the altar contained a waxwork of Notre Dame crowned with a crown of gold and diamonds, covered with a robe embroidered with precious stones.

At the end of five minutes, the shrine, whose walls of ice, the thief

---

[31] Picklocks which would make any lock sing like a nightingale.
[32] A cup to hold holy water.

could have broken, was opened, like the tabernacle, using a false key, and he was about to unite the robe and the crown with the monstrance, the burettes, and the holy ciborium, when, not wanting such a theft to be accomplished, I left the confessional and advanced towards the altar.

The noise I made when I opened the door made the thief turn. He leaned over and tried to look into the distant darkness of the church, but the confessional was beyond the reach of light, so he only really saw me when I entered the circle lit by the trembling flame of the candle.

On seeing a man, the thief leaned against the altar, pulled a pistol from his belt, and aimed it at me. But, in my long black dress, he could soon see that I was only a simple harmless priest, and having for my safeguard only faith, and speech my only weapon.

Despite the threat of the pistol aimed at me, I advanced to the steps of the altar. I felt that, if he shot at me, the gun would miss, or the bullet would deflect; I had my hand on my medal, and I felt completely covered with the holy love of Our Lady.

This tranquility of a poor vicar seemed to move the bandit.

- What do you want? he said to me in a tone that sounded more confident than the person speaking the words.

- Are you L'Artifaille? I said.

- Good Lord! He replied, who would dare, if not me, to enter a church alone, as I do?

- A poor hardened sinner who takes pride in your crime, I said to him, don't you understand that in this game that you play you lose not only your body, but also your soul?

- Bah! he said, as for my body, I have saved it so many times already, that I have good hopes of saving it again, and as for my soul...

- Well! As for your soul!

- That concerns my wife: she is holy enough for the both of us, and she will save my soul at the same time as hers.

- You are right, your wife is a holy woman, my friend, and she would certainly die of pain if she learned that you had accomplished the crime that you were carrying out.

- Oh! Oh! Do you think she will die of pain, my poor wife?

- I'm sure.

- Here! I'm going to be a widower, continued the brigand, bursting out laughing and extending his hands towards the sacred vessels.

But I went up the three steps of the altar and stopped his arm.

- No, I said to him, because you will not commit this sacrilege.

- And who will stop me?

- Me.

- By force?

- No, by persuasion. God did not send his ministers to earth to use force, which is human, but persuasion, which is a heavenly virtue. My friend, it is not for the church, which can get other vases, but for you, who cannot redeem your sin; my friend, you will not commit this sacrilege.

- Oh that old trope! Do you think you are the first to make this appeal, my good man?

- No, I know it might be the tenth, the twentieth, the thirtieth time maybe, but what does it matter? Until now your eyes were closed, your eyes will open tonight, that's all. Haven't you heard that there was a man named Paul who kept the coats of those who stoned Saint Stephen? Well, this man, his eyes were covered with scales, as he says himself; one day the scales fell from his eyes; he saw, and it was St. Paul. Yes, Saint Paul! ... the great, the illustrious Saint Paul! ...

- Tell me then, Father, was not Saint Paul hanged?

- Yes.

- Well! what was it good for him to see?

- It served him to be convinced that, sometimes, salvation is in torture. Today, Saint Paul has left a revered name on earth, and enjoys eternal bliss in heaven.

- At what age did Saint Paul come to see?

- At thirty-five.

- I'm past the age, I'm forty.

- There is always time to repent. On the cross, Jesus said to the bad thief, A word of prayer, and I save you.

- Oh that ! So you care about your silverware? said the bandit, looking at me.

- No. I care about your soul, which I want to save.

- My soul! You will make me believe that; you don't really care!

- Do you want me to prove to you that I care about your soul? I said.

- Yes, give me this proof, you will make me happy.

- How much do you estimate the robbery is worth that you are going to commit tonight?

- Well! said the brigand, looking with pleasure at the cruets, the chalice, the monstrance, and the robe of the Virgin, a thousand crowns.

- A thousand crowns?

- I know very well that it is worth double; but I will have to lose at least two-thirds of it; these Jewish devils are such thieves!

- Come to my house.

- To your home?

- Yes, my residence, at the presbytery. I have a sum of a thousand francs, I'll give it to you.

- And the other two thousand?

- The other two thousand? Well! I promise you, on my faith! That I will go to my country; my mother has some property, I will sell three or four acres of land to make the other two thousand francs, and I will give them to you.

- Yes, for you to give me an appointment and set a trap for me?

"You don't believe what you're saying there," I said, extending my hand to him.

- Well! That's right, I don't believe it, he said grimly. But your mother, is she rich?

- My mother is poor.

- Will she be ruined, then?

- When I tell her that at the cost of her ruin I saved a soul, she will bless me. Besides, if she has nothing left, she will come to stay with me, and I will always have enough for two.

- I accept, he said; let's go to your place.

- So be it, but wait.

- What?

- Lock in the tabernacle the objects that you took from there, close it with the key, that will bring you happiness.

The bandit's eyebrow frowned like that of a man who was invaded by faith despite himself: he replaced the sacred vessels in the tabernacle and closed it with the greatest care.

- Come on, he said.

"Make the sign of the cross first," I said.

He tried to laugh mockingly, but the laughter started and stopped by itself. Then he made the sign of the cross.

- Now follow me, I said.

We went out by the small door. In less than five minutes we were at home.

On the way, however short it was, the bandit had seemed very worried, looking around and fearful that I would want to place him in some ambush. When he got to my house, he stood by the door.

- Well! Those thousand francs? he asked.

- Wait, I replied.

I lit a candle at my dying fire; I opened a wardrobe, I pulled out a bag.

- Here they are, I said.

And I gave him the bag.

- Now the other two thousand, when will I have them?

- I'm asking you for six weeks.

- That is fine, I give you six weeks.

- Who will I give them to?

The bandit thought for a moment.

- To my wife, he said.

- Very well!

- But she won't know where they come from or how I got them?

- She won't know, neither she nor anyone. And never, in your turn, will you try nothing either against Our Lady of Étampes or against any other church under the invocation of the Virgin?

- Never!

- On your word?

- I swear by the faith of L'Artifaille!

- Go, brother, and don't sin anymore.

I greeted him with a wave of his hand that he was free to withdraw. He seemed to hesitate for a moment; then, opening the door carefully, he disappeared.

I knelt down and prayed for this man. I hadn't finished my prayer when I heard a knock on the door.

- Come in, I said without looking back.

Someone actually, seeing me in prayer, stopped on entering and stood behind me.

When I had finished my prayer, I turned around, and I saw L'Artifaille motionless and upright near the door, having his bag under his arm.

- Here, he said to me. I have brought you your thousand francs.

- My thousand francs?

- Yes, and I'm leaving you two thousand more.

- And yet the promise you made to me remains?

- Good Lord!

- So you repent?

- I don't know if I repent, yes or no, but I don't want your money, that's all.

And he put the bag on the edge of the sideboard. Then, the bag deposited, he stopped as if to ask for something; but this request, one felt, was hard to come out of his lips. His eyes questioned me.

- What would you like? I asked him. Speak, my friend. What you just did is good; don't be ashamed to do better.

- Do you have a great devotion to Notre-Dame? he asked me.

- The greatest.

- And do you believe that, by Her intercession, a man, however guilty he may be, can be saved at the time of death? Well then, in exchange for your three thousand francs, which I am leaving you, give me some relic, some rosary, some reliquary that I can kiss at the hour of my death.

I untied the medal and the gold chain that my mother had worn around my neck on the day of my birth, which had never left me since, and I gave them to the brigand.

The robber put his lips on the medal and fled.

A year went by without me hearing about L'Artifaille: no doubt he had left Étampes to go practice elsewhere. In the meantime, I received a letter from my colleague, the Vicar of Fleury. My good mother was sick and called me near her. I got a leave and I left.

Six weeks or two months of good care and prayer restored my mother's health. We parted, me joyful, she in good health, and I returned to Étampes.

I arrived on a Friday evening; the whole city was in turmoil. The famous thief L'Artifaille was caught in the Orleans quarter, had been judged by the provincial governor of this city, who, after conviction, had sent him to Étampes to be hanged, the canton of Étampes having been mainly the theater of its misdeeds.

The execution took place the same morning. This is what I learned on the street; but when I entered the presbytery I learned something else: that a woman from the lower town had come since the previous morning, that is to say from the moment when L'Artifaille had arrived at Étampes to suffer his torture, to inquire more than ten times if I was back.

This insistence was not surprising. I had written to announce my arrival, and I was expected from one moment to the next.

I only knew the poor woman who was going to become a widow in the region. I decided to go to her house before I even shook the dust off my feet.

From the presbytery to the lower town, there was only one step. Ten o'clock in the evening sounded; but I thought that, since the desire to see me was so ardent, the poor woman would not be disturbed by my visit.

So I went down to the suburb and asked for her house to be indicated. As everyone knew her as a saint, no one held her to account for the crime of her husband, no one made her ashamed of her shame.

I came to the door. The shutter was open, and through the windowpane I could see the poor woman at the foot of the bed, kneeling and praying. By the movement of her shoulders, you could guess that she was sobbing while praying.

I knocked on the door.

She got up and came quickly to open the door.

- Ah! Reverend Father! she exclaimed, I guessed you. When you knocked, I understood that it was you. Alas! alas! you arrive too late: my husband died without confession.

- Did he die in bad faith?

- No; on the contrary, I am sure that he was a Christian at heart, but he had declared that he wanted no other priest than you, that he would confess only to you, and that, he wouldn't confess to you, he wouldn't confess to anyone except Notre-Dame.

- Did he tell you that?

- Yes, and, while saying so, he kissed a medal of the Virgin hanging from his neck with a gold chain, recommending above all things that this medal should not be taken from her, and affirming that, if one managed to bury him with this medal, the evil spirit would have no hold on his body.

- Is that all he said?

- No. When he left me to walk on the scaffold, he told me again that you would arrive this evening, that you would come to see me as soon as you arrived; that's why I was waiting for you.

- Did he tell you that? I said in amazement.

- Yes, and then he charged me with one last prayer.

- For me?

- For you. He said that no matter what time you came, I should beg you ... My God! I would never dare say such a thing, would it be so painful for you?...

- Speak, my good woman, speak!

- Well! that I beg you to go to La Justice[33], and there, over his body, to say for the benefit of his soul five *Pater Nosters* and five *Ave Marias*. He said you wouldn't refuse me, Father.

- And he was right because I'm going to go.

- Oh! How good you are!

She took my hands and wanted to kiss me. I freed myself.

- Come on, my good lady, I said to her, courage!

- May God grant me some, Father, I'm not complaining.

- Did he ask for anything else?

- No.

- Very well then! If only this fulfilled desire is needed for the solace of his soul, his soul will be at rest.

I went out.

It was about half past ten. It was in the last days of April, the wind was still fresh. However the sky was beautiful, especially for a painter, because the moon rolled in a sea of dark waves which gave a great character to the horizon.

I turned around the old city walls and arrived at the Porte de Paris. After eleven o'clock in the evening, it was the only door of Étampes that remained open.

The object of my excursion was on an esplanade, which, today as then,

---

[33] Author's footnote: This was the name of the place where the thieves and the assassins were hung – *Ed.*

dominates the whole city. Only today, there remain few traces of the gallows, which was then erected on this esplanade, only three fragments of the masonry which secured the three posts connected together by two beams and which formed the gibbet.

To get to this esplanade, located to the left of the road when you come from Étampes to Paris, and to the right when you come from Paris to Étampes; to get to this esplanade, you had to pass at the foot of the Guinette tower, an advanced structure which seems to be a sentry standing alone on the plain to guard the city.

This tower, which you must be familiar with, Chevalier Lenoir, and which Louis XI tried to blow up in the past without succeeding, is ripped apart by the explosion and seems to be looking at the gallows of which it sees only the end with the black orbit of a big eye without a pupil.

By day it is the home of crows; at night, it is the palace of barn owls.

I took, in the midst of their cries and their hoots, the path to the esplanade, a narrow, difficult, rugged path, dug in the rock, pierced through the brushwood.

I cannot say that I was afraid. The man who believes in God, who confides in him must not be afraid of anything, but I was moved. All you could hear in the world was the monotonous ticking of the mill in the lower town, the hoots of owls, and the whistling of the wind in the brushwood.

The moon entered a black cloud, the ends of which it embroidered with a whitish fringe. She disappeared.

My heart was beating. It seemed to me that I was going to see, not what I had come to see, but something unexpected. I went ever upwards. Arriving at a certain point of the climb I began to distinguish the upper end of the gibbet, made up of its three pillars and this double oak crosspiece of which I have already spoken.

It is on these oak sleepers that hang the iron crosses to which the tortured are attached. I saw, like a moving shadow, the body of the unfortunate L'Artifaille, which the wind was swinging in space.

Suddenly I stopped; I now could discern the gibbet from its upper end to its base. I saw a shapeless mass nearby that looked like an animal on all fours and was moving.

I stopped and lay down behind a rock. This animal was larger than a dog and more massive than a wolf.

Suddenly he rose on his hind legs, and I recognized that this animal was none other than that which Plato called an animal with two feet and without feathers, that is to say, a man.

What could a man come to do at this hour under a gibbet, unless he came there with a religious heart to pray, or with an irreligious heart to make some sacrilege?

In any case, I resolved to remain quiet and wait. At that moment, the moon came out of the cloud it was hiding behind and lit up the gallows. I looked up.

I could see the man clearly, and even all the movements he was making. He picked up a ladder lying on the ground, then raised it against one of the poles, closest to the corpse of the hanged man. Then he climbed the ladder.

Then he formed with the hanged man a strange group, in which the living and the dead seemed to merge in a kiss.

Suddenly a terrible cry sounded. I saw the two bodies shake; I heard screaming in a strangled voice, which soon ceased to be distinct; then one of the two bodies broke away from the gallows, while the other hung on his rope and waved his arms and legs.

It was impossible for me to guess what was going on under the infamous machine; but finally, whether the work of man or of the devil, something extraordinary had happened, something that called for help.

I started.

At my sight, the hanged man appeared to be more agitated, while the one beneath him was motionless, lying on the body which had detached itself from the gallows.

I first ran to the aid of the living. I quickly climbed the steps of the ladder, and, with my knife, I cut the rope. The hanged man fell to the ground, I jumped down the ladder. The hanged man was rolling in horrible convulsions, the other body was still standing.

I understood that the noose continued to tighten the neck of the poor devil. I lay down on him to fix him, and with great difficulty I loosened the noose that was strangling him. During this operation, which forced me to look at this man in the face, I recognized with astonishment that this man was the executioner.

His eyes were out of their sockets, his face bluish, his jaw almost twisted, and a rattle more than a breath escaped from his chest. However, the air gradually returned to his lungs, and, with air, life.

I leaned him against a big stone; after a moment he seemed to regain his senses, coughed, turned his neck coughing, and finally looked me in the face.

His amazement was no less than mine had been.

- Oh ! Oh ! Father, he said, is that you?

- Yes, it's me.

- What are you doing here? he asked me.

- Me? What are you doing here yourself?

He seemed to regain his spirit. He looked around him again; but this time his eyes stopped on the corpse.

- Ah! He said, trying to get up, let's go, Father, in the name of heaven, let's go!

- Go away if you want, my friend; but I have a duty to perform.

- Here?

- Here.

- What is it then?

- This unfortunate man, who was hanged by you today, wanted me to come and say five *Paters* and five *Aves* at the foot of the gibbet for the salvation of his soul.

- For the salvation of his soul? Oh ! Father, you'll have a job if you save this one, he is Satan in person.

- What! He is Satan himself?

- No doubt, didn't you just see what he did to me?

- What did he do to you, and what were you doing to him?

- He hanged me, Good Lord!

- He hanged you? But it seemed to me, on the contrary, that it was you who had done him this sad service?

- Yes, my faith! And I thought I did hang him. It seems that I was wrong! But how did he take advantage of the moment when I was focused on my task to save himself?

I went to the corpse, I lifted it; he was stiff and cold.

- Because he died, I said.

- Dead! repeated the executioner. Dead! Ah! By the devil, that's worse;

so let's save ourselves, Father, let's save ourselves.

He got up.

- No, by my faith! he said, I still prefer to stay; he would only have to get up and run after me. You, at least, who are a holy man, will defend me.

- My friend, I said to the executioner, staring at him, there's something you're hiding. You were asking me earlier what I was doing here at this hour. In my turn, I will ask you: What did you come here to do?

- My faith! Father, I'll have to tell you, whether in confession or otherwise. Well ! I'll tell you now. But wait...

He stepped back.

- What?

- He does not move there, does he?

- No, don't worry, the poor fellow is dead.

- Oh ! Dead... dead... no matter! I will tell you why I came, and if I lie he will deny it, that's all.

- Tell me.

- I must tell you that this disbeliever did not want to hear about confession. He only said from time to time: *"Did Father Moulle arrive?"*

They replied: *"No, not yet."*

He sighed; they offered him a priest, he replied: *"No! Father Moulle ... and no other!"*

- Yes, I know that.

- At the foot of the Guinette tower, he stopped: *"Look, then,"* he said, *"if you do not see Father Moulle coming.*

"No," I told him, and we set off again. At the bottom of the ladder, he stopped again.

"Father Moulle is not coming?" He asked.

"No! There is nothing more impatient than a man who always repeats the same thing to you. Let's go!"

I put the rope around him. I stepped on the ladder and said, *"Go up."*

He went upstairs without being prodded too much; but when he got two-thirds of the way up, *"Wait,"* he said, *"until I make sure Father Moulle doesn't come."*

- Ah! look, I told him, it is not forbidden.

Then he looked one last time in the crowd; but, not seeing you, he sighed. I thought he was resolved and that there was nothing left but to push him; but he saw my movement.

"Wait," he said.

"What now?"

"I would like to kiss a medal of Notre-Dame, which is on my neck."

"Ah! that," I said to him, *"it is a fair thing,"*

And I put the medal against his lips.

"What else?" I asked.

"I want to be buried with this medal."

"Um! hum!" I said, *"it seems to me that all of the hanged man's clothes belong to the executioner."*

"That doesn't concern me, I want to be buried with my medal."

"I want! I want! Even as you go!"

"I want what!"

Patience escaped me; he was ready, he had the rope around his neck, the other end of the rope was on the hook.

"Go to hell!" I said.

And I threw him into space.

"Notre-Dame, have pity..."

- Well! That's all he could say – the rope strangled both the man and the sentence. At the same time, you know how it is done, I grabbed the rope, I jumped on his shoulders, and bang! Bang! All was said and done. He didn't have to complain about me, and I tell you that he didn't suffer.

- But all that does not explain why you came this evening.

- Oh ! that's the hardest thing to tell.

- Well ! I'll tell you – you came to take his medal from him.

- Well ! yes, the devil tempted me. I said to myself: Good! Well ! You know you want it – that's easy to say, but when the night comes, don't worry, we'll see.

So when night fell, I left the house. I had left my ladder around; I knew where to find it. I went for a walk; I came back by the longest route and then, when I heard no noise, I approached the gallows, I set up my ladder, I climbed up, I pulled the hanged man to myself, I unhooked his chain, and...

- And what?

- Well! Believe me if you want, but the moment the medal left his neck, the hanged man grabbed me, removed his head from the noose, put my head in place of his, and, well! he pushed me too, as I had pushed me. That's the thing.

- Impossible! You are wrong.

- Did you find me hanged, yes or no?

- Yes.

- Well! I promise you that I did not hang myself. That's all I can tell you.

I thought for a moment.

- And the medal, I asked him, where is it?

- Well! Look around, it must not be far. When I felt myself hanging, I let go of it.

I got up and looked down. A ray of the moon gave on it as if to guide my research.

I picked it up. I went to poor L'Artifaille's corpse and tied the medal around his neck. The moment it touched his chest, something like a shudder ran through his whole body, and a high, almost painful scream came out of his chest.

The executioner jumped back.

My mind had just been illuminated by this cry. I remembered what the Holy Scriptures said about exorcisms and the cry of the demons when they left the body of the possessed.

The executioner was trembling like a leaf.

"Come here, my friend," I said, "and fear nothing."

He approached hesitantly.

- What do you want from me? he asked.

- Here's a corpse that needs to be put back in its place.

- Never! Well then, am I to hang him again?

- There is no danger, my friend, I will answer for everything.

- But Father! Reverend sir!

- Come, I tell you.

He took another step.

- Um! he whispered; I don't trust it.

- And you are wrong, my friend. As long as the body has its medal, you will have nothing to fear.

- Why is that?

- Because the demon will have no control over him. This medal protected him, you took it away from him; instantly the evil genius which had driven him to evil, who had been dismissed by his good angel, entered the corpse, and you saw what the work of this bad genius was.

- So the cry we just heard?

- It was the demon's scream when he felt that his prey was escaping him.

- Well, said the executioner, indeed, it could well be.

- It is so.

- So, I'm going to put it back on its hook.

- Put it back; justice must have its course; the condemnation must be accomplished.

The poor devil still hesitated.

- Fear nothing, I said to him, I answer for everything.

- Never mind, continued the executioner, don't lose sight of me, and at the least cry come to my rescue.

- Keep calm.

He approached the corpse, gently lifted it by the shoulders and pulled it toward the ladder while speaking to it.

- Don't be afraid, L'Artifaille, he said, I am not taking your medal. You don't lose sight of us, do you, Father?

- No, my friend, don't worry.

- It's not to take your medal, continued the executioner in the most conciliatory tone; no, don't worry, since you wanted it, you will be buried with it. It's true, he does not move, Father.

- Do you see it.

- You will be buried with it; in the meantime, I put you back in your place, by the desire of the abbot, because, for me you understand! ...

- Yes, yes, I said, not being able to help smiling, but hurry.

- Well! it's done, he said, letting go of the body he had just attached to the hook again and jumping to the ground at the same time.

And the body swayed in the still, inanimate space.

I got down on my knees and started the prayers that L'Artifaille had asked of me.

- Father, said the executioner, kneeling next to me, would you like to say the prayers high and soft enough so that I can say them again?

- What! So you have forgotten them?

- I don't think I ever knew them.

I said the five *Pater Nosters* and the five *Ave Marias*, which the executioner conscientiously repeated after me.

The prayers finished, I got up.

- Artifaille, I said softly to the tortured, I did everything I could for the salvation of your soul, it is up to Blessed Notre Dame to do the rest.

- Amen! said my companion.

At that moment, a ray of moonlight illuminated the corpse like a cascade of silver. Midnight tolled at Notre-Dame.

Come on, I said to the executor, we have nothing more to do here.

- Father, said the poor devil, would you be good enough to give me one last favor?

- Which ?

- To accompany me home; as long as I don't feel my door closed tightly between me and this fellow, I won't be at ease.

- Come, my friend.

We left the esplanade, not without my companion, ten paces, every ten paces, turning to see if the hanged man was in his place.

Nothing moved.

We returned to the city. I led my man to his house. I waited until he had lit his candles, then he closed the door on me, said goodbye, and thanked me through the door. I returned home, perfectly calm in body and mind.

The next day, when I woke up, I was told that the thief's wife was waiting for me in my dining room.

Her face was calm and almost happy.

- Monsieur l'Abbé, she said to me, I come to thank you: my husband appeared to me yesterday as midnight struck at Notre Dame, and he said to me:

"Tomorrow morning, you will go and find Father Moulle, and tell him that, thanks to him and Notre-Dame, I am saved."

Chapter Eleven: The Bracelet of Hair

"**M**y dear abbot", said Alliette, "I have the greatest esteem for you and the greatest veneration for Cazotte; I perfectly admire the influence of your evil genius; but there is one thing that you forget and of which I am an example: that death does not kill life; death is just a way of transforming the human body; death kills memory, that's all."

If memory did not die, everyone would remember all the peregrinations of their soul, from the beginning of the world to us. The Philosopher's Stone is nothing but this secret; it is this secret that Pythagoras had found, and that the Count of Saint-Germain and Cagliostro found; it is this secret which I have in my turn, and which causes my body to die, as I remember positively that has already happened to it four or five times, and again, when I say that my body will die, I am wrong , there are certain bodies that do not die, and I am one of them."

- Mr. Alliette, said the doctor, would you like to give me permission in advance?

- Which ?

- It is to have your tomb opened a month after your death.

- A month, two months, a year, ten years, whenever you like, doctor; only take your precautions – because the harm you would do to my corpse could harm the other body into which my soul would have entered.

- So you believe in this madness?

- I have to believe it: I saw...

- What did you see? One of these living dead?

- Yes.

- Come on, Mr. Alliette, since everyone has told their story, tell yours too; it would be curious if it were the most believable one of our little society.

- Probable or not, doctor, here it is in all its truth. I was going from

Strasbourg to the waters of Louesche[34]. You know the road, doctor?

- No ; but no matter, always go.

- So I was going from Strasbourg to Louesche, and I went naturally through Basel, where I had to leave the public car to take a cart.

I arrived at the Hôtel de la Couronne, which I had been recommended. I inquired about a car and a buggy, asking my host to inquire if anyone in the city was not willing to take the same route as me; so he was responsible for proposing to the same person an association which was naturally to make both the road more pleasant and less expensive.

In the evening he returned, having found what I asked: the wife of a Basel merchant, who had just lost her three-month-old child whom she was nursing herself, had fallen prey, following this loss, to an illness for which she was advised the Louesche waters. This was the first child of the young couple, married less than a year.

My host told me that it was exceedingly difficult for the woman to leave her husband. She absolutely wanted to stay in Basel or have him come with her to Louesche; but, on the other hand, the state of her health required the waters, while the state of their trade required his presence in Basel.

She made up her mind and left with me the next morning. Her maid accompanied her. A Catholic priest, serving the church in a small village nearby, accompanied us and took fourth place in the car.

The next day, around eight in the morning, the car came to pick us up at the hotel; the priest was already on board. I climbed in too, and we went to collect the lady and her maid. We witnessed, from inside the car, the farewell of the two spouses, who, begun at the back of their apartment, continued in the store, and only ended in the street. No doubt the woman had a presentiment, for she could not console herself. It looked like, instead of going on a journey of about fifty leagues, she was leaving to go around the world. The husband appeared calmer than her, but nevertheless was more moved than was reasonably suitable for such a separation. We finally left.

Naturally, the priest and I gave the two best places to the traveler and

---

her maid, that is to say that we were at the front and they at the back. We took the road to Solothurn, and the first day we went to sleep in Mundischwyll.

All day long, our partner had been tormented, worried. In the evening, having seen a car passing in the opposite direction, she wanted to take the road back to Basel. Her maid however managed to persuade her to decide to continue on her way.

The next day we set off around nine in the morning. The day was short; we did not intend to go further than Solothurn. Towards evening, and as we began to see the city, our patient started.

- Ah! she said, stop, they are running after us.

I leaned out of the door.

"You are mistaken, madam," I replied, "the road is perfectly empty.

- It's strange, she insisted. I hear the gallop of a horse.

I thought I was mistaken. I got out of the car further.

"No one, madam," I said.

She looked herself and saw the deserted road like me.

- I was wrong, she said, throwing herself into the back of the car.

And she closed her eyes like a woman who wants to focus her thoughts on herself.

The next day we left at five in the morning. It was a long day on the road. Our driver entered into Bern at the same time as the day before, that is to say around five o'clock, just as our companion emerged from a kind of sleep where she was resting in the coach, and, stretching out her arms towards the coachman cried:

- Driver! she said, stop! This time, I'm sure, they're running after us.

"Madame is mistaken," replied the driver. I only see the three peasants who have just passed us, and who are quietly following their path.

- Oh! But I hear the gallop of a horse.

These words were said with such conviction that I couldn't help but look behind us.

As on the previous day, the road was absolutely deserted.

- It is impossible, madam, I replied, I do not see a jumper.

- How is it that you don't see a rider, since I see the shadow of a man and a horse?

I looked in the direction of her hand and saw, in fact, the shadow of a horse and a rider. But I looked in vain for the bodies to which the shadows belonged.

I pointed out this strange phenomenon to the priest, who crossed himself.

Little by little this shadow cleared up, became instantly less visible, and finally disappeared altogether.

We entered Bern.

All these omens seemed fatal to the poor woman; she kept saying she wanted to go back, and yet she kept going.

Either due to moral uneasiness or the natural progress of the disease, on arriving in Thun, the patient found herself in such a state of suffering that she had to continue her journey on a litter. This was how she crossed the Khander-Thal and the Gemmi. Arriving at Louesche, erysipelas[35] was diagnosed, and for more than a month she was deaf and blind.

Besides, her presentiments had not deceived her, scarcely had she made twenty leagues than her husband had been diagnosed with suffering from a cerebral fever.

The disease had progressed so quickly that the same day, feeling the gravity of his condition, he sent a man on horseback to warn his wife and invite her to return. But between Lauffen and Breinteinbach, the horse had fallen, and, the rider having fallen, his head had given against a stone, and he had remained in an inn, being able to do nothing for the one who had sent him other than to warn him of the accident that had happened.

So he had sent another letter; but no doubt there was a fatal curse on them; at the end of the Khander-Thal, the courier had left his horse and taken a guide to climb the Schwalbach plateau, which separates the Oberland from the Valais when, halfway, an avalanche, rolling from Mount Attels, had drawn him with it into an abyss; the guide had been saved as if by a miracle.

Meanwhile, the evil sickness was making terrible progress. They had to shave the head of the patient, who had very long hair, in order to apply ice to his head. From that moment on, the dying man had no hope left, and in a moment of calm, he had written to his wife:

---

[35] A severe skin disease caused by streptococcus infection in surface and surrounding tissue, marked by continued spreading inflammation.

Dear Bertha,

I'm going to die, but I don't want to part with you entirely. Get a bracelet from the hair that was just cut off and set it aside. Always wear it, and it seems to me that we will be together again.

Your Frédéric.

Then he delivered the letter to a third express courier, whom he ordered to leave as soon as he expired.

That evening he was dead. An hour after his death, the express had left, and, luckier than his two predecessors, he had arrived at Louesche by the end of the fifth day.

But he had found the woman blind and deaf. After only a month, thanks to the efficiency of the waters, this double infirmity had started to disappear. It had been another month before they had dared to share the woman the fatal news for which, moreover, her different visions had prepared her. She had stayed for the last month to fully recover; finally, after three months of absence, she left for Basel.

As for my part, I had finished my treatment – the infirmity for which I had taken the waters, and which was rheumatism, was much healed, I asked her permission to leave with her, which she accepted gratefully, having found in me a person to talk to about her husband, whom I had only glimpsed at the time of departure, but finally whom I had seen.

We left Louesche, and on the fifth day, in the evening, we were back in Basel. Nothing was more sad and painful than the return of this poor widow to her house; as the two young people were alone in the world, the husband dead, the store was closed, the trade had stopped as the movement stopped when a pendulum stopped. They sent for the doctor who had cared for the patient, the various people who had assisted him in his last moments, and, through them somehow resuscitated his agony. reconstructing this tragic death already almost forgotten in their indifferent hearts.

At last, she asked for the hair her husband had left her.

The doctor remembered having ordered them to be cut; the barber remembered shaving the patient well, but that was it. The hair had been thrown to the wind, scattered, lost.

The woman was desperate; this one and only desire of the dying man, that she wore a bracelet of his hair, was therefore impossible to realize.

Several nights passed: deeply sad nights, during which the widow, wandering in the house, seemed much more a shadow than a living being.

As soon as she was lying down, or rather barely asleep, she felt her right arm fall into numbness, and she did not wake up until the numbness seemed to win her heart.

This numbness started on the wrist, that is to say where the hair bracelet should have been and where she felt a pressure like that of an iron bracelet too narrow for the wrist, and as we said, numbness won the heart. It was evident that the dead man expressed regret that his wishes had been so poorly followed.

The widow understood these regrets, which came from the other side of the grave. She resolved to open the grave, and, if her husband's head had not been completely shaved, to gather enough hair there to fulfill his last wish. Consequently, without telling anyone about her plans, she sent for the gravedigger.

But the gravedigger who had buried her husband was dead. The new gravedigger, who had been practicing for only two weeks, did not know where the grave was.

So, hoping for a revelation, she who, by the double appearance of the horse, the ghostly rider, she who, by the pressure of the bracelet, had the right to believe in wonders, she went alone to the cemetery, sat down on a covered green mound with the perennial grass that grows on tombs, and there she invoked some new sign to which she could be directed for her research.

A *danse macabre* was painted on the wall of this cemetery. Her eyes fell on Death and fixed themselves for a long time on this mocking and terrible figure at the same time.

Then it seemed to her that Death raised its emaciated arm, and with the tip of its bony finger pointed to a grave in the middle of the last row.

The widow went straight to this tomb, and when she was there, she seemed to see Death very distinctly, letting his arm fall back to the original place.

So she made a mark at the grave, went to fetch the gravedigger, brought him back to the designated place, and said to him:

- Dig, it's here!

I attended this operation. I wanted to follow this wonderful adventure to the end.

192: Hans Holbein, Danse Macabre XXXVII, The Pedlar

The gravedigger dug. When he reached the coffin, he lifted the lid. At first he hesitated, but the widow said to him in a firm voice:

- Lift up, this is my husband's coffin.

So he obeyed, as this woman knew how to inspire in others the confidence she had herself. Then a miraculous thing appeared and that I saw with my eyes. Not only was the corpse that of her husband, not only was this corpse, except for the pallor, as he had been while alive, but also, even though he had been shaved, that is to say since the day of his death, his hair had grown so that it came out like roots through all the cracks in his bier.

Then the poor woman leaned over this corpse, which seemed only to be asleep; she kissed him on the forehead, cut a lock of her long hair, so wonderfully grown on the head of a dead man, and made it into a bracelet.

From that day, the night's numbness stopped. Only, whenever she was in some great danger, a gentle pressure, a friendly embrace of the bracelet warned her to be on her guard.

- Well ! Do you believe that this dead man was really dead? that this corpse was indeed a corpse? I don't believe it.

- And, asked the pale lady with such a peculiar tone, that she made us all start in the deep darkness of night, have you heard that this corpse was ever taken out of the tomb, have you heard that anybody might have suffered from his sight and contact?

- No, said Alliette, I left the country.

- Ah! said the doctor, you are wrong, Mr. Alliette, to be of such easy composition. Here is Mrs. Grégoriska who is willing to consider your good merchant from Basel in Switzerland to be a Polish, Wallachian or Hungarian vampire. During your stay in the Carpathian Mountains, continued the doctor, laughing, did you happen to see vampires?

- Listen, said the pale lady with a strange solemnity, since everyone here has told a story, I want to tell one too. Doctor, you will not say that the story is not true, it is mine. You will know why I am so pale.

At that moment, a ray of moon slipped through the window through the curtains, and, coming to play on the sofa where she was lying, enveloped her with a bluish light which seemed to make her a statue of reclining black marble on a tomb.

No voice welcomed the proposal; but the deep silence that reigned in the living room announced that everyone was waiting with anxiety.

Chapter Twelve: The Carpathian Mountains

J am Polish, born in Sandomir, that is to say, in a country where legends become articles of faith, where we believe in our family traditions as much as, perhaps more so than in the Gospel. There is not one of our castles that doesn't have its ghost, nor a cottage that does not have a familiar spirit. In the rich as in the poor, in the castle as in the little country house, one recognizes the principle of friends as much as that of enemies. Sometimes, these two principles go into battle and fight. So, there are such mysterious noises in the corridors, such appalling roars in the old towers, such frightening tremors in the walls, that one flees from the cottage as from the castle, and that makes peasants or gentlemen run to the church looking for the blessed cross or the holy relics of the saints, the only preservatives against the demons that torment us.

But there are two even more terrible, more bitter, more implacable principles at battle in our presence – those of tyranny and freedom.

The year 1825 saw one of these struggles between Russia and Poland, in which one would think that all the blood of a people was spilled, as often as the blood of all one's family.

My father and two brothers had risen against the new Tsar and had gone to take up arms under the flag of Polish independence, always cast down, ever raised.

One day, I learned that my younger brother had been killed; on another day, I was informed that my older brother had died from his wounds; finally, after a tense period when I listened with terror to the sound of the approaching guns, I saw my father arrive with a hundred riders, the remnants of a three thousand he commanded.

He came to seal himself in our castle, with the intention to be buried under its ruins. My father, who feared nothing for himself, trembled for me. Indeed, my father was only too prepared for death, because he was sure he would not let himself be taken alive by his enemies, but for me, he expected slavery, dishonor, shame. Among the hundred or so of his men left, he chose ten, summoned the steward and gave him all the gold and jewelry we had. He remembered that during the second partition of Poland, my mother, still a child, had found safe refuge in the monastery of Sahastru, located in the middle of the Carpathian Mountains.

He ordered the steward to lead me to this monastery, which, hospitable to the mother, would be no less hospitable, not doubt, to the daughter. Despite the great love my father had for me, the farewells were not long. In all probability, the Russians would be in sight of the castle by the next day, so there was no time to lose.

I hastily dressed like an Amazon, as I used to when I accompanied my brothers on the hunt. The grooms saddled the surest horse of the stable. My father slipped me his own cherished pistols, masterpieces manufactured by Toula, kissed me, and ordered us to depart.

During the night and the next day, we made twenty leagues following the banks of one of those unnamed rivers that falls into the Vistula. This first step, at double pace, had put us out of reach of the Russians.

In the last rays of the sun, we saw the snowy peaks of the Carpathians sparkle. Towards sunset, the next day, we reached their base. Finally, on the morning of the third day, we began our ascent through one of the deep gorges.

Our Carpathian Mountains are not like the civilized mountains of your Western lands. All that is strange and grandiose in nature is displayed in its most complete majesty. Their stormy peaks are lost in the clouds, covered with eternal snow. Their immense forests of fir trees reflect on the polished mirrors of lakes vast as seas, and scarcely have they been crisscrossed by a gondola, nor their crystal waters, deep as the azure of the sky, been disturbed by fishing nets. The human voice might ring out from time to time, a Moldovan song heard for miles, to which the cries of wild animals respond. The sound might awaken a solitary human echo, amazed that any other might breach his own existence.

For many miles, we traveled under dark wood arches cut through unexpected wonders revealed in each step, and which moved our minds from astonishment to admiration. Danger was everywhere, and multiplied a thousand different ways, but there was no time to be afraid – these dangers were so sublime. Sometimes, they were waterfalls improvised by the melting of the ice, which leaping from rock to rock, suddenly invade the narrow path we followed, a path traced by the passage of the wild beast and the pursuing hunter. Sometimes, it was trees weakened over time which detached themselves from the ground and fell with a terrible crash as if it were an earthquake. Sometimes, finally, it was storms enveloping us in clouds in the midst of which we saw, gushing out, lengthening, and twisting, lightning, like a fiery serpent.

Then, after these alpine peaks, after these primitive forests, like the giant mountains and endless woods, we had endless steppes, land seas with their waves and storms, arid and bumpy savannas where the view was lost in a boundless horizon. Then it was no longer terror that gripped us, but a flood of sadness. It was a vast and deep melancholy from which nothing could distract because the aspect of the country was the same, as far as one's gaze could extend. You go up and down slopes twenty times, vainly seeking a path, but you are still lost in isolation. As if amidst the deserts, you think you are alone, and your melancholy becomes desolation. Indeed, walking seems to have become a useless task, which will lead to nothing; you do not come across a village, a castle, or a cottage – there is no trace of human habitation. Sometimes, like one more sad sight in this bleak landscape, a small lake without reeds, without bushes, silent at the bottom of a ravine like another Dead Sea, blocks the path with its green waters, above which rise, as you approach, some aquatic birds with prolonged and discordant cries.

Then you make a detour; you climb the hill in front of you, you descend into another valley, then another hill, and it lasts like this until you have exhausted the chain of fleece, ever descending. If you make a turn towards the south, the landscape once again becomes imposing – there is a range of higher mountains, of picturesque form and richer aspect. These are covered in forests, dappled with streams, providing shade and water. Life is reborn in this landscape – we hear the bells of a hermitage; we see a caravan meandering on the side of some mountain. Finally, by the last rays of the sun, we are able to distinguish, like a band of white birds huddled together, the houses of a few small villages which seem to have grouped together to protect themselves from some nocturnal attack; for, with life, danger has returned, and it is no longer, as in the first mountains we crossed, bands of bears and wolves we must fear, but hordes of Moldovan brigands.

However, we were approaching our destination. Ten days of walking had passed without incident. We could already see the summit of Mount Pion, which overhangs this family of giants, and on the southern slope of which was the convent of Sahastru, where I was headed.

Three days more, and we had arrived.

It was the end of July, the day had been hot, and it was unparalleled pleasure that, around four o'clock, we started to savor the first freshness of the evening breeze. We had passed the ruined towers of Niantzo. We went down towards a plain which we began to glimpse through the opening of the mountains. We could already, from where we were, follow the course of the Bistriza, with its shores enameled with red affraine[36] trees and large white bellflowers. We crossed a precipice at the bottom of which the river flowed, at that point, only a torrent. At this stage, we could walk past only two at a time.

Our guide preceded us, leaning on his horse to one side, singing a Morlach[37] song, with monotonous modulations, and whose words I followed with singular interest. The singer was at the same time a poet. He had the air of one of those mountain men who expressed themselves in wild sadness and somber simplicity.

Here are the lyrics to his song:

In the swamp of Stavila,
Where so much warrior blood flowed,
Do you see that corpse?
He is not a son of Illyria[38];
He is a robber filled with fury
Who, deceiving the sweet Marie,
Exterminated, deceived, burned,
Striking a bullet in the brigand's heart,

---

[36] African?
[37] A Vlach pastoralist community in the mountains of Croatia, across the Venetian-Ottoman border, often referred to as the Black Latins or Black Wallachians, were epic singers, and used a single stringed instrument called the gusle.
38 Region in the western part of the Balkan Peninsula inhabited by numerous tribes of people collectively known as the Illyrians.

Like a hurricane,
In his throat is a yatagan[39],
But for three days, oh mystery!
Under the dreary and lonely pine,
His hot blood watered the earth,
And darkened the pale Ovigan.
His blue eyes will never leave him,
Let's all flee, woe to he
Who goes to the swamp near him
He is a vampire! The tan wolf,
Far from the impure corpse flees,
And on the bald mountain,
The funeral vulture does leave.

Suddenly, the detonation of a firearm was heard, a ball hissed in the air. The song stopped abruptly and the guide, shot to death, went tumbling to the bottom of the precipice, while his horse stopped midstep, quivering, stretching out his intelligent nose towards the bottom of the abyss where his master had disappeared.

At the same time, a great cry arose, and we saw thirty bandits rise up on both sides of the mountain. We were completely surrounded. Each one of us seized their weapons, and although taken unexpectedly, these were old soldiers used to gunfire, and were not intimidated, retaliating at once. I, setting an example myself, grabbed a gun and feeling the disadvantage of the position, shouted 'Forward!' and prodded my horse, who galloped away in the direction of the plain.

But, we were dealing with mountainfolk, leaping from rock to rock like real demons of the abyss, firing, while leaping, always keeping us to the side of their guns. Besides, the maneuver had been well planned. At a place where the path widened and the mountain made a small plateau, a young man was waiting for us at the head of a dozen mounted men. When they saw us, they turned their galloping mounts, and came to strike us from the front, while those who were chasing us let the sides of the mountain roar, and having cut off our retreat, enveloped us from all sides.

---

[39] A type of Ottoman knife or short sabre

The situation was serious and yet, accustomed from childhood to scenes of war, I could consider it in its entirety without losing a single detail.

All these men, dressed in sheepskin, wore huge round hats crowned with flowers, like the Hungarians. They each had a long Turkish rifle in their hand, which they waved after firing, uttering wild cries, and at their belts, they had a curved saber and a pair of pistols.

Their leader was a young man, barely twenty-two years old, with a pale complexion, dark black eyes and curly hair falling on his shoulders. His costume was the Moldavian dress trimmed with furs and tightened at the waist by a scarf with gold and silk bands. A curved saber shone in his hand, and four pistols sparkled on his belt. During the combat, he uttered raucous and inarticulate cries which seemed to not belong to any human language, yet nevertheless expressed his wishes, because his men obeyed them, throwing themselves to the ground to avoid the discharges of our soldiers, standing up to fire in turn, slaughtering those who were still standing, finishing off the wounded, and finally turning the fight into butchery.

I saw two-thirds of my defenders fall one after the other. Four were still standing, huddled around me, not asking for a pardon that they were certain they would be denied, and thinking only how they might sell their lives as dearly as possible.

Then, the young chief uttered a more expressive cry than before, extending the point of his saber towards us. No doubt this order was to surround us with a circle of fire, and to shoot us all together, because the long Moldovan muskets lowered in one movement.

I understood our last hour had come. I raised my eyes and my hands to heaven with a last silent prayer and awaited death.

At this moment, I saw, not descending, but rushing, leaping from rock to rock, a young man, who stopped, standing on a stone dominating the whole scene, like a statue on a pedestal, and who, stretching out his hand to the battlefield, said only one word: "Enough."

At that voice, all eyes rose, each appeared to obey this new master. One solitary bandit replaced his rifle on his shoulder and let loose a volley. One of our men cried out – the bullet had broken his left arm.

He immediately turned to charge on the man who had injured him, but before had taken four steps, a lightning bolt flashed above our heads, and the rebel bandit rolled to the ground, his head smashed by a bullet.

The shock of so many diverse emotions had driven me to the end of my strength, and I passed out. When I came to, I was lying on the grass, my head resting on the knees of a man, whose white hand covered with rings was around my waist, while standing before me, arms crossed, saber under one of his arms, stood the young Moldovan chief who had led the attack on us.

"Kostaki," the man supporting me said in French, with an authoritative tone, "have your men withdraw immediately and leave me be to care for this young woman."

"My brother, my brother," replied the one to whom these words were addressed and who seemed to restrain himself with difficulty, "my brother, take care not to tire my patience. I leave you the castle, pray leave the forest to me. At the castle, you are the master, but here I am all powerful. Here, one word would be enough to force you to obey me."

"Kostaki, I am the eldest – that is to say, I am the master everywhere, in the forest as well in the castle, there as here. Oh! I'm on Brankovan blood like you, royal blood used to command, and I do command!"

"You, Grégoriska, command you valets, yes – my soldiers, you do not."

"Your soldiers are brigands, Kostaki – brigands whom I will hang in the battlements of our towers, if they don't immediately obey me!"

"Well! So try to order them!"

Then, I felt the man supporting me withdrawing his knee and laying my head gently on a stone. I looked at him anxiously and I saw the young man who had fallen, so to speak, out of the sky, and only glimpsed, having passed out as soon as he halted the conflict.

He was a young man, about twenty-four years old, tall, with big blue eyes in which one saw a singular resolution and firmness. His long blond hair, one indication of his Slavic heritage, fell on his shoulders like that of the Archangel Michael, framing young and fresh cheeks. His lips were raised with a disdainful smile and revealed a double row of pearls. His gaze was eagle-like and sharp. He was dressed in a sort of black velvet tunic, with a small cap like that of Raphael adorned with a single eagle feather. He had on pantaloons and embroidered boots. His waist was tightened with a belt holding a hunting knife and he was carrying a small twin-barreled rifle, whose accuracy had been attested to by one of the bandits.

He stretched out his hand and that extended hand appeared to command his brother. He said a few words in the Moldovan language, which seemed to make a deep impression on the bandits.

Then, in the same language, the young chief spoke in his turn to the elder, and I guessed that his words were mixed with threats and imprecations. But, in this long and boisterous speech, the elder answered with only one word and the bandits bowed their heads at this point.

"Well then," Grégoriska said to Kostaki in French, "This will not go to the cave, but she will be mine no less. I find her beautiful, I have conquered her, and I want her."

Saying these words, he threw himself on me and took me in his arms.

"This woman will be taken to the castle and handed over to my mother, and I will not leave her until then," replied my protector.

"My horse!" cried Kostaki in Moldovan.

Ten bandits hastened to obey and brought horses for him to choose from. Grégoriska looked around, grabbed a horse by the bridle and leapt on it without touching the stirrups.

Kostaki got onto his horse almost as lightly as his brother, although he still held me in his arms, and started off at a gallop.

Grégoriska's horse appeared to have received the same impulse, and kept pace with Kostaki's horse, neck, and flank at par. It was a curious sight to see these two riders flying side by side, dark, silent, and not losing a moment of attention. The two did not seem to be looking at each other, surrendering to their horses whose desperate race took them over woods, rocks, and precipices.

My head tilted, allowing me to see the beautiful eyes of Grégoriska fixed on mine. Kostaki noticed it too, I looked up at him and saw only his dark gaze devouring me. I lowered my eyelids, but it was useless. Through their veil, I continued to see that haunting look which penetrated to the bottom of chest and pierced my heart. Then, a strange hallucination took hold of me. I seemed to be the Lenore of Burger's ballad[40], carried away

---

[40] A poem by German author Gottfried August Bürger in 1844, in which a ghostly rider, who Lenore believes to be her dead lover, carries her away on a ghostly ride through the night, at the end of which

by the ghost horse and rider, and when I felt we had stopped, it was only with terror that I opened my eyes. I was convinced I would see around me only broken crosses and open graves. What I saw was hardly more cheerful – it was the open courtyard of a Moldovan castle built in the fourteenth century.

---

the rider is revealed to be Death himself – 'a scythe and a sandglass the skeleton bore.'

Chapter Thirteen: The Castle of Brankovan

*K*ostaki let me slide from his arms to the ground and almost immediately glided down next to me, but as rapidly as he had done so, he had not matched Grégoriska's speed. As Grégoriska had said, at the castle, he was indeed the master.

Seeing the abrupt arrival of the two young men and the strange foreigner they brought with them, the servants ran up to help, and although they shared their attention to both Kostaki and Grégoriska, one sensed that the greatest regards, the deepest respects were for the latter.

Two women approached. Grégoriska gave them an order in Moldavan and signed to me with his hand to follow them.

There was so much respect in the look that accompanied this sign that I did not hesitate to comply. Five minutes later, I was in a room, which, bare and uninhabitable as it might have seemed to anyone, was obviously the most beautiful of the castle.

It was a large square room, with a green serge couch that served as a daytime seat and bed for the night. There were five or six large oak armchairs, one wide sideboard, and in one of the corners, a canopy like a grand and magnificent church stall. Curtains were hung from the windows to the bed.

We went up to this room by a staircase, where three Brankovan statues stood in niches, larger than life. The luggage was delivered to the room after a few moments, in the middle of which I found my trunks. The women offered me their services, but while fixing the mess these events had made of my condition, I retained the Amazon costume, seeing it to be more suitable with my hosts than any other I could have chosen.

Hardly had I completed these minor cosmetic adjustments, than I heard gentle knocking on my door.

"Come in," I said in French, naturally, as French was almost a mother tongue for the rest of us Polish folk, as you know.

Grégoriska entered.

"Ah! Madam, I'm glad you speak French."

"And me too, sir," I replied. "I'm happy to speak this language since I can thus appreciate your generous conduct towards me. It was in this language that you defended me against the designs of your brother, and so I offer the expression of my sincere gratitude in the same language."

"Thank you, my lady. It was very simply because I was interested in a woman in the position that you were. I was hunting in the mountains when I heard continuous irregular detonations. I understood that an armed attack was underway, and I marched on the fire, as we say in military terms. I arrived just in time, thank heavens, but will you kindly inform me, madam, by what chance has a woman of distinction like you ventured into our mountains?

"I am Polish, sir," I replied. "My two brothers were just killed in the war with Russia. My father chose to make his final stand defending our castle when I left, and the battle has probably been joined at this time. On my father's orders, fleeing all these massacres, I came to seek refuge at the monastery of Sahastru, where my mother, in her youth and in similar circumstances, had found safe asylum in the past."

"You are an enemy of the Russians; so much better," said the young man. "This news will be an enormous aid to the castle, and we need all our strength to support the fight which is being prepared for. First, since I know who you are, you should know, madam, who we are. The name of Brankovan is not foreign to you, is it, my lady?"

I bowed.

"My mother is the last princess of this name, the last descendant of the illustrious chief that had the Cantimir, those wretched courtiers killed by Peter I. My mother was married to my father, Serban Waivady, a prince like her, but of a less illustrious lineage."

"My father had been brought up in Vienna; he could appreciate the advantages of civilization. He resolved to make me a European. We left on a trip to France, Italy, Spain, and Germany."

"During my father's early trips, when I was still a child, my mother had certain guilty relationships with a partisan leader (no, not a son, I know that to tell you what I am about to say, for our salvation, you must appreciate this revelation). As I was saying, mother had relations with a count of the partisans, that is the way the men who attacked you are called in this country. This Count Giordaki Koproli, was half Greek, half Moldovan. She wrote to my father to tell him everything and ask him for a divorce, saying in this letter that she did not want a Brankovan princess to remain the wife of a man who made himself day by day more foreign to his country."

"Alas! My father did not see fit to consent to this request, which can seem strange to you, but which, to us, is the most common and natural thing. "

"In truth, my father had just died of an aneurysm which he had suffered from for a long time, and it was I who had received the letter."

"I had nothing to do, except express sincere good wishes for the happiness of my mother. These wishes were included in a letter from me, which also announced to her that she was a widow."

"This same letter asked her to grant me the permission to continue my travels, which was granted to me."

"My intention was to settle in France or Germany, so as to not be faced with a man who hated me, and who I could not love, that is to say, my mother's husband, when I suddenly learned that Count Giordaki Koproli had been assassinated, it was said, by my father's ancient Cossacks."

"I hastened to return; I loved my mother, I understood her isolation, her need to have around her, at such a time, the people who were dear to her heart. Without her ever having expressed such a tender love for me, I was nevertheless her son. I returned one morning, without being expected to the castle of our fathers."

"I found there a young man whom I first mistook for a stranger, and who I later learned was my brother."

"This was Kostaki, the son of adultery, which a second marriage had legitimized. Kostaki, that is to say, the indomitable creature that you have met, whose passions are the only law he obeys, and for whom nothing is more sacred in this world than my mother; who obeys me like the tiger obeys the arm which tamed him, with an eternal roar fueled by the vague hope of devouring me one day."

"In the interior of the castle, in the home of the Brankovans and the Waivadys, I am still the master, but once outside this enclosure, once in the middle of the countryside, he again becomes the savage child of the woods and the mountains, who wants to bend everything under his iron will."

"Why did he give in today? Why did his men give in? I do not know – an old habit, a remnant of respect, perhaps, but I would not want to hazard another test. Stay here, don't leave this room, this courtyard. Inside the walls, I answer for everything; a step outside the castle, I answer for nothing more than to be killed to defend you."

"Could I not therefore, according to the wishes of my father, continue my journey towards the convent of Sahastru?" I asked my protector.

"You can try, just order me and I will accompany you, but I will stay on the road, and you, you… you won't arrive."

"What should I do then?"

"Stay here, wait, watch events as they occur and take advantage of the circumstances. Tell yourself you have fallen into a den of bandits, and your courage alone can get you out of trouble; that your composure alone can save you."

"My mother, despite her preference for Kostaki, her lover's son, is good and generous. Besides, she is a Brankovan, that is to say, a true princess. You will see it; she will defend you from the brutal passions of Kostaki. Put yourself under her protection. You are beautiful – she will love you."

"Besides," (he looked at me with an indefinable expression), "who could see you and not love you?"

"Now, come to the supper chamber, where she is waiting for us. Do not show any embarrassment or distrust. Speak in Polish – nobody knows this language here. I will translate your words to my mother, and rest assured, I will only say what you say. Above all, not a word on what I have just revealed to you – no one should suspect that we get along with each other. You must still ignore the ruse and the dissimulation of the sincerest of us."

"Now, come."

I followed him down the staircase, lit by resin torches burning in iron hands which came out of the walls. It was obvious that it was for me that they had placed this unusual illumination.

We arrived in the dining room. As soon as Grégoriska opened the door, and in Moldovan, said a word that I knew, yet feigned it foreign, a tall woman came towards us.

It was the Princess Brankovan.

She wore her white hair braided around her head; she was wearing a little sable hat, topped with an egret, a testimony of her princely origin. She wore a kind of gold tunic, with a bodice strewn with jewels, covering a long Turkish dress, trimmed with fur like the hat.

She was holding a rosary of amber beads in her hand, which she quickly rolled between her fingers. Beside her was Kostaki, wearing the splendid and majestic Magyar costume, in which he seemed to me stranger still than he had before.

He had on a green velvet dress, with wide sleeves, falling below the knee, with red cashmere pants and gold embroidered morocco slippers. His head was uncovered, and his long hair, deepest black appearing almost blue, fell on his naked neck, which was set against the light white thread of a silk shirt.

He greeted me awkwardly and said a few words in Moldavian which remained unintelligible to me.

"You can speak French, my brother," said Grégoriska. "Madam is Polish and understands French."

So, Kostaki pronounced a few words in French almost as intelligible to me as those he had said in Moldovan, but the mother, gravely extending her arm, interrupted them. It was obvious to me that she was telling her son that it was she would receive me.

She started a speech in Moldavan of welcome, which her physiognomy expressed quite clearly. She showed me the table, offered me a seat near her, gestured to the whole house, as if to tell me that it was all for me, and sitting first with a benevolent dignity, she made the sign of the cross and began a prayer.

So, everyone took their place, marked by etiquette. Grégoriska was near me. I was the foreigner, and therefore was established in a place of honor for Kostaki, near his mother Smérande, for that was the princess' name. Grégoriska, too, had changed his costume. He wore the Magyar tunic like his brother, only his was of velvet garnet and he had on blue cashmere pants. A beautiful decoration was hanging around his neck – it was the Nisham or seal of Sultan Mahmoud.

The rest of the usual house guests supped at the same table, each sitting at their place by the rank given by their position among friends or servants.

The supper was sad; not once did Kostaki speak to me, although his brother encouraged him often to speak with me in French. As for the mother, she offered me everything herself with that solemn air that never left her. Grégoriska has said the truth – she was a real princess.

After supper, Grégoriska walked over to his mother. He explained to her in Moldovan the need I had to be alone, and how much rest I needed after such an emotional day. Smérande nodded her approval, held her hand out to me, kissed my forehead as she would have done with her daughter, and wished me a good night in her castle.

Grégoriska was not mistaken – I longed for a moment of solitude. So I thanked the princess, who came to escort me to the door, where the two women who had led me to the room earlier were waiting for me.

I acknowledged the princess and her two sons and returned to the same apartment I had left an hour before. The sofa had become a bed. This was the only change that had taken place in my absence.

I thanked the women and signaled to them that I would undress alone. They went out immediately with expressions of respect which indicated they had orders to obey me in all things.

I stayed in this huge room, dimly lit by my candle which illuminated only the parts I moved through without ever being able to brighten the whole room. There was a singular play of light, as if there was a battle between the glow of my candle and the rays of the moon, which passed by my bare window.

Besides the door by which I had entered, and which gave on to the staircase, two other doors opened into my room, but huge locks placed on them, closed from my side, were enough to reassure me that I was safe for the night.

I went to the front door of the room. This door, like the others, was well defended.

I opened my window and saw that it overlooked a precipice.

I understood that Grégoriska had made a thoughtful choice in selecting this room for me.

Finally, on returning to my sofa, I found a small folded note on a table placed by my bedside. I opened it and read in Polish:

"Sleep easy — you will have nothing to fear as long as you stay inside the castle. GRÉGORISKA"

I followed the advice I was given, and tiredness outweighing my concerns, I went to bed and fell asleep.

Chapter Fourteen: The Two Brothers

$\mathcal{F}$rom that moment on, I was established in the castle, and from the same moment, began the drama that I will recount to you.

The two brothers both fell in love with me, each with the nuances of his character on display. Kostaki, the next day, told me that he loved me, declared I would be his and not any other's, and that he would kill me rather than let me belong to anyone else.

Grégoriska said nothing, but he surrounded me with care and attention. All the resources of a brilliant education, all the memories of a youth passed in the most noble courts of Europe were used to please me. Alas! It was not difficult – at the first sound of his voice, I felt that it caressed my soul. At the first glance of his eyes, I felt as if it penetrated my heart.

After three months, Kostaki had told me a hundred time that he loved me, and I hated him; after three months, Grégoriska had not yet said a word of love to me, however I felt that when he expected it, I would be all his.

Kostaki had given up hunting and racing. He never left the castle. He had abdicated temporarily in favor of a lieutenant, who, from time to time, came to ask him for his orders, and then disappeared.

Smérande also loved me with a passionate friendship, the expression of which frightened me. She visibly protected Kostaki and seemed to be more jealous of me than he was himself. Only, as she neither understood Polish nor French, and I did not understand Moldavan, she could not make express requests in favor of her son, but she had learned to say in French three words, which she kept saying to me every time her lips landed on my forehead: *"Kostaki loves Hedwige."*

One day, I learned of terrible news which came to make the worst of my misfortunes. Freedom had been restored to the four men who had survived the conflict where I had been brought to the castle. They had left for Poland, pledging their word that one of them would come back, before three months had passed, to give me news of my father.

One of them reappeared, indeed, one morning. Our castle had been taken, burned and razed, and my father was killed, defending it.

I was now alone in the world.

Kostaki redoubled his attention, and Smérande her tenderness, but this time, I pretended to mourn my father. Kostaki insisted, saying that the more I was isolated, the more I needed support. His mother agreed with him and insisted too, perhaps even more so. Grégoriska had told me about this power that Moldovans have over themselves when they don't want their feelings to be read by others. He was a living example of this himself. It was impossible to be more certain of the love of a man than I was of his, and yet, if I were asked on what evidence I based this certainty, it would have been difficult to say; no one in the castle had seen his hand touch mine, nor his eyes look for mine. Only Kostaki could shed light on this rivalry as my love alone could enlighten me on this love.

I admit, however, that Grégoriska's power over himself worried me. I believed in him certainly, but it was not enough. I yearned to be convinced, when, one evening, as I had just returned to my room, I heard a soft knock on one of the doors I had described as locked from within. From the gentleness of the knock, I guessed it was that of a friend. I walked over and asked who was there.

"Grégoriska," replied a voice, in which there was no danger that I was mistaken.

"What do you want from me?" I asked him, trembling.

"If you trust me," said Grégoriska, "if you believe me to be a man of honor, grant me my request."

"What is it?"

"Extinguish your light, as if you were in bed, and, in half an hour, open your door for me."

"Come back in half an hour," was my only answer.

I blew out my candle and waited.

My heart was beating violently because I understood that this was something important.

Half an hour passed; I heard a knock softer than the first time. In the meantime, I had pulled open the locks, so I only had to open the door.

Grégoriska entered, and without even asking me, pushed the door shut behind him and locked it.

He remained mute and motionless for a moment, imposing silence on the scene. Then, when he was assured that no urgent danger was threating us, he took me into the middle of the large room and sensing from my trembling that I could stand no longer, he fetched me a chair. I sat down, or rather, I fell into the chair.

"Oh! My God!" I said to him, "what is it then and why have you taken so many precautions?"

"Because my life would be worth naught, and yours too, based on the conversation we are going to have if we were found out."

I took his hand, all frightened. He brought my hand to his lips, while looking at me to ask forgiveness for such daring. I looked down: it was consent.

"I love you," he said to me in his melodious voice like a song, "do you love me?"

"Yes," I replied.

"Would you consent to be my wife?"

"Yes."

He ran his hand over his forehead with a deep aspiration of happiness.

"So you won't refuse to follow me?"

"I will follow you everywhere!"

"Because I want you to understand," he continued, "that we can only be happy by fleeing from here."

"Oh yes!" I cried, "Let's run away!"

"Silence!" he said, trembling, "silence!"

"You are right."

I drew closer to him, trembling.

"This is what I have done," he said to me, "this is why it has taken so long before I could confess that I love you. I wanted to ensure, once confident of your love, that nothing could stand in the way of our union. I am rich, Hedwige, immensely rich, but in the manner of the Moldavan lords – rich with lands, herds, serfs."

"Well, I have sold to the monastery of Hango for a million francs my lands, herds, villages. They have given me three hundred thousand francs in precious stones, one hundred thousand francs in gold, and the rest in bills of exchange at Vienna. Will a million be enough for you?"

I took his hand in mine.

"Your love would have been enough, Grégoriska."

"Well! Listen – tomorrow, I am going to the monastery of Hango to make my final arrangements with the superior. He is keeping horses ready for us. These horses will be waiting for us at nine o'clock, hidden a hundred paces from the castle."

"After supper, go back up to your room as you did today, then turn off your light, and like today, I will come to your room. But tomorrow, instead of going out alone, you will follow me, we will reach the door that opens into the countryside, find our horses, run like the wind, and the day after tomorrow, in one day, we will have traveled thirty leagues."

"What are we to do until the day after tomorrow?"

"Dear Hedwige!"

Grégoriska pressed me to his chest, our lips met.

Oh! He had said it well – he was an honorable man to whom I had opened the door of my room, but he understood it well: if I did not belong to him in body, I belonged to him in soul.

The night went by without my being able to sleep for a moment.

I saw myself fleeing with Grégoriska. I felt myself carried away by him as I had been by Kostaki! Only this time, the race, which was earlier terrible, scary, funereal, had changed into a sweet and lovely embrace at which speed added pleasure, because speed had a voluptuousness to itself.

The day came.

I went down to the common area of the castle. It seemed to me that there was something even darker than usual in the way Kostaki greeted me. His smile was not more ironic; it was a threat. As for Smérande, she seemed to me the same as ever.

During lunch, Grégoriska ordered his horse to be made ready. Kostaki did not seem to care about this order. Around eleven o'clock, Grégoriska greeted us, announcing he would be back by evening, and prayed to his mother to not wait for him to have her dinner; then, turning to me, he asked me, in turn, to accept his apologies and he left. His brother's eye followed him until he had left the room, and at the same time, there spurted from that eye such a flash of hatred that I shivered.

The day passed almost in the midst of a trance. I had not told anyone about our plans; hardly even in my prayers, if I had even dared to speak to God about it, and it seemed to me that these projects were known to everyone; that every glance that fixed itself on me could penetrate and read what lay at the bottom of my heart.

Dinner was a dark and taciturn torment, Kostaki rarely spoke; this evening, he just spoke to his mother in Moldavan two or three times and each time the accent of his voice gave me a start.

When I got up to go back to my room, Smérande, as usual, kissed me and while doing so, she said to me this sentence, which for eight days, I had not heard come out of her mouth:

"Kostaki loves Hedwige."

This sentence pursued me menacingly. Once in my room, it seemed to me that a fatal voice whispered in my ear: *Kostaki loves Hedwige!*

Well, Kostaki's love, Grégoriska had told me, was death.

Around seven in the evening, and as the sun began to set, I saw Kostaki cross the courtyard. He turned to look at me, but I pulled myself back so that he could not see me.

I was worried, because, as long as my position at the window allowed me to follow him, I had seen him walking towards the stables. I ventured to pull the locks on my door and slip into the next room, from where I could see everything that he was going to do.

Indeed, he went to the stables. He took his favorite horse out himself, got it ready with his own hands and with the care of a man who attaches the greatest importance to the smallest details. He had on the same suit in which he had appeared to me for the first time. Only, for his weapon, he carried only his saber. His horse saddled, he cast his eyes again a few times towards my bedroom window. Then not seeing me, he jumped in the saddle, took the same door by which his brother had gone and would return, and galloped away, in the direction of the monastery of Hango.

My heart sank in a terrible way. I had aa fatal feeling told me that Kostaki was going to meet his brother. I stayed at this window as long as I could distinguish the road, which, a quarter of a league from the castle, bent and got lost in the beginning of a forest. As the night got darker every moment, the road eventually faded completely.

I stayed still.

Finally my concern, by its very excess, gave me back my strength, and, as it was obviously in the downstairs room I had to be in order to get the first news from either of the two brothers, I went down.

My first look was for Smérande. I saw, by the calmness of her face, for she never felt any apprehension, that she was giving her orders for the usual supper, and the cutlery of both brothers was in their places.

I dared not question anyone. Besides, who would I have questioned? No one at the castle, except Kostaki and Grégoriska, did not speak either of languages I spoke.

At the slightest noise I started.

It was usually nine o'clock that we met, and the table was laid for supper. I had come down at half past eight; I followed the minute hand with my eyes, its every step was almost visible on the large dial of the clock.

The traveling needle crossed the quarter mark and the bell tolled once. The vibration sounded dark and sad, then the needle resumed its silent walk, and I saw her again walk the distance with the regularity and the slowness of a compass point.

A few minutes before nine o'clock, I seemed to hear the gallop of a horse in the court. Smérande heard it too, because she turned her head to the side of the window; but the night was too thick for her to see too far into the darkness.

Oh ! if she had looked at me right now, she could have guessed what was going on in my heart!

We only heard the trotting of one horse; and it was remarkably simple. I knew well, me, that there would only be one rider.

But which one?

Footsteps echoed in the anteroom. These were not slow and seemed to weigh on my heart.

The door opened. I held my breath as a shadow was visible. This shadow stopped for a moment at the door.

My heart was suspended.

The shadow moved forward, and gradually as it entered the circle of light, I began breathing.

I recognized Grégoriska.

One more moment of pain, and my heart broke.

I recognized Grégoriska, but pale like a dead man. Just by looking at it, you could guess that something terrible had just happened.

"Is it you, Kostaki?" asked Smérande.

"No, mother," replied Grégoriska in a low voice.

"Ah! there you are," she said, "and since when should your mother wait for you?"

"Dear mother," said Grégoriska, glancing at the clock, "it is only nine o'clock." And, at the same time, indeed, the clock tolled nine times.

"It's true," said Smérande. "Where is your brother?"

In spite of myself, I thought it was the same question God had asked Cain.

Grégoriska did not reply.

"Has anyone seen Kostaki?" asked Smérande.

The vatar, or butler, inquired about him.

"At about seven o'clock," said he, "the count went to the stables, saddled his horse himself, and left by the road to Hango."

At that moment, my eyes met the eyes of Grégoriska. I do not know if it was a reality or a hallucination, it seemed to me that he had a drop of blood in the middle of the forehead.

I slowly put my finger to my own forehead, indicating where I thought I saw the stain.

Grégoriska understood me; he took his handkerchief and wiped himself.

"Yes, yes," murmured Smérande, "he will have met some bear, some wolf, whom he will have fun chasing. This is why a child keeps his mother waiting. Where did you leave him, Grégoriska? Tell me."

"Mother," replied Grégoriska in a touched but confident voice, "my brother and I did not go out together."

"That's good," said Smérande. "Let's have supper served, sit at the table and close the doors; those who are outside will sleep outside."

The first two parts of this order were carried out to the letter. Smérande took her place, Grégoriska sat on her right and I sat on her left. Then the servants went out to complete the third, that is, to close the doors of the castle.

At this moment, we heard a great noise in the courtyard and a bewildered valet entered the room saying:

"Princess, Count Kostaki's horse has just entered the courtyard, alone and covered in blood!"

"Oh!" murmured Smérande, standing up pale and grim, "that is how his father's horse came home one evening."

I looked at Grégoriska: he was no longer pale, he was livid.

In fact, Count Koproli's horse had returned one evening to the castle courtyard, all covered in blood, and an hour later the servants had found and brought back the body covered with wounds.

Smérande took a torch from one of the valets, walked towards the door, opened it, and went down into the courtyard.

The dismayed horse was contained in spite of itself by the three or four servants who joined forces to calm it.

Smérande walked towards the animal, looked at the blood staining his saddle, and recognized a wound on the top of its forehead.

"Kostaki was killed face to face," she said, "in a duel, and by a single enemy. Look for his body, children, later we will look for the murderer."

As the horse had returned by the door of Hango, all the servants rushed through this door, and we saw their torches go astray in the countryside and sink into the forest, as, in a beautiful summer evening, we see fireflies sparkle in the plains of Nice and Pisa.

Smérande, as if she had been convinced that the search would not be long, waited, standing at the door.

Not a tear streamed from the eyes of this desolate mother and yet one felt the rumble of despair deep in her heart. Grégoriska was standing behind her, and I was near Grégoriska.

When he left the room for a moment, it appeared he intended to offer me his arm, but he hadn't dared.

About a quarter of an hour later, at the turn of the road, we saw a torch, then two, then all the torches. Only this time, instead of scattering in the countryside, they were massed around a common center.

It was soon evident that this common center consisted of a litter and a man lying on that litter. The funeral procession was advancing slowly, but it was advancing. After ten minutes, it was at the door. When they saw the living mother who was waiting for the dead son, those who carried him discovered their instincts, then they entered the courtyard silently.

Smérande followed them, and we followed Smérande. We thus reached the great hall, in which the body was deposited. Then, making a gesture of supreme majesty, Smérande pushed everyone aside, and, approaching the corpse, she put one knee in front of him, parted the hair which made a veil on his face, contemplated it for a long time, dry eyes still, then, opening the Moldovan robe, parted the bloodstained shirt. The wound was on the right side of the chest.

It must have been made by a straight, cutting blade on both sides. I remembered having seen the same day, next to Grégoriska, the long hunting knife which served as a bayonet for his rifle. I looked at his side for this weapon; but she was gone.

Smérande asked for water, soaked her handkerchief in this water and washed the wound. Fresh, pure blood gushed from the lips of the wound. The show I had before me presented something excruciating and sublime at the same time. This vast room, smoked by resin torches, these barbaric faces, these eyes shining with ferocity, these strange costumes, this mother who calculated, at the sight of the blood still warm, how long it had been since death had taken her son, this great silence interrupted only by the sobs of these brigands of which Kostaki was the chief, all this, I repeat, was excruciating and sublime to see.

Finally Smérande brought her lips to her son's forehead, then stood up, then threw back the long braids of his white hair that had unfolded.

"Grégoriska!" she said, in a clear, still voice.

Grégoriska started, shook his head, and emerging from his dullness: "Mother?" he replied.

"Come here, son, and listen to me."

Grégoriska obeyed with a shudder, but he obeyed. As he approached the body, the blood, more abundant and ruddier, came out of the wound. Fortunately, Smérande was no longer looking that way, because, at the sight of this accusing blood, she would no longer have to look for who was the murderer.

"Grégoriska," she said, "I know very well that you and Kostaki don't love each other. I know that you are Waivady by your father, and he Koproli by his, but by your mother, you were both Brankovans. I know that you are a man from the western cities, and he a child from the eastern mountains; but finally, by the belly which carried you both, you are brothers. Well! Grégoriska, I want to know if we are going to take my son to his father without the oath having been taken; if I can cry quietly, finally, like a woman, resting on you, that is to say on a man, for punishment."

"Name my brother's murderer, my lady, and order; I swear to you that before an hour, if you demand it, he will have ceased to live."

"Swear, Grégoriska, swear, under penalty of my curse, do you hear, my son?"

"Swear that the murderer will die, that you will not leave stone on stone of his house; that his mother, children, brothers, wife or fiancée will perish from your hand. Swear, and, swearing, call upon yourself the wrath of heaven if you break this sacred oath. If you fail this sacred oath, submit yourself to misery, the cruelty of your friends, the curse of your mother."

Grégoriska stretched out his hand over the corpse.

"I swear the murderer will die," he said.

At this strange oath, the true meaning of which I and perhaps only the dead could understand, I saw or thought I saw an appalling wonder accomplished. The corpse's eyes opened and looked at me more alive than I had ever seen them, and I felt, as if this double ray had been palpable, a hot iron penetrate my heart.

It was more than I could bear; I fainted.

Chapter Fifteen: The Monastery of Hango

When I woke up, I was in my room, lying on my bed; one of the two women was waiting near me. I asked where Smérande was; I was told that she was watching over her son's body. I asked about Grégoriska; I was told that he was at Hango Monastery.

There was no longer any question of flight. Wasn't Kostaki dead?

There was no longer any question of marriage. Could I marry the fratricide?

Three days and three nights passed in the midst of strange dreams. Waking or asleep, I always saw those two living eyes in the middle of his dead face: it was a horrible vision.

It was on the third day that Kostaki's funeral was to take place.

On the morning of that day, I was brought from Smérande a full widow's costume. I got dressed and went downstairs.

The house seemed empty; everyone was in the chapel.

I made my way to the meeting place. As I crossed the threshold, Smérande, whom I had not seen for three days, crossed the threshold and came to me.

She looked like a statue of Pain. With a slow movement like that of a statue, she put her icy lips on my forehead, and, in a voice that already seemed to come out of the tomb, she uttered her usual words: "Kostaki loves you."

You cannot imagine the effect these words had on me. This love protest made in the present tense, instead of being expressed in the past; he loves you instead of loved you; this love from beyond the grave that came to seek me in life made a terrible impression on me.

At the same time, a strange feeling took hold of me, as if I had indeed been the wife of the one who had died, and not the bride of the one who was alive. This coffin drew me to him, in spite of myself, painfully, as they say that the snake attracts the bird that it fascinates. I looked for Grégoriska's eyes.

I saw him, pale and standing, against a column; his eyes looking to heaven. I cannot say if he saw me.

The monks of the Hango convent surrounded the body, singing chants from the Greek rite, sometimes harmonious, more often monotonous. I also wanted to pray; but the prayer expired on my lips. My mind was so upset, that it seemed to me much more like attending a consistory of demons than a meeting of priests.

When the body was removed, I wanted to follow it, but my strength refused. I felt my legs weaken under me and leaned against the door.

So Smérande came to me and made a sign to Grégoriska. Grégoriska obeyed and approached. So Smérande spoke to me in the Moldovan language.

"My mother orders me to repeat to you verbatim what she is going to say," said Grégoriska.

Then Smérande spoke again; when she had finished: - Here are my mother's words, he said: "You cry for my son, Hedwige, you love him, don't you?" Thank you for your tears and your love; henceforth you are as much my daughter as if Kostaki had been your husband; you now have a homeland, a mother, a family."

"Let's pour out the tears we owe to the dead, and then we both will become worthy of the one who is no longer – me his mother, you his wife! Farewell! go home: I will follow my son to his last home; when I return, I will lock myself in with my pain, and you will not see me until I have overcome it; don't worry, I will kill it because I don't want it to kill me. "

I could not answer these words of Smérande, translated by Grégoriska, save by a whimper.

I went up to my room, the convoy departed. I saw it disappear at the corner of the road. The Convent of Hango was only half a league from the castle in a straight line, but the obstacles on the ground forced the road to deviate, and, following the path, they were away for nearly two hours.

We were in November. The days had become cold and short again. At five in the evening it was dark. Around seven o'clock I saw torches reappear. It was the funeral procession that returned. The corpse lay in the tomb of his fathers. All was done.

I told you what a strange obsession I have lived in since the fatal event that had dressed us all in mourning, and especially since I saw the corpse reopen its eyes that death had closed and fix them on me. That evening, overwhelmed by the emotions of the day, I was even sadder. I listened to the various hours tolling on the castle clock, and I was saddened as the time that passed brought me closer to the moment when Kostaki had died.

I heard the bell tool a quarter to nine. Then a strange feeling took hold of me. It was a shivering terror that ran through my whole body and froze it; then, with this terror, something like an invincible sleep weighed down my senses; my chest tightened, my eyes clouded. I stretched out my arms, and I went backwards to fall on my bed.

However, my senses had not disappeared so much that I could not hear a step approaching my door; then it seemed to me that my door was opening; then I saw and heard nothing.

Only I felt a sharp pain in the neck.

After which I fell into complete lethargy.

At midnight, I woke up, my lamp was still burning; I wanted to get up, but I was so weak that I had to do it twice. However, I overcome this weakness, and awake, I felt the same pain in my neck as I had experienced in my sleep, I dragged myself, leaning against the wall, to the mirror and I looked at my neck.

Something like a pinprick marked the artery on my neck. I thought that some insect had bitten me during my sleep, and, as I was overcome with fatigue, I went to bed and fell asleep.

The next day I woke up as usual. As usual, I wanted to get up as soon as my eyes were opened; but I experienced a weakness that I had only experienced once in my life, the day after I had bled for the first time. I went over to my looking glass and was struck by my pallor.

The day passed sad and gloomy; I was experiencing a strange thing: where I had the need to stay motionless – any movement tired me.

Night came, they brought me my lamp. My ladies in waiting, I understood at least from their gestures, offered to stay close to me. I thanked them: they went out.

At the same time as the day before, I experienced the same symptoms. I wanted to get up then and call for help; but I couldn't go to the door. I vaguely heard the clock sounding a quarter to nine; footsteps echoed, the door opened; but I didn't see anyone, I couldn't hear anything; like the day before, I went to fall down on my bed.

Like the evening before, I experienced sharp pain in the same place on my neck.

Like the evening before, I woke up at midnight; only I woke up weaker and paler than last time.

The next day again, the horrible obsession was renewed.

I had decided to descend to be near Smérande, weak as I was, when one of the ladies entered my room and pronounced the name of Grégoriska.

Grégoriska came in behind her.

I wanted to get up to receive him, but I fell back into my chair. He cried out when he saw me and wanted to rush towards me; but I had the strength to reach for him.

"What are you doing here?" I asked him.

"Alas!" he said, "I came to say goodbye to you! I came to tell you that I am leaving this world which is unbearable to me without your love and without your presence; I came to tell you that I am retiring to the Hango monastery."

"My presence is taken from you, Grégoriska," I replied, "but not my love. Alas! I still love you, and my great pain is that now this love is almost a crime."

"Then I can hope that you will pray for me, Hedwige.

"Yes - only I will not pray long," I added with a smile.

"So what is it, and why are you so pale?"

"I have ... May God have mercy on me, no doubt, and call me to him soon!"

Grégoriska approached me, took my hand, which I did not have the strength to withdraw, and, staring at me:

"This pallor is not natural, Hedwige; where is it from?"

"If I told you, Grégoriska, you'd think I was crazy."

"No, no, tell me, Hedwige, I beg you. We are here in a country unlike any other country, in a family unlike any other family. Say, say everything, I beg you!"

I told him everything: this strange hallucination which was taking me at the hour when Kostaki must have died; this terror, this numbness, this cold ice, this prostration which lay me on my bed, this footstep that I thought I heard, this door that I thought I saw opening, finally this sharp pain followed by a pallor and then an ever-increasing weakness.

I had thought that my story would appear to Grégoriska to be the beginning of madness, and I ended it with a certain timidity, when, on the contrary, I saw that he was paying close attention to my experiences.

After I stopped talking, he thought for a moment.

"So," he asked, "do you fall asleep every evening at a quarter to nine?"

"Yes, even I make every effort to resist sleep."

"So you think you see your door open?"

"Yes, although I close it with the bolt."

"So you feel sharp neck pain?"

"Yes, although barely my neck keeps track of an injury."

"Will you allow me to see?" he asked.

I turned my head to my shoulder. He examined the scar.

"Hedwige," he said after a moment, "do you trust me?"

"You doubt it!" I exclaimed.

"Do you believe my word?"

"As I believe in the Holy Gospels."

"Well ! Hedwige, on my word! I swear you don't have eight days to live, if you don't agree to do, today, what I'm going to tell you ..."

"What if I agree?"

"If you agree, you may be saved."

"Perhaps?"

He was silent.

"Whatever happens, Grégoriska," I said, "I'll do what you tell me to do."

"Well! listen," he said, "and above all don't be afraid. In your country as in Hungary, as in our Romania, there is a tradition."

I shivered because this tradition came back to my mind.

"Ah!" he said, "you know what I mean?"

"Yes," I replied, "I have seen people in Poland subjected to this horrible sickness and then death."

"You mean vampires, right?"

"Yes, in my childhood, I saw forty people dead in a village cemetery belonging to my father, forty dead in a fortnight without anyone being able to guess the cause of their death. Seventeen gave all the signs of vampirism, that is to say that they were found fresh, ruddy and like the living; the rest were their victims."

"And what was done to deliver the country from it?"

"They stuck a stake in their hearts, and then burned them."

"Yes, that's how we usually do it, but for us it's not enough. To deliver you from the ghost I first want to know him, and by heaven I will know him. Yes, and, if necessary, I will fight hand to hand with him, whatever he may be."

"Ah! Grégoriska!" I cried, scared.

"I said "whatever it is", and I repeat it. But to carry out this terrible adventure, you must consent to everything that I am going to demand of you."

"Tell me," I said, faintly.

"Get ready at seven. Go down to the chapel, go down there alone; you must overcome your weakness, Hedwige, you must. There we will receive the nuptial blessing. Agree, my beloved; In order to defend yourself, I must have the right to watch over you before God and before men. We will go up here and then we will see."

"Oh ! Grégoriska," I cried, "what if he is the one who will kill you?"

"Have no fear, my beloved Hedwige. Only, consent."

"You know I will do whatever you want, Grégoriska."

"See you tonight then."

"Yes, do what you can on your part, and I will assist you as best I can."

He went. A quarter of an hour later, I saw a cavalier leaping on the road to the monastery: it was him!

No sooner had I lost sight of him than I fell on my knees and prayed as one no longer prays in those faithless lands these days, and I continued for seven hours, offering to God and the Saints the burnt offering of my thoughts; I did not get up until seven o'clock struck.

I was weak like a dying woman, pale like a dead woman. I threw a large black veil over my head, went down the stairs, supporting myself against the walls, and went to the chapel without having met anyone.

Grégoriska was waiting for me with Father Bazile, superior of the Convent of Hango. He was carrying a holy sword alongside, a relic of an old crusader who had taken Constantinople with Villehardouin and Beaudouin of Flanders.

"Hedwige," he said, clapping his sword, "with the help of God, this will break the spell that threatens your life. Come therefore resolutely, here is a holy man who, after having received my confession, will receive our oaths."

The ceremony began; never perhaps was there one more simple and more solemn at the same time. No one attended the priest; he himself placed the bridal crowns on our heads. Dressed in mourning, we walked around the altar with a candle in hand; then the monk having pronounced the holy words, added:

"Go now, my children, and may God give you the strength and the courage to fight against the enemy of mankind. You are armed with your innocence and its justice; you will defeat the demon. Go, and be blessed."

We kissed the holy books and left the chapel.

So, for the first time, I leaned on Grégoriska's arm, and it seemed to me that at the touch of this valiant arm, in contact with this noble heart, life returned to my veins. I thought I was certain to triumph, since Grégoriska was with me; we went back up to my room.

The clock tolled the half hour.

"Hedwige," said Grégoriska to me, "we have no time to waste. Do you want to fall asleep as usual, and everything happens while you sleep? Or do you want to stay dressed and see everything?"

"Beside you, I fear nothing, I want to stay awake, I want to see everything."

Grégoriska drew a blessed branch of boxwood, still moist with holy water, from his chest and gave it to me.

"Take this branch, then, he said, lie down on your bed, recite the prayers to the Virgin and wait without fear. God is with us."

"Above all, don't drop your branch; with it, you will command in hell itself. Don't call me, don't yell; pray, hope and wait."

I lay down on the bed, crossed my hands on my chest, on which I rested the blessed twig.

As for Grégoriska, he hid behind the canopy I had mentioned, which cut across the corners of my room.

I counted the minutes, and no doubt Grégoriska also counted them.

The bell tolled three quarters of the hour.

The sound of the hammer still vibrated, I felt the same numbness, the same terror, the same freezing cold; but I pressed the blessed twig to my lips, and the feeling dissipated.

So I distinctly heard the noise of this slow and measured step which resounded on the staircase and which approached my door. Then my door opened slowly, quietly, as if pushed by a supernatural force, and then ...

The voice stopped as if stifled in the narrator's throat.

- And so, she continued with an effort, I saw Kostaki, pale as I had seen on the litter; his long black hair, scattered on his shoulders, dripped with blood; he wore his usual costume; only he was cut open on his chest and showed his bleeding wound.

He was dead, a walking corpse ... flesh, clothes, gait ... the eyes alone, those terrible eyes, were alive.

At this sight, I felt a strange feeling! Instead of feeling my terror redoubled, I felt my courage grow. No doubt God sent him to me so that I could judge my position and defend myself from hell. At the first step that the ghost took towards my bed, I boldly met its gaze with that leaden look, and presented him the blessed twig.

The specter tried to move forward; but a power stronger than his own kept him in his place. He stopped himself :

"Oh!" it murmured, "she doesn't sleep, she knows everything."

It spoke in Moldovan, and yet I heard it as if these words had been spoken in a language I understood.

We were thus opposite each other, the ghost and me, without my eyes being able to detach from his, when I saw, without needing to turn my head to his side, Grégoriska come out from behind the wooden stall, like an exterminating angel, and holding his sword in his hand. He made the sign of the cross with his left hand and advanced slowly, the sword stretched out towards the ghost; the latter, like his brother, had in turn drawn his saber with a terrible laugh; but as soon as the saber touched the blessed iron, the ghost's arm fell inert close to his body.

Kostaki sighed, full of struggle and despair.

"What do you want?" he said to his brother.

"In the name of the living God! said Grégoriska, "I command you to answer."

"Speak," said the ghost, gnashing his teeth.

"Did I wait for you?"

"No."

"Was it me who attacked you?"

"No."

"Was it me who hit you?"

"No."

"You threw yourself on my sword, and that's what happened, am I speaking the truth?"

"So, in the eyes of God and men, I am not guilty of the crime of fratricide; therefore you did not receive a divine mission, but an infernal mission; so you came out of the grave, not like a holy shadow, but like a cursed specter, and now you are going to enter your grave forever more."

"With her, yes!" cried Kostaki, making a supreme effort to take me.

"Never!" cried Grégoriska in his turn; "this woman is mine!"

And, speaking these words, with the tip of the blessed iron, he touched the living wound.

Kostaki cried out as if a sword of flame had touched him, and, bringing his left hand to his chest, he took a step back.

At the same time, and with a movement that seemed to be nested with his, Grégoriska took a step forward; then, eyes on the eyes of the dead man, the sword on his brother's chest, began a slow, terrible, solemn march; something like the passage of Don Juan and the Commander; the specter receding under the sacred sword, under the irresistible will of the champion of God; the latter followed him step by step without speaking a word; both breathless, both livid, the living pushing the dead man before him and forcing him to abandon this castle which was his abode in the past, for the tomb which was his abode in the future.

Oh ! it was horrible to see, I swear.

And yet, moving myself by a superior force, invisible, unknown, without realizing what I was doing, I got up and followed them. We went down the stairs, lit only by Kostaki's fiery eyes. We crossed the gallery and the courtyard. We crossed the door in this same measured step: the specter backwards, Grégoriska with outstretched arm, me following them.

This fantastic race lasted an hour: the dead had to be taken back to his grave; only, instead of following the usual path, Kostaki and Grégoriska had cut through the ground in a straight line, caring little for the obstacles that had ceased to exist under their feet, the ground leveled, the torrents dried up, the trees retreated, the rocks spread apart. The same miracle worked for me as for them; only the whole sky seemed to me covered with a black pancake, the moon and the stars had disappeared, and I still saw in the night shining only the eyes of flame of the vampire.

So we got to Hango, so we passed through the strawberry tree hedge that served as a fence at the cemetery. As soon as I entered, I saw in the shadows the tomb of Kostaki placed next to that of his father; I didn't know she was there, and yet I recognized her.

That night I knew everything.

At the edge of the open pit, Grégoriska stopped.

"Kostaki, he said, it's not all over yet for you, and a voice from heaven tells me that you will be forgiven if you repent: do you promise to return to your grave? Do you promise not to leave? Do you promise to finally dedicate your worship to hell to God?"

"No!" replied Kostaki.

"Do you repent?" asked Grégoriska.

"No!"

"For the last time, Kostaki?"

"No!"

"Well ! call Satan to your aid, as I call God to mine, and let us see, this time again, to whom will be the victory.

Two cries were heard at the same time; the irons crossed, sparking out with sparks, and the fight lasted a minute which seemed to me a century.

Kostaki fell, I saw the terrible sword rise, I saw it sink into his body and nail that body to the freshly stirred earth.

A supreme, and nothing human-like cry passed through the air.

I ran.

Grégoriska remained standing but faltering. I ran up and held him in my arms.

"Are you hurt?" I asked him anxiously.

"No, he said, but in such a duel, dear Hedwige, it is not the wound that kills, it is the struggle. I struggled with death; I belong to death."

"Dearest friend," I cried, "walk away, get away from here, and life may come back."

"No," said he, "here is my grave, Hedwige; but let's not waste time; take a little of this soil impregnated with his blood and apply it to the bite he gave you; it's the only way to save yourself in the future from his horrible love.

I obeyed, shivering. I stooped to pick up the bloody earth, and, stooping down, I saw the corpse nailed to the ground; the blessed sword through his heart, and a profuse black blood flowed from his wound, as if he had died just then.

I kneaded some soil with the blood and applied the horrible talisman to my wound.

"Now, my beloved Hedwige," said Grégoriska in a weak voice, "listen to my last instructions. Leave the country as soon as you can. Distance alone is security for you. Father Bazile has received my final will today, and he will execute it."

"Hedwige! A kiss! The last, the only, Hedwige! I die."

Saying these words, Grégoriska fell close to his brother.

In any other circumstance, in the middle of this cemetery, near this open grave, with these two corpses lying next to each other, I would have gone mad; but, as I said before, God had put in me a force equal to the events of which I was not only a witness, but a supreme actress.

As I looked around, looking for some help, I saw the cloister doors open, and the monks, led by Father Bazile, advanced two by two, carrying burning torches and chanting the prayers of the dead .

Father Bazile had just arrived at the convent; he had foreseen what had happened, and, at the head of the whole community, he went to the cemetery. He found me alive near the two bodies.

Kostaki's face was upset by a last convulsion.

Grégoriska, on the contrary, was calm and almost smiling.

As Grégoriska had recommended, he was buried near his brother: the Christian guarding the damned.

Smérande, learning of this new misfortune and the share that I had taken in it, wanted to see me; she came to find me at the Convent of Hango, and learned from me everything that had happened on that terrible night.

I told her in all its details the fantastic story; but she listened to me as

Grégoriska had listened to me, without surprise, without fear.

"Hedwige," she replied after a moment of silence, "strange as you may have said, you have only spoken the purest truth. The Brankovan race is cursed, up to the third and fourth generation, because a Brankovan killed a priest. But the end of the curse has arrived; for, though a wife, you are a virgin, and in me the race is dying out. If my son left you a million, take it."

"After me, apart from the pious legacies that I intend to make, you will have the rest of my fortune. Now follow your husband's advice. Return as quickly as possible to the countries where God does not allow these terrible wonders to take place. I don't need anyone to mourn my sons with me. Goodbye. Don't ask about me anymore. My fate to come belongs only to me and to God."

And, having kissed me on the forehead as usual, she left me and went to lock herself in Brankovan Castle.

Eight days later, I left for France. As Grégoriska had hoped, my nights ceased to be frequented by the terrible ghost.

My health has recovered, and I have kept from this event only that deadly pallor which accompanies to the grave any creature which has undergone the kiss of a vampire.

The lady fell silent, midnight rang, and I would almost dare say that the bravest of us started with the sound of the tolling bell.

It was time to retire; we took leave of Mr. Ledru.

A year later, this excellent man died. It is the first time since this death that I have had the opportunity to pay a tribute to the good citizen, the modest scientist, especially the honest man. I hasten to do so.

I never went back to Fontenay-aux-Roses.

But the memory of that day left such a deep impression on my life, but all these strange stories, which had accumulated in one evening, made such a deep furrow in my memory, that hoping to arouse interest in others that I had experienced it myself, I collected in the different countries that I have traveled for eighteen years, that is to say in Switzerland, Germany, Italy, Spain, Sicily, Greece and in England, all the traditions of the same genre as the stories of the different peoples revived in my ear, and I have composed this collection which I deliver today to my usual readers, under the title: *The Thousand & One Ghosts*.

THE LEPER OF THE CITY OF AOSTA

By Xavier de Maistre

203: Original Image of Xavier de Maistre by Michael Gallant

he southern part of the city of Aosta is almost deserted and seems to have never been very inhabited. One can see plowed fields and meadows terminated on one side by ancient ramparts that the Romans built to serve as its enclosure, and on the other by the walls of some gardens. This solitary location is perhaps of interest to travelers.

Near the city gate, we see the ruins of an ancient castle in which, if we believe popular tradition, Count René de Chalans, driven by the fury of jealousy, left to starve, in the fifteenth century, his wife Princess Marie of Braganza, hence the name of *Bramafam* (which means *the cry of hunger*) was given to this castle by the locals. This anecdote, the authenticity of which could be disputed, makes these hovels interesting for sensitive people who believe it to be true.

214: Torre Bramafam, Aosta, Italy, Artist Unknown, Public Domain

Farther on, a few hundred steps away, is a square tower, leaning against the ancient wall and built with the marble with which it was already coated: it is called the Tower of Fear, because the people believed it had long been inhabited by ghosts. The old women of the city of Aosta remember all too well that they have seen a tall woman in white coming out of the tower during dark nights, holding a lamp in her hand.

This tower was repaired about fifteen years ago by order of the government and surrounded by an enclosure, to house a leper and thus separate him from society, providing him with all the amenities of which his sad situation was susceptible. Saint-Maurice Hospital was responsible for providing for his subsistence, and he was provided with some furniture and tools necessary for cultivating a garden.

It was there that he lived for a long time, left to himself, never seeing anyone, except the priest who went from time to time to help him with the help of religion, and the man who every week brought him his provisions of hospital.

During the Alpine War, in the year 1797, a soldier, being in the city of Aosta, passed one day, by chance near the garden of the leper whose door was ajar, and he had the curiosity to enter. There he found a man dressed simply, leaning against a tree, and immersed in deep meditation. At the noise made by the officer as he entered, the solitary recluse, without turning around and looking, cried in a sad voice, "Who is there, and what do they want of me?"

"Excuse me, I am a stranger," replied the soldier, "who has perhaps been indiscreet about the pleasant appearance of your garden, but who doesn't want to disturb you."

"Do not advance," replied the inhabitant of the tower, waving to him, "Do not advance; you are near the victim of an unfortunate attack of leprosy."

"Whatever be your misfortune," replied the traveler, "I will not go away. I have never fled from the poor; however if my presence annoys you, I am ready to withdraw."

"Welcome," said the leper, then, turning suddenly, "and stay if you dare after looking at me."

The soldier was for a time motionless with terror and dread at the appearance of this unfortunate man whom leprosy had totally disfigured.

"I will gladly stay," he said, "if you will accept the visit of a man whom chance leads here, but who is keenly interested in your tale."

The leper smiled grimly. "Interest! I have never excited any emotion but pity from others."

The soldier didn't move away, instead he said with a compassionate tone, "I would consider myself happy if I could offer you some consolation."

The leper said, "It is a great feeling for me to see men, to hear the sound of the human voice, when it is not running away from me in fear."

The military man encouraged the leper to continue, saying, "So then allow me to speak with you for a few moments and walk with you through your sanctuary."

"Very gladly, if that gives you pleasure." Saying these words, the leper covered his head with a large felt cap, the folded edges of which hid his face. "Come on," he added, "at noon, I tend to a small flowerbed that you may like. You will find some quite rare flowers here. I obtained the seeds of all those flowers which grow by themselves on the Alps, and I have tried to make them reproduce and embellish them by my horticulture."

The soldier, looking at the beautiful flowers, said, "Indeed, these flowers are completely unfamiliar to me."

The leper pointed to a bush with his misshapen hands, "notice this little bush of roses; it is the thornless rose, which only grows in the high Alps; but it already loses this property, and it grows thorns as it is cultivated and multiplied."

- It should be the emblem of ingratitude!

- If some of these flowers look beautiful to you, you can take them without fear, and you won't be taking any risks by carrying them with you. I sowed them, I have the pleasure of watering them and seeing them, but I never touch them."

- Why is that? asked the soldier.

- I would fear to defile them, and I would not dare to offer them any more, the leper said.

The soldier asked him, "who are you growing them for?"

The leper replied, "the people who bring me provisions from the hospital are not afraid to make bouquets from these flowers. Sometimes the children of the city also appear at the door of my garden. I immediately climb into the tower, for fear of frightening them or harming them. I see them frolicking from my window and stealing some flowers from me. When they leave, they look up at me: "*Hello, Leper*" they tell me laughing and that makes me happy."

The soldier asked him curiously, while feeling the leaves of a young tree that grew by the path, "you knew how to bring together so many different plants here are vines and fruit trees of several species."

The leper, seeing his visitor's object of attention, said, "the trees are still young. I planted them myself, as well as this vine, which I raised to the top of the ancient wall here it is, and the width of which forms a small promenade is my favorite place . Go up along these stones; it is a staircase of which I am the architect. Stand on the wall."

The military man was captivated by the sight. "Such a charming and cheaply prepared spot! It is well made for the meditations of a solitary man."

The leper said, "I also love how much of the countryside and the ploughmen in the fields I can see from my eyrie. I see everything that happens in the meadow and I am not seen by anyone.

The soldier said, appreciatively, "I admire how peaceful and lonely this retreat is. We are in a city, and it seems we are in a desert."

The leper added, "loneliness is not always in the middle of forests and rocks. Misfortune alone is found everywhere."

The soldier asked, "what sequence of events have brought you to this retreat? Is this country your homeland?"

The leper replied, "I was born on the seaside, in the Principality of Orielle, and I have only lived here for fifteen years. As for my story, it is a long and uniform calamity."

The soldier asked him, gently, "have you always lived alone?"

"I lost my parents in my childhood and I never knew them. A sister who stayed with me died two years ago. I have never had a friend," the leper replied, with a distant, wistful look on his face.

"That is unfortunate!"

"These are the purposes of God."

The soldier asked, "what is your name, please?"

The leper exclaimed, "Ah! my name is terrible! my name is The Leper! The name I was given by my family and that religion gave me on the day of my birth is unknown in the world. I am The Leper, that is the only title I have for the benevolence of men. May they forever ignore who I am!"

The military man asked him, "did this sister you lost live with you?"

The leper replied, "she lived five years with me in the same house where you see me. As unhappy as I was, she shared my sorrows, and I tried to soften hers."

"What can you do now, in such deep solitude?"

"The detail of the occupations of a solitary soul like me could not be too monotonous for a man of the world, who finds his happiness in activity of the social life."

The soldier said, "Ah! You know little about this world which has never given me happiness. I am often lonely by choice, and there is perhaps more similarity between our ideas than you think. However, I admit, the thought of an eternal loneliness terrifies me. I can hardly imagine it."

The leper remarked, "*Whosoever cherishes his cell will find peace there,*" then continued, "The Imitation of Jesus Christ teaches us this. I begin to experience the truth of these consoling words. The feeling of loneliness also eases through work. The working man is never completely unhappy, and I am proof of that. During the beautiful season, the care of my garden and my flowerbed occupies me sufficiently during the winter, I make baskets and mats; I work to make clothes, I prepare my own food every day with the provisions that are brought to me from the hospital and prayer fills the hours that work leaves me. Finally the year passes, and when it has passed, it still seems to me to have been too short."

The soldier said, "It should seem like a century."

The leper replied, "the evils and sorrows make the hours appear long, but the years always fly away with the same speed. There is also, at the last moment of misfortune, a pleasure that ordinary people cannot know, and which will seem very singular to you – that of simply existing and breathing. I spend whole days of the beautiful season motionless on this rampart enjoying the air and beauty of nature: all my ideas are vague and indecisive, sadness rests in my heart without overwhelming it; my eyes wander over this countryside and over the rocks which surround us. These different aspects are so imprinted in my memory that are, so to speak, a part of me, and each site is a friend who I see with pleasure each day."

The military man agreed, "I have often experienced something similar. When sorrow is heavy on me, and I do not find in the hearts of men what mine despises, the aspect of nature and inanimate things consoles me; I love rocks and trees, and it seems to me that all beings in creation are friends that God has given me.

The leper said, "you encourage me to explain to you in turn what is happening in me. I really like the objects which are, so to speak, my life companions, and which I see every day, and also every evening. Before retiring to the tower, I come to greet the glaciers of Ruitorts, the dark woods of the Saint-Bernard mountain, and the bizarre points which dominate the Rhéme valley. Although the power of God is as visible in the creation of an ant as in that of the whole universe, the great spectacle of the mountains imposes more on my senses, however, I cannot see these enormous masses covered with eternal ice, without experiencing religious surprise; but, in this vast table which surrounds me, I have my favorite sites and one which I prefer is the hermitage which you see up there on the top of the mountain of Charvensol."

"Isolated in the middle of the woods, near a deserted field, it receives the last rays of the setting sun. Although I have never been there, I have a particular pleasure in seeing it. When the day falls, sitting in my garden, I fix my eyes on this lonely hermitage, and my imagination rests there. It has become for me a kind of property. It seems to me that a confused reminiscence teaches me that I lived there formerly in happier times, and whose memory has been erased in me. I especially like to contemplate the distant mountains which merge with the sky in the horizon. As well as the future, the remoteness gives birth to me the feeling of hope, my oppressed heart believes that there may be a far distant land, where, at a future time I will finally be able to taste the happiness for which I sigh, and that a secret instinct constantly presents me as possible."

The soldier said, in a sympathetic tone, "with an ardent soul like yours, it probably took a lot of effort to resign yourself to your destiny, and not to abandon yourself to despair."

The leper said, "I would deceive you by letting you believe that I am always resigned to my fate. I have not reached this state of self-denial which some anchorites have realized. This complete sacrifice of all human affections has not yet been accomplished; my life is spent in continuous combat with my emotions and the powerful help from religion itself is not always able to repress them in my imagination. She often leads me in spite of myself in an ocean of chimerical desires, which all bring me back to this world of which I have no idea and whose fantastic image is always present to torment me."

The soldier said, "If I could make you look into my soul, and give you the wrinkled world that I have, then all your desires and your regrets would vanish instantly."

The leper said, "In vain, some books have informed me of the perversity of men and the inseparable misfortunes of humanity; my heart refuses to believe them. I always imagine societies of sincere and virtuous friends; matched spouses, whom health, youth, and fortune combined fill with happiness. I think I see them wandering together in hedgerows greener and fresher than those who lend me their shade, lit by a sun brighter than the one that lights me up and their fate seems to me more worthy of envy, as mine is more miserable. At the beginning of spring ~ when the Piedmont wind blows in our valley, I feel penetrated by its invigorating heat, and I tremble.

I experience an inexplicable desire and the confused feeling of an immense bliss which I could enjoy and which is denied me. So I flee from my cell, I wander in the countryside to breathe more freely. I avoid being seen by the same men my Heart burns to meet; and from the top of the hill, hidden among the undergrowth like a wild beast, my eyes are on the city of Aosta.

I see its happy inhabitants from afar with envious eyes. They ignore me as I reach out to them groaning, and I ask them for my portion of happiness. In my transport, will I admit it to you? I have sometimes hugged the trees in my arms, praying to God to animate them for me, and to give me a friend. But the trees are silent; their cold bark repels me – they have nothing in common with my heart, which pulsates and burns. Overwhelmed with the weary fatigue of life I drag myself back into my retirement, I expose my torments to God and prayer brings a little calm to my soul."

The soldier asked, "So, poor unhappy man, do you suffer all the ailments of the soul and of the body?"

The leper replied, "These are not the cruelest."

The soldier asked him, "do they sometimes leave you with a rash?"

The leper replied, "They increase and decrease each month with the course of the moon. When it begins to show itself, I usually suffer more; the disease then decreases and seems to change in nature. My skin dries up and whitens, and I hardly feel my pain anymore, but it would still be bearable if not for the insomnia which it causes me."

"What! Even sleep abandons you!"

The leper said, "Ah, sir! Insomnia! Insomnia! You cannot imagine how long and sad it is a night that an unhappy one spends entirely without closing his eye, his mind fixed on a dreadful situation and on a hopeless future. No! no one can understand it.

My worries increase as the night progresses and when it is close to ending, my agitation is such that I no longer know what I have become; my thoughts get confused. I have an extraordinary feeling that I never experience except in these sad moments. Sometimes it seems to me that an irresistible force draws me into a bottomless pit; sometimes I see black spots in front of my eyes but while I examine them, they cross with the rapidity of lightning, they get bigger as they approach me, and soon they are mountains which overwhelm me with their weight.

At other times, I see clouds coming out of the earth around me, like swelling waves, which pile up and threaten to engulf me; and when I want to get up to distract myself from these ideas I feel like I am held in by invisible ties that take my strength away. You may believe that these are dreams; but no, I'm awake. I keep seeing the same things over and over, and it's a feeling of horror that surpasses all my other ills.

- It is possible that you have a fever during these cruel bouts of insomnia, and it is no doubt that which is causing you this kind of delirium.

- Do you think this can be the case? Ah! I would like you to disagree with me, truly. I had hitherto feared that these visions were a symptom of madness, and I confess that this worries me a lot. I pray to God that it was indeed fever!

- You interest me very much. I admit that I would never have imagined a situation similar to yours. I think, however, that it must have been less sad when your sister was alive.

- God only knows what I lost by the death of my sister.

- But aren't you afraid of being so close to me? Sit here on this stone. I will place myself behind the foliage, and we can converse without seeing each other.

- Why is that? No, you will not leave me; stand near me."

(Saying these words, the traveler made an involuntary movement to seize the hand of the Leper, who withdrew it quickly.)

- Imprudent fool! You were going to grab my hand!

- Well, I would have gladly hugged you.

- It would be the first time that this happiness would have been granted to me – my hand has never been shaken by anybody.

- What! Apart from this sister that you told me about, have you never had an affair – have you never been cherished by any of your fellow men?

- Fortunately for humanity, I have no loved ones on earth.

- You make me shudder!

- Forgive me, compassionate stranger! You know that the unhappy love to talk about their misfortunes.

- Speak, speak, you interesting man! You told me that a sister once lived with you and helped you to bear your sufferings.

- It was the only link which I still held to the rest of men. It pleased God to break it and leave me isolated and alone in the middle of the world. Her soul was worthy of the heaven that now possesses it, and her example supported me against the discouragement that has often overwhelmed me since her death.

However, we did not live in that delicious intimacy of which I have an idea, and which should unite my friends – that of being happy. The sorrow of our ills deprived us of this consolation. Even as we got closer to God in our prayers, we reciprocally avoided looking at each other, lest the sight of our evils disturb our meditations, and our eyes dared to meet only in heaven. After our prayers, my sister usually retired to her cell or under the hazelnut trees which are at the garden's end, and we almost always lived apart.

- But why impose such a constraint on yourselves?

- When my sister was attacked by the contagious disease which had infected my whole family, she came to share my retirement in this tower. We had never seen each other – she had an expression of extreme terror on seeing me for the first time. Her greater fear was the pain she felt in adopting my sad manner of existence. Leprosy had only attacked her chest, and I still had some hope of seeing it heal.

You see this trellis that I have neglected; it was then a hedge of hops which I maintained with care and which divided the garden into two parts. I had made a small path on each side, along which we could walk and converse together without getting too close to each other.

- It looks like the heavens wished to poison the sad pleasures left you.

- At least I was not alone anymore. The presence of my sister made my retirement more vibrant. I could hear the sound of her steps in my solitude. When I awoke at dawn to pray to God under these trees, the door of the tower opened slowly, and my sister's voice gradually mixed with mine. In the evening, when I watered my garden, she sometimes walked by in the setting sun, here in the same place where I am speaking with you, and I saw her shadow pass over my flowers. Even when I didn't see her, I found traces of her presence everywhere.

Now, I no longer happen to meet on my way a leafless flower, or a few branches that she might have dropped here and there while passing by. I am alone and there is no more movement or life around me, and the path which led to her favorite copse in the garden is already disappearing under the overgrown grass.

Without seeming to take care of me, she constantly watched what would make me happy. When I returned to my room, I was sometimes surprised to find vases of new flowers, or some beautiful fruit that she had tended for herself. I did not dare to render the same services, and I had even asked her never to enter my room, but who can limit the affections of a sister!

A single example will give you an idea of her tenderness for me. I strode one night in my cell, tormented by terrible pain. In the middle of the night, sitting for a moment to rest, I heard a slight noise at the entrance to my room. I approached, I listened. You can judge my astonishment when I found that it was my sister who prayed to God outside, on the threshold of my door. She had heard my complaints. Her tenderness had made her fearful of disturbing me; but she came to be able to help me if necessary. I heard her reciting the *Miserere*[41] in a low voice. I began to cry near the door and without interrupting I mentally followed her words. My eyes were full of tears – who would not have been touched by such affection?

When I thought her prayer was over, I said to her in a low voice, "Farewell, my sister, farewell, withdraw, I feel a little better; may God bless you and reward you for your devotion!"

She retired in silence, and no doubt her prayer was answered because I finally slept a few hours of a peaceful sleep.

---

[41] *Miserere mei, Deus,* or Have Mercy on me, Lord, a setting of Psalm 51 by Gregorio Allegri for Pope Urban VIII in the 1630s. It begins:
Have mercy upon me, O God: after Thy great goodness.
According to the multitude of Thy mercies, do away my offences.
Wash me thoroughly from my wickedness: and cleanse me from my sin.

225: Gregori Allegri, composer of the Miserere, Mei Deus, Artist Unknown, Public Domain

- How sad you must have been in the first days after the death of your dear sister.

- I was in a kind of stupor for a long time which made it easy for me to feel the whole extent of my misfortune when I finally came to my senses. When I was able to judge my situation I was ready to abandon all reason. This time will always be doubly sad for me it reminded me of the greatest of my misfortunes, and the crime that almost followed.

I can't believe you are capable of a crime!

It is only too true – and by telling you about this period of my life, I feel too much that I will lose a lot in your esteem; but I don't want to paint myself better than I am, and you might pity me by condemning me. Already, in some bouts of melancholy, the idea of leaving this life voluntarily had presented itself to me, however the fear of God had always made me reject it, when the most simple and trivial circumstance gave me consideration to surrender myself to eternal damnation.

I had just experienced a new sorrow. For a few years, a little dog had adopted us. My sister had loved it, and I confess that since she was no longer alive, this poor animal was a real consolation to me. We no doubt owed to his ugliness the choice he had made of our home for his refuge. He had been put off by everyone, but he was still a treasure for our little Leper home. In recognition of the favor that God had granted us by giving us this friend, my sister called him *Miracle*; and its name, which contrasted with its ugliness, as well as with its continued gaiety, had often distracted us from our sorrows.

Despite the care I took of it, he sometimes escaped from our sanctuary, and I never thought that he could be harmful to anyone. However, some of the town's inhabitants were alarmed by this, and believed that he could carry the germ of his illness among them; they determined to file complaints with the commander, who ordered that my dog be killed immediately. Soldiers, accompanied by some inhabitants, came to carry out this cruel order. They passed a rope around his neck in my presence and dragged him away. When he was at the garden gate, I couldn't help but look at him again: I saw him turn my eyes towards me to ask for help that I could not give him. They wanted to drown him in the Doire, but the populace waiting outside knocked him out with stones.

I heard his screams, and I returned to my tower more dead than alive; my trembling knees could not support me. I threw myself on my bed in a state impossible to describe. My pain only allowed me to see, in this just but severe order, a barbarism as excruciating as it was useless, and although I am ashamed today of the feeling which animated me then, I cannot still think of it in cold blood. I spent the whole day in the greatest agitation. He was the last living being in my life who had just been torn from me, and this new blow had reopened all the wounds of my heart.

Such was my situation when the same day, at sunset, I came to sit here, on this bed of ivy where you are sitting now. I had been thinking for some time on my sad fate, when over there, towards these two birch trees which turn the hedge, I saw appear a young couple who had just recently united in marriage. They advanced along the path through the meadow and passed by me. The delicious tranquility that inspires certain happiness was imprinted on their beautiful faces – they walked slowly; their arms were intertwined. Suddenly I saw them stop: the young woman tilted her head on the breast of her husband, who hugged her, transported with ardor. I felt my heart tighten. I confess that envy slipped for the first time into my heart: the image of happiness had never presented itself to me with so much force. I followed them with my eyes to the end of the meadow, and I was going to lose sight of them in the trees when cries of joy came to strike my ear: it was their families reuniting with them. Old men, women, children surrounded them. I heard the confused murmur of joy; I saw shiny glimpses of their clothes between the trees, and this whole group seemed surrounded by a cloud of happiness.

I could not bear this spectacle – the torments of hell had entered my heart. I looked away, and I rushed into my cell. God! what had seemed to me deserted, somber, appalling!

It is here that my abode is fixed forever; it is here where, dragging out my deplorable life, I will wait for the end of my days! The Eternal Lord has poured out happiness, He has poured it out in torrents over all that breathes; and me, me alone! without help, without friends, without companions. What a terrible destiny!

Full of these sad thoughts, I forgot that he is a comforting being, I forgot myself.

Why, I said to myself, *was life given to me? Why is nature only unfair and stepmotherly towards me? Like a disinherited child, I have before me the rich heritage of human starvation, and the miserly heavens refuse me my share.*

No, no, I cried at last in a fit of rage, *there is no happiness for you on earth; die, unfortunate soul, die! For long enough, you defiled the earth by your presence. May it engulf you alive and leave no trace of your odious existence.*

My insane fury increasing by degrees, the desire to destroy me took hold of me and fixed all my thoughts. I finally conceived the resolution to burn down my retreat, and to let myself be consumed with everything that could have left anything to remember me. Restless, furious, I went out into the countryside. I wandered for a while in the shadows around my house. Involuntary howls came from my oppressed chest and frightened me in the silence of the night. I came home full of rage, shouting: *Woe unto you, Lepers, woe unto you!*

As if the world agreed with my sorrow and had contributed to my loss, I heard the echo which, from the middle of the ruins of the castle of Bramafan, distinctly repeated to me, *Woe unto you!*

I stopped, seized with horror, on the door of the tower, and the faint echo of the mountain repeated long afterwards, *Woe unto you!*

I took a lamp, and, resolving to set my house on fire, I went down to the lowest room, taking with me some dry branches. It was the room my sister had lived in, and I hadn't been inside since her death. Her chair was still as comfortable as when I had removed it for the last time. I felt a shiver of fear when I saw her veil and some of her clothes scattered in her room: the last words she had said before leaving them were brought back to me. *"I will not leave you even if I die,"* she had said to me; *"remember that I will be present in your anxieties."*

As I placed the lamp on the table, I saw the cord of the cross which she wore around her neck, and which she had placed herself between two sheets of her Bible. At this aspect I stepped back full of holy dread. The depth of the abyss into which I was going to rush suddenly presented itself to my unshaven eyes. I approached, trembling with the sacred book.

As I removed the cross from the book, I found a sealed letter that my good sister had left there for me. My tears, hitherto held back by pain, escaped in torrents: all my fatal projects vanished instantly. I pressed this precious letter to my heart for a long time before I could read it; and, throwing myself on my knees to implore divine mercy, I opened it, and I read there sobbing these words which will be eternally etched in my heart:

> *My brother, I will soon leave you: but I will not abandon you. From heaven, where I hope to go, I will watch over you. I will pray to God that he will give you the courage to endure life with resignation, until he deigns to bring us together in another world, then I can show you all my affection: nothing will prevent me from approaching you anymore, and nothing can separate us. I leave you the little cross that I have carried all my life; she has often comforted me in my troubles, and my tears never had other witnesses than her. Remember, when you see it, that my last wish was that you would live and die in good Christian faith.*

The dearest words I have ever received! She will never leave me: I will take her words with me to the grave, she is the one who will open the doors of heaven to me, which would have been closed forever to me by my crime.

As I finished reading, I felt exhausted from all that I had just experienced. I saw a cloud spread over my life, and for some time I lost both the memory of my ills and the feeling of my existence. When I came to, it was late in the night. As my thoughts clear, I felt an indefinable feeling of peace. Everything that had happened that evening seemed to me a dream. My first movement was to raise my eyes to the heavens to thank God for having saved me from the greatest of misfortunes. Never had the firmament seemed so serene and beautiful to me: a brilliant star shone in front of my window; I contemplated it for a long time with inexpressible pleasure, thanking God for the mercy he still granted me in the pleasure of seeing it, and I felt a secret consolation at thinking that one of its rays was intended for the sad cell of the Leper.

I went home more calmly. I spent the rest of the night reading the Book of Job, and the holy enthusiasm that it spread to my soul ended by entirely dissipating the dark ideas that had obsessed me. I had never experienced such terrible moments while my sister lived: it was enough for me to know she was close to me to be calm, and the mere thought of her affection for me was enough to console me and give me courage.

Compassionate stranger! God save you from ever having to live alone! My sister, my companion is no more, but heaven will grant me the strength to bear life courageously; it will connect me, I hope, because I pray in the sincerity of my heart.

- How old was your sister when you lost her?

- She was barely twenty-five years old; but her sufferings made her look older. Despite the illness which burdened her, and which had altered her features, she would still have been beautiful without a frightening pallor which upset her demeanor: she was the image of living death, and I could not see her groaning.

- You lost her too young.

- Her weak and delicate constitution could not resist so many evils for too long. I realized that her loss was inevitable, and such was her sad fate, that I was forced to desire it. Seeing her languish and destroy herself every day, I watched with fatal joy the approaching end of her sufferings. Already for a month, her weakness had been increased; frequent fainting threatened her life hour by hour. One night. (it was around the beginning of August) I saw her so depressed that I did not want to leave her: she was in her chair, unable to support herself on the bed for a few days since. I sat down next to her, and in the profound obscurity of her cell, we had our last talk together. My tears would not stop – a flood of presentiment agitated me.

"Why are you crying?" she said to me, *"why do you grieve so? I will not leave you even after I die, and I will be with you in your anxieties!"*

A few moments later, she expressed to me the desire to be transported out of the tower and to say her prayers in her grove of hazelnut trees: this is where she spent most of the summer. *"I want,"* she said, *"to look at the sky."*

However, I did not believe her hour was so close. I took her in my arms, only for her to push me away.

"Help me stand," she said to me, *"I may still have the strength to walk."*

I led her slowly to the hazel trees; I formed a cushion for her with dry leaves which she had collected there herself, and, having covered her with a veil, in order to preserve her from the night's humidity, I placed myself near her, but she wanted to be alone in her last meditation. I moved away without losing sight of her. I saw her veil rise from time to time, and her white hands reaching for the sky. As I approached the grove, she asked for water; I brought her some in her cup; she dipped her lips in it, but she couldn't drink.

"I feel my end," she said to me, turning her head away, *"my thirst will soon be quenched forever. Support me, my brother; help your sister to cross this desired but terrible passage. Support me, recite the prayers of the dying."*

These were the last words she spoke to me. I leaned her head against my breast; I recited the prayers of the dying: *Go to your eternal rest!* I said to her, *my dear sister; free yourself from life; leave this body in my arms!*

For three hours I supported her in the last struggle of nature; it finally died out gently, and its soul detached itself effortlessly from the earth.

The Leper, at the end of this tale, covered his face with his hands; the sorrowful scene stifled the traveler's voice. After a moment of silence, the Leper got up:

"Foreigner," he said, "when sorrow or discouragement envelops you, think of the solitary recluse of the city of Aosta, you will not have paid him a useless visit."

They went together towards the gate of garden. As the soldier was about to leave, he put his glove on his right hand.

"You have never shaken a person's hand," he said to the Leper.

The leper retreated a few steps with a sort of dread and raised his eyes and hands to the heavens: "Great and good God," he cried, "shower this compassionate man with your blessings!"

"Give me yet another grace," replied the traveler. "I am going to leave; we may not see each other very well for a long time: could we not, with necessary precautions, write to each other sometimes? A similar relationship could distract you and would give me great pleasure."

The Leper reflected for some time. "Why," he said finally, "should I seek to deceive myself? I must have no other society than myself, no friend other than God; we will see each other again in him. Farewell, generous stranger – be happy. Farewell, forever!"

The traveler went out. The Leper closed and locked the door.

ABOUT THE AUTHOR

Aaman Lamba is a poet, occultist and student of magic, astrology, and philosophy, as well as a computer science professional. His articles have been published in leading newspapers. He was the editor and publisher of an online magazine. He lives in Virginia.

Other books by Aaman include The Complete Illustrated Grand Grimoire and The Odontiad. He is currently working on additional translations of texts that deserve greater attention as well as a book on ways of engaging with the world for solitary magicians.

THE ARTIST

Deepti Lamba is an accomplished self-taught artist with her works in private collections and featured in shows. Her art can be found at BlueSigil.com

THE COVER DESIGNER

Matthew Lacasse is an artist and designer who can be found on Twitter at @AnomaliGraphics and on Instagram.

THE ILLUSTRATOR

Michael Gallant is an artist, student of astrology, tarot interpreter, occultist, collector of books, and an avid reader living in the wilderness of Southern Oregon. He enjoys the change of seasons and is especially fond of Oregon's winters with the snow that blankets the mountains around him. He stays physically fit chopping firewood, rowing, working on his house, and caring for the five acres that surrounds him in the mountains. He can be contacted at gallant.productions@mac.com. Art is available on Instagram at Gallant Productions